Youth/Heart of Darkness/ Typhoon/The Secret Sharer

WITH READER'S GUIDE

AMSCO LITERATURE PROGRAM

WILBERT J. LEVY, *Program Editor*

D1560288

Joseph Conrad

YOUTH / HEART OF DARKNESS / TYPHOON / THE SECRET SHARER

Amsco Literature Program

When ordering this book, you may specify:
R 153 ALP (Paperback)
R 153 H (Hardbound)

WITH READER'S GUIDE

Julie Stern

Teacher of English
Newtown High School
New York City

Amsco School Publications, Inc.
315 HUDSON STREET NEW YORK, N.Y. 10013

ISBN 0-87720-819-0 (Paperback)
ISBN 0-87720-832-8 (Hardbound)

Youth / Heart of Darkness / Typhoon / The Secret Sharer
    with Reader's Guide

Amsco School Publications, Inc.

Printed in the United States of America

CONTENTS

Youth   *page* 1

Heart of Darkness   37

Typhoon   137

The Secret Sharer   221

    Reader's Guide   267

YOUTH

This could have occurred nowhere but in England, where men and sea interpenetrate, so to speak—the sea entering into the life of most men, and the men knowing something or everything about the sea, in the way of amusement, of travel, or of breadwinning.   5

We were sitting round a mahogany table that reflected the bottle, the claret-glasses, and our faces as we leaned on our elbows. There was a director of companies, an accountant, a lawyer, Marlow, and myself. The director had been a *Conway* boy, the accountant had served four years at sea, the lawyer—a fine crusted Tory, High Churchman, the best of old fellows, the soul of honour—had been chief officer in the P. & O. service in the good old days when mail-boats were square-rigged at least on two masts, and used to come down the China Sea before a fair monsoon with stun'-sails set alow and aloft. We all began life in 15 the merchant service. Between the five of us there was the strong bond of the sea, and also the fellowship of the craft, which no amount of enthusiasm for yachting, cruising, and so on can give, since one is only the amusement of life and the other is life itself.

1

Marlow (at least I think that is how he spelt his name) told the story, or rather the chronicle, of a voyage:—

"Yes, I have seen a little of the Eastern seas; but what I remember best is my first voyage there. You fellows know there are those voyages that seem ordered for the illustration of life, that might stand for a symbol of existence. You fight, work, sweat, nearly kill yourself, sometimes do kill yourself, trying to accomplish something—and you can't. Not from any fault of yours. You simply can do nothing, neither great nor little—not a thing in the world—not even marry an old maid, or get a wretched 600-ton cargo of coal to its port of destination.

"It was altogether a memorable affair. It was my first voyage to the East, and my first voyage as second mate; it was also my skipper's first command. You'll admit it was time. He was sixty if a day; a little man, with a broad, not very straight back, with bowed shoulders and one leg more bandy than the other, he had that queer twisted-about appearance you see so often in men who work in the fields. He had a nutcracker face—chin and nose trying to come together over a sunken mouth—and it was framed in iron-gray fluffy hair, that looked like a chin-strap of cotton-wool sprinkled with coal-dust. And he had blue eyes in that old face of his, which were amazingly like a boy's, with that candid expression some quite common men preserve to the end of their days by a rare internal gift of simplicity of heart and rectitude of soul. What induced him to accept me was a wonder. I had come out of a crack Australian clipper, where I had been third officer, and he seemed to have a prejudice against crack clippers as aristocratic and high-toned. He said to me, 'You know, in this ship you will have to work.' I said I had to work in every ship I had ever been in. 'Ah, but this is different, and you gentlemen out of them big ships; . . . but there! I dare say you will do. Join to-morrow.'

"I joined to-morrow. It was twenty-two years ago; and I was just twenty. How time passes! It was one of the happiest days of my life. Fancy! Second mate for the first time—a really responsible officer! I wouldn't have thrown up my new billet for a fortune. The mate looked me over carefully. He was also an old chap, but of another stamp. He had a Roman nose, a snow-white, long beard, and his name was Mahon, but he insisted that it should be pronounced Mann. He was well connected; yet there was something wrong with his luck, and he had never got on.

"As to the captain, he had been for years in coasters, then in the Mediterranean, and last in the West Indian trade. He had never been round the Capes. He could just write a kind of sketchy hand, and didn't care for writing at all. Both were thorough good seamen of course, and between those two old chaps I felt like a small boy between two grandfathers.

"The ship also was old. Her name was the *Judea*. Queer name, isn't it? She belonged to a man Wilmer, Wilcox—some name like that; but he has been bankrupt and dead these twenty years or more, and his name don't matter. She had been laid up in Shadwell basin for ever so long. You may imagine her state. She was all rust, dust, grime—soot aloft, dirt on deck. To me it was like coming out of a palace into a ruined cottage. She was about 400 tons, had a primitive windlass, wooden latches to the doors, not a bit of brass about her, and a big square stern. There was on it, below her name in big letters, a lot of scrollwork, with the gilt off, and some sort of a coat of arms, with the motto 'Do or Die' underneath. I remember it took my fancy immensely. There was a touch of romance in it, something that made me love the old thing—something that appealed to my youth!

"We left London in ballast—sand ballast—to load a cargo of coal in a northern port for Bankok. Bankok! I thrilled. I had been six years at sea, but had only seen Melbourne and Sydney, very good places, charming places in their way—but Bankok!

"We worked out of the Thames under canvas, with a North Sea pilot on board. His name was Jermyn, and he dodged all day long about the galley drying his handkerchief before the stove. Apparently he never slept. He was a dismal man, with a perpetual tear sparkling at the end of his nose, who either had been in trouble, or was in trouble, or expected to be in trouble

5

15

25

35

—couldn't be happy unless something went wrong. He mistrusted my youth, my common-sense, and my seamanship, and made a point of showing it in a hundred little ways. I dare say he was right. It seems to me I knew very little then, and I
5   know not much more now; but I cherish a hate for that Jermyn to this day.

"We were a week working up as far as Yarmouth Roads, and then we got into a gale—the famous October gale of twenty-two years ago. It was wind, lightning, sleet, snow, and a terrific sea. We were flying light, and you may imagine how bad it was when I tell you we had smashed bulwarks and a flooded deck. On the second night she shifted her ballast into the lee bow, and by that time we had been blown off somewhere on the Dogger Bank. There was nothing for it but go below with shov-
15   els and try to right her, and there we were in that vast hold, gloomy like a cavern, the tallow dips stuck and flickering on the beams, the gale howling above, the ship tossing about like mad on her side; there we all were, Jermyn, the captain, every one, hardly able to keep our feet, engaged on that gravedigger's work, and trying to toss shovelfuls of wet sand up to windward. At every tumble of the ship you could see vaguely in the dim light men falling down with a great flourish of shovels. One of the ship's boys (we had two), impressed by the weirdness of the scene, wept as if his heart would break. We could hear him blub-
25   bering somewhere in the shadows.

"On the third day the gale died out, and by and by a north-country tug picked us up. We took sixteen days in all to get from London to the Tyne! When we got into dock we had lost our turn for loading, and they hauled us off to a tier where we remained for a month. Mrs. Beard (the captain's name was Beard) came from Colchester to see the old man. She lived on board. The crew of runners had left, and there remained only the officers, one boy and the steward, a mulatto who answered to the name of Abraham. Mrs. Beard was an old woman, with
35   a face all wrinkled and ruddy like a winter apple, and the fig-ure of a young girl. She caught sight of me once, sewing on a

button, and insisted on having my shirts to repair. This was something different from the captains' wives I had known on board crack clippers. When I brought her the shirts, she said: 'And the socks? They want mending, I am sure, and John's—Captain Beard's—things are all in order now. I would be glad of something to do.' Bless the old woman. She overhauled my outfit for me, and meantime I read for the first time *Sartor Resartus* and Burnaby's *Ride to Khiva*. I didn't understand much of the first then; but I remember I preferred the soldier to the philosopher at the time; a preference which life has only confirmed. One was a man, and the other was either more—or less. However, they are both dead and Mrs. Beard is dead, and youth, strength, genius, thoughts, achievements, simple hearts —all die. . . . No matter.

"They loaded us at last. We shipped a crew. Eight able seamen and two boys. We hauled off one evening to the buoys at the dock-gates, ready to go out, and with a fair prospect of beginning the voyage next day. Mrs. Beard was to start for home by a late train. When the ship was fast we went to tea. We sat rather silent through the meal—Mahon, the old couple, and I. I finished first, and slipped away for a smoke, my cabin being in a deck-house just against the poop. It was high water, blowing fresh with a drizzle; the double dock-gates were opened, and the steam-colliers were going in and out in the darkness with their lights burning bright, a great plashing of propellers, rattling of winches, and a lot of hailing on the pier-heads. I watched the procession of head-lights gliding high and of green lights gliding low in the night, when suddenly a red gleam flashed at me, vanished, came into view again, and re-mained. The fore-end of a steamer loomed up close. I shouted down the cabin, 'Come up, quick!' and then heard a startled voice saying afar in the dark, 'Stop her, sir.' A bell jingled. Another voice cried warningly, 'We are going right into that barque, sir.' The answer to this was a gruff 'All right,' and the next thing was a heavy crash as the steamer struck a glancing blow with the bluff of her bow about our fore-rigging. There

was a moment of confusion, yelling, and running about. Steam
roared. Then somebody was heard saying, 'All clear, sir.' . . .
'Are you all right?' asked the gruff voice. I had jumped forward
to see the damage, and hailed back, 'I think so.' 'Easy astern,'
5 said the gruff voice. A bell jingled. 'What steamer is that?'
screamed Mahon. By that time she was no more to us than a
bulky shadow manœuvring a little way off. They shouted at us
some name—a woman's name, Miranda or Melissa—or some
such thing. 'This means another month in this beastly hole,'
said Mahon to me, as we peered with lamps about the splin-
tered bulwarks and broken braces. 'But where's the captain?'

"We had not heard or seen anything of him all that time.
We went aft to look. A doleful voice arose hailing somewhere
in the middle of the dock, '*Judea* ahoy!' . . . How the devil
15 did he get there? . . . 'Hallo!' we shouted. 'I am adrift in our
boat without oars,' he cried. A belated water-man offered his
services, and Mahon struck a bargain with him for half-a-crown
to tow our skipper alongside; but it was Mrs. Beard that came
up the ladder first. They had been floating about the dock in
that mizzly cold rain for nearly an hour. I was never so surprised in my life.

"It appears that when he heard my shout 'Come up' he understood at once what was the matter, caught up his wife, ran
on deck, and across, and down into our boat, which was fast to
25 the ladder. Not bad for a sixty-year-old. Just imagine that old
fellow saving heroically in his arms that old woman—the
woman of his life. He set her down on a thwart, and was ready
to climb back on board when the painter came adrift somehow,
and away they went together. Of course in the confusion we
did not hear him shouting. He looked abashed. She said cheerfully, 'I suppose it does not matter my losing the train now?'
'No, Jenny—you go below and get warm,' he growled. Then to
us: 'A sailor has no business with a wife—I say. There I was,
out of the ship. Well, no harm done this time. Let's go and
35 look at what that fool of a steamer smashed.'

"It wasn't much, but it delayed us three weeks. At the end

of that time, the captain being engaged with his agents, I carried Mrs. Beard's bag to the railway-station and put her all comfy into a third-class carriage. She lowered the window to say, 'You are a good young man. If you see John—Captain Beard—without his muffler at night, just remind him from me to keep his throat well wrapped up.' 'Certainly, Mrs. Beard,' I said. 'You are a good young man; I noticed how attentive you are to John—to Captain——' The train pulled out suddenly; I took my cap off to the old woman: I never saw her again. . . . Pass the bottle.

"We went to sea next day. When we made that start for Bankok we had been already three months out of London. We had expected to be a fortnight or so—at the outside.

"It was January, and the weather was beautiful—the beautiful sunny winter weather that has more charm than in the summer-time, because it is unexpected, and crisp, and you know it won't, it can't, last long. It's like a windfall, like a godsend, like an unexpected piece of luck.

"It lasted all down the North Sea, all down Channel; and it lasted till we were three hundred miles or so to the westward of the Lizards: then the wind went round to the sou'west and began to pipe up. In two days it blew a gale. The *Judea*, hove to, wallowed on the Atlantic like an old candle-box. It blew day after day: it blew with spite, without interval, without mercy, without rest. The world was nothing but an immensity of great foaming waves rushing at us, under a sky low enough to touch with the hand and dirty like a smoked ceiling. In the stormy space surrounding us there was as much flying spray as air. Day after day and night after night there was nothing round the ship but the howl of the wind, the tumult of the sea, the noise of water pouring over her deck. There was no rest for her and no rest for us. She tossed, she pitched, she stood on her head, she sat on her tail, she rolled, she groaned, and we had to hold on while on deck and cling to our bunks when below, in a constant effort of body and worry of mind.

"One night Mahon spoke through the small window of my

berth. It opened right into my very bed, and I was lying there
sleepless, in my boots, feeling as though I had not slept
for years, and could not if I tried. He said excitedly—

5 " 'You got the sounding-rod in here, Marlow? I can't get the
pumps to suck. By God! It's no child's play.'

"I gave him the sounding-rod and lay down again, trying
to think of various things—but I thought only of the pumps.
When I came on deck they were still at it, and my watch relieved at the pumps. By the light of the lantern brought on deck
to examine the sounding-rod I caught a glimpse of their weary,
serious faces. We pumped all the four hours. We pumped all
night, all day, all the week—watch and watch. She was working herself loose, and leaked badly—not enough to drown us
at once, but enough to kill us with the work at the pumps. And
15 while we pumped the ship was going from us piecemeal: the
bulwarks went, the stanchions were torn out, the ventilators
smashed, the cabin-door burst in. There was not a dry spot in
the ship. She was being gutted bit by bit. The long-boat
changed, as if by magic, into matchwood where she stood in
her gripes. I had lashed her myself, and was rather proud of my
handiwork, which had withstood so long the malice of the sea.
And we pumped. And there was no break in the weather. The
sea was white like a sheet of foam, like a caldron of boiling
milk; there was not a break in the clouds, no—not the size of a
25 man's hand—no, not for so much as ten seconds. There was for
us no sky, there were for us no stars, no sun, no universe—
nothing but angry clouds and an infuriated sea. We pumped
watch and watch, for dear life; and it seemed to last for months,
for years, for all eternity, as though we had been dead and gone
to a hell for sailors. We forgot the day of the week, the name
of the month, what year it was, and whether we had ever been
ashore. The sails blew away, she lay broadside on under a
weather-cloth, the ocean poured over her, and we did not care.
We turned those handles, and had the eyes of idiots. As soon as
35 we had crawled on deck I used to take a round turn with a
rope about the men, the pumps, and the mainmast, and we

turned, we turned incessantly, with the water to our waists, to our necks, over our heads. It was all one. We had forgotten how it felt to be dry.

"And there was somewhere in me the thought: By Jove! this is the deuce of an adventure—something you read about; and 5 it is my first voyage as second mate—and I am only twenty— and here I am lasting it out as well as any of these men, and keeping my chaps up to the mark. I was pleased. I would not have given up the experience for worlds. I had moments of exultation. Whenever the old dismantled craft pitched heavily with her counter high in the air, she seemed to me to throw up, like an appeal, like a defiance, like a cry to the clouds without mercy, the words written on her stern: 'Judea, London. Do or Die.'

"O youth! The strength of it, the faith of it, the imagination 15 of it! To me she was not an old rattle-trap carting about the world a lot of coal for a freight—to me she was the endeavour, the test, the trial of life. I think of her with pleasure, with affection, with regret—as you would think of someone dead you have loved. I shall never forget her.   Pass the bottle.

"One night when tied to the mast, as I explained, we were pumping on, deafened with the wind, and without spirit enough in us to wish ourselves dead, a heavy sea crashed aboard and swept clean over us. As soon as I got my breath I shouted, as in duty bound, 'Keep on, boys!' when suddenly I felt some- 25 thing hard floating on deck strike the calf of my leg. I made a grab at it and missed. It was so dark we could not see each other's faces within a foot—you understand.

"After that thump the ship kept quiet for a while, and the thing, whatever it was, struck my leg again. This time I caught it—and it was a saucepan. At first, being stupid with fatigue and thinking of nothing but the pumps, I did not understand what I had in my hand. Suddenly it dawned upon me, and I shouted, 'Boys, the house on deck is gone. Leave this, and let's look for the cook.' 35

"There was a deck-house forward, which contained the gal-

ley, the cook's berth, and the quarters of the crew. As we had
expected for days to see it swept away, the hands had been
ordered to sleep in the cabin—the only safe place in the ship.
The steward, Abraham, however, persisted in clinging to his
berth, stupidly, like a mule—from sheer fright I believe, like an
animal that won't leave a stable falling in an earthquake. So
we went to look for him. It was chancing death, since once out
of our lashings we were as exposed as if on a raft. But we went.
The house was shattered as if a shell had exploded inside. Most
of it had gone overboard—stove, men's quarters, and their
property, all was gone; but two posts, holding a portion of the
bulkhead to which Abraham's bunk was attached, remained as
if by a miracle. We groped in the ruins and came upon this, and
there he was, sitting in his bunk, surrounded by foam and
wreckage, jabbering cheerfully to himself. He was out of his
mind; completely and for ever mad, with this sudden shock
coming upon the fag-end of his endurance. We snatched him
up, lugged him aft, and pitched him head-first down the cabin
companion. You understand there was no time to carry him
down with infinite precautions and wait to see how he got
on. Those below would pick him up at the bottom of the stairs
all right. We were in a hurry to go back to the pumps. That
business could not wait. A bad leak is an inhuman thing.

"One would think that the sole purpose of that fiendish
gale had been to make a lunatic of that poor devil of a mulatto.
It eased before morning, and next day the sky cleared, and as
the sea went down the leak took up. When it came to bending a fresh set of sails the crew demanded to put back—and
really there was nothing else to do. Boats gone, decks swept
clean, cabin gutted, men without a stitch but what they stood
in, stores spoiled, ship strained. We put her head for home, and
—would you believe it? The wind came east right in our teeth.
It blew fresh, it blew continuously. We had to beat up every
inch of the way, but she did not leak so badly, the water keeping comparatively smooth. Two hours' pumping in every four
is no joke—but it kept her afloat as far as Falmouth.

"The good people there live on casualties of the sea, and no doubt were glad to see us. A hungry crowd of shipwrights sharpened their chisels at the sight of that carcass of a ship. And, by Jove! they had pretty pickings off us before they were done. I fancy the owner was already in a tight place. There were delays. Then it was decided to take part of the cargo out and caulk her topsides. This was done, the repairs finished, cargo reshipped; a new crew came on board, and we went out —for Bankok. At the end of a week we were back again. The crew said they weren't going to Bankok—a hundred and fifty days' passage—in a something hooker that wanted pumping eight hours out of the twenty-four; and the nautical papers inserted again the little paragraph: 'Judea. Barque. Tyne to Bankok; coals; put back to Falmouth leaky and with crew refusing duty.'

"There were more delays—more tinkering. The owner came down for a day, and said she was as right as a little fiddle. Poor old Captain Beard looked like the ghost of a Geordie skipper —through the worry and humiliation of it. Remember he was sixty, and it was his first command. Mahon said it was a foolish business, and would end badly. I loved the ship more than ever, and wanted awfully to get to Bankok. To Bankok! Magic name, blessed name. Mesopotamia wasn't a patch on it. Remember I was twenty, and it was my first second-mate's billet, and the East was waiting for me.

"We went out and anchored in the outer roads with a fresh crew—the third. She leaked worse than ever. It was as if those confounded shipwrights had actually made a hole in her. This time we did not even go outside. The crew simply refused to man the windlass.

"They towed us back to the inner harbour, and we became a fixture, a feature, an institution of the place. People pointed us out to visitors as 'That 'ere barque that's going to Bankok —has been here six months—put back three times.' On holidays the small boys pulling about in boats would hail, 'Judea, ahoy!' and if a head showed above the rail shouted, 'Where you bound to?—Bankok?' and jeered. We were only three on board. The poor old skipper mooned in the cabin. Mahon undertook the cooking, and unexpectedly developed all a Frenchman's genius for preparing nice little messes. I looked languidly after the rigging. We became citizens of Falmouth. Every shopkeeper knew us. At the barber's or tobacconist's they asked familiarly, 'Do you think you will ever get to Bankok?' Meantime the owner, the underwriters, and the charterers squabbled amongst themselves in London, and our pay went on. . . . Pass the bottle.

"It was horrid. Morally it was worse than pumping for life. It seemed as though we had been forgotten by the world, belonged to nobody, would go nowhere; it seemed that, as if bewitched, we would have to live for ever and ever in that inner harbour, a derision and a byword to generations of long-shore loafers and dishonest boatmen. I obtained three months' pay and a five days' leave, and made a rush for London. It took me a day to get there and pretty well another to come back— but three months' pay went all the same. I don't know what I did with it. I went to a music-hall, I believe, lunched, dined, and supped in a swell place in Regent Street, and was back in time, with nothing but a complete set of Byron's works and a new railway rug to show for three months' work. The boatman who pulled me off to the ship said: 'Hallo! I thought you had left the old thing. *She* will never get to Bankok.' 'That's all *you* know about it,' I said scornfully—but I didn't like that prophecy at all.

"Suddenly a man, some kind of agent to somebody, appeared with full powers. He had grog-blossoms all over his face, an indomitable energy, and was a jolly soul. We leaped into life again. A hulk came alongside, took our cargo, and then we went into dry dock to get our copper stripped. No wonder she leaked. The poor thing, strained beyond endurance by the gale, had, as if in disgust, spat out all the oakum of her lower seams. She was recaulked, new coppered, and made as tight as a bottle. We went back to the hulk and reshipped our cargo.

"Then, on a fine moonlight night, all the rats left the ship.

"We had been infested with them. They had destroyed our sails, consumed more stores than the crew, affably shared our beds and our dangers, and now, when the ship was made seaworthy, concluded to clear out. I called Mahon to enjoy the spectacle. Rat after rat appeared on our rail, took a last look over his shoulder, and leaped with a hollow thud into the empty hulk. We tried to count them, but soon lost the tale. Mahon said: 'Well, well! don't talk to me about the intelligence of rats. They ought to have left before, when we had that narrow squeak from foundering. There you have the proof how silly is the superstition about them. They leave a good ship for an old rotten hulk, where there is nothing to eat, too, the fools! . . . I don't believe they know what is safe or what is good for them, any more than you or I.'

"And after some more talk we agreed that the wisdom of rats had been grossly overrated, being in fact no greater than that of men.

"The story of the ship was known, by this, all up the Channel from Land's End to the Forelands, and we could get no crew on the south coast. They sent us one all complete from Liverpool, and we left once more—for Bankok.

"We had fair breezes, smooth water right into the tropics, and the old *Judea* lumbered along in the sunshine. When she went eight knots everything cracked aloft, and we tied our caps to our heads; but mostly she strolled on at the rate of three miles an hour. What could you expect? She was tired—that old ship. Her youth was where mine is—where yours is—you fellows who listen to this yarn; and what friend would throw your years and your weariness in your face? We didn't grumble at her. To us aft, at least, it seemed as though we had been born in her, reared in her, had lived in her for ages, had never known any other ship. I would just as soon have abused the old village church at home for not being a cathedral.

"And for me there was also my youth to make me patient. There was all the East before me, and all life, and the thought

that I had been tried in that ship and had come out pretty well. And I thought of men of old who, centuries ago, went that road in ships that sailed no better, to the land of palms, and spices, and yellow sands, and of brown nations ruled by kings
5 more cruel than Nero the Roman, and more splendid than Solomon the Jew. The old barque lumbered on, heavy with her age and the burden of her cargo, while I lived the life of youth in ignorance and hope. She lumbered on through an interminable procession of days; and the fresh gilding flashed back at the setting sun, seemed to cry out over the darkening sea the words painted on her stern, '*Judea*, London. Do or Die.'

"Then we entered the Indian Ocean and steered northerly for Java Head. The winds were light. Weeks slipped by. She crawled on, do or die, and people at home began to think of
15 posting us as overdue.

"One Saturday evening, I being off duty, the men asked me to give them an extra bucket of water or so—for washing clothes. As I did not wish to screw on the fresh-water pump so late, I went forward whistling, and with a key in my hand to unlock the forepeak scuttle, intending to serve the water out of a spare tank we kept there.

"The smell down below was as unexpected as it was frightful. One would have thought hundreds of paraffin-lamps had been flaring and smoking in that hole for days. I was glad
25 to get out. The man with me coughed and said, 'Funny smell, sir.' I answered negligently, 'It's good for the health, they say,' and walked aft.

"The first thing I did was to put my head down the square of the midship ventilator. As I lifted the lid a visible breath, something like a thin fog, a puff of faint haze, rose from the opening. The ascending air was hot, and had a heavy, sooty, paraffiny smell. I gave one sniff, and put down the lid gently. It was no use choking myself. The cargo was on fire.

"Next day she began to smoke in earnest. You see it was to
35 be expected, for though the coal was of a safe kind, that cargo

had been so handled, so broken up with handling, that it looked more like smithy coal than anything else. Then it had been wetted—more than once. It rained all the time we were taking it back from the hulk, and now with this long passage it got heated, and there was another case of spontaneous combustion. 5

"The captain called us into the cabin. He had a chart spread on the table, and looked unhappy. He said, 'The coast of West Australia is near, but I mean to proceed to our destination. It is the hurricane month, too; but we will just keep her head for Bankok, and fight the fire. No more putting back anywhere, if we all get roasted. We will try first to stifle this 'ere damned combustion by want of air.'

"We tried. We battened down everything, and still she smoked. The smoke kept coming out through imperceptible 15 crevices; it forced itself through bulkheads and covers; it oozed here and there and everywhere in slender threads, in an invisible film, in an incomprehensible manner. It made its way into the cabin, into the forecastle; it poisoned the sheltered places on the deck, it could be sniffed as high as the mainyard. It was clear that if the smoke came out the air came in. This was disheartening. This combustion refused to be stifled.

"We resolved to try water, and took the hatches off. Enormous volumes of smoke, whitish, yellowish, thick, greasy, misty, choking, ascended as high as the trucks. All hands cleared out 25 aft. Then the poisonous cloud blew away, and we went back to work in a smoke that was no thicker now than that of an ordinary factory chimney.

"We rigged the force-pump, got the hose along, and by and by it burst. Well, it was as old as the ship—a prehistoric hose, and past repair. Then we pumped with the feeble head-pump, drew water with buckets, and in this way managed in time to pour lots of Indian Ocean into the main hatch. The bright stream flashed in sunshine, fell into a layer of white crawling smoke, and vanished on the black surface of coal. Steam as- 35

cended mingling with the smoke. We poured salt water as into a barrel without a bottom. It was our fate to pump in that ship, to pump out of her, to pump into her; and after keeping water out of her to save ourselves from being drowned, we fran-
5 tically poured water into her to save ourselves from being burnt.

"And she crawled on, do or die, in the serene weather. The sky was a miracle of purity, a miracle of azure. The sea was polished, was blue, was pellucid, was sparkling like a precious stone, extending on all sides, all round to the horizon—as if the whole terrestrial globe had been one jewel, one colossal sapphire, a single gem fashioned into a planet. And on the lustre of the great calm waters the *Judea* glided imperceptibly, enveloped in languid and unclean vapours, in a lazy cloud that drifted to leeward, light and slow; a pestiferous cloud defiling
15 the splendour of sea and sky.

"All this time of course we saw no fire. The cargo smouldered at the bottom somewhere. Once Mahon, as we were working side by side, said to me with a queer smile: 'Now, if she only would spring a tidy leak—like that time when we first left the Channel—it would put a stopper on this fire. Wouldn't it?' I remarked irrelevantly, 'Do you remember the rats?'

"We fought the fire and sailed the ship too as carefully as though nothing had been the matter. The steward cooked and attended on us. Of the other twelve men, eight worked while
25 four rested. Everyone took his turn, captain included. There was equality, and if not exactly fraternity, then a deal of good feeling. Sometimes a man, as he dashed a bucketful of water down the hatchway, would yell out, 'Hurrah for Bankok!' and the rest laughed. But generally we were taciturn and serious—and thirsty. Oh! how thirsty! And we had to be careful with the water. Strict allowance. The ship smoked, the sun blazed. . . . Pass the bottle.

"We tried everything. We even made an attempt to dig down to the fire. No good, of course. No man could remain
35 more than a minute below. Mahon, who went first, fainted there, and the man who went to fetch him out did likewise. We

lugged them out on deck. Then I leaped down to show how easily it could be done. They had learned wisdom by that time, and contented themselves by fishing for me with a chain-hook tied to a broom-handle, I believe. I did not offer to go and fetch up my shovel, which was left down below.

"Things began to look bad. We put the long-boat into the water. The second boat was ready to swing out. We had also another, a 14-foot thing, on davits aft, where it was quite safe.

"Then, behold, the smoke suddenly decreased. We redoubled our efforts to flood the bottom of the ship. In two days there was no smoke at all. Everybody was on the broad grin. This was on a Friday. On Saturday no work, but sailing the ship, of course, was done. The men washed their clothes and their faces for the first time in a fortnight, and had a special dinner given them. They spoke of spontaneous combustion with contempt, and implied *they* were the boys to put out combustions. Somehow we all felt as though we each had inherited a large fortune. But a beastly smell of burning hung about the ship. Captain Beard had hollow eyes and sunken cheeks. I had never noticed so much before how twisted and bowed he was. He and Mahon prowled soberly about hatches and ventilators, sniffing. It struck me suddenly poor Mahon was a very, very old chap. As to me, I was as pleased and proud as though I had helped to win a great naval battle. O! Youth!

"The night was fine. In the morning a homeward-bound ship passed us hull down—the first we had seen for months; but we were nearing the land at last, Java Head being about 190 miles off, and nearly due north.

"Next day it was my watch on deck from eight to twelve. At breakfast the captain observed, 'It's wonderful how that smell hangs about the cabin.' About ten, the mate being on the poop, I stepped down on the main-deck for a moment. The carpenter's bench stood abaft the mainmast: I leaned against it sucking at my pipe, and the carpenter, a young chap, came to talk to me. He remarked, 'I think we have done very well, haven't we?' and then I perceived with annoyance the fool was trying to

tilt the bench. I said curtly, 'Don't, Chips,' and immediately became aware of a queer sensation, of an absurd delusion— I seemed somehow to be in the air. I heard all round me like a pent-up breath released—as if a thousand giants simultane-
5 ously had said Phoo!—and felt a dull concussion which made my ribs ache suddenly. No doubt about it—I was in the air, and my body was describing a short parabola. But short as it was, I had the time to think several thoughts in, as far as I can remember, the following order: This can't be the carpenter—What is it?—Some accident—Submarine volcano?—Coals, gas!—By Jove! we are being blown up—Everybody's dead—I am falling into the after-hatch—I see fire in it.

"The coal-dust suspended in the air of the hold had glowed dull-red at the moment of the explosion. In the twinkling of an
15 eye, in an infinitesimal fraction of a second since the first tilt of the bench, I was sprawling full length on the cargo. I picked myself up and scrambled out. It was quick like a rebound. The deck was a wilderness of smashed timber, lying crosswise like trees in a wood after a hurricane; an immense curtain of soiled rags waved gently before me—it was the main-sail blown to strips. I thought, The masts will be toppling over directly; and to get out of the way bolted on all-fours towards the poop-ladder. The first person I saw was Mahon, with eyes like saucers, his mouth open, and the long white hair standing straight on
25 end round his head like a silver halo. He was just about to go down when the sight of the main-deck stirring, heaving up, and changing into splinters before his eyes, petrified him on the top step. I stared at him in unbelief, and he stared at me with a queer kind of shocked curiosity. I did not know that I had no hair, no eyebrows, no eyelashes, that my young moustache was burnt off, that my face was black, one cheek laid open, my nose cut, and my chin bleeding. I had lost my cap, one of my slippers, and my shirt was torn to rags. Of all this I was not aware. I was amazed to see the ship still afloat, the poop-deck
35 whole—and, most of all, to see anybody alive. Also the

peace of the sky and the serenity of the sea were distinctly surprising. I suppose I expected to see them convulsed with horror. . . . Pass the bottle.

"There was a voice hailing the ship from somewhere—in the
air, in the sky—I couldn't tell. Presently I saw the captain— 5
and he was mad. He asked me eagerly, 'Where's the cabin-
table?' and to hear such a question was a frightful shock. I had
just been blown up, you understand, and vibrated with that
experience—I wasn't quite sure whether I was alive. Mahon
began to stamp with both feet and yelled at him, 'Good God!
don't you see the deck's blown out of her?' I found my voice,
and stammered out as if conscious of some gross neglect of
duty, 'I don't know where the cabin-table is.' It was like an absurd dream.

"Do you know what he wanted next? Well, he wanted to 15
trim the yards. Very placidly, and as if lost in thought, he insisted on having the foreyard squared. 'I don't know if there's
anybody alive,' said Mahon, almost tearfully. 'Surely,' he said,
gently, 'there will be enough left to square the foreyard.'

"The old chap, it seems, was in his own berth winding up the
chronometers, when the shock sent him spinning. Immediately it occurred to him—as he said afterwards—that the ship
had struck something, and he ran out into the cabin. There, he
saw, the cabin-table had vanished somewhere. The deck being
blown up, it had fallen down into the lazarette of course. Where 25
we had our breakfast that morning he saw only a great hole in
the floor. This appeared to him so awfully mysterious, and impressed him so immensely, that what he saw and heard after
he got on deck were mere trifles in comparison. And, mark,
he noticed directly the wheel deserted and his barque off her
course—and his only thought was to get that miserable,
stripped, undecked, smouldering shell of a ship back again with
her head pointing at her port of destination. Bankok! That's
what he was after. I tell you this quiet, bowed, bandy-legged,
almost deformed little man was immense in the singleness of 35

his idea and in his placid ignorance of our agitation. He motioned us forward with a commanding gesture, and went to take the wheel himself.

"Yes; that was the first thing we did—trim the yards of that
5   wreck! No one was killed, or even disabled, but everyone was more or less hurt. You should have seen them! Some were in rags, with black faces, like coal-heavers, like sweeps, and had bullet heads that seemed closely cropped, but were in fact singed to the skin. Others, of the watch below, awakened by being shot out from their collapsing bunks, shivered incessantly, and kept on groaning even as we went about our work. But they all worked. That crew of Liverpool hard cases had in them the right stuff. It's my experience they always have. It is the sea that gives it—the vastness, the loneliness sur-
15   rounding their dark stolid souls. Ah! Well! we stumbled, we crept, we fell, we barked our shins on the wreckage, we hauled. The masts stood, but we did not know how much they might be charred down below. It was nearly calm, but a long swell ran from the west and made her roll. They might go at any moment. We looked at them with apprehension. One could not foresee which way they would fall.

"Then we retreated aft and looked about us. The deck was a tangle of planks on edge, of planks on end, of splinters, of ruined woodwork. The masts rose from that chaos like big
25   trees above a matted undergrowth. The interstices of that mass of wreckage were full of something whitish, sluggish, stirring— of something that was like a greasy fog. The smoke of the invisible fire was coming up again, was trailing, like a poisonous thick mist in some valley choked with dead wood. Already lazy wisps were beginning to curl upwards amongst the mass of splinters. Here and there a piece of timber, stuck upright, resembled a post. Half of a fife-rail had been shot through the foresail, and the sky made a patch of glorious blue in the ignobly soiled canvas. A portion of several boards holding to-
35   gether had fallen across the rail, and one end protruded overboard, like a gangway leading upon nothing, like a gangway

.leading over the deep sea, leading to death—as if inviting us to walk the plank at once and be done with our ridiculous troubles. And still the air, the sky—a ghost, something invisible was hailing the ship.

"Someone had the sense to look over, and there was the helmsman, who had impulsively jumped overboard, anxious to come back. He yelled and swam lustily like a merman, keeping up with the ship. We threw him a rope, and presently he stood amongst us streaming with water and very crestfallen. The captain had surrendered the wheel, and apart, elbow on rail and chin in hand, gazed at the sea wistfully. We asked ourselves, What next? I thought, Now, this is something like. This is great. I wonder what will happen. O youth!

"Suddenly Mahon sighted a steamer far astern. Captain Beard said, 'We may do something with her yet.' We hoisted two flags, which said in the international language of the sea, 'On fire. Want immediate assistance.' The steamer grew bigger rapidly, and by and by spoke with two flags on her foremast, 'I am coming to your assistance.'

"In half an hour she was abreast, to windward, within hail, and rolling slightly, with her engines stopped. We lost our composure, and yelled all together with excitement, 'We've been blown up.' A man in a white helmet, on the bridge, cried, 'Yes! All right! all right!' and he nodded his head, and smiled, and made soothing motions with his hand as though at a lot of frightened children. One of the boats dropped in the water, and walked towards us upon the sea with her long oars. Four Calashes pulled a swinging stroke. This was my first sight of Malay seamen. I've known them since, but what struck me then was their unconcern: they came alongside, and even the bowman standing up and holding to our main-chains with the boat-hook did not deign to lift his head for a glance. I thought people who had been blown up deserved more attention.

"A little man, dry like a chip and agile like a monkey, clambered up. It was the mate of the steamer. He gave one look, and cried, 'O boys—you had better quit.'

"We were silent. He talked apart with the captain for a time —seemed to argue with him. Then they went away together to the steamer.

"When our skipper came back we learned that the steamer was the *Somerville*, Captain Nash, from West Australia to Singapore *via* Batavia with mails, and that the agreement was she should tow us to Anjer or Batavia, if possible, where we could extinguish the fire by scuttling, and then proceed on our voyage—to Bankok! The old man seemed excited. 'We will do it yet,' he said to Mahon, fiercely. He shook his fist at the sky. Nobody else said a word.

"At noon the steamer began to tow. She went ahead slim and high, and what was left of the *Judea* followed at the end of seventy fathom of tow-rope—followed her swiftly like a cloud of smoke with mastheads protruding above. We went aloft to furl the sails. We coughed on the yards, and were careful about the bunts. Do you see the lot of us there, putting a neat furl on the sails of that ship doomed to arrive nowhere? There was not a man who didn't think that at any moment the masts would topple over. From aloft we could not see the ship for smoke, and they worked carefully, passing the gaskets with even turns. 'Harbour furl—aloft there!' cried Mahon from below.

"You understand this? I don't think one of those chaps expected to get down in the usual way. When we did I heard them saying to each other, 'Well, I thought we would come down overboard, in a lump—sticks and all—blame me if I didn't.' 'That's what I was thinking to myself,' would answer wearily another battered and bandaged scarecrow. And, mind, these were men without the drilled-in habit of obedience. To an onlooker they would be a lot of profane scallywags without a redeeming point. What made them do it—what made them obey me when I, thinking consciously how fine it was, made them drop the bunt of the foresail twice to try and do it better? What? They had no professional reputation—no examples, no praise. It wasn't a sense of duty; they all knew well enough how to shirk, and laze, and dodge—when they had a mind to it—and mostly they had. Was it the two pounds ten-a-month that sent them there? They didn't think their pay half good enough. No; it was something in them, something inborn and subtle and everlasting. I don't say positively that the crew of a French or German merchantman wouldn't have done it, but I doubt whether it would have been done in the same way. There was a completeness in it, something solid like a principle, and masterful like an instinct—a disclosure of something secret—of that hidden something, that gift of good or evil that makes racial difference, that shapes the fate of nations.

"It was that night at ten that, for the first time since we had been fighting it, we saw the fire. The speed of the towing had fanned the smouldering destruction. A blue gleam appeared forward, shining below the wreck of the deck. It wavered in patches, it seemed to stir and creep like the light of a glow-worm. I saw it first, and told Mahon. 'Then the game's up,' he said. 'We had better stop this towing, or she will burst out suddenly fore and aft before we can clear out.' We set up a yell; rang bells to attract their attention; they towed on. At last Mahon and I had to crawl forward and cut the rope with an axe. There was no time to cast off the lashings. Red tongues could be seen licking the wilderness of splinters under our feet as we made our way back to the poop.

"Of course they very soon found out in the steamer that the rope was gone. She gave a loud blast of her whistle, her lights were seen sweeping in a wide circle, she came up ranging close alongside, and stopped. We were all in a tight group on the poop looking at her. Every man had saved a little bundle or a bag. Suddenly a conical flame with a twisted top shot up forward and threw upon the black sea a circle of light, with the two vessels side by side and heaving gently in its centre. Captain Beard had been sitting on the gratings still and mute for hours, but now he rose slowly and advanced in front of us, to the mizzen-shrouds. Captain Nash hailed: 'Come along! Look sharp. I have mail-bags on board. I will take you and your boats to Singapore.'

"   'Thank you! No!' said our skipper. 'We must see the last of the ship.'

"   'I can't stand by any longer,' shouted the other. 'Mails— you know.'

5   "   'Ay! ay! We are all right.'

"   'Very well! I'll report you in Singapore. . . . Good-bye!'

"He waved his hand. Our men dropped their bundles quietly. The steamer moved ahead, and passing out of the circle of light, vanished at once from our sight, dazzled by the fire which burned fiercely. And then I knew that I would see the East first as commander of a small boat. I thought it fine; and the fidelity to the old ship was fine. We should see the last of her. Oh, the glamour of youth! Oh, the fire of it, more daz- zling than the flames of the burning ship, throwing a magic 15   light on the wide earth, leaping audaciously to the sky, pres- ently to be quenched by time, more cruel, more pitiless, more bitter than the sea—and like the flames of the burning ship sur- rounded by an impenetrable night.

"The old man warned us in his gentle and inflexible way that it was part of our duty to save for the underwriters as much as we could of the ship's gear. Accordingly we went to work aft, while she blazed forward to give us plenty of light. We lugged out a lot of rubbish. What didn't we save? An old barometer fixed with an absurd quantity of screws nearly cost me my life: 25   a sudden rush of smoke came upon me, and I just got away in time. There were various stores, bolts of canvas, coils of rope; the poop looked like a marine bazaar, and the boats were lum- bered to the gunwales. One would have thought the old man wanted to take as much as he could of his first command with him. He was very, very quiet, but off his balance evidently. Would you believe it? He wanted to take a length of old stream-cable and a kedge-anchor with him in the long-boat. We said, 'Ay, ay, sir,' deferentially, and on the quiet let the things slip overboard. The heavy medicine-chest went that way, two bags of green coffee, tins of paint—fancy, paint!—a whole lot of things. Then I was ordered with two hands into the boats to make a stowage and get them ready against the time it would be proper for us to leave the ship.

"We put everything straight, stepped the long-boat's mast for our skipper, who was to take charge of her, and I was not sorry to sit down for a moment. My face felt raw, every limb ached as if broken, I was aware of all my ribs, and would have sworn to a twist in the backbone. The boats, fast astern, lay in a deep shadow, and all around I could see the circle of the sea lighted by the fire. A gigantic flame arose forward straight and clear. It flared fierce, with noises like the whirr of wings, with rumbles as of thunder. There were cracks, detonations, and from the cone of flame the sparks flew upwards, as man is born to trouble, to leaky ships, and to ships that burn.

"What bothered me was that the ship, lying broadside to the swell and to such wind as there was—a mere breath—the boats would not keep astern where they were safe, but persisted, in a pig-headed way boats have, in getting under the counter and then swinging alongside. They were knocking about dangerously and coming near the flame, while the ship rolled on them, and, of course, there was always the danger of the masts going over the side at any moment. I and my two boat-keepers kept them off as best we could, with oars and boat-hooks; but to be constantly at it became exasperating, since there was no reason why we should not leave at once. We could not see those on board, nor could we imagine what caused the delay. The boat-keepers were swearing feebly, and I had not only my share of the work but also had to keep at it two men who showed a constant inclination to lay themselves down and let things slide.

"At last I hailed, 'On deck there,' and someone looked over. 'We're ready here,' I said. The head disappeared, and very soon popped up again. 'The captain says, All right, sir, and to keep the boats well clear of the ship.'

"Half an hour passed. Suddenly there was a frightful racket, rattle, clanking of chain, hiss of water, and millions of sparks flew up into the shivering column of smoke that stood leaning slightly above the ship. The cat-heads had burned away, and the 5 two red-hot anchors had gone to the bottom, tearing out after them two hundred fathom of red-hot chain. The ship trembled, the mass of flame swayed as if ready to collapse, and the fore top-gallant-mast fell. It darted down like an arrow of fire, shot under, and instantly leaping up within an oar's-length of the boats, floated quietly, very black on the luminous sea. I hailed the deck again. After some time a man in an unexpectedly cheerful but also muffled tone, as though he had been trying to speak with his mouth shut, informed me, 'Coming directly, sir,' and vanished. For a long time I heard nothing 15 but the whirr and roar of the fire. There were also whistling sounds. The boats jumped, tugged at the painters, ran at each other playfully, knocked their sides together, or, do what we would, swung in a bunch against the ship's side. I couldn't stand it any longer, and swarming up a rope, clambered aboard over the stern.

"It was as bright as day. Coming up like this, the sheet of fire facing me was a terrifying sight, and the heat seemed hardly bearable at first. On a settee cushion dragged out of the cabin Captain Beard, his legs drawn up and one arm under his 25 head, slept with the light playing on him. Do you know what the rest were busy about? They were sitting on deck right aft, round an open case, eating bread and cheese and drinking bottled stout.

"On the background of flames twisting in fierce tongues above their heads they seemed at home like salamanders, and looked like a band of desperate pirates. The fire sparkled in the whites of their eyes, gleamed on patches of white skin seen through the torn shirts. Each had the marks as of a battle about him—bandaged heads, tied-up arms, a strip of dirty rag 35 round a knee—and each man had a bottle between his legs and a chunk of cheese in his hand. Mahon got up. With his hand-

some and disreputable head, his hooked profile, his long
white beard, and with an uncorked bottle in his hand, he resembled one of those reckless sea-robbers of old making merry
amidst violence and disaster. 'The last meal on board,' he explained solemnly. 'We had nothing to eat all day, and it was no   5
use leaving all this.' He flourished the bottle and indicated
the sleeping skipper. 'He said he couldn't swallow anything, so
I got him to lie down,' he went on; and as I stared, 'I
don't know whether you are aware, young fellow, the man had
no sleep to speak of for days—and there will be dam' little
sleep in the boats.' 'There will be no boats by and by if you fool
about much longer,' I said, indignantly. I walked up to the skipper and shook him by the shoulder. At last he opened his eyes,
but did not move. 'Time to leave her, sir,' I said quietly.

"He got up painfully, looked at the flames, at the sea spar-   15
kling round the ship, and black, black as ink farther away; he
looked at the stars shining dim through a thin veil of smoke in
a sky black, black as Erebus.

" 'Youngest first,' he said.

"And the ordinary seaman, wiping his mouth with the back
of his hand, got up, clambered over the taffrail, and vanished.
Others followed. One, on the point of going over, stopped
short to drain his bottle, and with a great swing of his arm flung
it at the fire. 'Take this!' he cried.

"The skipper lingered disconsolately, and we left him to com-   25
mune alone for a while with his first command. Then I went
up again and brought him away at last. It was time. The iron-
work on the poop was hot to the touch.

"Then the painter of the long-boat was cut, and the three
boats, tied together, drifted clear of the ship. It was just sixteen hours after the explosion when we abandoned her. Mahon
had charge of the second boat, and I had the smallest—the
14-foot thing. The long-boat would have taken the lot of us; but
the skipper said we must save as much property as we could—
for the underwriters—and so I got my first command. I had two   35
men with me, a bag of biscuits, a few tins of meat, and a breaker

of water. I was ordered to keep close to the long-boat, that in case of bad weather we might be taken into her.

"And do you know what I thought? I thought I would part company as soon as I could. I wanted to have my first command all to myself. I wasn't going to sail in a squadron if there were a chance for independent cruising. I would make land by myself. I would beat the other boats. Youth! All youth! The silly, charming, beautiful youth.

"But we did not make a start at once. We must see the last of the ship. And so the boats drifted about that night, heaving and setting on the swell. The men dozed, waked, sighed, groaned. I looked at the burning ship.

"Between the darkness of earth and heaven she was burning fiercely upon a disc of purple sea shot by the blood-red play of gleams; upon a disc of water glittering and sinister. A high, clear flame, an immense and lonely flame, ascended from the ocean, and from its summit the black smoke poured continuously at the sky. She burned furiously; mournful and imposing like a funeral pile kindled in the night, surrounded by the sea, watched over by the stars. A magnificent death had come like a grace, like a gift, like a reward to that old ship at the end of her laborious days. The surrender of her weary ghost to the keeping of stars and sea was stirring like the sight of a glorious triumph. The masts fell just before daybreak, and for a moment there was a burst and turmoil of sparks that seemed to fill with flying fire the night patient and watchful, the vast night lying silent upon the sea. At daylight she was only a charred shell, floating still under a cloud of smoke and bearing a glowing mass of coal within.

"Then the oars were got out, and the boats forming in a line moved round her remains as if in procession—the long-boat leading. As we pulled across her stern a slim dart of fire shot out viciously at us, and suddenly she went down, head first, in a great hiss of steam. The unconsumed stern was the last to sink; but the paint had gone, had cracked, had peeled off, and

there were no letters, there was no word, no stubborn device
that was like her soul, to flash at the rising sun her creed and
her name.

"We made our way north. A breeze sprang up, and about
noon all the boats came together for the last time. I had no mast   5
or sail in mine, but I made a mast out of a spare oar and hoisted
a boat-awning for a sail, with a boat-hook for a yard. She was
certainly overmasted, but I had the satisfaction of knowing
that with the wind aft I could beat the other two. I had to wait
for them. Then we all had a look at the captain's chart, and,
after a sociable meal of hard bread and water, got our last instructions. These were simple: steer north, and keep together
as much as possible. 'Be careful with that jury-rig, Marlow,' said
the captain; and Mahon, as I sailed proudly past his boat, wrinkled his curved nose and hailed, 'You will sail that ship of   15
yours under water, if you don't look out, young fellow.' He was
a malicious old man—and may the deep sea where he sleeps
now rock him gently, rock him tenderly to the end of time!

"Before sunset a thick rain-squall passed over the two boats,
which were far astern, and that was the last I saw of them for a
time. Next day I sat steering my cockle-shell—my first command—with nothing but water and sky around me. I did sight
in the afternoon the upper sails of a ship far away, but
said nothing, and my men did not notice her. You see I was
afraid she might be homeward bound, and I had no mind to   25
turn back from the portals of the East. I was steering for Java
—another blessed name—like Bankok, you know. I steered
many days.

"I need not tell you what it is to be knocking about in an
open boat. I remember nights and days of calm, when we
pulled, we pulled, and the boat seemed to stand still, as if bewitched within the circle of the sea horizon. I remember the
heat, the deluge of rain-squalls that kept us baling for dear
life (but filled our water-cask), and I remember sixteen hours
on end with a mouth dry as a cinder and a steering-oar over   35

the stern to keep my first command head on to a breaking sea.
I did not know how good a man I was till then. I remember
the drawn faces, the dejected figures of my two men, and I remember my youth and the feeling that will never come back
5   any more—the feeling that I could last for ever, outlast the
sea, the earth, and all men; the deceitful feeling that lures us
on to joys, to perils, to love, to vain effort—to death; the triumphant conviction of strength, the heat of life in the handful
of dust, the glow in the heart that with every year grows dim,
grows cold, grows small, and expires—and expires, too soon, too
soon—before life itself.

"And this is how I see the East. I have seen its secret places
and have looked into its very soul; but now I see it always from
a small boat, a high outline of mountains, blue and afar in the
15 morning; like faint mist at noon; a jagged wall of purple at sunset. I have the feel of the oar in my hand, the vision of
a scorching blue sea in my eyes. And I see a bay, a wide bay,
smooth as glass and polished like ice, shimmering in the dark.
A red light burns far off upon the gloom of the land, and the
night is soft and warm. We drag at the oars with aching
arms, and suddenly a puff of wind, a puff faint and tepid and
laden with strange odours of blossoms, of aromatic wood,
comes out of the still night—the first sigh of the East on my
face. That I can never forget. It was impalpable and enslaving,
25 like a charm, like a whispered promise of mysterious delight.

"We had been pulling this finishing spell for eleven hours.
Two pulled, and he whose turn it was to rest sat at the tiller.
We had made out the red light in that bay and steered for
it, guessing it must mark some small coasting port. We passed
two vessels, outlandish and high-sterned, sleeping at anchor,
and, approaching the light, now very dim, ran the boat's nose
against the end of a jutting wharf. We were blind with fatigue.
My men dropped the oars and fell off the thwarts as if dead. I
made fast to a pile. A current rippled softly. The scented ob-
35 scurity of the shore was grouped into vast masses, a density of
colossal clumps of vegetation, probably—mute and fantastic

shapes. And at their foot the semicircle of a beach gleamed faintly, like an illusion. There was not a light, not a stir, not a sound. The mysterious East faced me, perfumed like a flower, silent like death, dark like a grave.

"And I sat weary beyond expression, exulting like a conqueror, sleepless and entranced as if before a profound, a fateful enigma.

"A splashing of oars, a measured dip reverberating on the level of water, intensified by the silence of the shore into loud claps, made me jump up. A boat, a European boat, was coming in. I invoked the name of the dead; I hailed: *Judea* ahoy! A thin shout answered.

"It was the captain. I had beaten the flagship by three hours, and I was glad to hear the old man's voice again, tremulous and tired. 'Is it you, Marlow?' 'Mind the end of that jetty, sir,' I cried.

"He approached cautiously, and brought up with the deepsea lead-line which we had saved—for the underwriters. I eased my painter and fell alongside. He sat, a broken figure at the stern, wet with dew, his hand clasped in his lap. His men were asleep already. 'I had a terrible time of it,' he murmured. 'Mahon is behind—not very far.' We conversed in whispers, in low whispers, as if afraid to wake up the land. Guns, thunder, earthquakes would not have awakened the men just then.

"Looking round as we talked, I saw away at sea a bright light travelling in the night. 'There's a steamer passing the bay,' I said. She was not passing, she was entering, and she even came close and anchored. 'I wish,' said the old man, 'you would find out whether she is English. Perhaps they could give us a passage somewhere.' He seemed nervously anxious. So by dint of punching and kicking I started one of my men into a state of somnambulism, and giving him an oar, took another and pulled towards the lights of the steamer.

"There was a murmur of voices in her, metallic hollow clangs of the engine-room, footsteps on the deck. Her ports shone, round like dilated eyes. Shapes moved about, and there was a shadowy man high up on the bridge. He heard my oars.

"And then, before I could open my lips, the East spoke to me, but it was in a Western voice. A torrent of words was poured into the enigmatical, the fateful silence; outlandish,
5 angry words, mixed with words and even whole sentences of good English, less strange but even more surprising. The voice swore and cursed violently; it riddled the solemn peace of the bay by a volley of abuse. It began by calling me Pig, and from that went crescendo into unmentionable adjectives—in English. The man up there raged aloud in two languages, and with a sincerity in his fury that almost convinced me I had, in some way, sinned against the harmony of the universe. I could hardly see him, but began to think he would work himself into a fit.

15 "Suddenly he ceased, and I could hear him snorting and blowing like a porpoise. I said—

" 'What steamer is this, pray?'

" 'Eh? What's this? And who are you?'

" 'Castaway crew of an English barque burnt at sea. We came here to-night. I am the second mate. The captain is in the long-boat, and wishes to know if you would give us a passage somewhere.'

" 'Oh, my goodness! I say. . . . This is the *Celestial* from Singapore on her return trip. I'll arrange with your captain in
25 the morning, . . . and, . . . I say, . . . did you hear me just now?'

" 'I should think the whole bay heard you.'

" 'I thought you were a shore-boat. Now, look here—this infernal lazy scoundrel of a caretaker has gone to sleep again—curse him. The light is out, and I nearly ran foul of the end of this damned jetty. This is the third time he plays me this trick. Now, I ask you, can anybody stand this kind of thing? It's enough to drive a man out of his mind. I'll report him. . . . I'll get the Assistant Resident to give him the sack, by . . . I
35 See—there's no light. It's out, isn't it? I take you to witness the

light's out. There should be a light, you know. A red light on the——'

" 'There was a light,' I said mildly.

" 'But it's out, man! What's the use of talking like this? You can see for yourself it's out—don't you? If you had to take a valuable steamer along this God-forsaken coast you would want a light, too. I'll kick him from end to end of his miserable wharf. You'll see if I don't. I will——'

" 'So I may tell my captain you'll take us?' I broke in.

" 'Yes, I'll take you. Good-night,' he said, brusquely.

"I pulled back, made fast again to the jetty, and then went to sleep at last. I had faced the silence of the East. I had heard some of its language. But when I opened my eyes again the silence was as complete as though it had never been broken. I was lying in a flood of light, and the sky had never looked so far, so high, before. I opened my eyes and lay without moving.

"And then I saw the men of the East—they were looking at me. The whole length of the jetty was full of people. I saw brown, bronze, yellow faces, the black eyes, the glitter, the colour of an Eastern crowd. And all these beings stared without a murmur, without a sigh, without a movement. They stared down at the boats, at the sleeping men who at night had come to them from the sea. Nothing moved. The fronds of palms stood still against the sky. Not a branch stirred along the shore, and the brown roofs of hidden houses peeped through the green foliage, through the big leaves that hung shining and still like leaves forged of heavy metal. This was the East of the ancient navigators, so old, so mysterious, resplendent and sombre, living and unchanged, full of danger and promise. And these were the men. I sat up suddenly. A wave of movement passed through the crowd from end to end, passed along the heads, swayed the bodies, ran along the jetty like a ripple on the water, like a breath of wind on a field—and all was still again. I see it now—the wide sweep of the bay, the glittering sands, the wealth of green infinite and varied, the sea blue like the sea of a dream, the crowd of attentive faces, the blaze of vivid colour—the water reflecting it all, the curve of the shore, the jetty, the high-sterned outlandish craft floating still, and the three boats with the tired men from the West sleeping, unconscious of the land and the people and of the violence of sunshine. They slept thrown across the thwarts, curled on bottom-boards, in the careless attitudes of death. The head of the old skipper, leaning back in the stern of the long-boat, had fallen on his breast, and he looked as though he would never wake. Farther out old Mahon's face was up-turned to the sky, with the long white beard spread out on his breast, as though he had been shot where he sat at the tiller; and a man, all in a heap in the bows of the boat, slept with both arms embracing the stem-head and with his cheek laid on the gunwale. The East looked at them without a sound.

"I have known its fascination since; I have seen the mysteri-ous shores, the still water, the lands of brown nations, where a stealthy Nemesis lies in wait, pursues, overtakes so many of the conquering race, who are proud of their wisdom, of their knowledge, of their strength. But for me all the East is con-tained in that vision of my youth. It is all in that moment when I opened my young eyes on it. I came upon it from a tussle with the sea—and I was young—and I saw it looking at me. And this is all that is left of it! Only a moment; a moment of strength, of romance, of glamour—of youth! . . . A flick of sunshine upon a strange shore, the time to remember, the time for a sigh, and—good-bye!—Night—Good-bye . . . !"

He drank.

"Ah! The good old time—the good old time. Youth and the sea. Glamour and the sea! The good, strong sea, the salt, bitter sea, that could whisper to you and roar at you and knock your breath out of you."

He drank again.

"By all that's wonderful it is the sea, I believe, the sea itself —or is it youth alone? Who can tell? But you here—you all had something out of life: money, love—whatever one gets on shore

—and, tell me, wasn't that the best time, that time when we were young at sea; young and had nothing, on the sea that gives nothing, except hard knocks—and sometimes a chance to feel your strength—that only—what you all regret?"

And we all nodded at him: the man of finance, the man of accounts, the man of law, we all nodded at him over the polished table that like a still sheet of brown water reflected our faces, lined, wrinkled; our faces marked by toil, by deceptions, by success, by love; our weary eyes looking still, looking always, looking anxiously for something out of life, that while it is expected is already gone—has passed unseen, in a sigh, in a flash—together with the youth, with the strength, with the romance of illusions.

HEART OF DARKNESS

Chapter One   Dover Beach - calm
~~~~~~~~   @beginning

The *Nellie,* a cruising yawl, swung to her anchor without a
flutter of the sails, and was at rest. The flood had made, the
wind was nearly calm, and being bound down the river, the only
thing for it was to come to and wait for the turn of the tide.

The sea-reach of the Thames stretched before us like the be-   5
ginning of an interminable waterway. In the offing the sea and
the sky were welded together without a joint, and in the luminous space the tanned sails of the barges drifting up with the
tide seemed to stand still in red clusters of canvas sharply
peaked, with gleams of varnished sprits. A haze rested on the
low shores that ran out to sea in vanishing flatness. The air was
dark above Gravesend, and farther back still seemed condensed
into a mournful gloom, brooding motionless over the biggest,
and the greatest, town on earth.

The Director of Companies was our captain and our host.   15
We four affectionately watched his back as he stood in the
bows looking to seaward. On the whole river there was nothing
that looked half so nautical. He resembled a pilot, which to a
seaman is trustworthiness personified. It was difficult to realize
his work was not out there in the luminous estuary, but behind
him, within the brooding gloom.

Between us there was, as I have already said somewhere, the bond of the sea. Besides holding our hearts together through long periods of separation, it had the effect of making us tolerant of each other's yarns—and even convictions. The Lawyer—the best of old fellows—had, because of his many years and many virtues, the only cushion on deck, and was lying on the only rug. The Accountant had brought out already a box of dominoes, and was toying architecturally with the bones. Marlow sat cross-legged right aft, leaning against the mizzen-mast. He had sunken cheeks, a yellow complexion, a straight back, an ascetic aspect, and, with his arms dropped, the palms of hands outwards, resembled an idol. The director, satisfied the anchor had good hold, made his way aft and sat down amongst us. We exchanged a few words lazily. Afterwards there was silence on board the yacht. For some reason or other we did not begin that game of dominoes. We felt meditative, and fit for nothing but placid staring. The day was ending in a serenity of still and exquisite brilliance. The water shone pacifically; the sky, without a speck, was a benign immensity of unstained light; the very mist on the Essex marshes was like a gauzy and radiant fabric, hung from the wooded rises inland, and draping the low shores in diaphanous folds. Only the gloom to the west, brooding over the upper reaches, became more sombre every minute, as if angered by the approach of the sun.

And at last, in its curved and imperceptible fall, the sun sank low, and from glowing white changed to a dull red without rays and without heat, as if about to go out suddenly, stricken to death by the touch of that gloom brooding over a crowd of men.

Forthwith a change came over the waters, and the serenity became less brilliant but more profound. The old river in its broad reach rested unruffled at the decline of day, after ages of good service done to the race that peopled its banks, spread out in the tranquil dignity of a waterway leading to the uttermost ends of the earth. We looked at the venerable stream not

in the vivid flush of a short day that comes and departs for
ever, but in the august light of abiding memories. And indeed
nothing is easier for a man who has, as the phrase goes, "followed the sea" with reverence and affection, than to evoke the
great spirit of the past upon the lower reaches of the Thames.
The tidal current runs to and fro in its unceasing service,
crowded with memories of men and ships it had borne to the
rest of home or to the battles of the sea. It had known and
served all the men of whom the nation is proud, from Sir Fran-
cis Drake to Sir John Franklin, knights all, titled and untitled
—the great knights-errant of the sea. It had borne all the ships
whose names are like jewels flashing in the night of time, from
the *Golden Hind* returning with her round flanks full of treasure, to be visited by the Queen's Highness and thus pass out
of the gigantic tale, to the *Erebus* and *Terror*, bound on other
conquests—and that never returned. It had known the ships
and the men. They had sailed from Deptford, from Greenwich,
from Erith—the adventurers and the settlers; kings' ships and
the ships of men on 'Change; captains, admirals, the dark "in-
terlopers" of the Eastern trade, and the commissioned "Gen-
erals" of East India fleets. Hunters for gold or pursuers of fame,
they all had gone out on that stream, bearing the sword, and
often the torch, messengers of the might within the land,
bearers of a spark from the sacred fire. What greatness had not
floated on the ebb of that river into the mystery of an unknown
earth! . . . The dreams of men, the seed of commonwealths,
the germs of empires.

The sun set; the dusk fell on the stream, and lights began to
appear along the shore. The Chapman lighthouse, a three-
legged thing erect on a mud-flat, shone strongly. Lights of ships
moved in the fairway—a great stir of lights going up and going
down. And farther west on the upper reaches the place of the
monstrous town was still marked ominously on the sky, a
brooding gloom in sunshine, a lurid glare under the stars.

"And this also," said Marlow suddenly, "has been one of the
dark places of the earth."

He was the only man of us who still "followed the sea." The worst that could be said of him was that he did not represent his class. He was a seaman, but he was a wanderer, too, while most seamen lead, if one may so express it, a sedentary life. Their minds are of the stay-at-home order, and their home is always with them—the ship; and so is their country—the sea. One ship is very much like another, and the sea is always the same. In the immutability of their surroundings the foreign shores, the foreign faces, the changing immensity of life, glide past, veiled not by a sense of mystery but by a slightly disdainful ignorance; for there is nothing mysterious to a seaman unless it be the sea itself, which is the mistress of his existence and as inscrutable as Destiny. For the rest, after his hours of work, a casual stroll or a casual spree on shore suffices to unfold for him the secret of a whole continent, and generally he finds the secret not worth knowing. The yarns of seamen have a direct simplicity, the whole meaning of which lies within the shell of a cracked nut. But Marlow was not typical (if his propensity to spin yarns be excepted), and to him the meaning of an episode was not inside like a kernel but outside, enveloping the tale which brought it out only as a glow brings out a haze, in the likeness of one of these misty halos that sometimes are made visible by the spectral illumination of moonshine.

His remark did not seem at all surprising. It was just like Marlow. It was accepted in silence. No one took the trouble to grunt even; and presently he said, very slow—

"I was thinking of very old times, when the Romans first came here, nineteen hundred years ago—the other day. . . . Light came out of this river since—you say Knights? Yes; but it is like a running blaze on a plain, like a flash of lightning in the clouds. We live in the flicker—may it last as long as the old earth keeps rolling! But darkness was here yesterday. Imagine the feelings of a commander of a fine—what d'ye call 'em? —trireme in the Mediterranean, ordered suddenly to the north; run overland across the Gauls in a hurry; put in charge of one of these craft the legionaries—a wonderful lot of handy men they must have been, too—used to build, apparently by the hundred, in a month or two, if we may believe what we read. Imagine him here—the very end of the world, a sea the colour of lead, a sky the colour of smoke, a kind of ship about as rigid 5 as a concertina—and going up this river with stores, or orders, or what you like. Sand-banks, marshes, forests, savages—precious little to eat fit for a civilized man, nothing but Thames water to drink. No Falernian wine here, no going ashore. Here and there a military camp lost in a wilderness, like a needle in a bundle of hay—cold, fog, tempests, disease, exile, and death —death skulking in the air, in the water, in the bush. They must have been dying like flies here. Oh, yes—he did it. Did it very well, too, no doubt, and without thinking much about it either, except afterwards to brag of what he had gone through 15 in his time, perhaps. They were men enough to face the darkness. And perhaps he was cheered by keeping his eye on a chance of promotion to the fleet at Ravenna by and by, if he had good friends in Rome and survived the awful climate. Or think of a decent young citizen in a toga—perhaps too much dice, you know—coming out here in the train of some prefect, or tax-gatherer, or trader even, to mend his fortunes. Land in a swamp, march through the woods, and in some inland post feel the savagery, the utter savagery, had closed round him —all that mysterious life of the wilderness that stirs in the 25 forest, in the jungles, in the hearts of wild men. There's no initiation either into such mysteries. He has to live in the midst of the incomprehensible, which is also detestable. And it has a fascination, too, that goes to work upon him. The fascination of the abomination—you know, imagine the growing regrets, the longing to escape, the powerless disgust, the surrender, the hate."

He paused.

"Mind," he began again, lifting one arm from the elbow, the palm of the hand outwards, so that, with his legs folded before 35 him, he had the pose of a Buddha preaching in European clothes and without a lotus-flower—"Mind, none of us would feel exactly like this. What saves us is efficiency—the devotion to efficiency. But these chaps were not much account, really. They were no colonists; their administration was merely a squeeze, and nothing more, I suspect. They were conquerors, and for that you want only brute force—nothing to boast of, when you have it, since your strength is just an accident arising from the weakness of others. They grabbed what they could get for the sake of what was to be got. It was just robbery with violence, aggravated murder on a great scale, and men going at it blind—as is very proper for those who tackle a darkness. The conquest of the earth, which mostly means the taking it away from those who have a different complexion or slightly flatter noses than ourselves, is not a pretty thing when you look into it too much. What redeems it is the idea only. An idea at the back of it; not a sentimental pretence but an idea; and an unselfish belief in the idea—something you can set up, and bow down before, and offer a sacrifice to. . . ."

He broke off. Flames glided in the river, small green flames, red flames, white flames, pursuing, overtaking, joining, crossing each other—then separating slowly or hastily. The traffic of the great city went on in the deepening night upon the sleepless river. We looked on, waiting patiently—there was nothing else to do till the end of the flood; but it was only after a long silence, when he said, in a hesitating voice, "I suppose you fellows remember I did once turn fresh-water sailor for a bit," that we knew we were fated, before the ebb began to run, to hear about one of Marlow's inconclusive experiences.

"I don't want to bother you much with what happened to me personally," he began, showing in this remark the weakness of many tellers of tales who seem so often unaware of what their audience would best like to hear; "yet to understand the effect of it on me you ought to know how I got out there, what I saw, how I went up that river to the place where I first met the poor chap. It was the farthest point of navigation and the culminating point of my experience. It seemed somehow to throw a kind of light on everything about me—and into my thoughts. It was sombre enough, too—and pitiful—not extraordinary in any way—not very clear either. No, not very clear. And yet it seemed to throw a kind of light.

"I had then, as you remember, just returned to London after a lot of Indian Ocean, Pacific, China Seas—a regular dose of the East—six years or so, and I was loafing about, hindering you fellows in your work and invading your homes, just as though I had got a heavenly mission to civilize you. It was very fine for a time, but after a bit I did get tired of resting. Then I began to look for a ship—I should think the hardest work on earth. But the ships wouldn't even look at me. And I got tired of that game, too.

"Now when I was a little chap I had a passion for maps. I would look for hours at South America, or Africa, or Australia, and lose myself in all the glories of exploration. At that time there were many blank spaces on the earth, and when I saw one that looked particularly inviting on a map (but they all look that) I would put my finger on it and say, When I grow up I will go there. The North Pole was one of these places, I remember. Well, I haven't been there yet, and shall not try now. The glamour's off. Other places were scattered about the Equator, and in every sort of latitude all over the two hemispheres. I have been in some of them, and . . . well, we won't talk about that. But there was one yet—the biggest, the most blank, so to speak—that I had a hankering after.

"True, by this time it was not a blank space any more. It had got filled since my boyhood with rivers and lakes and names. It had ceased to be a blank space of delightful mystery—a white patch for a boy to dream gloriously over. It had become a place of darkness. But there was in it one river especially, a mighty big river, that you could see on the map, resembling an immense snake uncoiled, with its head in the sea, its body at rest curving afar over a vast country, and its tail lost in the depths of the land. And as I looked at the map of it in a shop-window, it fascinated me as a snake would a bird—a silly little bird.

Then I remembered there was a big concern, a Company for trade on that river. Dash it all! I thought to myself, they can't trade without using some kind of craft on that lot of fresh water—steamboats! Why shouldn't I try to get charge of one?
5   I went on along Fleet Street, but could not shake off the idea. The snake had charmed me.

"You understand it was a Continental concern, that Trading society; but I have a lot of relations living on the Continent, because it's cheap and not so nasty as it looks, they say.

"I am sorry to own I began to worry them. This was already a fresh departure for me. I was not used to get things that way, you know. I always went my own road and on my own legs where I had a mind to go. I wouldn't have believed it of myself; but, then—you see—I felt somehow I must get
15   there by hook or by crook. So I worried them. The men said 'My dear fellow,' and did nothing. Then—would you believe it?—I tried the women. I, Charlie Marlow, set the women to work—to get a job. Heavens! Well, you see, the notion drove me. I had an aunt, a dear enthusiastic soul. She wrote: 'It will be delightful. I am ready to do anything, anything for you. It is a glorious idea. I know the wife of a very high personage in the Administration, and also a man who has lots of influence with,' etc., etc. She was determined to make no end of fuss to get me appointed skipper of a river steamboat, if such was my
25   fancy.

"I got my appointment—of course; and I got it very quick. It appears the Company had received news that one of their captains had been killed in a scuffle with the natives. This was my chance, and it made me the more anxious to go. It was only months and months afterwards, when I made the attempt to recover what was left of the body, that I heard the original quarrel arose from a misunderstanding about some hens. Yes, two black hens. Fresleven—that was the fellow's name, a Dane —thought himself wronged somehow in the bargain, so he
35   went ashore and started to hammer the chief of the village with a stick. Oh, it didn't surprise me in the least to hear this, and

at the same time to be told that Fresleven was the gentlest,
quietest creature that ever walked on two legs. No doubt he
was; but he had been a couple of years already out there engaged in the noble cause, you know, and he probably felt the
need at last of asserting his self-respect in some way. There-   5
fore he whacked the old nigger mercilessly, while a big crowd
of his people watched him, thunderstruck, till some man—I
was told the chief's son—in desperation at hearing the old
chap yell, made a tentative jab with a spear at the white man
—and of course it went quite easy between the shoulder-blades.
Then the whole population cleared into the forest, expecting
all kinds of calamities to happen, while, on the other hand, the
steamer Fresleven commanded left also in a bad panic, in
charge of the engineer, I believe. Afterwards nobody seemed
to trouble much about Fresleven's remains, till I got out and   15
stepped into his shoes. I couldn't let it rest, though; but when
an opportunity offered at last to meet my predecessor, the grass
growing through his ribs was tall enough to hide his bones.
They were all there. The supernatural being had not been
touched after he fell. And the village was deserted, the huts
gaped black, rotting, all askew within the fallen enclosures. A
calamity had come to it, sure enough. The people had vanished.
Mad terror had scattered them, men, women, and children,
through the bush, and they had never returned. What became
of the hens I don't know either. I should think the cause of   25
progress got them, anyhow. However, through this glorious
affair I got my appointment, before I had fairly begun to hope
for it.

"I flew around like mad to get ready, and before forty-eight
hours I was crossing the Channel to show myself to my employ-
ers, and sign the contract. In a very few hours I arrived in a
city that always makes me think of a whited sepulchre. Prejudice no doubt. I had no difficulty in finding the Company's
offices. It was the biggest thing in the town, and everybody I
met was full of it. They were going to run an over-sea empire,   35
and make no end of coin by trade.

"A narrow and deserted street in deep shadow, high houses, innumerable windows with venetian blinds, a dead silence, grass sprouting between the stones, imposing carriage archways right and left, immense double doors standing ponderously ajar. I slipped through one of these cracks, went up a swept and ungarnished staircase, as arid as a desert, and opened the first door I came to. Two women, one fat and the other slim, sat on straw-bottomed chairs, knitting black wool. The slim one got up and walked straight at me—still knitting with downcast eyes—and only just as I began to think of getting out of her way, as you would for a somnambulist, stood still, and looked up. Her dress was as plain as an umbrella-cover, and she turned round without a word and preceded me into a waiting-room. I gave my name, and looked about. Deal table in the middle, plain chairs all round the walls, on one end a large shining map, marked with all the colours of a rainbow. There was a vast amount of red—good to see at any time, because one knows that some real work is done in there, a deuce of a lot of blue, a little green, smears of orange, and, on the East Coast, a purple patch, to show where the jolly pioneers of progress drink the jolly lager-beer. However, I wasn't going into any of these. I was going into the yellow. Dead in the centre. And the river was there—fascinating—deadly—like a snake. Ough! A door opened, a white-haired secretarial head, but wearing a compassionate expression, appeared, and a skinny forefinger beckoned me into the sanctuary. Its light was dim, and a heavy writing-desk squatted in the middle. From behind that structure came out an impression of pale plumpness in a frock-coat. The great man himself. He was five feet six, I should judge, and had his grip on the handle-end of ever so many millions. He shook hands, I fancy, murmured vaguely, was satisfied with my French. *Bon voyage.*

"In about forty-five seconds I found myself again in the waiting-room with the compassionate secretary, who, full of desolation and sympathy, made me sign some document. I believe I undertook amongst other things not to disclose any trade secrets. Well, I am not going to.

"I began to feel slightly uneasy. You know I am not used to such ceremonies, and there was something ominous in the atmosphere. It was just as though I had been let into some conspiracy—I don't know—something not quite right; and I was glad to get out. In the outer room the two women knitted black wool feverishly. People were arriving, and the younger one was walking back and forth introducing them. The old one sat on her chair. Her flat cloth slippers were propped up on a foot-warmer, and a cat reposed on her lap. She wore a starched white affair on her head, had a wart on one cheek, and silver-rimmed spectacles hung on the tip of her nose. She glanced at me above the glasses. The swift and indifferent placidity of that look troubled me. Two youths with foolish and cheery countenances were being piloted over, and she threw at them the same quick glance of unconcerned wisdom. She seemed to know all about them and about me, too. An eerie feeling came over me. She seemed uncanny and fateful. Often far away there I thought of these two, guarding the door of Darkness, knitting black wool as for a warm pall, one introducing, introducing continuously to the unknown, the other scrutinizing the cheery and foolish faces with unconcerned old eyes. *Ave!* Old knitter of black wool. *Morituri te salutant.* Not many of those she looked at ever saw her again—not half, by a long way.

"There was yet a visit to the doctor. 'A simple formality,' assured me the secretary, with an air of taking an immense part in all my sorrows. Accordingly a young chap wearing his hat over the left eyebrow, some clerk I suppose—there must have been clerks in the business, though the house was as still as a house in a city of the dead—came from somewhere up-stairs, and led me forth. He was shabby and careless, with ink-stains on the sleeves of his jacket, and his cravat was large and billowy, under a chin shaped like the toe of an old boot. It was a little too early for the doctor, so I proposed a drink, and

thereupon he developed a vein of joviality. As we sat over our
vermouths he glorified the Company's business, and by and by
I expressed casually my surprise at him not going out there.
He became very cool and collected all at once. 'I am not such
a fool as I look, quoth Plato to his disciples,' he said senten-
tiously, emptied his glass with great resolution, and we rose.

"The old doctor felt my pulse, evidently thinking of something else the while. 'Good, good for there,' he mumbled, and
then with a certain eagerness asked me whether I would let
him measure my head. Rather surprised, I said Yes, when he
produced a thing like calipers and got the dimensions back
and front and every way, taking notes carefully. He was an
unshaven little man in a threadbare coat like a gaberdine, with
his feet in slippers, and I thought him a harmless fool. 'I always ask leave, in the interests of science, to measure the crania
of those going out there,' he said. 'And when they come back,
too?' I asked. 'Oh, I never see them,' he remarked; 'and, moreover, the changes take place inside, you know.' He smiled, as
if at some quiet joke. 'So you are going out there. Famous. Interesting, too.' He gave me a searching glance, and made another note. 'Ever any madness in your family?' he asked, in
a matter-of-fact tone. I felt very annoyed. 'Is that question in
the interests of science, too?' 'It would be,' he said, without
taking notice of my irritation, 'interesting for science to watch
the mental changes of individuals, on the spot, but . . .' 'Are
you an alienist?' I interrupted. 'Every doctor should be—a
little,' answered that original, imperturbably. 'I have a little
theory which you Messieurs who go out there must help me
to prove. This is my share in the advantages my country shall
reap from the possession of such a magnificent dependency.
The mere wealth I leave to others. Pardon my questions, but
you are the first Englishman coming under my observation
. . .' I hastened to assure him I was not in the least typical. 'If
I were,' said I, 'I wouldn't be talking like this with you.' 'What
you say is rather profound, and probably erroneous,' he said,
with a laugh. 'Avoid irritation more than exposure to the sun.

Adieu. How do you English say, eh? Good-bye. Ah! Good-bye.
Adieu. In the tropics one must before everything keep calm.'
. . . He lifted a warning forefinger. . . . *'Du calme, du calme.
Adieu.'*

"One thing more remained to do—say good-bye to my ex- 5
cellent aunt. I found her triumphant. I had a cup of tea—the
last decent cup of tea for many days—and in a room that most
soothingly looked just as you would expect a lady's drawing-
room to look, we had a long quiet chat by the fireside. In the
course of these confidences it became quite plain to me I had
been represented to the wife of the high dignitary, and goodness knows to how many more people besides, as an exceptional and gifted creature—a piece of good fortune for the
Company—a man you don't get hold of every day. Good heavens! and I was going to take charge of a two-penny-half-penny 15
river-steamboat with a penny whistle attached! It appeared,
however, I was also one of the Workers, with a capital—you
know. Something like an emissary of light, something like a
lower sort of apostle. There had been a lot of such rot let loose
in print and talk just about that time, and the excellent woman,
living right in the rush of all that humbug, got carried off her
feet. She talked about 'weaning those ignorant millions from
their horrid ways,' till, upon my word, she made me quite uncomfortable. I ventured to hint that the Company was run for
profit. 25

" 'You forget, dear Charlie, that the labourer is worthy of
his hire,' she said, brightly. It's queer how out of touch with
truth women are. They live in a world of their own, and there
has never been anything like it, and never can be. It is too
beautiful altogether, and if they were to set it up it would go
to pieces before the first sunset. Some confounded fact we
men have been living contentedly with ever since the day of
creation would start up and knock the whole thing over.

"After this I got embraced, told to wear flannel, be sure to
write often, and so on—and I left. In the street—I don't know 35
why—a queer feeling came to me that I was an impostor. Odd

thing that I, who used to clear out for any part of the world at twenty-four hours' notice, with less thought than most men give to the crossing of a street, had a moment—I won't say of hesitation, but of startled pause, before this commonplace af-
5   fair. The best way I can explain it to you is by saying that, for a second or two, I felt as though, instead of going to the centre of a continent, I were about to set off for the centre of the earth.

"I left in a French steamer, and she called in every blamed port they have out there, for, as far as I could see, the sole pur-pose of landing soldiers and custom-house officers. I watched the coast. Watching a coast as it slips by the ship is like think-ing about an enigma. There it is before you—smiling, frown-ing, inviting, grand, mean, insipid, or savage, and always mute
15   with an air of whispering, Come and find out. This one was al-most featureless, as if still in the making, with an aspect of mo-notonous grimness. The edge of a colossal jungle, so dark-green as to be almost black, fringed with white surf, ran straight, like a ruled line, far, far away along a blue sea whose glitter was blurred by a creeping mist. The sun was fierce, the land seemed to glisten and drip with steam. Here and there grayish-whitish specks showed up clustered inside the white surf, with a flag flying above them perhaps. Settlements some centuries old, and still no bigger than pinheads on the untouched expanse
25   of their background. We pounded along, stopped, landed sol-diers; went on, landed custom-house clerks to levy toll in what looked like a God-forsaken wilderness, with a tin shed and a flag-pole lost in it; landed more soldiers—to take care of the custom-house clerks, presumably. Some, I heard, got drowned in the surf; but whether they did or not, nobody seemed par-ticularly to care. They were just flung out there, and on we went. Every day the coast looked the same, as though we had not moved; but we passed various places—trading places—with names like Gran' Bassam, Little Popo; names that seemed to
35   belong to some sordid farce acted in front of a sinister back-cloth. The idleness of a passenger, my isolation amongst all

these men with whom I had no point of contact, the oily and languid sea, the uniform sombreness of the coast, seemed to keep me away from the truth of things, within the toil of a mournful and senseless delusion. The voice of the surf heard now and then was a positive pleasure, like the speech of a brother. It was something natural, that had its reason, that had a meaning. Now and then a boat from the shore gave one a momentary contact with reality. It was paddled by black fellows. You could see from afar the white of their eyeballs glistening. They shouted, sang; their bodies streamed with perspiration; they had faces like grotesque masks—these chaps; but they had bone, muscle, a wild vitality, an intense energy of movement, that was as natural and true as the surf along their coast. They wanted no excuse for being there. They were a great comfort to look at. For a time I would feel I belonged still to a world of straightforward facts; but the feeling would not last long. Something would turn up to scare it away. Once, I remember, we came upon a man-of-war anchored off the coast. There wasn't even a shed there, and she was shelling the bush. It appears the French had one of their wars going on thereabouts. Her ensign dropped limp like a rag; the muzzles of the long six-inch guns stuck out all over the low hull; the greasy, slimy swell swung her up lazily and let her down, swaying her thin masts. In the empty immensity of earth, sky, and water, there she was, incomprehensible, firing into a continent. Pop, would go one of the six-inch guns; a small flame would dart and vanish, a little white smoke would disappear, a tiny projectile would give a feeble screech—and nothing happened. Nothing could happen. There was a touch of insanity in the proceeding, a sense of lugubrious drollery in the sight; and it was not dissipated by somebody on board assuring me earnestly there was a camp of natives—he called them enemies! —hidden out of sight somewhere.

"We gave her her letters (I heard the men in that lonely ship were dying of fever at the rate of three a day) and went on. We called at some more places with farcical names, where the

merry dance of death and trade goes on in a still and earthy
atmosphere as of an overheated catacomb; all along the form-
less coast bordered by dangerous surf, as if Nature herself had
tried to ward off intruders; in and out of rivers, streams of death
5 in life, whose banks were rotting into mud, whose waters,
thickened into slime, invaded the contorted mangroves, that
seemed to writhe at us in the extremity of an impotent despair.
Nowhere did we stop long enough to get a particularized impression, but the general sense of vague and oppressive wonder
grew upon me. It was like a weary pilgrimage amongst hints
for nightmares.

"It was upward of thirty days before I saw the mouth of the
big river. We anchored off the seat of the government. But
my work would not begin till some two hundred miles farther
15 on. So as soon as I could I made a start for a place thirty miles
higher up.

"I had my passage on a little sea-going steamer. Her captain
was a Swede, and knowing me for a seaman, invited me on the
bridge. He was a young man, lean, fair, and morose, with lanky
hair and a shuffling gait. As we left the miserable little
wharf, he tossed his head contemptuously at the shore. 'Been
living there?' he asked. I said, 'Yes.' 'Fine lot these government
chaps—are they not?' he went on, speaking English with great
precision and considerable bitterness. 'It is funny what some
25 people will do for a few francs a month. I wonder what becomes of that kind when it goes up-country?' I said to him I
expected to see that soon. 'So-o-o!' he exclaimed. He shuffled
athwart, keeping one eye ahead vigilantly. 'Don't be too sure,'
he continued. 'The other day I took up a man who hanged
himself on the road. He was a Swede, too.' 'Hanged himself!
Why, in God's name?' I cried. He kept on looking out watchfully. 'Who knows? The sun too much for him, or the country
perhaps.'

"At last we opened a reach. A rocky cliff appeared, mounds of
35 turned-up earth by the shore, houses on a hill, others with
iron roofs, amongst a waste of excavations, or hanging to the

declivity. A continuous noise of the rapids above hovered over this scene of inhabited devastation. A lot of people, mostly black and naked, moved about like ants. A jetty projected into the river. A blinding sunlight drowned all this at times in a sudden recrudescence of glare. 'There's your Company's sta- 5 tion,' said the Swede, pointing to three wooden barrack-like structures on the rocky slope. 'I will send your things up. Four boxes did you say? So. Farewell.'

"I came upon a boiler wallowing in the grass, then found a path leading up the hill. It turned aside for the boulders, and also for an undersized railway-truck lying there on its back with its wheels in the air. One was off. The thing looked as dead as the carcass of some animal. I came upon more pieces of decaying machinery, a stack of rusty rails. To the left a clump of trees made a shady spot, where dark things seemed to stir fee- 15 bly. I blinked, the path was steep. A horn tooted to the right, and I saw the black people run. A heavy and dull detonation shook the ground, a puff of smoke came out of the cliff, and that was all. No change appeared on the face of the rock. They were building a railway. The cliff was not in the way or any- thing; but this objectless blasting was all the work going on.

"A slight clinking behind me made me turn my head. Six black men advanced in a file, toiling up the path. They walked erect and slow, balancing small baskets full of earth on their heads, and the clink kept time with their footsteps. Black rags 25 were wound round their loins and the short ends behind wag- gled to and fro like tails. I could see every rib, the joints of their limbs were like knots in a rope; each had an iron collar on his neck, and all were connected together with a chain whose bights swung between them, rhythmically clinking. An- other report from the cliff made me think suddenly of that ship of war I had seen firing into a continent. It was the same kind of ominous voice; but these men could by no stretch of imagination be called enemies. They were called criminals, and the outraged law, like the bursting shells, had come to them, 35 an insoluble mystery from the sea. All their meagre breasts

panted together, the violently dilated nostrils quivered, the
eyes stared stonily up-hill. They passed me within six inches,
without a glance, with that complete, deathlike indifference of
unhappy savages. Behind this raw matter one of the reclaimed,
the product of the new forces at work, strolled despondently,
carrying a rifle by its middle. He had a uniform jacket with
one button off, and seeing a white man on the path, hoisted
his weapon to his shoulder with alacrity. This was simple prudence, white men being so much alike at a distance that he
could not tell who I might be. He was speedily reassured, and
with a large, white, rascally grin, and a glance at his charge,
seemed to take me into partnership in his exalted trust. After
all, I also was a part of the great cause of these high and just
proceedings.

"Instead of going up, I turned and descended to the left.
My idea was to let that chain-gang get out of sight before I
climbed the hill. You know I am not particularly tender; I've
had to strike and to fend off. I've had to resist and to attack
sometimes—that's only one way of resisting—without count-
ing the exact cost, according to the demands of such sort of
life as I had blundered into. I've seen the devil of violence, and
the devil of greed, and the devil of hot desire; but, by all the
stars! these were strong, lusty, red-eyed devils, that swayed and
drove men—men, I tell you. But as I stood on this hillside
I foresaw that in the blinding sunshine of that land I would
become acquainted with a flabby, pretending, weak-eyed devil
of a rapacious and pitiless folly. How insidious he could be,
too, I was only to find out several months later and a thousand
miles farther. For a moment I stood appalled, as though by a
warning. Finally I descended the hill, obliquely, towards the
trees I had seen.

"I avoided a vast artificial hole somebody had been digging
on the slope, the purpose of which I found it impossible to
divine. It wasn't a quarry or a sandpit, anyhow. It was just a
hole. It might have been connected with the philanthropic
desire of giving the criminals something to do. I don't know.

Then I nearly fell into a very narrow ravine, almost no more than a scar in the hillside. I discovered that a lot of imported drainage-pipes for the settlement had been tumbled in there. There wasn't one that was not broken. It was a wanton smash-up. At last I got under the trees. My purpose was to stroll into 5 the shade for a moment; but no sooner within than it seemed to me I had stepped into the gloomy circle of some Inferno. The rapids were near, and an uninterrupted, uniform, head-long, rushing noise filled the mournful stillness of the grove, where not a breath stirred, not a leaf moved, with a mysterious sound—as though the tearing pace of the launched earth had suddenly become audible.

"Black shapes crouched, lay, sat between the trees leaning against the trunks, clinging to the earth, half coming out, half effaced within the dim light, in all the attitudes of pain, aban- 15 donment, and despair. Another mine on the cliff went off, followed by a slight shudder of the soil under my feet. The work was going on. The work! And this was the place where some of the helpers had withdrawn to die.

"They were dying slowly—it was very clear. They were not enemies, they were not criminals, they were nothing earthly now—nothing but black shadows of disease and starvation, lying confusedly in the greenish gloom. Brought from all the recesses of the coast in all the legality of time contracts, lost in uncongenial surroundings, fed on unfamiliar food, they 25 sickened, became inefficient, and were then allowed to crawl away and rest. These moribund shapes were free as air—and nearly as thin. I began to distinguish the gleam of the eyes under the trees. Then, glancing down, I saw a face near my hand. The black bones reclined at full length with one shoul-der against the tree, and slowly the eyelids rose and the sunken eyes looked up at me, enormous and vacant, a kind of blind, white flicker in the depths of the orbs, which died out slowly. The man seemed young—almost a boy—but you know with them it's hard to tell. I found nothing else to do but to offer 35 him one of my good Swede's ship's biscuits I had in my pocket.

The fingers closed slowly on it and held—there was no other movement and no other glance. He had tied a bit of white worsted round his neck—Why? Where did he get it? Was it a badge—an ornament—a charm—a propitiatory act? Was
5 there any idea at all connected with it? It looked startling round his black neck, this bit of white thread from beyond the seas.

"Near the same tree two more bundles of acute angles sat with their legs drawn up. One, with his chin propped on his knees, stared at nothing, in an intolerable and appalling manner: his brother phantom rested its forehead, as if overcome with a great weariness; and all about others were scattered in every pose of contorted collapse, as in some picture of a massacre or a pestilence. While I stood horror-struck, one of these
15 creatures rose to his hands and knees, and went off on all-fours towards the river to drink. He lapped out of his hand, then sat up in the sunlight, crossing his shins in front of him, and after a time let his woolly head fall on his breastbone.

"I didn't want any more loitering in the shade, and I made haste towards the station. When near the buildings I met a white man, in such an unexpected elegance of get-up that in the first moment I took him for a sort of vision. I saw a high starched collar, white cuffs, a light alpaca jacket, snowy trousers, a clean necktie, and varnished boots. No hat. Hair parted,
25 brushed, oiled, under a green-lined parasol held in a big white hand. He was amazing, and had a penholder behind his ear.

"I shook hands with this miracle, and I learned he was the Company's chief accountant, and that all the bookkeeping was done at this station. He had come out for a moment, he said, 'to get a breath of fresh air.' The expression sounded wonderfully odd, with its suggestion of sedentary desk-life. I wouldn't have mentioned the fellow to you at all, only it was from his lips that I first heard the name of the man who is so indissolubly connected with the memories of that time. More-
35 over, I respected the fellow. Yes; I respected his collars, his vast cuffs, his brushed hair. His appearance was certainly that

of a hairdresser's dummy; but in the great demoralization of the land he kept up his appearance. That's backbone. His starched collars and got-up shirt-fronts were achievements of character. He had been out nearly three years; and, later, I could not help asking him how he managed to sport such linen. He had just the faintest blush, and said modestly, 'I've been teaching one of the native women about the station. It was difficult: She had a distaste for the work.' Thus this man had verily accomplished something. And he was devoted to his books, which were in apple-pie order.

"Everything else in the station was in a muddle—heads, things, buildings. Strings of dusty niggers with splay feet arrived and departed; a stream of manufactured goods, rubbishy cottons, beads, and brass-wire set into the depths of darkness, and in return came a precious trickle of ivory.

"I had to wait in the station for ten days—an eternity. I lived in a hut in the yard, but to be out of the chaos I would sometimes get into the accountant's office. It was built of horizontal planks, and so badly put together that, as he bent over his high desk, he was barred from neck to heels with narrow strips of sunlight. There was no need to open the big shutter to see. It was hot there, too; big flies buzzed fiendishly, and did not sting, but stabbed. I sat generally on the floor, while, of faultless appearance (and even slightly scented), perching on a high stool, he wrote, he wrote. Sometimes he stood up for exercise. When a truckle-bed with a sick man (some invalid agent from up-country) was put in there, he exhibited a gentle annoyance. 'The groans of this sick person,' he said, 'distract my attention. And without that it is extremely difficult to guard against clerical errors in this climate.'

"One day he remarked, without lifting his head, 'In the interior you will no doubt meet Mr. Kurtz.' On my asking who Mr. Kurtz was, he said he was a first-class agent; and seeing my disappointment at this information, he added slowly, laying down his pen, 'He is a very remarkable person.' Further questions elicited from him that Mr. Kurtz was at present in

58

charge of a trading post, a very important one, in the true
ivory-country, at 'the very bottom of there. Sends in as much
ivory as all the others put together . . .' He began to write
again. The sick man was too ill to groan. The flies buzzed in a
5 great peace.

"Suddenly there was a growing murmur of voices and a
great tramping of feet. A caravan had come in. A violent babble of uncouth sounds burst out on the other side of the planks.
All the carriers were speaking together, and in the midst of the
uproar the lamentable voice of the chief agent was heard 'giving it up' tearfully for the twentieth time that day. . . . He
rose slowly. 'What a frightful row,' he said. He crossed the
room gently to look at the sick man, and returning, said to me,
'He does not hear.' 'What! Dead?' I asked, startled. 'No, not
15 yet,' he answered, with great composure. Then, alluding with
a toss of the head to the tumult in the station-yard, 'When one
has got to make correct entries, one comes to hate those savages—hate them to the death.' He remained thoughtful for a
moment. 'When you see Mr. Kurtz,' he went on, 'tell him
from me that everything here'—he glanced at the desk—'is
very satisfactory. I don't like to write to him—with those messengers of ours you never know who may get hold of your letter
—at that Central Station.' He stared at me for a moment with
his mild, bulging eyes. 'Oh, he will go far, very far,' he began
25 again. 'He will be a somebody in the Administration before
long. They, above—the Council in Europe, you know—mean
him to be.'

"He turned to his work. The noise outside had ceased, and
presently in going out I stopped at the door. In the steady buzz
of flies the homeward-bound agent was lying flushed and in-
sensible; the other, bent over his books, was making correct
entries of perfectly correct transactions; and fifty feet below
the doorstep I could see the still tree-tops of the grove of death.

"Next day I left that station at last, with a caravan of sixty
35 men, for a two-hundred-mile tramp.

"No use telling you much about that. Paths, paths, every-

where; a stamped-in network of paths spreading over the empty
land, through long grass, through burnt grass, through thickets,
down and up chilly ravines, up and down stony hills ablaze
with heat; and a solitude, a solitude, nobody, not a hut. The
population had cleared out a long time ago. Well, if a lot of   5
mysterious niggers armed with all kinds of fearful weapons
suddenly took to travelling on the road between Deal and
Gravesend, catching the yokels right and left to carry heavy
loads for them, I fancy every farm and cottage thereabouts
would get empty very soon. Only here the dwellings were
gone, too. Still I passed through several abandoned villages.
There's something pathetically childish in the ruins of grass
walls. Day after day, with the stamp and shuffle of sixty pair
of bare feet behind me, each pair under a 60-lb. load. Camp,
cook, sleep, strike camp, march. Now and then a carrier dead   15
in harness, at rest in the long grass near the path, with an
empty water-gourd and his long staff lying by his side. A great
silence around and above. Perhaps on some quiet night the
tremor of far-off drums, sinking, swelling, a tremor vast, faint;
a sound weird, appealing, suggestive, and wild—and perhaps
with as profound a meaning as the sound of bells in a Christian country. Once a white man in an unbuttoned uniform,
camping on the path with an armed escort of lank Zanzibaris,
very hospitable and festive—not to say drunk. Was looking
after the upkeep of the road, he declared. Can't say I saw any   25
road or any upkeep, unless the body of a middle-aged Negro,
with a bullet-hole in the forehead, upon which I absolutely
stumbled three miles farther on, may be considered as a per-
manent improvement. I had a white companion, too, not a
bad chap, but rather too fleshy and with the exasperating habit
of fainting on the hot hillsides, miles away from the least bit
of shade and water. Annoying, you know, to hold your own
coat like a parasol over a man's head while he is coming-to. I
couldn't help asking him once what he meant by coming there
at all. 'To make money, of course. What do you think?' he said,   35
scornfully. Then he got fever, and had to be carried in a ham-

mock slung under a pole. As he weighed sixteen stone I had no
end of rows with the carriers. They jibbed, ran away, sneaked
off with their loads in the night—quite a mutiny. So, one
evening, I made a speech in English with gestures, not one of
which was lost to the sixty pairs of eyes before me, and the
next morning I started the hammock off in front all right. An
hour afterwards I came upon the whole concern wrecked in a
bush—man, hammock, groans, blankets, horrors. The heavy
pole had skinned his poor nose. He was very anxious for me
to kill somebody, but there wasn't the shadow of a carrier
near. I remembered the old doctor—'It would be interesting for
science to watch the mental changes of individuals, on the
spot.' I felt I was becoming scientifically interesting. However,
all that is to no purpose. On the fifteenth day I came in sight
of the big river again, and hobbled into the Central Station.
It was on a backwater surrounded by scrub and forest, with a
pretty border of smelly mud on one side, and on the three
others enclosed by a crazy fence of rushes. A neglected gap was
all the gate it had, and the first glance at the place was enough
to let you see the flabby devil was running that show. White
men with long staves in their hands appeared languidly from
amongst the buildings, strolling up to take a look at me, and
then retired out of sight somewhere. One of them, a stout,
excitable chap with black moustaches, informed me with great
volubility and many digressions, as soon as I told him who I
was, that my steamer was at the bottom of the river. I was
thunderstruck. What, how, why? Oh, it was 'all right.' The
'manager himself' was there. All quite correct. 'Everybody had
behaved splendidly! splendidly!'—'you must,' he said in agitation, 'go and see the general manager at once. He is waiting!'

"I did not see the real significance of that wreck at once. I
fancy I see it now, but I am not sure—not at all. Certainly
the affair was too stupid—when I think of it—to be altogether
natural. Still . . . But at the moment it presented itself simply
as a confounded nuisance. The steamer was sunk. They had
started two days before in a sudden hurry up the river with the

manager on board, in charge of some volunteer skipper, and
before they had been out three hours they tore the bottom out
of her on stones, and she sank near the south bank. I asked myself what I was to do there, now my boat was lost. As a matter
of fact, I had plenty to do in fishing my command out of the 5
river. I had to set about it the very next day. That, and the repairs when I brought the pieces to the station, took some
months.

"My first interview with the manager was curious. He did
not ask me to sit down after my twenty-mile walk that morning.
He was commonplace in complexion, in feature, in manners, and
in voice. He was of middle size and of ordinary build. His eyes,
of the usual blue, were perhaps remarkably cold, and he certainly could make his glance fall on one as trenchant and heavy
as an axe. But even at these times the rest of his person seemed 15
to disclaim the intention. Otherwise there was only an indefinable, faint expression of his lips, something stealthy—a smile
—not a smile—I remember it, but I can't explain. It was unconscious, this smile was, though just after he had said something it got intensified for an instant. It came at the end of
his speeches like a seal applied on the words to make the meaning of the commonest phrase appear absolutely inscrutable.
He was a common trader, from his youth up employed in
these parts—nothing more. He was obeyed, yet he inspired
neither love nor fear, nor even respect. He inspired uneasiness. 25
That was it! Uneasiness. Not a definite mistrust—just uneasiness—nothing more. You have no idea how effective such a
. . . a . . . faculty can be. He had no genius for organizing,
for initiative, or for order even. That was evident in such
things as the deplorable state of the station. He had no learning, and no intelligence. His position had come to him—
why? Perhaps because he was never ill . . . He had served
three terms of three years out there . . . Because triumphant
health in the general rout of constitutions is a kind of power
in itself. When he went home on leave he rioted on a large 35
scale—pompously. Jack ashore—with a difference—in exter-

nals only. This one could gather from his casual talk. He origi-
nated nothing, he could keep the routine going—that's all.
But he was great. He was great by this little thing that it was
impossible to tell what could control such a man. He never
gave that secret away. Perhaps there was nothing within him.
Such a suspicion made one pause—for out there there were no
external checks. Once when various tropical diseases had laid
low almost every 'agent' in the station, he was heard to say,
'Men who come out here should have no entrails.' He sealed
the utterance with that smile of his, as though it had been a
door opening into a darkness he had in his keeping. You fancied you had seen things—but the seal was on. When annoyed
at meal-times by the constant quarrels of the white men about
precedence, he ordered an immense round table to be made,
for which a special house had to be built. This was the station's mess-room. Where he sat was the first place—the rest
were nowhere. One felt this to be his unalterable conviction.
He was neither civil nor uncivil. He was quiet. He allowed his
'boy'—an overfed young Negro from the coast—to treat the
white men, under his very eyes, with provoking insolence.

"He began to speak as soon as he saw me. I had been very
long on the road. He could not wait. Had to start without me.
The up-river stations had to be relieved. There had been so
many delays already that he did not know who was dead and
who was alive, and how they got on—and so on, and so on.
He paid no attention to my explanations, and, playing with a
stick of sealing-wax, repeated several times that the situation
was 'very grave, very grave.' There were rumours that a very
important station was in jeopardy, and its chief, Mr. Kurtz,
was ill. Hoped it was not true. Mr. Kurtz was . . . I felt weary
and irritable. Hang Kurtz, I thought. I interrupted him by saying I had heard of Mr. Kurtz on the coast. 'Ah! So they talk
of him down there,' he murmured to himself. Then he began
again, assuring me Mr. Kurtz was the best agent he had, an
exceptional man, of the greatest importance to the Company;
therefore I could understand his anxiety. He was, he said, 'very,

very uneasy.' Certainly he fidgeted on his chair a good deal, exclaimed 'Ah, Mr. Kurtz!' broke the stick of sealing-wax and seemed dumfounded by the accident. Next thing he wanted to know 'how long it would take to' . . . I interrupted him again. Being hungry, you know, and kept on my feet too, I was getting savage. 'How can I tell?' I said. 'I haven't even seen the wreck yet—some months, no doubt.' All this talk seemed to me so futile. 'Some months,' he said. 'Well, let us say three months before we can make a start. Yes. That ought to do the affair.' I flung out of his hut (he lived all alone in a clay hut with a sort of verandah) muttering to myself my opinion of him. He was a chattering idiot. Afterwards I took it back when it was borne in upon me startlingly with what extreme nicety he had estimated the time requisite for the 'affair.'

"I went to work the next day, turning, so to speak, my back on that station. In that way only it seemed to me I could keep my hold on the redeeming facts of life. Still, one must look about sometimes; and then I saw this station, these men strolling aimlessly about in the sunshine of the yard. I asked myself sometimes what it all meant. They wandered here and there with their absurd long staves in their hands, like a lot of faithless pilgrims bewitched inside a rotten fence. The word 'ivory' rang in the air, was whispered, was sighed. You would think they were praying to it. A taint of imbecile rapacity blew through it all, like a whiff from some corpse. By Jove! I've never seen anything so unreal in my life. And outside, the silent wilderness surrounding this cleared speck on the earth struck me as something great and invincible, like evil or truth, waiting patiently for the passing away of this fantastic invasion.

"Oh, these months! Well, never mind. Various things happened. One evening a grass shed full of calico, cotton prints, beads, and I don't know what else, burst into a blaze so suddenly that you would have thought the earth had opened to let an avenging fire consume all that trash. I was smoking my pipe quietly by my dismantled steamer, and saw them all cut-

ting capers in the light, with their arms lifted high, when the
stout man with moustaches came tearing down to the river, a
tin pail in his hand, assured me that everybody was 'behaving
splendidly, splendidly,' dipped about a quart of water and
5   tore back again. I noticed there was a hole in the bottom of
his pail.

"I strolled up. There was no hurry. You see the thing had
gone off like a box of matches. It had been hopeless from the
very first. The flame had leaped high, driven everybody back,
lighted up everything—and collapsed. The shed was already a
heap of embers glowing fiercely. A nigger was being beaten near
by. They said he had caused the fire in some way; be that as it
may, he was screeching most horribly. I saw him, later, for
several days, sitting in a bit of shade looking very sick and try-
15   ing to recover himself: afterwards he arose and went out—and
the wilderness without a sound took him into its bosom again.
As I approached the glow from the dark I found myself at
the back of two men, talking. I heard the name of Kurtz
pronounced, then the words, 'take advantage of this unfortunate accident.' One of the men was the manager. I wished
him a good evening. 'Did you ever see anything like it—eh? it
is incredible,' he said, and walked off. The other man remained.
He was a first-class agent, young, gentlemanly, a bit reserved,
with a forked little beard and a hooked nose. He was stand-
25   offish with the other agents, and they on their side said he
was the manager's spy upon them. As to me, I had hardly ever
spoken to him before. We got into talk, and by and by we
strolled away from the hissing ruins. Then he asked me to his
room, which was in the main building of the station. He struck
a match, and I perceived that this young aristocrat had not
only a silver-mounted dressing-case but also a whole candle
all to himself. Just at that time the manager was the only man
supposed to have any right to candles. Native mats covered the
clay walls; a collection of spears, assegais, shields, knives was
35   hung up in trophies. The business intrusted to this fellow was
the making of bricks—so I had been informed; but there wasn't

a fragment of a brick anywhere in the station, and he had been
there more than a year—waiting. It seems he could not make
bricks without something, I don't know what—straw maybe.
Anyway, it could not be found there, and as it was not likely
to be sent from Europe, it did not appear clear to me what he
was waiting for. An act of special creation perhaps. However,
they were all waiting—all the sixteen or twenty pilgrims of
them—for something; and upon my word it did not seem an
uncongenial occupation, from the way they took it, though the
only thing that ever came to them was disease—as far as I could
see. They beguiled the time by backbiting and intriguing
against each other in a foolish kind of way. There was an air
of plotting about that station, but nothing came of it, of course.
It was as unreal as everything else—as the philanthropic pretence of the whole concern, as their talk, as their government,
as their show of work. The only real feeling was a desire to get
appointed to a trading-post where ivory was to be had, so that
they could earn percentages. They intrigued and slandered and
hated each other only on that account—but as to effectually
lifting a little finger—oh, no. By heavens! there is something
after all in the world allowing one man to steal a horse while
another must not look at a halter. Steal a horse straight out.
Very well. He has done it. Perhaps he can ride. But there is
a way of looking at a halter that would provoke the most
charitable of saints into a kick.

"I had no idea why he wanted to be sociable, but as we
chatted in there it suddenly occurred to me the fellow was trying to get at something—in fact, pumping me. He alluded
constantly to Europe, to the people I was supposed to know
there—putting leading questions as to my acquaintances in
the sepulchral city, and so on. His little eyes glittered like
mica discs—with curiosity—though he tried to keep up a bit
of superciliousness. At first I was astonished, but very soon I
became awfully curious to see what he would find out from
me. I couldn't possibly imagine what I had in me to make it
worth his while. It was very pretty to see how he baffled him-

self, for in truth my body was full only of chills, and my head
had nothing in it but that wretched steamboat business. It was
evident he took me for a perfectly shameless prevaricator. At
last he got angry, and, to conceal a movement of furious an-
5   noyance, he yawned. I rose. Then I noticed a small sketch in
oils, on a panel, representing a woman, draped and blindfolded, carrying a lighted torch. The background was sombre—
almost black. The movement of the woman was stately, and the
effect of the torch-light on the face was sinister.

"It arrested me, and he stood by civilly, holding an empty
half-pint champagne bottle (medical comforts) with the
candle stuck in it. To my question he said Mr. Kurtz had
painted this—in this very station more than a year ago—
while waiting for means to go to his trading post. 'Tell me,
15   pray,' said I, 'who is this Mr. Kurtz?'

" 'The chief of the Inner Station,' he answered in a short
tone, looking away. 'Much obliged,' I said, laughing. 'And you
are the brick-maker of the Central Station. Everyone knows
that.' He was silent for a while. 'He is a prodigy,' he said at
last. 'He is an emissary of pity, and science, and progress, and
devil knows what else. We want,' he began to declaim suddenly,
'for the guidance of the cause intrusted to us by Europe, so to
speak, higher intelligence, wide sympathies, a singleness of
purpose.' 'Who says that?' I asked. 'Lots of them,' he replied.
25   'Some even write that; and so *he* comes here, a special being,
as you ought to know.' 'Why ought I to know?' I interrupted,
really surprised. He paid no attention. 'Yes. To-day he is chief
of the best station, next year he will be assistant-manager, two
years more and . . . but I daresay you know what he will be
in two years' time. You are of the new gang—the gang of virtue. The same people who sent him specially also recommended
you. Oh, don't say no. I've my own eyes to trust.' Light dawned
upon me. My dear aunt's influential acquaintances were producing an unexpected effect upon that young man. I nearly
35   burst into a laugh. 'Do you read the Company's confidential
correspondence?' I asked. He hadn't a word to say. It was

great fun. 'When Mr. Kurtz,' I continued, severely, 'is General Manager, you won't have the opportunity.'

"He blew the candle out suddenly, and we went outside. The moon had risen. Black figures strolled about listlessly, pouring water on the glow, whence proceeded a sound of hissing; steam ascended in the moonlight, the beaten nigger groaned somewhere. 'What a row the brute makes!' said the indefatigable man with the moustaches, appearing near us. 'Serve him right. Transgression—punishment—bang! Pitiless, pitiless. That's the only way. This will prevent all conflagrations for the future. I was just telling the manager . . .' He noticed my companion, and became crestfallen all at once. 'Not in bed yet,' he said, with a kind of servile heartiness; 'it's so natural. Ha! Danger—agitation.' He vanished. I went on to the river-side, and the other followed me. I heard a scathing murmur at my ear, 'Heap of muffs—go to.' The pilgrims could be seen in knots gesticulating, discussing. Several had still their staves in their hands. I verily believe they took these sticks to bed with them. Beyond the fence the forest stood up spectrally in the moonlight, and through the dim stir, through the faint sounds of that lamentable courtyard, the silence of the land went home to one's very heart—its mystery, its greatness, the amazing reality of its concealed life. The hurt nigger moaned feebly somewhere near by, and then fetched a deep sigh that made me mend my pace away from there. I felt a hand introducing itself under my arm. 'My dear sir,' said the fellow, 'I don't want to be misunderstood, and especially by you, who will see Mr. Kurtz long before I can have that pleasure. I wouldn't like him to get a false idea of my disposition. . . .'

"I let him run on, this papier-mâché Mephistopheles, and it seemed to me that if I tried I could poke my forefinger through him, and would find nothing inside but a little loose dirt, maybe. He, don't you see, had been planning to be assistant-manager by and by under the present man, and I could see that the coming of that Kurtz had upset them both not a little. He talked precipitately, and I did not try to stop him. I had my shoulders against the wreck of my steamer, hauled up on the slope like a carcass of some big river animal. The smell of mud, of primeval mud, by Jove! was in my nostrils, the high stillness of primeval forest was before my eyes; there were shiny patches on the black creek. The moon had spread over everything a thin layer of silver—over the rank grass, over the mud, upon the wall of matted vegetation standing higher than the wall of a temple, over the great river I could see through a sombre gap glittering, glittering, as it flowed broadly by without a murmur. All this was great, expectant, mute, while the man jabbered about himself. I wondered whether the stillness on the face of the immensity looking at us two were meant as an appeal or as a menace. What were we who had strayed in here? Could we handle that dumb thing, or would it handle us? I felt how big, how confoundedly big, was that thing that couldn't talk, and perhaps was deaf as well. What was in there? I could see a little ivory coming out from there, and I had heard Mr. Kurtz was in there. I had heard enough about it, too —God knows! Yet somehow it didn't bring any image with it—no more than if I had been told an angel or a fiend was in there. I believed it in the same way one of you might believe there are inhabitants in the planet Mars. I knew once a Scotch sailmaker who was certain, dead sure, there were people in Mars. If you asked him for some idea how they looked and behaved, he would get shy and mutter something about 'walking on all-fours.' If you as much as smiled, he would—though a man of sixty—offer to fight you. I would not have gone so far as to fight for Kurtz, but I went for him near enough to a lie. You know I hate, detest, and can't bear a lie, not because I am straighter than the rest of us, but simply because it appalls me. There is a taint of death, a flavour of mortality in lies—which is exactly what I hate and detest in the world—what I want to forget. It makes me miserable and sick, like biting something rotten would do. Temperament, I suppose. Well, I went near enough to it by letting the young fool there believe anything he liked to imagine as to my influence in Europe. I became in an instant as much of a pretence as the rest of the bewitched pilgrims. This simply because I had a notion it somehow would be of help to that Kurtz whom at the time I did not see—you understand. He was just a word for me. I did not see the man in the name any more 5 than you do. Do you see him? Do you see the story? Do you see anything? It seems to me I am trying to tell you a dream—making a vain attempt, because no relation of a dream can convey the dream-sensation, that commingling of absurdity, surprise, and bewilderment in a tremor of struggling revolt, that notion of being captured by the incredible which is of the very essence of dreams. . . ."

He was silent for a while.

". . . No, it is impossible; it is impossible to convey the life-sensation of any given epoch of one's existence—that which 15 makes its truth, its meaning—its subtle and penetrating essence. It is impossible. We live, as we dream—alone. . . ."

He paused again as if reflecting, then added—

"Of course in this you fellows see more than I could then. You see me, whom you know. . . ."

It had become so pitch dark that we listeners could hardly see one another. For a long time already he, sitting apart, had been no more to us than a voice. There was not a word from anybody. The others might have been asleep, but I was awake. I listened, I listened on the watch for the sentence, for the word, 25 that would give me the clue to the faint uneasiness inspired by this narrative that seemed to shape itself without human lips in the heavy night-air of the river.

". . . Yes—I let him run on," Marlow began again, "and think what he pleased about the powers that were behind me. I did! And there was nothing behind me! There was nothing but that wretched, old, mangled steamboat I was leaning against, while he talked fluently about 'the necessity for every man to get on.' 'And when one comes out here, you conceive, it is not to gaze at the moon.' Mr. Kurtz was a 'universal genius,' 35 but even a genius would find it easier to work with 'adequate tools—intelligent men.' He did not make bricks—why, there was a physical impossibility in the way—as I was well aware; and if he did secretarial work for the manager, it was because 'no sensible man rejects wantonly the confidence of his superiors.' Did I see it? I saw it. What more did I want? What I really wanted was rivets, by heaven! Rivets. To get on with the work—to stop the hole. Rivets I wanted. There were cases of them down at the coast—cases—piled up—burst—split! You kicked a loose rivet at every second step in that station yard on the hillside. Rivets had rolled into the grove of death. You could fill your pockets with rivets for the trouble of stooping down—and there wasn't one rivet to be found where it was wanted. We had plates that would do, but nothing to fasten them with. And every week the messenger, a lone Negro, letter-bag on shoulder and staff in hand, left our station for the coast. And several times a week a coast caravan came in with trade goods—ghastly glazed calico that made you shudder only to look at it, glass beads value about a penny a quart, confounded spotted cotton handkerchiefs. And no rivets. Three carriers could have brought all that was wanted to set that steamboat afloat.

"He was becoming confidential now, but I fancy my unresponsive attitude must have exasperated him at last, for he judged it necessary to inform me he feared neither God nor devil, let alone any mere man. I said I could see that very well, but what I wanted was a certain quantity of rivets—and rivets were what really Mr. Kurtz wanted, if he had only known it. Now letters went to the coast every week. . . . 'My dear sir,' he cried, 'I write from dictation.' I demanded rivets. There was a way—for an intelligent man. He changed his manner; became very cold, and suddenly began to talk about a hippopotamus; wondered whether sleeping on board the steamer (I stuck to my salvage night and day) I wasn't disturbed. There was an old hippo that had the bad habit of getting out on the bank and roaming at night over the station grounds. The pilgrims used to turn out in a body and empty every rifle they could lay

hands on at him. Some even had sat up o' nights for him. All
this energy was wasted, though. 'That animal has a charmed
life,' he said; 'but you can say this only of brutes in this country.
No man—you apprehend me?—no man here bears a charmed
life.' He stood there for a moment in the moonlight with his   5
delicate hooked nose set a little askew, and his mica eyes glittering without a wink, then, with a curt Good-night, he strode
off. I could see he was disturbed and considerably puzzled,
which made me feel more hopeful than I had been for days. It
was a great comfort to turn from that chap to my influential
friend, the battered, twisted, ruined, tin-pot steamboat. I
clambered on board. She rang under my feet like an empty
Huntley & Palmer biscuit-tin kicked along a gutter; she was
nothing so solid in make, and rather less pretty in shape, but I
had expended enough hard work on her to make me love her.   15
No influential friend would have served me better. She had
given me a chance to come out a bit—to find out what I could
do. No, I don't like work. I had rather laze about and think of
all the fine things that can be done. I don't like work—no man
does—but I like what is in the work—the chance to find yourself. Your own reality—for yourself, not for others—what no
other man can ever know. They can only see the mere show,
and never can tell what it really means.

"I was not surprised to see somebody sitting aft, on the
deck, with his legs dangling over the mud. You see I rather   25
chummed with the few mechanics there were in that station,
whom the other pilgrims naturally despised—on account of
their imperfect manners, I suppose. This was the foreman—a
boiler-maker by trade—a good worker. He was a lank, bony,
yellow-faced man, with big intense eyes. His aspect was worried,
and his head was as bald as the palm of my hand; but his hair
in falling seemed to have stuck to his chin, and had prospered
in the new locality, for his beard hung down to his waist. He
was a widower with six young children (he had left them in
charge of a sister of his to come out there), and the passion of   35
his life was pigeon-flying. He was an enthusiast and a connois-

seur. He would rave about pigeons. After work hours he used
sometimes to come over from his hut for a talk about his children and his pigeons; at work, when he had to crawl in the
mud under the bottom of the steamboat, he would tie up that
5   beard of his in a kind of white serviette he brought for the
purpose. It had loops to go over his ears. In the evening he
could be seen squatted on the bank rinsing that wrapper
in the creek with great care, then spreading it solemnly on a
bush to dry.

"I slapped him on the back and shouted, 'We shall have
rivets!' He scrambled to his feet exclaiming, 'No! Rivets!' as
though he couldn't believe his ears. Then in a low voice, 'You
. . . eh?' I don't know why we behaved like lunatics. I put
my finger to the side of my nose and nodded mysteriously.
15   'Good for you!' he cried, snapped his fingers above his head,
lifting one foot. I tried a jig. We capered on the iron deck. A
frightful clatter came out of that hulk, and the virgin forest
on the other bank of the creek sent it back in a thundering
roll upon the sleeping station. It must have made some of the
pilgrims sit up in their hovels. A dark figure obscured the lighted
doorway of the manager's hut, vanished, then, a second or so
after, the doorway itself vanished, too. We stopped, and the
silence driven away by the stamping of our feet flowed back
again from the recesses of the land. The great wall of vegeta-
25   tion, an exuberant and entangled mass of trunks, branches,
leaves, boughs, festoons, motionless in the moonlight was like
a rioting invasion of soundless life, a rolling wave of plants,
piled up, crested, ready to topple over the creek, to sweep
every little man of us out of his little existence. And it moved
not. A deadened burst of mighty splashes and snorts reached
us from afar, as though an ichthyosaurus had been taking a bath
of glitter in the great river. 'After all,' said the boiler-maker in
a reasonable tone, 'why shouldn't we get the rivets?' Why not,
indeed! I did not know of any reason why we shouldn't.
35   'They'll come in three weeks,' I said, confidently.

"But they didn't. Instead of rivets there came an invasion, an infliction, a visitation. It came in sections during the next three weeks, each section headed by a donkey carrying a white man in new clothes and tan shoes bowing from that elevation right and left to the impressed pilgrims. A quarrelsome band   5
of footsore sulky niggers trod on the heels of the donkey; a lot of tents, camp-stools, tin boxes, white cases, brown bales would be shot down in the courtyard, and the air of mystery would deepen a little over the muddle of the station. Five such in-stalments came, with their absurd air of disorderly flight with the loot of innumerable outfit shops and provision stores, that, one would think, they were lugging, after a raid, into the wilderness for equitable division. It was an inextricable mess of things decent in themselves but that human folly made look like the spoils of thieving.   15
"This devoted band called itself the Eldorado Exploring Expedition, and I believe they were sworn to secrecy. Their talk, however, was the talk of sordid buccaneers: it was reckless without hardihood, greedy without audacity, and cruel without courage; there was not an atom of foresight or of serious inten-tion in the whole batch of them, and they did not seem aware these things are wanted for the work of the world. To tear treasure out of the bowels of the land was their desire, with no more moral purpose at the back of it than there is in bur-glars breaking into a safe. Who paid the expenses of the noble   25
enterprise I don't know; but the uncle of our manager was leader of that lot.
"In exterior he resembled a butcher in a poor neighbourhood, and his eyes had a look of sleepy cunning. He carried his fat paunch with ostentation on his short legs, and during the time his gang infested the station spoke to no one but his nephew. You could see these two roaming about all day long with their heads close together in an everlasting confab.
"I had given up worrying myself about the rivets. One's capacity for that kind of folly is more limited than you would   35

suppose. I said Hang!—and let things slide. I had plenty of time for meditation, and now and then I would give some thought to Kurtz. I wasn't very interested in him. No. Still, I was curious to see whether this man, who had come out equipped with moral ideas of some sort, would climb to the top after all and how he would set about his work when there."

Chapter Two

"One evening as I was lying flat on the deck of my steamboat, I heard voices approaching—and there were the nephew and the uncle strolling along the bank. I laid my head on my arm again, and had nearly lost myself in a doze, when somebody said in my ear, as it were: 'I am as harmless as a little child, but I don't like to be dictated to. Am I the manager—or am I not? I was ordered to send him there. It's incredible.' . . . I became aware that the two were standing on the shore alongside the forepart of the steamboat, just below my head. I did not move; it did not occur to me to move: I was sleepy. 'It *is* unpleasant,' grunted the uncle. 'He has asked the Administration to be sent there,' said the other, 'with the idea of showing what he could do; and I was instructed accordingly. Look at the influence that man must have. Is it not frightful?' They both agreed it was frightful, then made several bizarre remarks: 'Make rain and fine weather—one man—the Council—by the nose' —bits of absurd sentences that got the better of my drowsiness, so that I had pretty near the whole of my wits about me when the uncle said, 'The climate may do away with this difficulty for you. Is he alone there?' 'Yes,' answered the manager; 'he sent his assistant down the river with a note to me in these terms: "Clear this poor devil out of the country, and don't bother sending more of that sort. I had rather be alone than have the kind of men you can dispose of with me." It was more than a year ago. Can you imagine such impudence!' 'Anything since then?' asked the other, hoarsely. 'Ivory,' jerked the nephew; 'lots of it—prime sort—lots—most annoying, from him.' 'And with that?' questioned the heavy rumble. 'Invoice,' 5 was the reply fired out, so to speak. Then silence. They had been talking about Kurtz.

"I was broad awake by this time, but, lying perfectly at ease, remained still, having no inducement to change my position. 'How did that ivory come all this way?' growled the elder man, who seemed very vexed. The other explained that it had come with a fleet of canoes in charge of an English half-caste clerk Kurtz had with him; that Kurtz had apparently intended to re- turn himself, the station being by that time bare of goods and stores, but after coming three hundred miles, had suddenly 15 decided to go back, which he started to do alone in a small dugout with four paddlers, leaving the half-caste to continue down the river with the ivory. The two fellows there seemed astounded at anybody attempting such a thing. They were at a loss for an adequate motive. As to me, I seemed to see Kurtz for the first time. It was a distinct glimpse: the dugout, four paddling savages, and the lone white man turning his back suddenly on the headquarters, on relief, on thoughts of home—perhaps; setting his face towards the depths of the wilderness, towards his empty and desolate station. I did not 25 know the motive. Perhaps he was just simply a fine fellow who stuck to his work for its own sake. His name, you understand, had not been pronounced once. He was 'that man.' The half- caste, who, as far as I could see, had conducted a difficult trip with great prudence and pluck, was invariably alluded to as 'that scoundrel.' The 'scoundrel' had reported that the 'man' had been very ill—had recovered imperfectly. . . . The two below me moved away then a few paces, and strolled back and forth at some little distance. I heard: 'Military post—doctor— two hundred miles—quite alone now—unavoidable delays— 35 nine months—no news—strange rumours.' They approached

again, just as the manager was saying, 'No one, as far as I know,
unless a species of wandering trader—a pestilential fellow,
snapping ivory from the natives.' Who was it they were talking
about now? I gathered in snatches that this was some man sup-
5   posed to be in Kurtz's district, and of whom the manager did
not approve. 'We will not be free from unfair competition till
one of these fellows is hanged for an example,' he said. 'Certainly,' grunted the other; 'get him hanged! Why not? Anything—anything can be done in this country. That's what I
say; nobody here, you understand, *here*, can endanger your
position. And why? You stand the climate—you outlast them
all. The danger is in Europe; but there before I left I took care
to——' They moved off and whispered, then their voices rose
again. 'The extraordinary series of delays is not my fault. I did
15   my best.' The fat man sighed. 'Very sad.' 'And the pestiferous
absurdity of his talk,' continued the other; 'he bothered me
enough when he was here. "Each station should be like a beacon on the road towards better things, a centre for trade of
course, but also for humanizing, improving, instructing." Conceive you—that ass! And he wants to be manager! No, it's——'
Here he got choked by excessive indignation, and I lifted my
head the least bit. I was surprised to see how near they were
—right under me. I could have spat upon their hats. They were
looking on the ground, absorbed in thought. The manager was
25   switching his leg with a slender twig: his sagacious relative
lifted his head. 'You have been well since you came out this
time?' he asked. The other gave a start. 'Who? I? Oh! Like a
charm—like a charm. But the rest—oh, my goodness! All
sick. They die so quick, too, that I haven't the time to send
them out of the country—it's incredible!' 'H'm. Just so,' grunted
the uncle. 'Ah! my boy, trust to this—I say, trust to this.' I
saw him extend his short flipper of an arm for a gesture that
took in the forest, the creek, the mud, the river—seemed to
beckon with a dishonouring flourish before the sunlit face of
35   the land a treacherous appeal to the lurking death, to the
hidden evil, to the profound darkness of its heart. It was so

startling that I leaped to my feet and looked back at the edge
of the forest, as though I had expected an answer of some sort
to that black display of confidence. You know the foolish notions that come to one sometimes. The high stillness confronted these two figures with its ominous patience, waiting   5
for the passing away of a fantastic invasion.

"They swore aloud together—out of sheer fright, I believe—
then pretending not to know anything of my existence, turned
back to the station. The sun was low; and leaning forward side
by side, they seemed to be tugging painfully uphill their two
ridiculous shadows of unequal length, that trailed behind them
slowly over the tall grass without bending a single blade.

"In a few days the Eldorado Expedition went into the patient wilderness, that closed upon it as the sea closes over a
diver. Long afterwards the news came that all the donkeys were   15
dead. I know nothing as to the fate of the less valuable animals.
They, no doubt, like the rest of us, found what they deserved.
I did not inquire. I was then rather excited at the prospect of
meeting Kurtz very soon. When I say very soon I mean it comparatively. It was just two months from the day we left the
creek when we came to the bank below Kurtz's station.

"Going up that river was like travelling back to the earliest
beginnings of the world, when vegetation rioted on the earth
and the big trees were kings. An empty stream, a great silence,
an impenetrable forest. The air was warm, thick, heavy, slug-   25
gish. There was no joy in the brilliance of sunshine. The long
stretches of the waterway ran on, deserted, into the gloom of
overshadowed distances. On silvery sandbanks hippos and
alligators sunned themselves side by side. The broadening
waters flowed through a mob of wooded islands; you lost your
way on that river as you would in a desert, and butted all day
long against shoals, trying to find the channel, till you thought
yourself bewitched and cut off for ever from everything you
had known once—somewhere—far away—in another existence perhaps. There were moments when one's past came   35
back to one, as it will sometimes when you have not a moment

to spare to yourself; but it came in the shape of an unrestful
and noisy dream, remembered with wonder amongst the overwhelming realities of this strange world of plants, and water,
and silence. And this stillness of life did not in the least
5   resemble a peace. It was the stillness of an implacable force
brooding over an inscrutable intention. It looked at you with
a vengeful aspect. I got used to it afterwards; I did not see it
any more; I had no time. I had to keep guessing at the channel; I had to discern, mostly by inspiration, the signs of hidden
banks; I watched for sunken stones; I was learning to clap my
teeth smartly before my heart flew out, when I shaved by a
fluke some infernal sly old snag that would have ripped the
life out of the tin-pot steamboat and drowned all the pilgrims;
I had to keep a look-out for the signs of dead wood we could
15   cut up in the night for next day's steaming. When you have to
attend to things of that sort, to the mere incidents of the surface, the reality—the reality, I tell you—fades. The inner
truth is hidden—luckily, luckily. But I felt it all the same; I
felt often its mysterious stillness watching me at my monkey
tricks, just as it watches you fellows performing on your respective tight-ropes for—what is it? half-a-crown a tumble——"

"Try to be civil, Marlow," growled a voice, and I knew there
was at least one listener awake besides myself.

"I beg your pardon. I forgot the heartache which makes up
25   the rest of the price. And indeed what does the price matter,
if the trick be well done? You do your tricks very well. And I
didn't do badly either, since I managed not to sink that steamboat on my first trip. It's a wonder to me yet. Imagine a blindfolded man set to drive a van over a bad road. I sweated and
shivered over that business considerably, I can tell you. After
all, for a seaman, to scrape the bottom of the thing that's supposed to float all the time under his care is the unpardonable
sin. No one may know of it, but you never forget the thump—
eh? A blow on the very heart. You remember it, you dream of
35   it, you wake up at night and think of it—years after—and go
hot and cold all over. I don't pretend to say that steamboat

floated all the time. More than once she had to wade for a
bit, with twenty cannibals splashing around and pushing. We
had enlisted some of these chaps on the way for a crew. Fine
fellows—cannibals—in their place. They were men one could
work with, and I am grateful to them. And, after all, they did 5
not eat each other before my face: they had brought along a
provision of hippo-meat which went rotten, and made the mystery of the wilderness stink in my nostrils Phoo! I can sniff it
now. I had the manager on board and three or four pilgrims
with their staves—all complete. Sometimes we came upon
a station close by the bank, clinging to the skirts of the unknown, and the white men rushing out of a tumble-down hovel,
with great gestures of joy and surprise and welcome, seemed
very strange—had the appearance of being held there captive
by a spell. The word ivory would ring in the air for a while— 15
and on we went again into the silence, along empty reaches,
round the still bends, between the high walls of our winding
way, reverberating in hollow claps the ponderous beat of the
stern-wheel. Trees, trees, millions of trees, massive, immense,
running up high; and at their foot, hugging the bank against
the stream, crept the little begrimed steamboat, like a sluggish
beetle crawling on the floor of a lofty portico. It made you
feel very small, very lost, and yet it was not altogether de-
pressing, that feeling. After all, if you were small, the grimy
beetle crawled on—which was just what you wanted it to do. 25
Where the pilgrims imagined it crawled to I don't know. To
some place where they expected to get something, I bet! For
me it crawled towards Kurtz—exclusively; but when the steam-
pipes started leaking we crawled very slow. The reaches opened
before us and closed behind, as if the forest had stepped
leisurely across the water to bar the way for our return. We
penetrated deeper and deeper into the heart of darkness. It
was very quiet there. At night sometimes the roll of drums behind the curtain of trees would run up the river and remain
sustained faintly, as if hovering in the air high over our heads, 35
till the first break of day. Whether it meant war, peace, or

prayer we could not tell. The dawns were heralded by the descent of a chill stillness; the wood-cutters slept, their fires burned low; the snapping of a twig would make you start. We were wanderers on a prehistoric earth, on an earth that
5 wore the aspect of an unknown planet. We could have fancied ourselves the first of men taking possession of an accursed inheritance, to be subdued at the cost of profound anguish and of excessive toil. But suddenly, as we struggled round a bend, there would be a glimpse of rush walls, of peaked grass-roofs, a burst of yells, a whirl of black limbs, a mass of hands clapping, of feet stamping, of bodies swaying, of eyes rolling, under the droop of heavy and motionless foliage. The steamer toiled along slowly on the edge of a black and incomprehensible frenzy. The prehistoric man was cursing us, praying to us,
15 welcoming us—who could tell? We were cut off from the comprehension of our surroundings; we glided past like phantoms, wondering and secretly appalled, as sane men would be before an enthusiastic outbreak in a madhouse. We could not understand because we were too far and could not remember, because we were travelling in the night of first ages, of those ages that are gone, leaving hardly a sign—and no memories.

"The earth seemed unearthly. We are accustomed to look upon the shackled form of a conquered monster, but there—there you could look at a thing monstrous and free. It was un-
25 earthly, and the men were—— No, they were not inhuman. Well, you know, that was the worst of it—this suspicion of their not being inhuman. It would come slowly to one. They howled and leaped, and spun, and made horrid faces; but what thrilled you was just the thought of their humanity—like yours —the thought of your remote kinship with this wild and passionate uproar. Ugly. Yes, it was ugly enough; but if you were man enough you would admit to yourself that there was in you just the faintest trace of a response to the terrible frankness of that noise, a dim suspicion of there being a meaning
35 in it which you—you so remote from the night of first ages— could comprehend. And why not? The mind of man is capa-

ble of anything—because everything is in it, all the past as well as all the future. What was there after all? Joy, fear, sorrow, devotion, valour, rage—who can tell?—but truth—truth stripped of its cloak of time. Let the fool gape and shudder—the man knows, and can look on without a wink. But he must 5
at least be as much of a man as these on the shore. He must meet that truth with his own true stuff—with his own inborn strength. Principles won't do. Acquisitions, clothes, pretty rags—rags that would fly off at the first good shake. No; you want a deliberate belief. An appeal to me in this fiendish row —is there? Very well; I hear; I admit, but I have a voice, too, and for good or evil mine is the speech that cannot be silenced. Of course, a fool, what with sheer fright and fine sentiments, is always safe. Who's that grunting? You wonder I didn't go ashore for a howl and a dance? Well, no—I didn't. Fine senti- 15
ments, you say? Fine sentiments, be hanged! I had no time. I had to mess about with white-lead and strips of woollen blanket helping to put bandages on those leaky steam-pipes—I tell you. I had to watch the steering, and circumvent those snags, and get the tin-pot along by hook or by crook. There was surface-truth enough in these things to save a wiser man. And between whiles I had to look after the savage who was fire-man. He was an improved specimen; he could fire up a vertical boiler. He was there below me, and, upon my word, to look at him was as edifying as seeing a dog in a parody of breeches 25
and a feather hat, walking on his hind-legs. A few months of training had done for that really fine chap. He squinted at the steam-gauge and at the water-gauge with an evident effort of intrepidity—and he had filed teeth, too, the poor devil, and the wool of his pate shaved into queer patterns, and three orna-mental scars on each of his cheeks. He ought to have been clap-ping his hands and stamping his feet on the bank, instead of which he was hard at work, a thrall to strange witchcraft, full of improving knowledge. He was useful because he had been instructed; and what he knew was this—that should the 35
water in that transparent thing disappear, the evil spirit inside

the boiler would get angry through the greatness of his thirst, and take a terrible vengeance. So he sweated and fired up and watched the glass fearfully (with an impromptu charm, made of rags, tied to his arm, and a piece of polished bone, as big
5 as a watch, stuck flatways through his lower lip), while the wooded banks slipped past us slowly, the short noise was left behind, the interminable miles of silence—and we crept on, towards Kurtz. But the snags were thick, the water was treacherous and shallow, the boiler seemed indeed to have a sulky devil in it, and thus neither that fireman nor I had any time to peer into our creepy thoughts.

    "Some fifty miles below the Inner Station we came upon a hut of reeds, an inclined and melancholy pole, with the unrecognizable tatters of what had been a flag of some sort flying
15 from it, and a neatly stacked woodpile. This was unexpected. We came to the bank, and on the stack of firewood found a flat piece of board with some faded pencil-writing on it. When deciphered it said: 'Wood for you. Hurry up. Approach cautiously.' There was a signature, but it was illegible—not Kurtz —a much longer word. 'Hurry up.' Where? Up the river? 'Approach cautiously.' We had not done so. But the warning could not have been meant for the place where it could be only found after approach. Something was wrong above. But what —and how much? That was the question. We commented
25 adversely upon the imbecility of that telegraphic style. The bush around said nothing, and would not let us look very far, either. A torn curtain of red twill hung in the doorway of the hut, and flapped sadly in our faces. The dwelling was dismantled; but we could see a white man had lived there not very long ago. There remained a rude table—a plank on two posts; a heap of rubbish reposed in a dark corner, and by the door I picked up a book. It had lost its covers, and the pages had been thumbed into a state of extremely dirty softness; but the back had been lovingly stitched afresh with white cotton
35 thread, which looked clean yet. It was an extraordinary find. Its title was *An Inquiry into Some Points of Seamanship,*

by a man Towser, Towson—some such name—Master in His
Majesty's Navy. The matter looked dreary reading enough,
with illustrative diagrams and repulsive tables of figures, and
the copy was sixty years old. I handled this amazing antiquity
with the greatest possible tenderness, lest it should dissolve   5
in my hands. Within, Towson or Towser was inquiring earnestly
into the breaking strain of ships' chains and tackle, and other
such matters. Not a very enthralling book; but at the first glance
you could see there a singleness of intention, an honest concern for the right way of going to work, which made these
humble pages, thought out so many years ago, luminous with
another than a professional light. The simple old sailor, with
his talk of chains and purchases, made me forget the jungle and
the pilgrims in a delicious sensation of having come upon
something unmistakably real. Such a book being there was   15
wonderful enough; but still more astounding were the notes
pencilled in the margin, and plainly referring to the text. I
couldn't believe my eyes! They were in cipher! Yes, it looked
like cipher. Fancy a man lugging with him a book of that description into this nowhere and studying it—and making notes
—in cipher at that! It was an extravagant mystery.

"I had been dimly aware for some time of a worrying noise,
and when I lifted my eyes I saw the wood-pile was gone, and
the manager, aided by all the pilgrims, was shouting at me
from the river-side. I slipped the book into my pocket. I as-   25
sure you to leave off reading was like tearing myself away from
the shelter of an old and solid friendship.

"I started the lame engine ahead. 'It must be this miserable
trader—this intruder,' exclaimed the manager, looking back
malevolently at the place we had left. 'He must be English,'
I said. 'It will not save him from getting into trouble if he is
not careful,' muttered the manager darkly. I observed with
assumed innocence that no man was safe from trouble in this
world.

"The current was more rapid now, the steamer seemed at   35
her last gasp, the stern-wheel flopped languidly, and I caught

myself listening on tip-toe for the next beat of the boat, for in
sober truth I expected the wretched thing to give up every
moment. It was like watching the last flickers of a life. But
still we crawled. Sometimes I would pick out a tree a little way
5   ahead to measure our progress towards Kurtz by, but I lost it
invariably before we got abreast. To keep the eyes so long on
one thing was too much for human patience. The manager
displayed a beautiful resignation. I fretted and fumed and took
to arguing with myself whether or no I would talk openly with
Kurtz; but before I could come to any conclusion it occurred
to me that my speech or my silence, indeed any action of
mine, would be a mere futility. What did it matter what anyone knew or ignored? What did it matter who was manager?
One gets sometimes such a flash of insight. The essentials of
15   this affair lay deep under the surface, beyond my reach, and
beyond my power of meddling.

"Towards the evening of the second day we judged ourselves about eight miles from Kurtz's station. I wanted to
push on; but the manager looked grave, and told me the navigation up there was so dangerous that it would be advisable,
the sun being very low already, to wait where we were till next
morning. Moreover, he pointed out that if the warning to approach cautiously were to be followed, we must approach in
daylight—not at dusk, or in the dark. This was sensible
25   enough. Eight miles meant nearly three hours' steaming
for us, and I could also see suspicious ripples at the upper end
of the reach. Nevertheless, I was annoyed beyond expression at
the delay, and most unreasonably, too, since one night more
could not matter much after so many months. As we had
plenty of wood, and caution was the word, I brought up in
the middle of the stream. The reach was narrow, straight, with
high sides like a railway cutting. The dusk came gliding into it
long before the sun had set. The current ran smooth and swift,
but a dumb immobility sat on the banks. The living trees,
35   lashed together by the creepers and every living bush of the
undergrowth, might have been changed into stone, even to

the slenderest twig, to the lightest leaf. It was not sleep—it
seemed unnatural, like a state of trance. Not the faintest sound
of any kind could be heard. You looked on amazed, and began
to suspect yourself of being deaf—then the night came suddenly, and struck you blind as well. About three in the morning   5
some large fish leaped, and the loud splash made me jump as
though a gun had been fired. When the sun rose there was a
white fog, very warm and clammy, and more blinding than
the night. It did not shift or drive; it was just there, standing
all round you like something solid. At eight or nine, perhaps, it
lifted as a shutter lifts. We had a glimpse of the towering multitude of trees, of the immense matted jungle, with the blazing
little ball of the sun hanging over it—all perfectly still—and
then the white shutter came down again, smoothly, as if sliding in greased grooves. I ordered the chain, which we had begun   15
to heave in, to be paid out again. Before it stopped running
with a muffled rattle, a cry, a very loud cry as of infinite
desolation, soared slowly in the opaque air. It ceased. A complaining clamour, modulated in savage discords, filled our ears.
The sheer unexpectedness of it made my hair stir under my
cap. I don't know how it struck the others: to me it seemed as
though the mist itself had screamed, so suddenly, and apparently from all sides at once, did this tumultuous and mournful
uproar arise. It culminated in a hurried outbreak of almost
intolerably excessive shrieking, which stopped short, leaving   25
us stiffened in a variety of silly attitudes, and obstinately listening to the nearly as appalling and excessive silence. 'Good God!
What is the meaning——' stammered at my elbow one of the
pilgrims—a little fat man, with sandy hair and red whiskers,
who wore side-spring boots, and pink pyjamas tucked into his
socks. Two others remained open-mouthed a whole minute,
then dashed into the little cabin, to rush out incontinently and
stand darting scared glances, with Winchesters at 'ready' in
their hands. What we could see was just the steamer we were
on, her outlines blurred as though she had been on the point   35
of dissolving, and a misty strip of water, perhaps two feet broad,

around her—and that was all. The rest of the world was nowhere, as far as our eyes and ears were concerned. Just nowhere. Gone, disappeared; swept off without leaving a whisper
or a shadow behind.

5   "I went forward, and ordered the chain to be hauled in short,
so as to be ready to trip the anchor and move the steamboat
at once if necessary. 'Will they attack?' whispered an awed
voice. 'We will be all butchered in this fog,' murmured another.
The faces twitched with the strain, the hands trembled slightly,
the eyes forgot to wink. It was very curious to see the contrast
of expressions of the white men and of the black fellows of
our crew, who were as much strangers to that part of the river
as we, though their homes were only eight hundred miles away.
The whites, of course greatly discomposed, had besides a curious
15   look of being painfully shocked by such an outrageous row.
The others had an alert, naturally interested expression; but
their faces were essentially quiet, even those of the one or two
who grinned as they hauled at the chain. Several exchanged
short, grunting phrases, which seemed to settle the matter to
their satisfaction. Their headman, a young, broad-chested
black, severely draped in dark-blue fringed cloths, with fierce
nostrils and his hair all done up artfully in oily ringlets, stood
near me. 'Aha!' I said, just for good fellowship's sake. 'Catch
'im,' he snapped, with a bloodshot widening of his eyes and a
25   flash of sharp teeth—'catch 'im. Give 'im to us.' 'To you, eh?'
I asked; 'what would you do with them?' 'Eat 'im!' he said,
curtly, and, leaning his elbow on the rail, looked out into the
fog in a dignified and profoundly pensive attitude. I would
no doubt have been properly horrified, had it not occurred to
me that he and his chaps must be very hungry: that they must
have been growing increasingly hungry for at least this month
past. They had been engaged for six months (I don't think a
single one of them had any clear idea of time, as we at the
end of countless ages have. They still belonged to the begin-
35   nings of time—had no inherited experience to teach them as
it were), and of course, as long as there was a piece of paper

written over in accordance with some farcical law or other
made down the river, it didn't enter anybody's head to trouble
how they would live. Certainly they had brought with them
some rotten hippo-meat, which couldn't have lasted very long,
anyway, even if the pilgrims hadn't, in the midst of a shocking   5
hullabaloo, thrown a considerable quantity of it overboard. It
looked like a high-handed proceeding; but it was really a case of
legitimate self-defence. You can't breathe dead hippo waking,
sleeping, and eating, and at the same time keep your precarious
grip on existence. Besides that, they had given them every
week three pieces of brass wire, each about nine inches long;
and the theory was they were to buy their provisions with
that currency in river-side villages. You can see how *that* worked.
There were either no villages, or the people were hostile, or the
director, who like the rest of us fed out of tins, with an occa-   15
sional old he-goat thrown in, didn't want to stop the steamer
for some more or less recondite reason. So, unless they swallowed the wire itself, or made loops of it to snare the fishes
with, I don't see what good their extravagant salary could be
to them. I must say it was paid with a regularity worthy of a
large and honourable trading company. For the rest, the only
thing to eat—though it didn't look eatable in the least—I saw
in their possession was a few lumps of some stuff like half-
cooked dough, of a dirty lavender colour, they kept wrapped in
leaves, and now and then swallowed a piece of, but so small   25
that it seemed done more for the looks of the thing than for
any serious purpose of sustenance. Why in the name of all the
gnawing devils of hunger they didn't go for us—they were
thirty to five—and have a good tuck-in for once, amazes me
now when I think of it. They were big powerful men, with
not much capacity to weigh the consequences, with courage,
with strength, even yet, though their skins were no longer
glossy and their muscles no longer hard. And I saw that something restraining, one of those human secrets that baffle prob-
ability, had come into play there. I looked at them with a   35
swift quickening of interest—not because it occurred to me I

might be eaten by them before very long, though I own to
you that just then I perceived—in a new light, as it were—
how unwholesome the pilgrims looked, and I hoped, yes I
positively hoped, that my aspect was not so—what shall I say?
5   —so—unappetizing: a touch of fantastic vanity which fitted
well with the dream-sensation that pervaded all my days at
that time. Perhaps I had a little fever, too. One can't live with
one's finger everlastingly on one's pulse. I had often 'a little
fever,' or a little touch of other things—the playful paw-strokes
of the wilderness, the preliminary trifling before the more
serious onslaught which came in due course. Yes; I looked at
them as you would on any human being, with a curiosity of
their impulses, motives, capacities, weaknesses, when brought
to the test of an inexorable physical necessity. Restraint! What
15   possible restraint? Was it superstition, disgust, patience, fear
—or some kind of primitive honour? No fear can stand up to
hunger, no patience can wear it out, disgust simply does not
exist where hunger is; and as to superstition, beliefs, and what
you may call principles, they are less than chaff in a breeze.
Don't you know the devilry of lingering starvation, its exasperating torment, its black thoughts, its sombre and brooding
ferocity? Well, I do. It takes a man all his inborn strength to
fight hunger properly. It's really easier to face bereavement,
dishonour, and the perdition of one's soul—than this kind of
25   prolonged hunger. Sad, but true. And these chaps, too, had
no earthly reason for any kind of scruple. Restraint! I would
just as soon have expected restraint from a hyena prowling
amongst the corpses of a battlefield. But there was the fact
facing me—the fact dazzling, to be seen, like the foam on the
depths of the sea, like a ripple on an unfathomable enigma, a
mystery greater—when I thought of it—than the curious, inexplicable note of desperate grief in this savage clamour that had
swept by us on the river-bank, behind the blind whiteness of
the fog.
35   "Two pilgrims were quarrelling in hurried whispers as to
which bank. 'Left.' 'No, no; how can you? Right, right, of

course.' 'It is very serious,' said the manager's voice behind me;
'I would be desolated if anything should happen to Mr. Kurtz
before we came up.' I looked at him, and had not the slightest
doubt he was sincere. He was just the kind of man who would
wish to preserve appearances. That was his restraint. But when   5
he muttered something about going on at once, I did not
even take the trouble to answer him. I knew, and he knew, that
it was impossible. Were we to let go our hold of the bottom,
we would be absolutely in the air—in space. We wouldn't be
able to tell where we were going to—whether up or down
stream, or across—till we fetched against one bank or the
other—and then we wouldn't know at first which it was. Of
course I made no move. I had no mind for a smash-up. You
couldn't imagine a more deadly place for a shipwreck. Whether
drowned at once or not, we were sure to perish speedily in   15
one way or another. 'I authorize you to take all the risks,' he
said, after a short silence. 'I refuse to take any,' I said shortly;
which was just the answer he expected, though its tone might
have surprised him. 'Well, I must defer to your judgment. You
are captain,' he said, with marked civility. I turned my shoulder
to him in sign of my appreciation, and looked into the fog.
How long would it last? It was the most hopeless look-out. The
approach to this Kurtz grubbing for ivory in the wretched bush
was beset by as many dangers as though he had been an en-
chanted princess sleeping in a fabulous castle. 'Will they   25
attack, do you think?' asked the manager, in a confidential tone.

"I did not think they would attack, for several obvious reasons. The thick fog was one. If they left the bank in their canoes
they would get lost in it, as we would be if we attempted to
move. Still, I had also judged the jungle of both banks quite
impenetrable—and yet eyes were in it, eyes that had seen us.
The river-side bushes were certainly very thick; but the undergrowth behind was evidently penetrable. However, during the
short lift I had seen no canoes anywhere in the reach—certainly
not abreast of the steamer. But what made the idea of attack   35
inconceivable to me was the nature of the noise—of the cries

we had heard. They had not the fierce character boding immediate hostile intention. Unexpected, wild, and violent as they
had been, they had given me an irresistible impression of sorrow. The glimpse of the steamboat had for some reason filled
5 those savages with unrestrained grief. The danger, if any, I
expounded, was from our proximity to a great human passion
let loose. Even extreme grief may ultimately vent itself in violence—but more generally takes the form of apathy. . . .

"You should have seen the pilgrims stare! They had no heart
to grin, or even to revile me: but I believe they thought me
gone mad—with fright, maybe. I delivered a regular lecture.
My dear boys, it was no good bothering. Keep a look-out? Well,
you may guess I watched the fog for the signs of lifting as a cat
watches a mouse; but for anything else our eyes were of no
15 more use to us than if we had been buried miles deep in a
heap of cotton-wool. It felt like it, too—choking, warm, stifling.
Besides, all I said, though it sounded extravagant, was absolutely
true to fact. What we afterwards alluded to as an attack was
really an attempt at repulse. The action was very far from being
aggressive—it was not even defensive, in the usual sense: it
was undertaken under the stress of desperation, and in its
essence was purely protective.

"It developed itself, I should say, two hours after the fog
lifted, and its commencement was at a spot, roughly speaking,
25 about a mile and a half below Kurtz's station. We had just
floundered and flopped round a bend, when I saw an islet,
a mere grassy hummock of bright green, in the middle of the
stream. It was the only thing of the kind; but as we opened the
reach more, I perceived it was the head of a long sand-bank, or
rather of a chain of shallow patches stretching down the middle
of the river. They were discoloured, just awash, and the whole
lot was seen just under the water, exactly as a man's backbone
is seen running down the middle of his back under the skin.
Now, as far as I did see, I could go to the right or to the left
35 of this. I didn't know either channel, of course. The banks

looked pretty well alike, the depth appeared the same; but as I
had been informed the station was on the west side, I naturally
headed for the western passage.

"No sooner had we fairly entered it than I became aware
it was much narrower than I had supposed. To the left of us   5
there was the long uninterrupted shoal, and to the right a high,
steep bank heavily overgrown with bushes. Above the bush
the trees stood in serried ranks. The twigs overhung the current
thickly, and from distance to distance a large limb of some
tree projected rigidly over the stream. It was then well on in
the afternoon, the face of the forest was gloomy, and a broad
strip of shadow had already fallen on the water. In this shadow
we steamed up—very slowly, as you may imagine. I sheered
her well inshore—the water being deepest near the bank, as
the sounding-pole informed me.   15

"One of my hungry and forbearing friends was sounding
in the bows just below me. This steamboat was exactly like
a decked scow. On the deck, there were two little teak-wood
houses, with doors and windows. The boiler was in the fore-end,
and the machinery right astern. Over the whole there was a
light roof, supported on stanchions. The funnel projected
through that roof, and in front of the funnel a small cabin
built of light planks served for a pilot-house. It contained a
couch, two camp-stools, a loaded Martini-Henry leaning in
one corner, a tiny table, and the steering-wheel. It had a wide   25
door in front and a broad shutter at each side. All these were
always thrown open, of course. I spent my days perched up
there on the extreme fore-end of that roof, before the door. At
night I slept, or tried to, on the couch. An athletic black
belonging to some coast tribe, and educated by my poor predecessor, was the helmsman. He sported a pair of brass ear-
rings, wore a blue cloth wrapper from the waist to the ankles,
and thought all the world of himself. He was the most un-
stable kind of fool I had ever seen. He steered with no end of
a swagger while you were by; but if he lost sight of you, he be- 35

came instantly the prey of an abject funk, and would let that cripple of a steamboat get the upper hand of him in a minute.

"I was looking down at the sounding-pole, and feeling much annoyed to see at each try a little more of it stick out of that river, when I saw my poleman give up the business suddenly, and stretch himself flat on the deck, without even taking the trouble to haul his pole in. He kept hold on it though, and it trailed in the water. At the same time the fireman, whom I could also see below me, sat down abruptly before his furnace and ducked his head. I was amazed. Then I had to look at the river mighty quick, because there was a snag in the fairway. Sticks, little sticks, were flying about—thick: they were whizzing before my nose, dropping below me, striking behind me against my pilot-house. All this time the river, the shore, the woods, were very quiet—perfectly quiet. I could only hear the heavy splashing thump of the stern-wheel and the patter of these things. We cleared the snag clumsily. Arrows, by Jove! We were being shot at! I stepped in quickly to close the shutter on the land-side. That fool-helmsman, his hands on the spokes, was lifting his knees high, stamping his feet, champing his mouth, like a reined-in horse. Confound him! And we were staggering within ten feet of the bank. I had to lean right out to swing the heavy shutter, and I saw a face amongst the leaves on the level with my own, looking at me very fierce and steady; and then suddenly, as though a veil had been removed from my eyes, I made out, deep in the tangled gloom, naked breasts, arms, legs, glaring eyes—the bush was swarming with human limbs in movement, glistening, of bronze colour. The twigs shook, swayed, and rustled, the arrows flew out of them, and then the shutter came to. 'Steer her straight,' I said to the helmsman. He held his head rigid, face forward; but his eyes rolled, he kept on lifting and setting down his feet gently, his mouth foamed a little. 'Keep quiet!' I said in a fury. I might just as well have ordered a tree not to sway in the wind. I darted out. Below me there was a great scuffle of feet on the iron deck; confused exclamations; a voice screamed, 'Can you turn back?' I caught sight of a V-shaped ripple on the water ahead. What? Another snag! A fusillade burst out under my feet. The pilgrims had opened with their Winchesters, and were simply squirting lead into that bush. A deuce of a lot of smoke came up and drove slowly forward. I swore at it. Now I couldn't see the ripple or the snag either. I stood in the doorway, peering, and the arrows came in swarms. They might have been poisoned, but they looked as though they wouldn't kill a cat. The bush began to howl. Our wood-cutters raised a warlike whoop; the report of a rifle just at my back deafened me. I glanced over my shoulder, and the pilot-house was yet full of noise and smoke when I made a dash at the wheel. The foolnigger had dropped everything, to throw the shutter open and let off that Martini-Henry. He stood before the wide opening, glaring, and I yelled at him to come back, while I straightened the sudden twist out of that steamboat. There was no room to turn even if I had wanted to, the snag was somewhere very near ahead in that confounded smoke, there was no time to lose, so I just crowded her into the bank—right into the bank, where I knew the water was deep.

"We tore slowly along the overhanging bushes in a whirl of broken twigs and flying leaves. The fusillade below stopped short, as I had foreseen it would when the squirts got empty. I threw my head back to a glinting whizz that traversed the pilot-house, in at one shutter hole and out at the other. Looking past that mad helmsman, who was shaking the empty rifle and yelling at the shore, I saw vague forms of men running bent double, leaping, gliding, distinct, incomplete, evanescent. Something big appeared in the air before the shutter, the rifle went overboard, and the man stepped back swiftly, looked at me over his shoulder in an extraordinary, profound, familiar manner, and fell upon my feet. The side of his head hit the wheel twice, and the end of what appeared a long cane clattered round and knocked over a little camp-stool. It looked as though after wrenching that thing from somebody ashore he

had lost his balance in the effort. The thin smoke had blown away, we were clear of the snag, and looking ahead I could see that in another hundred yards or so I would be free to sheer off, away from the bank; but my feet felt so very warm and wet
5   that I had to look down. The man had rolled on his back and stared straight up at me; both his hands clutched that cane. It was the shaft of a spear that, either thrown or lunged through the opening, had caught him in the side just below the ribs; the blade had gone in out of sight, after making a frightful gash; my shoes were full; a pool of blood lay very still, gleaming dark-red under the wheel; his eyes shone with an amazing lustre. The fusillade burst out again. He looked at me anxiously, gripping the spear like something precious, with an air of being afraid I would try to take it away from him. I
15 had to make an effort to free my eyes from his gaze and attend to the steering. With one hand I felt above my head for the line of the steam whistle, and jerked out screech after screech hurriedly. The tumult of angry and warlike yells was checked instantly, and then from the depths of the woods went out such a tremulous and prolonged wail of mournful fear and utter despair as may be imagined to follow the flight of the last hope from the earth. There was a great commotion in the bush; the shower of arrows stopped, a few dropping shots rang out sharply—then silence, in which the languid beat of the
25 stern-wheel came plainly to my ears. I put the helm hard a-starboard at the moment when the pilgrim in pink pyjamas, very hot and agitated, appeared in the doorway. 'The manager sends me——' he began in an official tone, and stopped short. 'Good God!' he said, glaring at the wounded man.

"We two whites stood over him, and his lustrous and inquiring glance enveloped us both. I declare it looked as though he would presently put to us some question in an understandable language; but he died without uttering a sound, without moving a limb, without twitching a muscle. Only in the very last
35 moment, as though in response to some sign we could not see, to some whisper we could not hear, he frowned heavily, and

that frown gave to his black death-mask an inconceivably sombre, brooding, and menacing expression. The lustre of inquiring glance faded swiftly into vacant glassiness. 'Can you steer?'
I asked the agent eagerly. He looked very dubious; but I made
a grab at his arm, and he understood at once I meant him to   5
steer whether or no. To tell you the truth, I was morbidly anxious to change my shoes and socks. 'He is dead,' murmured the
fellow, immensely impressed. 'No doubt about it,' said I, tugging like mad at the shoelaces. 'And by the way, I suppose Mr.
Kurtz is dead as well by this time.'

    "For the moment that was the dominant thought. There was
a sense of extreme disappointment, as though I had found out
I had been striving after something altogether without a substance. I couldn't have been more disgusted if I had travelled all
this way for the sole purpose of talking with Mr. Kurtz. Talk-   15
ing with . . . I flung one shoe overboard, and became aware
that that was exactly what I had been looking forward to—a
talk with Kurtz. I made the strange discovery that I had never
imagined him as doing, you know, but as discoursing. I didn't
say to myself, 'Now I will never see him,' or 'Now I will never
shake him by the hand,' but, 'Now I will never hear him.' The
man presented himself as a voice. Not of course that I did not
connect him with some sort of action. Hadn't I been told in all
the tones of jealousy and admiration that he had collected, bar-
tered, swindled, or stolen more ivory than all the other agents   25
together? That was not the point. The point was in his being a
gifted creature, and that of all his gifts the one that stood out
preëminently, that carried with it a sense of real presence, was
his ability to talk, his words—the gift of expression, the bewildering, the illuminating, the most exalted and the most con-
temptible, the pulsating stream of light, or the deceitful flow
from the heart of an impenetrable darkness.

    "The other shoe went flying unto the devil-god of that river.
I thought, By Jove! it's all over. We are too late; he has vanished—the gift has vanished, by means of some spear, arrow, or   35
club. I will never hear that chap speak after all—and my sor-

row had a startling extravagance of emotion, even such as I had
noticed in the howling sorrow of these savages in the bush. I
couldn't have felt more of lonely desolation somehow, had I
been robbed of a belief or had missed my destiny in life. . . .
Why do you sigh in this beastly way, somebody? Absurd?
Well, absurd. Good Lord! mustn't a man ever—— Here, give
me some tobacco." . . .

There was a pause of profound stillness, then a match flared,
and Marlow's lean face appeared, worn, hollow, with down-
ward folds and dropped eyelids, with an aspect of concentrated
attention; and as he took vigorous draws at his pipe, it seemed
to retreat and advance out of the night in the regular flicker of
the tiny flame. The match went out.

"Absurd!" he cried. "This is the worst of trying to tell. . . .
Here you all are, each moored with two good addresses, like a
hulk with two anchors, a butcher round one corner, a policeman round another, excellent appetites, and temperature normal—you hear—normal from year's end to year's end. And you
say, Absurd! Absurd be—exploded! Absurd! My dear boys,
what can you expect from a man who out of sheer nervousness
had just flung overboard a pair of new shoes! Now I think of it,
it is amazing I did not shed tears. I am, upon the whole, proud
of my fortitude. I was cut to the quick at the idea of having
lost the inestimable privilege of listening to the gifted Kurtz.
Of course I was wrong. The privilege was waiting for me. Oh,
yes, I heard more than enough. And I was right, too. A voice.
He was very little more than a voice. And I heard—him—it—
this voice—other voices—all of them were so little more than
voices—and the memory of that time itself lingers around me,
impalpable, like a dying vibration of one immense jabber, silly,
atrocious, sordid, savage, or simply mean, without any kind of
sense. Voices, voices—even the girl herself—now——"

He was silent for a long time.

"I laid the ghost of his gifts at last with a lie," he began, suddenly. "Girl! What? Did I mention a girl? Oh, she is out of it—
completely. They—the women I mean—are out of it—should

be out of it. We must help them to stay in that beautiful world
of their own, lest ours gets worse. Oh, she had to be out of it.
You should have heard the disinterred body of Mr. Kurtz saying, 'My Intended.' You would have perceived directly then
how completely she was out of it. And the lofty frontal bone of 5
Mr. Kurtz! They say the hair goes on growing sometimes, but
this—ah—specimen, was impressively bald. The wilderness had
patted him on the head, and, behold, it was like a ball—an
ivory ball; it had caressed him, and—lo!—he had withered; it
had taken him, loved him, embraced him, got into his veins,
consumed his flesh, and sealed his soul to its own by the inconceivable ceremonies of some devilish initiation. He was its
spoiled and pampered favourite. Ivory? I should think so.
Heaps of it, stacks of it. The old mud shanty was bursting with
it. You would think there was not a single tusk left either 15
above or below the ground in the whole country. 'Mostly
fossil,' the manager had remarked, disparagingly. It was no
more fossil than I am; but they call it fossil when it is dug up.
It appears these niggers do bury the tusks sometimes—but evidently they couldn't bury this parcel deep enough to save the
gifted Mr. Kurtz from his fate. We filled the steamboat with it,
and had to pile a lot on the deck. Thus he could see and enjoy
as long as he could see, because the appreciation of this favour
had remained with him to the last. You should have heard him
say, 'My ivory.' Oh yes, I heard him. 'My Intended, my ivory, 25
my station, my river, my——' everything belonged to him. It
made me hold my breath in expectation of hearing the wilderness burst into a prodigious peal of laughter that would shake
the fixed stars in their places. Everything belonged to him—but
that was a trifle. The thing was to know what he belonged to,
how many powers of darkness claimed him for their own. That
was the reflection that made you creepy all over. It was impossible—it was not good for one either—trying to imagine. He
had taken a high seat amongst the devils of the land—I mean
literally. You can't understand. How could you?—with solid 35
pavement under your feet, surrounded by kind neighbours

ready to cheer you or to fall on you, stepping delicately between the butcher and the policeman, in the holy terror of scandal and gallows and lunatic asylums—how can you imagine what particular region of the first ages a man's untrammelled
5 feet may take him into by the way of solitude—utter solitude without a policeman—by the way of silence—utter silence, where no warning voice of a kind neighbour can be heard whispering of public opinion? These little things make all the great difference. When they are gone you must fall back upon your own innate strength, upon your own capacity for faithfulness. Of course you may be too much of a fool to go wrong—too dull even to know you are being assaulted by the powers of darkness. I take it, no fool ever made a bargain for his soul with the devil: the fool is too much of a fool, or the devil too much of a
15 devil—I don't know which. Or you may be such a thunderingly exalted creature as to be altogether deaf and blind to anything but heavenly sights and sounds. Then the earth for you is only a standing place—and whether to be like this is your loss or your gain I won't pretend to say. But most of us are neither one nor the other. The earth for us is a place to live in, where we must put up with sights, with sounds, with smells, too, by Jove!—breathe dead hippo, so to speak, and not be contaminated. And there, don't you see? your strength comes in, the faith in your ability for the digging of unostentatious holes to
25 bury the stuff in—your power of devotion, not to yourself, but to an obscure, backbreaking business. And that's difficult enough. Mind, I am not trying to excuse or even explain—I am trying to account to myself for—for—Mr. Kurtz—for the shade of Mr. Kurtz. This initiated wraith from the back of Nowhere honoured me with its amazing confidence before it vanished altogether. This was because it could speak English to me. The original Kurtz had been educated partly in England, and—as he was good enough to say himself—his sympathies were in the right place. His mother was half-English, his father was half-
35 French. All Europe contributed to the making of Kurtz; and by and by I learned that, most appropriately, the International So-

ciety for the Suppression of Savage Customs had intrusted him
with the making of a report, for its future guidance. And he
had written it, too. I've seen it, I've read it. It was eloquent, vibrating with eloquence, but too high-strung, I think. Seventeen
pages of close writing he had found time for! But this must   5
have been before his—let us say—nerves, went wrong, and
caused him to preside at certain midnight dances ending with
unspeakable rites, which—as far as I reluctantly gathered from
what I heard at various times—were offered up to him—do you
understand?—to Mr. Kurtz himself. But it was a beautiful
piece of writing. The opening paragraph, however, in the light
of later information, strikes me now as ominous. He began
with the argument that we whites, from the point of development we had arrived at, 'must necessarily appear to them [sav-
ages] in the nature of supernatural beings—we approach them   15
with the might as of a deity,' and so on, and so on. 'By the simple exercise of our will we can exert a power for good practically
unbounded,' etc. etc. From that point he soared and took me
with him. The peroration was magnificent, though difficult to
remember, you know. It gave me the notion of an exotic Immensity ruled by an august Benevolence. It made me tingle
with enthusiasm. This was the unbounded power of eloquence
—of words—of burning noble words. There were no practical
hints to interrupt the magic current of phrases, unless a kind of
note at the foot of the last page, scrawled evidently much later,   25
in an unsteady hand, may be regarded as the exposition of a
method. It was very simple, and at the end of that moving appeal to every altruistic sentiment it blazed at you, luminous
and terrifying, like a flash of lightning in a serene sky: 'Exterminate all the brutes!' The curious part was that he had
apparently forgotten all about that valuable postscriptum, because, later on, when he in a sense came to himself, he repeatedly entreated me to take good care of 'my pamphlet' (he
called it), as it was sure to have in the future a good influence
upon his career. I had full information about all these things,   35
and, besides, as it turned out, I was to have the care of his

memory. I'd done enough for it to give me the indisputable right to lay it, if I choose, for an everlasting rest in the dust-bin of progress amongst all the sweepings and, figuratively speaking, all the dead cats of civilization. But then, you see, I can't choose. He won't be forgotten. Whatever he was, he was not common. He had the power to charm or frighten rudimentary souls into an aggravated witch-dance in his honour; he could also fill the small souls of the pilgrims with bitter misgivings: he had one devoted friend at least, and he had conquered one soul in the world that was neither rudimentary nor tainted with self-seeking. No; I can't forget him, though I am not prepared to affirm the fellow was exactly worth the life we lost in getting to him. I missed my late helmsman awfully—I missed him even while his body was still lying in the pilot-house. Perhaps you will think it passing strange this regret for a savage who was no more account than a grain of sand in a black Sahara. Well, don't you see, he had done something, he had steered; for months I had him at my back—a help—an instrument. It was a kind of partnership. He steered for me—I had to look after him, I worried about his deficiencies, and thus a subtle bond had been created, of which I only became aware when it was suddenly broken. And the intimate profundity of that look he gave me when he received his hurt remains to this day in my memory—like a claim of distant kinship affirmed in a supreme moment.

"Poor fool! If he had only left that shutter alone. He had no restraint, no restraint—just like Kurtz—a tree swayed by the wind. As soon as I had put on a dry pair of slippers, I dragged him out, after first jerking the spear out of his side, which operation I confess I performed with my eyes shut tight. His heels leaped together over the little door-step; his shoulders were pressed to my breast; I hugged him from behind desperately. Oh! he was heavy, heavy; heavier than any man on earth, I should imagine. Then without more ado I tipped him overboard. The current snatched him as though he had been a wisp of grass, and I saw the body roll over twice before I lost sight of it for ever. All the pilgrims and the manager were then congregated on the awning-deck about the pilot-house, chattering at each other like a flock of excited magpies, and there was a scandalized murmur at my heartless promptitude. What they wanted to keep that body hanging about for I can't guess. Embalm it, maybe. But I had also heard another, and a very ominous, murmur on the deck below. My friends the woodcutters were likewise scandalized, and with a better show of reason—though I admit that the reason itself was quite inadmissible. Oh, quite! I had made up my mind that if my late helmsman was to be eaten, the fishes alone should have him. He had been a very second-rate helmsman while alive, but now he was dead he might have become a first-class temptation, and possibly cause some startling trouble. Besides, I was anxious to take the wheel, the man in pink pyjamas showing himself a hopeless duffer at the business.

"This I did directly the simple funeral was over. We were going half-speed, keeping right in the middle of the stream, and I listened to the talk about me. They had given up Kurtz, they had given up the station; Kurtz was dead, and the station had been burnt—and so on—and so on. The red-haired pilgrim was beside himself with the thought that at least this poor Kurtz had been properly avenged. 'Say! We must have made a glorious slaughter of them in the bush. Eh? What do you think? Say?' He positively danced, the bloodthirsty little gingery beggar. And he had nearly fainted when he saw the wounded man! I could not help saying, 'You made a glorious lot of smoke, anyhow.' I had seen, from the way the tops of the bushes rustled and flew, that almost all the shots had gone too high. You can't hit anything unless you take aim and fire from the shoulder; but these chaps fired from the hip with their eyes shut. The retreat, I maintained—and I was right—was caused by the screeching of the steam whistle. Upon this they forgot Kurtz, and began to howl at me with indignant protests.

"The manager stood by the wheel murmuring confidentially about the necessity of getting well away down the river before dark at all events, when I saw in the distance a clearing on the river-side and the outlines of some sort of building. 'What's this?' I asked. He clapped his hands in wonder. 'The station!' he cried. I edged in at once, still going half-speed.

5   "Through my glasses I saw the slope of a hill interspersed with rare trees and perfectly free from undergrowth. A long decaying building on the summit was half buried in the high grass; the large holes in the peaked roof gaped black from afar; the jungle and the woods made a background. There was no enclosure or fence of any kind; but there had been one apparently, for near the house half-a-dozen slim posts remained in a row, roughly trimmed, and with their upper ends ornamented with round carved balls. The rails, or whatever there had been between, had disappeared. Of course the forest surrounded all

15   that. The river-bank was clear, and on the water-side I saw a white man under a hat like a cart-wheel beckoning persistently with his whole arm. Examining the edge of the forest above and below, I was almost certain I could see movements— human forms gliding here and there. I steamed past prudently, then stopped the engines and let her drift down. The man on the shore began to shout, urging us to land. 'We have been attacked,' screamed the manager. 'I know—I know. It's all right,' yelled back the other, as cheerful as you please. 'Come along. It's all right. I am glad.'

25   "His aspect reminded me of something I had seen—something funny I had seen somewhere. As I manœuvred to get alongside, I was asking myself, 'What does this fellow look like?' Suddenly I got it. He looked like a harlequin. His clothes had been made of some stuff that was brown holland probably, but it was covered with patches all over, with bright patches, blue, red, and yellow—patches on the back, patches on the front, patches on elbows, on knees; coloured binding around his jacket, scarlet edging at the bottom of his trousers; and the sunshine made him look extremely gay and wonderfully neat

35   withal, because you could see how beautifully all this patching had been done. A beardless, boyish face, very fair, no features

to speak of, nose peeling, little blue eyes, smiles and frowns chasing each other over that open countenance like sunshine and shadow on a wind-swept plain. 'Look out, captain!' he cried; 'there's a snag lodged in here last night.' What! Another snag? I confess I swore shamefully. I had nearly holed my crip- 5 ple, to finish off that charming trip. The harlequin on the bank turned his little pug-nose up to me. 'You English?' he asked, all smiles. 'Are you?' I shouted from the wheel. The smiles vanished, and he shook his head as if sorry for my disappointment. Then he brightened up. 'Never mind!' he cried, encouragingly. 'Are we in time?' I asked. 'He is up there,' he replied, with a toss of the head up the hill, and becoming gloomy all of a sudden. His face was like the autumn sky, overcast one moment and bright the next.

"When the manager, escorted by the pilgrims, all of them 15 armed to the teeth, had gone to the house this chap came on board. 'I say, I don't like this. These natives are in the bush,' I said. He assured me earnestly it was all right. 'They are simple people,' he added; 'well, I am glad you came. It took me all my time to keep them off.' 'But you said it was all right,' I cried. 'Oh, they meant no harm,' he said; and as I stared he corrected himself, 'Not exactly.' Then vivaciously, 'My faith, your pilot-house wants a clean-up!' In the next breath he advised me to keep enough steam on the boiler to blow the whistle in case of any trouble. 'One good screech will do more for you than all 25 your rifles. They are simple people,' he repeated. He rattled away at such a rate he quite overwhelmed me. He seemed to be trying to make up for lots of silence, and actually hinted, laughing, that such was the case. 'Don't you talk with Mr. Kurtz?' I said. 'You don't talk with that man—you listen to him,' he exclaimed with severe exaltation. 'But now——' He waved his arm, and in the twinkling of an eye was in the uttermost depths of despondency. In a moment he came up again with a jump, possessed himself of both my hands, shook them continuously, while he gabbled: 'Brother sailor . . . honour . . . pleasure 35 . . . delight . . . introduce myself . . . Russian . . . son of

an archpriest . . . Government of Tambov . . . What? Tobacco! English tobacco; the excellent English tobacco! Now,
that's brotherly. Smoke? Where's a sailor that does not smoke?'

"The pipe soothed him, and gradually I made out he had run
5   away from school, had gone to sea in a Russian ship; ran away
again; served some time in English ships; was now reconciled
with the archpriest. He made a point of that. 'But when one is
young one must see things, gather experience, ideas; enlarge
the mind.' 'Here!' I interrupted. 'You can never tell! Here I
met Mr. Kurtz,' he said, youthfully solemn and reproachful. I
held my tongue after that. It appears he had persuaded a
Dutch trading-house on the coast to fit him out with stores and
goods, and had started for the interior with a light heart, and
no more idea of what would happen to him than a baby. He
15   had been wandering about that river for nearly two years alone,
cut off from everybody and everything. 'I am not so young as I
look. I am twenty-five,' he said. 'At first old Van Shuyten
would tell me to go to the devil,' he narrated with keen enjoyment; 'but I stuck to him, and talked and talked, till at last he
got afraid I would talk the hind-leg off his favourite dog, so he
gave me some cheap things and a few guns, and told me he
hoped he would never see my face again. Good old Dutchman,
Van Shuyten. I've sent him one small lot of ivory a year ago, so
that he can't call me a little thief when I get back. I hope he
25   got it. And for the rest I don't care. I had some wood stacked
for you. That was my old house. Did you see?'

"I gave him Towson's book. He made as though he would
kiss me, but restrained himself. 'The only book I had left, and
I thought I had lost it,' he said, looking at it ecstatically. 'So
many accidents happen to a man going about alone, you know.
Canoes get upset sometimes—and sometimes you've got to
clear out so quick when the people get angry.' He thumbed the
pages. 'You made notes in Russian?' I asked. He nodded. 'I
thought they were written in cipher,' I said. He laughed, then
35   became serious. 'I had lots of trouble to keep these people off,'
he said. 'Did they want to kill you?' I asked. 'Oh, no!' he cried,

and checked himself. 'Why did they attack us?' I pursued. He hesitated, then said shamefacedly, 'They don't want him to go.' 'Don't they?' I said, curiously. He nodded a nod full of mystery and wisdom. 'I tell you,' he cried, 'this man has enlarged my mind.' He opened his arms wide, staring at me with his little blue eyes that were perfectly round." 5

Chapter Three

"I looked at him, lost in astonishment. There he was before me, in motley, as though he had absconded from a troupe of mimes, enthusiastic, fabulous. His very existence was improbable, inexplicable, and altogether bewildering. He was an insoluble problem. It was inconceivable how he had existed, how he had succeeded in getting so far, how he had managed to remain —why he did not instantly disappear. 'I went a little farther,' he said, 'then still a little farther—till I had gone so far that I don't know how I'll ever get back. Never mind. Plenty time. I 15 can manage. You take Kurtz away quick—quick—I tell you.' The glamour of youth enveloped his parti-coloured rags, his destitution, his loneliness, the essential desolation of his futile wanderings. For months—for years—his life hadn't been worth a day's purchase; and there he was gallantly, thoughtlessly alive, to all appearance indestructible solely by the virtue of his few years and of his unreflecting audacity. I was seduced into something like admiration—like envy. Glamour urged him on, glamour kept him unscathed. He surely wanted nothing from the wilderness but space to breathe in and to push on through. 25 His need was to exist, and to move onwards at the greatest possible risk, and with a maximum of privation. If the absolutely pure, uncalculating, unpractical spirit of adventure had ever ruled a human being, it ruled this be-patched youth. I almost

envied him the possession of this modest and clear flame. It seemed to have consumed all thought of self so completely, that even while he was talking to you, you forgot that it was he —the man before your eyes—who had gone through these
5　things. I did not envy him his devotion to Kurtz, though. He had not meditated over it. It came to him, and he accepted it with a sort of eager fatalism. I must say that to me it appeared about the most dangerous thing in every way he had come upon so far.

"They had come together unavoidably, like two ships becalmed near each other, and lay rubbing sides at last. I suppose Kurtz wanted an audience, because on a certain occasion, when encamped in the forest, they had talked all night, or more probably Kurtz had talked. 'We talked of everything,' he said, quite
15　transported at the recollection. 'I forgot there was such a thing as sleep. The night did not seem to last an hour. Everything! Everything! . . . . Of love, too.' 'Ah, he talked to you of love!' I said, much amused. 'It isn't what you think,' he cried, almost passionately. 'It was in general. He made me see things— things.'

"He threw his arms up. We were on deck at the time, and the headman of my wood-cutters, lounging near by, turned upon him his heavy and glittering eyes. I looked around, and I don't know why, but I assure you that never, never before, did
25　this land, this river, this jungle, the very arch of this blazing sky, appear to me so hopeless and so dark, so impenetrable to human thought, so pitiless to human weakness. 'And, ever since, you have been with him, of course?' I said.

"On the contrary. It appears their intercourse had been very much broken by various causes. He had, as he informed me proudly, managed to nurse Kurtz through two illnesses (he alluded to it as you would to some risky feat), but as a rule Kurtz wandered alone, far in the depths of the forest. 'Very often coming to this station, I had to wait days and days
35　before he would turn up,' he said. 'Ah, it was worth waiting for!—sometimes.' 'What was he doing? exploring or what?' I

asked. 'Oh, yes, of course'; he had discovered lots of villages, a
lake, too—he did not know exactly in what direction; it was
dangerous to inquire too much—but mostly his expeditions
had been for ivory. 'But he had no goods to trade with by that
time,' I objected. 'There's a good lot of cartridges left even yet,' 5
he answered, looking away. 'To speak plainly, he raided the
country,' I said. He nodded. 'Not alone, surely!' He muttered
something about the villages round that lake. 'Kurtz got the
tribe to follow him, did he?' I suggested. He fidgeted a little.
'They adored him,' he said. The tone of these words was so extraordinary that I looked at him searchingly. It was curious to
see his mingled eagerness and reluctance to speak of Kurtz.
The man filled his life, occupied his thoughts, swayed his
emotions. 'What can you expect?' he burst out; 'he came to
them with thunder and lightning, you know—and they had 15
never seen anything like it—and very terrible. He could be very
terrible. You can't judge Mr. Kurtz as you would an ordinary
man. No, no, no! Now—just to give you an idea—I don't mind
telling you, he wanted to shoot me, too, one day—but I don't
judge him.' 'Shoot you!' I cried. 'What for?' 'Well, I had a small
lot of ivory the chief of that village near my house gave me.
You see I used to shoot game for them. Well, he wanted it, and
wouldn't hear reason. He declared he would shoot me unless I
gave him the ivory and then cleared out of the country, because
he could do so, and had a fancy for it, and there was nothing 25
on earth to prevent him killing whom he jolly well pleased.
And it was true, too. I gave him the ivory. What did I care! But
I didn't clear out. No, no. I couldn't leave him. I had to be
careful, of course, till we got friendly again for a time. He had
his second illness then. Afterwards I had to keep out of the
way; but I didn't mind. He was living for the most part in
those villages on the lake. When he came down to the river,
sometimes he would take to me, and sometimes it was better
for me to be careful. This man suffered too much. He hated all
this, and somehow he couldn't get away. When I had a chance 35
I begged him to try and leave while there was time; I offered to

go back with him. And he would say yes, and then he would remain; go off on another ivory hunt; disappear for weeks; forget
himself amongst these people—forget himself—you know.'
'Why! he's mad,' I said. He protested indignantly. Mr. Kurtz
5 couldn't be mad. If I had heard him talk, only two days ago, I
wouldn't dare hint at such a thing. . . . I had taken up my bin-
oculars while we talked, and was looking at the shore, sweeping
the limit of the forest at each side and at the back of the
house. The consciousness of there being people in that bush,
so silent, so quiet—as silent and quiet as the ruined house on
the hill—made me uneasy. There was no sign on the face of
nature of this amazing tale that was not so much told as suggested to me in desolate exclamations, completed by shrugs, in
interrupted phrases, in hints ending in deep sighs. The woods
15 were unmoved, like a mask—heavy, like the closed door of a
prison—they looked with their air of hidden knowledge, of patient expectation, of unapproachable silence. The Russian was
explaining to me that it was only lately that Mr. Kurtz had
come down to the river, bringing along with him all the
fighting men of that lake tribe. He had been absent for several
months—getting himself adored, I suppose—and had come
down unexpectedly, with the intention to all appearance of
making a raid either across the river or down stream. Evidently
the appetite for more ivory had got the better of the—what
25 shall I say?—less material aspirations. However he had got
much worse suddenly. 'I heard he was lying helpless, and so I
came up—took my chance,' said the Russian. 'Oh, he is bad,
very bad.' I directed my glass to the house. There were no signs
of life, but there was the ruined roof, the long mud wall peep-
ing above the grass, with three little square window-holes, no
two of the same size; all this brought within reach of my hand,
as it were. And then I made a brusque movement, and one of
the remaining posts of that vanished fence leaped up in the
field of my glass. You remember I told you I had been struck at
35 the distance by certain attempts at ornamentation, rather remarkable in the ruinous aspect of the place. Now I had sud-

denly a nearer view, and its first result was to make me throw my head back as if before a blow. Then I went carefully from post to post with my glass, and I saw my mistake. These round knobs were not ornamental but symbolic; they were expressive and puzzling, striking and disturbing—food for thought and 5 also for vultures if there had been any looking down from the sky; but at all events for such ants as were industrious enough to ascend the pole. They would have been even more impressive, those heads on the stakes, if their faces had not been turned to the house. Only one, the first I had made out, was facing my way. I was not so shocked as you may think. The start back I had given was really nothing but a movement of surprise. I had expected to see a knob of wood there, you know. I returned deliberately to the first I had seen—and there it was, black, dried, sunken, with closed eyelids—a head that 15 seemed to sleep at the top of that pole, and with the shrunken dry lips showing a narrow white line of the teeth, was smiling, too, smiling continuously at some endless and jocose dream of that eternal slumber.

"I am not disclosing any trade secrets. In fact, the manager said afterwards that Mr. Kurtz's methods had ruined the district. I have no opinion on that point, but I want you clearly to understand that there was nothing exactly profitable in these heads being there. They only showed that Mr. Kurtz lacked restraint in the gratification of his various lusts, that there was 25 something wanting in him—some small matter which, when the pressing need arose, could not be found under his magnificent eloquence. Whether he knew of this deficiency himself I can't say. I think the knowledge came to him at last—only at the very last. But the wilderness had found him out early, and had taken on him a terrible vengeance for the fantastic invasion. I think it had whispered to him things about himself which he did not know, things of which he had no conception till he took counsel with this great solitude—and the whisper had proved irresistibly fascinating. It echoed loudly within him 35 because he was hollow at the core. . . . I put down the glass, and the head that had appeared near enough to be spoken to seemed at once to have leaped away from me into inaccessible distance.

"The admirer of Mr. Kurtz was a bit crestfallen. In a hurried, indistinct voice he began to assure me he had not dared to take these—say, symbols—down. He was not afraid of the natives; they would not stir till Mr. Kurtz gave the word. His ascendancy was extraordinary. The camps of these people surrounded the place, and the chiefs came every day to see him. They would crawl. . . . 'I don't want to know anything of the ceremonies used when approaching Mr. Kurtz,' I shouted. Curious, this feeling that came over me that such details would be more intolerable than those heads drying on the stakes under Mr. Kurtz's windows. After all, that was only a savage sight, while I seemed at one bound to have been transported into some lightless region of subtle horrors, where pure, uncomplicated savagery was a positive relief, being something that had a right to exist—obviously—in the sunshine. The young man looked at me with surprise. I suppose it did not occur to him that Mr. Kurtz was no idol of mine. He forgot I hadn't heard any of these splendid monologues on, what was it? on love, justice, conduct of life—or what not. If it had come to crawling before Mr. Kurtz, he crawled as much as the veriest savage of them all. I had no idea of the conditions, he said: these heads were the heads of rebels. I shocked him excessively by laughing. Rebels! What would be the next definition I was to hear? There had been enemies, criminals, workers—and these were rebels. Those rebellious heads looked very subdued to me on their sticks. 'You don't know how such a life tries a man like Kurtz,' cried Kurtz's last disciple. 'Well, and you?' I said. 'I! I! I am a simple man. I have no great thoughts. I want nothing from anybody. How can you compare me to . . . ?' His feelings were too much for speech, and suddenly he broke down. 'I don't understand,' he groaned. 'I've been doing my best to keep him alive, and that's enough. I had no hand in all this. I have no abilities. There hasn't been a drop of medicine or a

mouthful of invalid food for months here. He was shamefully
abandoned. A man like this, with such ideas. Shamefully!
Shamefully! I—I—haven't slept for the last ten nights. . . .'

"His voice lost itself in the calm of the evening. The long
shadows of the forest had slipped down hill while we talked,   5
had gone far beyond the ruined hovel, beyond the symbolic
row of stakes. All this was in the gloom, while we down there
were yet in the sunshine, and the stretch of the river abreast of
the clearing glittered in a still and dazzling splendour, with a
murky and overshadowed bend above and below. Not a living
soul was seen on the shore. The bushes did not rustle.

"Suddenly round the corner of the house a group of men appeared, as though they had come up from the ground. They
waded waist-deep in the grass, in a compact body, bearing an
improvised stretcher in their midst. Instantly, in the emptiness   15
of the landscape, a cry arose whose shrillness pierced the still
air like a sharp arrow flying straight to the very heart of the
land; and, as if by enchantment, streams of human beings—of
naked human beings—with spears in their hands, with bows,
with shields, with wild glances and savage movements, were
poured into the clearing by the dark-faced and pensive forest.
The bushes shook, the grass swayed for a time, and then everything stood still in attentive immobility.

" 'Now, if he does not say the right thing to them we are all
done for,' said the Russian at my elbow. The knot of men with   25
the stretcher had stopped, too, halfway to the steamer, as if petrified. I saw the man on the stretcher sit up, lank and with an
uplifted arm, above the shoulders of the bearers. 'Let us hope
that the man who can talk so well of love in general will find
some particular reason to spare us this time,' I said. I resented
bitterly the absurd danger of our situation, as if to be at the
mercy of that atrocious phantom had been a dishonouring necessity. I could not hear a sound, but through my glasses I saw
the thin arm extended commandingly, the lower jaw moving,
the eyes of that apparition shining darkly far in its bony head   35
that nodded with grotesque jerks. Kurtz—Kurtz—that means

short in German—don't it? Well, the name was as true as everything else in his life—and death. He looked at least seven feet long. His covering had fallen off, and his body emerged from it pitiful and appalling as from a winding-sheet. I could
5   see the cage of his ribs all astir, the bones of his arm waving. It was as though an animated image of death carved out of old ivory had been shaking its hand with menaces at a motionless crowd of men made of dark and glittering bronze. I saw him open his mouth wide—it gave him a weirdly voracious aspect, as though he had wanted to swallow all the air, all the earth, all the men before him. A deep voice reached me faintly. He must have been shouting. He fell back suddenly. The stretcher shook as the bearers staggered forward again, and almost at the same time I noticed that the crowd of savages was vanishing without
15   any perceptible movement of retreat, as if the forest that had ejected these beings so suddenly had drawn them in again as the breath is drawn in a long aspiration.

"Some of the pilgrims behind the stretcher carried his arms —two shot-guns, a heavy rifle, and a light revolver-carbine—the thunderbolts of that pitiful Jupiter. The manager bent over him murmuring as he walked beside his head. They laid him down in one of the little cabins—just a room for a bedplace and a camp-stool or two, you know. We had brought his belated correspondence, and a lot of torn envelopes and open let-
25   ters littered his bed. His hand roamed feebly amongst these papers. I was struck by the fire of his eyes and the composed languor of his expression. It was not so much the exhaustion of disease. He did not seem in pain. This shadow looked satiated and calm, as though for the moment it had had its fill of all the emotions.

"He rustled one of the letters, and looking straight in my face said, 'I am glad.' Somebody had been writing to him about me. These special recommendations were turning up again. The volume of tone he emitted without effort, almost without
35   the trouble of moving his lips, amazed me. A voice! A voice! It was grave, profound, vibrating, while the man did not seem ca-

pable of a whisper. However, he had enough strength in him—
factitious no doubt—to very nearly make an end of us, as you
shall hear directly.

"The manager appeared silently in the doorway; I stepped
out at once and he drew the curtain after me. The Russian,   5
eyed curiously by the pilgrims, was staring at the shore. I followed the direction of his glance.

"Dark human shapes could be made out in the distance,
flitting indistinctly against the gloomy border of the forest, and
near the river two bronze figures, leaning on tall spears, stood
in the sunlight under fantastic headdresses of spotted skins,
warlike and still in statuesque repose. And from right to left
along the lighted shore moved a wild and gorgeous apparition
of a woman.

"She walked with measured steps, draped in striped and   15
fringed cloths, treading the earth proudly, with a slight jingle
and flash of barbarous ornaments. She carried her head high;
her hair was done in the shape of a helmet; she had brass leg-
gings to the knee, brass wire gauntlets to the elbow, a crimson
spot on her tawny cheek, innumerable necklaces of glass beads
on her neck; bizarre things, charms, gifts of witch-men, that
hung about her, glittered and trembled at every step. She must
have had the value of several elephant tusks upon her. She was
savage and superb, wild-eyed and magnificent; there was something ominous and stately in her deliberate progress. And in   25
the hush that had fallen suddenly upon the whole sorrowful
land, the immense wilderness, the colossal body of the fecund
and mysterious life seemed to look at her, pensive, as though it
had been looking at the image of its own tenebrous and
passionate soul.

"She came abreast of the steamer, stood still, and faced us.
Her long shadow fell to the water's edge. Her face had a tragic
and fierce aspect of wild sorrow and dumb pain mingled with
the fear of some struggling, half-shaped resolve. She stood looking at us without a stir, and like the wilderness itself, with an   35
air of brooding over an inscrutable purpose. A whole minute

passed, and then she made a step forward. There was a low jingle, a glint of yellow metal, a sway of fringed draperies, and she
stopped as if her heart had failed her. The young fellow by my
side growled. The pilgrims murmured at my back. She looked
5 at us all as if her life had depended upon the unswerving steadiness of her glance. Suddenly she opened her bared arms and
threw them up rigid above her head, as though in an uncontrol-
lable desire to touch the sky, and at the same time the swift
shadows darted out on the earth, swept around on the river,
gathering the steamer into a shadowy embrace. A formidable silence hung over the scene.

"She turned away slowly, walked on, following the bank, and
passed into the bushes to the left. Once only her eyes gleamed
back at us in the dusk of the thickets before she disappeared.

15 " 'If she had offered to come aboard I really think I would
have tried to shoot her,' said the man of patches, nervously. 'I
have been risking my life every day for the last fortnight to
keep her out of the house. She got in one day and kicked up a
row about those miserable rags I picked up in the storeroom to
mend my clothes with. I wasn't decent. At least it must have
been that, for she talked like a fury to Kurtz for an hour,
pointing at me now and then. I don't understand the dialect of
this tribe. Luckily for me, I fancy Kurtz felt too ill that day to
care, or there would have been mischief. I don't understand.
25 . . . No—it's too much for me. Ah, well, it's all over now.'

"At this moment I heard Kurtz's deep voice behind the curtain: 'Save me!—save the ivory, you mean. Don't tell me. Save
me! Why, I've had to save you. You are interrupting my plans
now. Sick! Sick! Not so sick as you would like to believe. Never
mind. I'll carry my ideas out yet—I will return. I'll show you
what can be done. You with your little peddling notions—you
are interfering with me. I will return. I. . . .'

"The manager came out. He did me the honour to take me
under the arm and lead me aside. 'He is very low, very low,' he
35 said. He considered it necessary to sigh, but neglected to be
consistently sorrowful. 'We have done all we could for him—

haven't we? But there is no disguising the fact, Mr. Kurtz has done more harm than good to the Company. He did not see the time was not ripe for vigorous action. Cautiously, cautiously—that's my principle. We must be cautious yet. The district is closed to us for a time. Deplorable! Upon the whole, the trade will suffer. I don't deny there is a remarkable quantity of ivory—mostly fossil. We must save it, at all events —but look how precarious the position is—and why? Because the method is unsound.' 'Do you,' said I, looking at the shore, 'call it "unsound method"?' 'Without doubt,' he exclaimed hotly. 'Don't you?' . . .

"'No method at all,' I murmured after a while. 'Exactly,' he exulted. 'I anticipated this. Shows a complete want of judgment. It is my duty to point it out in the proper quarter.' 'Oh,' said I, 'that fellow—what's his name?—the brickmaker, will make a readable report for you.' He appeared confounded for a moment. It seemed to me I had never breathed an atmosphere so vile, and I turned mentally to Kurtz for relief—positively for relief. 'Nevertheless I think Mr. Kurtz is a remarkable man,' I said with emphasis. He started, dropped on me a cold heavy glance, said very quietly, 'he *was*,' and turned his back on me. My hour of favour was over; I found myself lumped along with Kurtz as a partisan of methods for which the time was not ripe: I was unsound! Ah! but it was something to have at least a choice of nightmares.

"I had turned to the wilderness really, not to Mr. Kurtz, who, I was ready to admit, was as good as buried. And for a moment it seemed to me as if I also were buried in a vast grave full of unspeakable secrets. I felt an intolerable weight oppressing my breast, the smell of the damp earth, the unseen presence of victorious corruption, the darkness of an impenetrable night. . . . The Russian tapped me on the shoulder. I heard him mumbling and stammering something about 'brother seaman—couldn't conceal—knowledge of matters that would affect Mr. Kurtz's reputation.' I waited. For him evidently Mr. Kurtz was not in his grave; I suspect that for him Mr. Kurtz was one of the immortals. 'Well!' said I at last, 'speak out. As it happens, I am Mr. Kurtz's friend—in a way.'

"He stated with a good deal of formality that had we not been 'of the same profession,' he would have kept the matter to himself without regard to consequences. 'He suspected there was an active ill will towards him on the part of these white men that——' 'You are right,' I said, remembering a certain conversation I had overheard. 'The manager thinks you ought to be hanged.' He showed a concern at this intelligence which amused me at first. 'I had better get out of the way quietly,' he said, earnestly. 'I can do no more for Kurtz now, and they would soon find some excuse. What's to stop them? There's a military post three hundred miles from here.' 'Well, upon my word,' said I, 'perhaps you had better go if you have any friends amongst the savages near by.' 'Plenty,' he said. 'They are simple people—and I want nothing, you know.' He stood biting his lip, then: 'I don't want any harm to happen to these whites here, but of course I was thinking of Mr. Kurtz's reputation—but you are a brother seaman and——' 'All right,' said I, after a time. 'Mr. Kurtz's reputation is safe with me.' I did not know how truly I spoke.

"He informed me, lowering his voice, that it was Kurtz who had ordered the attack to be made on the steamer. 'He hated sometimes the idea of being taken away—and then again. . . . But I don't understand these matters. I am a simple man. He thought it would scare you away—that you would give it up, thinking him dead. I could not stop him. Oh, I had an awful time of it this last month.' 'Very well,' I said. 'He is all right now.' 'Ye-e-es,' he muttered, not very convinced apparently. 'Thanks,' said I; 'I shall keep my eyes open.' 'But quiet—eh?' he urged, anxiously. 'It would be awful for his reputation if anybody here——' I promised a complete discretion with great gravity. 'I have a canoe and three black fellows waiting not very far. I am off. Could you give me a few Martini-Henry cartridges?' I could, and did, with proper secrecy. He helped himself, with a wink at me, to a handful of my tobacco. 'Between

sailors—you know—good English tobacco.' At the door of the
pilot-house he turned round—'I say, haven't you a pair of shoes
you could spare?' He raised one leg. 'Look.' The soles were tied
with knotted strings sandal-wise under his bare feet. I rooted
out an old pair, at which he looked with admiration before   5
tucking it under his left arm. One of his pockets (bright red)
was bulging with cartridges, from the other (dark blue) peeped
'Towson's Inquiry,' etc., etc. He seemed to think himself excel-
lently well equipped for a renewed encounter with the wilderness. 'Ah! I'll never, never meet such a man again. You ought
to have heard him recite poetry—his own, too, it was, he told
me. Poetry!' He rolled his eyes at the recollection of these delights. 'Oh, he enlarged my mind!' 'Good-bye,' said I. He shook
hands and vanished in the night. Sometimes I ask myself
whether I had ever really seen him—whether it was possible to   15
meet such a phenomenon! . . .

"When I woke up shortly after midnight his warning came to
my mind with its hint of danger that seemed, in the starred
darkness, real enough to make me get up for the purpose of
having a look round. On the hill a big fire burned, illuminating
fitfully a crooked corner of the station-house. One of the agents
with a picket of a few of our blacks, armed for the purpose, was
keeping guard over the ivory; but deep within the forest, red
gleams that wavered, that seemed to sink and rise from the
ground amongst confused columnar shapes of intense black-   25
ness, showed the exact position of the camp where Mr. Kurtz's
adorers were keeping their uneasy vigil. The monotonous beating of a big drum filled the air with muffled shocks and a lingering vibration. A steady droning sound of many men chant-
ing each to himself some weird incantation came out from the
black, flat wall of the woods as the humming of bees comes out
of a hive, and had a strange narcotic effect upon my half-awake
senses. I believe I dozed off leaning over the rail, till an abrupt
burst of yells, an overwhelming outbreak of a pent-up and mysterious frenzy, woke me up in a bewildered wonder. It was cut   35
short all at once, and the low droning went on with an effect

of audible and soothing silence. I glanced casually into the little cabin. A light was burning within, but Mr. Kurtz was not there.

"I think I would have raised an outcry if I had believed my eyes. But I didn't believe them at first—the thing seemed so impossible. The fact is I was completely unnerved by a sheer blank fright, pure abstract terror, unconnected with any distinct shape of physical danger. What made this emotion so overpowering was—how shall I define it?—the moral shock I received, as if something altogether monstrous, intolerable to thought and odious to the soul, had been thrust upon me unexpectedly. This lasted of course the merest fraction of a second, and then the usual sense of commonplace, deadly danger, the possibility of a sudden onslaught and massacre, or something of the kind, which I saw impending, was positively welcome and composing. It pacified me, in fact, so much, that I did not raise an alarm.

"There was an agent buttoned up inside an ulster and sleeping on a chair on deck within three feet of me. The yells had not awakened him; he snored very slightly; I left him to his slumbers and leaped ashore. I did not betray Mr. Kurtz—it was ordered I should never betray him—it was written I should be loyal to the nightmare of my choice. I was anxious to deal with this shadow by myself alone—and to this day I don't know why I was so jealous of sharing with any one the peculiar blackness of that experience.

"As soon as I got on the bank I saw a trail—a broad trail through the grass. I remember the exaltation with which I said to myself, 'He can't walk—he is crawling on all-fours—I've got him.' The grass was wet with dew. I strode rapidly with clenched fists. I fancy I had some vague notion of falling upon him and giving him a drubbing. I don't know. I had some imbecile thoughts. The knitting old woman with the cat obtruded herself upon my memory as a most improper person to be sitting at the other end of such an affair. I saw a row of pilgrims squirting lead in the air out of Winchesters held to the hip. I thought I would never get back to the steamer, and imagined myself living alone and unarmed in the woods to an advanced age. Such silly things—you know. And I remember I confounded the beat of the drum with the beating of my heart, and was pleased at its calm regularity.

"I kept to the track though—then stopped to listen. The night was very clear; a dark blue space, sparkling with dew and starlight, in which black things stood very still. I thought I could see a kind of motion ahead of me. I was strangely cocksure of everything that night. I actually left the track and ran in a wide semicircle (I verily believe chuckling to myself) so as to get in front of that stir, of that motion I had seen—if indeed I had seen anything. I was circumventing Kurtz as though it had been a boyish game.

"I came upon him, and, if he had not heard me coming, I would have fallen over him, too, but he got up in time. He rose, unsteady, long, pale, indistinct, like a vapour exhaled by the earth, and swayed slightly, misty and silent before me; while at my back the fires loomed between the trees, and the murmur of many voices issued from the forest. I had cut him off cleverly; but when actually confronting him I seemed to come to my senses, I saw the danger in its right proportion. It was by no means over yet. Suppose he began to shout? Though he could hardly stand, there was still plenty of vigour in his voice. 'Go away—hide yourself,' he said, in that profound tone. It was very awful. I glanced back. We were within thirty yards from the nearest fire. A black figure stood up, strode on long black legs, waving long black arms, across the glow. It had horns—antelope horns, I think—on its head. Some sorcerer, some witch-man, no doubt; it looked fiendlike enough. 'Do you know what you are doing?' I whispered. 'Perfectly,' he answered, raising his voice for that single word: it sounded to me far off and yet loud, like a hail through a speaking-trumpet. If he makes a row we are lost, I thought to myself. This clearly was not a case for fisticuffs, even apart from the very natural aversion I had to beat that Shadow—this wandering and tor-

mented thing. 'You will be lost,' I said—'utterly lost.' One gets
sometimes such a flash of inspiration, you know. I did say the
right thing, though indeed he could not have been more irretrievably lost than he was at this very moment, when the foundations of our intimacy were being laid—to endure—to endure
—even to the end—even beyond.

   " 'I had immense plans,' he muttered irresolutely. 'Yes,' said
I; 'but if you try to shout I'll smash your head with——' There
was not a stick or a stone near. 'I will throttle you for good,' I
corrected myself. 'I was on the threshold of great things,' he
pleaded, in a voice of longing, with a wistfulness of tone that
made my blood run cold. 'And now for this stupid scoundrel
——' 'Your success in Europe is assured in any case,' I affirmed,
steadily. I did not want to have the throttling of him, you understand—and indeed it would have been very little use for any
practical purpose. I tried to break the spell—the heavy, mute
spell of the wilderness—that seemed to draw him to its pitiless
breast by the awakening of forgotten and brutal instincts, by
the memory of gratified and monstrous passions. This alone, I
was convinced, had driven him out to the edge of the forest, to
the bush, towards the gleam of fires, the throb of drums, the
drone of weird incantations; this alone had beguiled his unlawful soul beyond the bounds of permitted aspirations. And,
don't you see, the terror of the position was not in being
knocked on the head—though I had a very lively sense of that
danger, too—but in this, that I had to deal with a being to
whom I could not appeal in the name of anything high or low.
I had, even like the niggers, to invoke him—himself—his own
exalted and incredible degradation. There was nothing either
above or below him, and I knew it. He had kicked himself
loose of the earth. Confound the man! he had kicked the very
earth to pieces. He was alone, and I before him did not know
whether I stood on the ground or floated in the air. I've been
telling you what we said—repeating the phrases we pronounced—but what's the good? They were common everyday
words—the familiar, vague sounds exchanged on every waking

day of life. But what of that? They had behind them, to my
mind, the terrific suggestiveness of words heard in dreams, of
phrases spoken in nightmares. Soul! If anybody had ever struggled with a soul, I am the man. And I wasn't arguing with a lunatic either. Believe me or not, his intelligence was perfectly   5
clear—concentrated, it is true, upon himself with horrible
intensity, yet clear; and therein was my only chance—barring,
of course, the killing him there and then, which wasn't so good,
on account of unavoidable noise. But his soul was mad. Being
alone in the wilderness, it had looked within itself, and, by
heavens! I tell you, it had gone mad. I had—for my sins, I suppose—to go through the ordeal of looking into it myself. No
eloquence could have been so withering to one's belief in
mankind as his final burst of sincerity. He struggled with himself, too. I saw it—I heard it. I saw the inconceivable mystery   15
of a soul that knew no restraint, no faith, and no fear, yet
struggling blindly with itself. I kept my head pretty well; but
when I had him at last stretched on the couch, I wiped my
forehead, while my legs shook under me as though I had carried
half a ton on my back down that hill. And yet I had only supported him, his bony arm clasped round my neck—and he was
not much heavier than a child.

"When next day we left at noon, the crowd, of whose presence behind the curtain of trees I had been acutely conscious
all the time, flowed out of the woods again, filled the clearing,   25
covered the slope with a mass of naked, breathing, quivering,
bronze bodies. I steamed up a bit, then swung downstream,
and two thousand eyes followed the evolutions of the splashing, thumping, fierce river-demon beating the water with its
terrible tail and breathing black smoke into the air. In front of
the first rank, along the river, three men, plastered with bright
red earth from head to foot, strutted to and fro restlessly.
When we came abreast again, they faced the river, stamped
their feet, nodded their horned heads, swayed their scarlet
bodies; they shook towards the fierce river-demon a bunch of   35
black feathers, a mangy skin with a pendent tail—something

that looked like a dried gourd; they shouted periodically together strings of amazing words that resembled no sounds of
human language; and the deep murmurs of the crowd, interrupted suddenly, were like the responses of some satanic litany.

5   "We had carried Kurtz into the pilot-house: there was more
air there. Lying on the couch, he stared through the open shutter. There was an eddy in the mass of human bodies, and the
woman with helmeted head and tawny cheeks rushed out to
the very brink of the stream. She put out her hands, shouted
something, and all that wild mob took up the shout in a roaring chorus of articulated, rapid, breathless utterance.

" 'Do you understand this?' I asked.

"He kept on looking out past me with fiery, longing eyes,
with a mingled expression of wistfulness and hate. He made no
15   answer, but I saw a smile, a smile of indefinable meaning, appear on his colourless lips that a moment after twitched convulsively. 'Do I not?' he said slowly, gasping, as if the words
had been torn out of him by a supernatural power.

"I pulled the string of the whistle, and I did this because I
saw the pilgrims on deck getting out their rifles with an air of
anticipating a jolly lark. At the sudden screech there was a
movement of abject terror through that wedged mass of bodies.
'Don't! don't you frighten them away,' cried someone on deck
disconsolately. I pulled the string time after time. They broke
25   and ran, they leaped, they crouched, they swerved, they dodged
the flying terror of the sound. The three red chaps had fallen
flat, face down on the shore, as though they had been shot
dead. Only the barbarous and superb woman did not so much
as flinch, and stretched tragically her bare arms after us over
the sombre and glittering river.

"And then that imbecile crowd down on the deck started
their little fun, and I could see nothing more for smoke.

"The brown current ran swiftly out of the heart of darkness,
bearing us down towards the sea with twice the speed of our
35   upward progress; and Kurtz's life was running swiftly, too, ebb-

ing, ebbing out of his heart into the sea of inexorable time.
The manager was very placid, he had no vital anxieties now, he
took us both in with a comprehensive and satisfied glance: the
'affair' had come off as well as could be wished. I saw the time
approaching when I would be left alone of the party of 'un-   5
sound method.' The pilgrims looked upon me with disfavour. I
was, so to speak, numbered with the dead. It is strange how I
accepted this unforeseen partnership, this choice of nightmares
forced upon me in the tenebrous land invaded by these mean
and greedy phantoms.

"Kurtz discoursed. A voice! a voice! It rang deep to the very
last. It survived his strength to hide in the magnificent folds of
eloquence the barren darkness of his heart. Oh, he struggled!
he struggled! The wastes of his weary brain were haunted by
shadowy images now—images of wealth and fame revolving ob-   15
sequiously round his unextinguishable gift of noble and lofty
expression. My Intended, my station, my career, my ideas—
these were the subjects for the occasional utterances of
elevated sentiments. The shade of the original Kurtz frequented the bedside of the hollow sham, whose fate it was to
be buried presently in the mould of primeval earth. But both
the diabolic love and the unearthly hate of the mysteries it had
penetrated fought for the possession of that soul satiated with
primitive emotions, avid of lying fame, of sham distinction, of
all the appearances of success and power.   25

"Sometimes he was contemptibly childish. He desired to
have kings meet him at railway-stations on his return from
some ghastly Nowhere, where he intended to accomplish great
things. 'You show them you have in you something that is
really profitable, and then there will be no limits to the recog-
nition of your ability,' he would say. 'Of course you must take
care of the motives—right motives—always.' The long reaches
that were like one and the same reach, monotonous bends that
were exactly alike, slipped past the steamer with their multitude of secular trees looking patiently after this grimy fragment   35
of another world, the forerunner of change, of conquest, of

trade, of massacres, of blessings. I looked ahead—piloting. 'Close the shutter,' said Kurtz suddenly one day; 'I can't bear to look at this.' I did so. There was a silence. 'Oh, but I will wring your heart yet!' he cried at the invisible wilderness.

5   "We broke down—as I had expected—and had to lie up for repairs at the head of an island. This delay was the first thing that shook Kurtz's confidence. One morning he gave me a packet of papers and a photograph—the lot tied together with a shoe-string. 'Keep this for me,' he said. 'This noxious fool' (meaning the manager) 'is capable of prying into my boxes when I am not looking.' In the afternoon I saw him. He was lying on his back with closed eyes, and I withdrew quietly, but I heard him mutter, 'Live rightly, die, die . . .' I listened. There was nothing more. Was he rehearsing some speech in his 15   sleep, or was it a fragment of a phrase from some newspaper article? He had been writing for the papers and meant to do so again, 'for the furthering of my ideas. It's a duty.'

"His was an impenetrable darkness. I looked at him as you peer down at a man who is lying at the bottom of a precipice where the sun never shines. But I had not much time to give him, because I was helping the engine-driver to take to pieces the leaky cylinders, to straighten a bent connecting-rod, and in other such matters. I lived in an infernal mess of rust, filings, nuts, bolts, spanners, hammers, ratchet-drills—things I abomi- 25   nate, because I don't get on with them. I tended the little forge we fortunately had aboard; I toiled wearily in a wretched scrap-heap—unless I had the shakes too bad to stand.

"One evening coming in with a candle I was startled to hear him say a little tremulously, 'I am lying here in the dark wait- ing for death.' The light was within a foot of his eyes. I forced myself to murmur, 'Oh, nonsense!' and stood over him as if transfixed.

"Anything approaching the change that came over his fea- tures I have never seen before, and hope never to see again. 35   Oh, I wasn't touched. I was fascinated. It was as though a veil had been rent. I saw on that ivory face the expression of som-

bre pride, of ruthless power, of craven terror—of an intense
and hopeless despair. Did he live his life again in every detail of
desire, temptation, and surrender during that supreme moment
of complete knowledge? He cried in a whisper at some image,
at some vision—he cried out twice, a cry that was no more 5
than a breath—

" 'The horror! The horror!'

"I blew the candle out and left the cabin. The pilgrims were
dining in the mess-room, and I took my place opposite the
manager, who lifted his eyes to give me a questioning glance,
which I successfully ignored. He leaned back, serene, with that
peculiar smile of his sealing the unexpressed depths of his
meanness. A continuous shower of small flies streamed upon
the lamp, upon the cloth, upon our hands and faces. Suddenly
the manager's boy put his insolent black head in the doorway, 15
and said in a tone of scathing contempt—

" 'Mistah Kurtz—he dead.'

"All the pilgrims rushed out to see. I remained, and went on
with my dinner. I believe I was considered brutally callous.
However, I did not eat much. There was a lamp in there
—light, don't you know—and outside it was so beastly, beastly
dark. I went no more near the remarkable man who had pronounced a judgment upon the adventures of his soul on this
earth. The voice was gone. What else had been there? But I am
of course aware that next day the pilgrims buried something in 25
a muddy hole.

"And then they very nearly buried me.

"However, as you see, I did not go to join Kurtz there and
then. I did not. I remained to dream the nightmare out to the
end, and to show my loyalty to Kurtz once more. Destiny. My
destiny! Droll thing life is—that mysterious arrangement of
merciless logic for a futile purpose. The most you can hope
from it is some knowledge of yourself—that comes too late—a
crop of unextinguishable regrets. I have wrestled with death. It
is the most unexciting contest you can imagine. It takes place 35
in an impalpable grayness, with nothing underfoot, with noth-

ing around, without spectators, without clamour, without glory, without the great desire of victory, without the great fear of defeat, in a sickly atmosphere of tepid scepticism, without much belief in your own right, and still less in that of your adversary.
If such is the form of ultimate wisdom, then life is a greater riddle than some of us think it to be. I was within a hair's breadth of the last opportunity for pronouncement, and I found with humiliation that probably I would have nothing to say. This is the reason why I affirm that Kurtz was a remarkable man. He had something to say. He said it. Since I had peeped over the edge myself, I understand better the meaning of his stare, that could not see the flame of the candle, but was wide enough to embrace the whole universe, piercing enough to penetrate all the hearts that beat in the darkness. He had summed up—he had judged. 'The horror!' He was a remarkable man. After all, this was the expression of some sort of belief; it had candour, it had conviction, it had a vibrating note of revolt in its whisper, it had the appalling face of a glimpsed truth—the strange commingling of desire and hate. And it is not my own extremity I remember best—a vision of grayness without form filled with physical pain, and a careless contempt for the evanescence of all things—even of this pain itself. No! It is his extremity that I seem to have lived through. True, he had made that last stride, he had stepped over the edge, while I had been permitted to draw back my hesitating foot. And perhaps in this is the whole difference; perhaps all the wisdom, and all truth, and all sincerity, are just compressed into that inappreciable moment of time in which we step over the threshold of the invisible. Perhaps! I like to think my summing-up would not have been a word of careless contempt. Better his cry—much better. It was an affirmation, a moral victory paid for by innumerable defeats, by abominable terrors, by abominable satisfactions. But it was a victory! That is why I have remained loyal to Kurtz to the last, and even beyond, when a long time after I heard once more, not his own voice, but the echo of his magnificent elo-

quence thrown to me from a soul as translucently pure as a
cliff of crystal.

"No, they did not bury me, though there is a period of time
which I remember mistily, with a shuddering wonder, like a
passage through some inconceivable world that had no hope in 5
it and no desire. I found myself back in the sepulchral city resenting the sight of people hurrying through the streets to filch
a little money from each other, to devour their infamous cook-
ery, to gulp their unwholesome beer, to dream their insignificant and silly dreams. They trespassed upon my thoughts. They
were intruders whose knowledge of life was to me an irritating
pretence, because I felt so sure they could not possibly know
the things I knew. Their bearing, which was simply the bearing
of commonplace individuals going about their business in the
assurance of perfect safety, was offensive to me like the outra- 15
geous flauntings of folly in the face of a danger it is unable to
comprehend. I had no particular desire to enlighten them, but
I had some difficulty in restraining myself from laughing in
their faces, so full of stupid importance. I daresay I was not
very well at that time. I tottered about the streets—there were
various affairs to settle—grinning bitterly at perfectly respectable persons. I admit my behaviour was inexcusable, but then
my temperature was seldom normal in these days. My dear
aunt's endeavours to 'nurse up my strength' seemed altogether
beside the mark. It was not my strength that wanted nursing, it 25
was my imagination that wanted soothing. I kept the bundle of
papers given me by Kurtz, not knowing exactly what to do with
it. His mother had died lately, watched over, as I was told, by
his Intended. A clean-shaved man, with an official manner and
wearing gold-rimmed spectacles, called on me one day and
made inquiries, at first circuitous, afterwards suavely pressing,
about what he was pleased to denominate certain 'documents.'
I was not surprised, because I had had two rows with the manager on the subject out there. I had refused to give up the
smallest scrap out of that package, and I took the same atti- 35

tude with the spectacled man. He became darkly menacing at
last, and with much heat argued that the Company had the
right to every bit of information about its 'territories.' And said
he, 'Mr. Kurtz's knowledge of unexplored regions must have
5   been necessarily extensive and peculiar—owing to his great
abilities and to the deplorable circumstances in which he had
been placed: therefore——' I assured him that Mr. Kurtz's
knowledge, however extensive, did not bear upon the problems
of commerce or administration. He invoked then the name of
science. 'It would be an incalculable loss if,' etc., etc. I offered
him the report on the 'Suppression of Savage Customs,' with
the postscriptum torn off. He took it up eagerly, but ended by
sniffing at it with an air of contempt. 'This is not what we had
a right to expect,' he remarked. 'Expect nothing else,' I said.
15   'There are only private letters.' He withdrew upon some threat
of legal proceedings, and I saw him no more; but another fellow, calling himself Kurtz's cousin, appeared two days later,
and was anxious to hear all the details about his dear relative's
last moments. Incidentally he gave me to understand that
Kurtz had been essentially a great musician. 'There was the
making of an immense success,' said the man, who was an or-
ganist, I believe, with lank gray hair flowing over a greasy coat-
collar. I had no reason to doubt his statement; and to this day
I am unable to say which was Kurtz's profession, whether
25   he ever had any—which was the greatest of his talents. I had
taken him for a painter who wrote for the papers, or else for a
journalist who could paint—but even the cousin (who took
snuff during the interview) could not tell me what he had been
—exactly. He was a universal genius—on that point I agreed
with the old chap, who thereupon blew his nose noisily into a
large cotton handkerchief and withdrew in senile agitation,
bearing off some family letters and memoranda without importance. Ultimately a journalist anxious to know something of
the fate of his 'dear colleague' turned up. This visitor informed
35   me Kurtz's proper sphere ought to have been politics 'on the
popular side.' He had furry straight eyebrows, bristly hair

cropped short, an eye-glass on a broad ribbon, and, becoming expansive, confessed his opinion that Kurtz really couldn't write a bit—'but heavens! how that man could talk. He electrified large meetings. He had faith—don't you see?—he had the faith. He could get himself to believe anything—anything. He would have been a splendid leader of an extreme party.' 'What party?' I asked. 'Any party,' answered the other. 'He was an—an—extremist.' Did I not think so? I assented. Did I know, he asked, with a sudden flash of curiosity, 'what it was that induced him to go out there?' 'Yes,' said I, and forthwith handed him the famous Report for publication, if he thought fit. He glanced through it hurriedly, mumbling all the time, judged 'it would do,' and took himself off with this plunder.

"Thus I was left at last with a slim packet of letters and the girl's portrait. She struck me as beautiful—I mean she had a beautiful expression. I know that the sunlight can be made to lie, too, yet one felt that no manipulation of light and pose could have conveyed the delicate shade of truthfulness upon those features. She seemed ready to listen without mental reservation, without suspicion, without a thought for herself. I concluded I would go and give her back her portrait and those letters myself. Curiosity? Yes; and also some other feeling perhaps. All that had been Kurtz's had passed out of my hands: his soul, his body, his station, his plans, his ivory, his career. There remained only his memory and his Intended—and I wanted to give that up, too, to the past, in a way—to surrender personally all that remained of him with me to that oblivion which is the last word of our common fate. I don't defend myself. I had no clear perception of what it was I really wanted. Perhaps it was an impulse of unconscious loyalty, or the fulfilment of one of those ironic necessities that lurk in the facts of human existence. I don't know. I can't tell. But I went.

"I thought his memory was like the other memories of the dead that accumulate in every man's life—a vague impress on the brain of shadows that had fallen on it in their swift and final passage; but before the high and ponderous door, between the tall houses of a street as still and decorous as a well-kept alley in a cemetery, I had a vision of him on the stretcher, opening his mouth voraciously, as if to devour all the earth with all its mankind. He lived then before me; he lived as much as he had ever lived—a shadow insatiable of splendid appearances, of frightful realities; a shadow darker than the shadow of the night, and draped nobly in the folds of a gorgeous eloquence. The vision seemed to enter the house with me—the stretcher, the phantom-bearers, the wild crowd of obedient worshippers, the gloom of the forests, the glitter of the reach between the murky bends, the beat of the drum, regular and muffled like the beating of a heart—the heart of a conquering darkness. It was a moment of triumph for the wilderness, an invading and vengeful rush which, it seemed to me, I would have to keep back alone for the salvation of another soul. And the memory of what I had heard him say afar there, with the horned shapes stirring at my back, in the glow of fires, within the patient woods, those broken phrases came back to me, were heard again in their ominous and terrifying simplicity. I remembered his abject pleading, his abject threats, the colossal scale of his vile desires, the meanness, the torment, the tempestuous anguish of his soul. And later on I seemed to see his collected languid manner, when he said one day, 'This lot of ivory now is really mine. The Company did not pay for it. I collected it myself at a very great personal risk. I am afraid they will try to claim it as theirs though. H'm. It is a difficult case. What do you think I ought to do—resist? Eh? I want no more than justice.' . . . He wanted no more than justice—no more than justice. I rang the bell before a mahogany door on the first floor, and while I waited he seemed to stare at me out of the glassy panel—stare with that wide and immense stare embracing, condemning, loathing all the universe. I seemed to hear the whispered cry, 'The horror! The horror!'

"The dusk was falling. I had to wait in a lofty drawing-room with three long windows from floor to ceiling that were like three luminous and bedraped columns. The bent gilt legs and backs of the furniture shone in indistinct curves. The tall marble fireplace had a cold and monumental whiteness. A grand piano stood massively in a corner; with dark gleams on the flat surfaces like a sombre and polished sarcophagus. A high door opened—closed. I rose.

"She came forward, all in black, with a pale head, floating towards me in the dusk. She was in mourning. It was more than a year since his death, more than a year since the news came; she seemed as though she would remember and mourn for ever. She took both my hands in hers and murmured, 'I had heard you were coming.' I noticed she was not very young—I mean not girlish. She had a mature capacity for fidelity, for belief, for suffering. The room seemed to have grown darker, as if all the sad light of the cloudy evening had taken refuge on her forehead. This fair hair, this pale visage, this pure brow, seemed surrounded by an ashy halo from which the dark eyes looked out at me. Their glance was guileless, profound, confident, and trustful. She carried her sorrowful head as though she were proud of that sorrow, as though she would say, I—I alone know how to mourn for him as he deserves. But while we were still shaking hands, such a look of awful desolation came upon her face that I perceived she was one of those creatures that are not the playthings of Time. For her he had died only yesterday. And, by Jove! the impression was so powerful that for me, too, he seemed to have died only yesterday—nay, this very minute. I saw her and him in the same instant of time—his death and her sorrow—I saw her sorrow in the very moment of his death. Do you understand? I saw them together—I heard them together. She had said, with a deep catch of the breath, 'I have survived' while my strained ears seemed to hear distinctly, mingled with her tone of despairing regret, the summing up whisper of his eternal condemnation. I asked myself what I was doing there, with a sensation of panic in my heart as though I had blundered into a place of cruel and absurd mysteries not fit for a human being to behold. She motioned me to a chair. We sat down. I laid the packet gently on the little table, and she put her hand over it. . . . 'You knew him well,' she murmured, after a moment of mourning silence.

5   " 'Intimacy grows quickly out there,' I said. 'I knew him as well as it is possible for one man to know another.'

" 'And you admired him,' she said. 'It was impossible to know him and not to admire him. Was it?'

" 'He was a remarkable man,' I said, unsteadily. Then before the appealing fixity of her gaze, that seemed to watch for more words on my lips, I went on, 'It was impossible not to——'

" 'Love him,' she finished eagerly, silencing me into an appalled dumbness. 'How true! how true! But when you think that no one knew him so well as I! I had all his noble confi-
15   dence. I knew him best.'

" 'You knew him best,' I repeated. And perhaps she did. But with every word spoken the room was growing darker, and only her forehead, smooth and white, remained illumined by the unextinguishable light of belief and love.

" 'You were his friend,' she went on. 'His friend,' she repeated, a little louder. 'You must have been, if he had given you this, and sent you to me. I feel I can speak to you—and oh! I must speak. I want you—you who have heard his last words—to know I have been worthy of him. . . . It is not
25   pride. . . . Yes! I am proud to know I understood him better than any one on earth—he told me so himself. And since his mother died I have had no one—no one—to—to——'

"I listened. The darkness deepened. I was not even sure whether he had given me the right bundle. I rather suspect he wanted me to take care of another batch of his papers which, after his death, I saw the manager examining under the lamp. And the girl talked, easing her pain in the certitude of my sympathy; she talked as thirsty men drink. I had heard that her engagement with Kurtz had been disapproved by her people. He
35   wasn't rich enough or something. And indeed I don't know whether he had not been a pauper all his life. He had given me

some reason to infer that it was his impatience of comparative poverty that drove him out there.

" '. . . Who was not his friend who had heard him speak once?' she was saying. 'He drew men towards him by what was best in them.' She looked at me with intensity. 'It is the gift of the great,' she went on, and the sound of her low voice seemed to have the accompaniment of all the other sounds, full of mystery, desolation, and sorrow, I had ever heard—the ripple of the river, the soughing of the trees swayed by the wind, the murmurs of the crowds, the faint ring of incomprehensible words cried from afar, the whisper of a voice speaking from beyond the threshold of an eternal darkness. 'But you have heard him! You know!' she cried.

" 'Yes, I know,' I said with something like despair in my heart, but bowing my head before the faith that was in her, before that great and saving illusion that shone with an unearthly glow in the darkness, in the triumphant darkness from which I could not have defended her—from which I could not even defend myself.

" 'What a loss to me—to us!'—she corrected herself with beautiful generosity; then added in a murmur, 'To the world.' By the last gleams of twilight I could see the glitter of her eyes, full of tears—of tears that would not fall.

" 'I have been very happy—very fortunate—very proud,' she went on. 'Too fortunate. Too happy for a little while. And now I am unhappy for—for life.'

"She stood up; her fair hair seemed to catch all the remaining light in a glimmer of gold. I rose, too.

" 'And of all this,' she went on, mournfully, 'of all his promise, and of all his greatness, of his generous mind, of his noble heart, nothing remains—nothing but a memory. You and I——'

" 'We shall always remember him,' I said, hastily.

" 'No!' she cried. 'It is impossible that all this should be lost —that such a life should be sacrificed to leave nothing—but sorrow. You know what vast plans he had. I knew of them, too —I could not perhaps understand—but others knew of them.

Something must remain. His words, at least, have not died.'

" 'His words will remain,' I said.

" 'And his example,' she whispered to herself. 'Men looked up to him—his goodness shone in every act. His example——'

5   " 'True,' I said; 'his example, too. Yes, his example. I forgot that.'

" 'But I do not. I cannot—I cannot believe—not yet. I cannot believe that I shall never see him again, that nobody will see him again, never, never, never.'

"She put out her arms as if after a retreating figure, stretching them back and with clasped pale hands across the fading and narrow sheen of the window. Never see him! I saw him clearly enough then. I shall see this eloquent phantom as long as I live, and I shall see her, too, a tragic and familiar Shade, re-
15   sembling in this gesture another one, tragic also, and bedecked with powerless charms, stretching bare brown arms over the glitter of the infernal stream, the stream of darkness. She said suddenly very low, 'He died as he lived.'

" 'His end,' said I, with dull anger stirring in me, 'was in every way worthy of his life.'

" 'And I was not with him,' she murmured. My anger subsided before a feeling of infinite pity.

" 'Everything that could be done——' I mumbled.

" 'Ah, but I believed in him more than any one on earth—
25   more than his own mother, more than—himself. He needed me! Me! I would have treasured every sigh, every word, every sign, every glance.'

"I felt like a chill grip on my chest. 'Don't,' I said, in a muffled voice.

" 'Forgive me. I—I—have mourned so long in silence—in silence. . . . You were with him—to the last? I think of his loneliness. Nobody near to understand him as I would have understood. Perhaps no one to hear. . . .'

" 'To the very end,' I said, shakily. 'I heard his very last
35   words. . . .' I stopped in a fright.

" 'Repeat them,' she murmured in a heartbroken tone. 'I want—I want—something—something—to—to live with.'

"I was on the point of crying at her, 'Don't you hear them?' The dusk was repeating them in a persistent whisper all around us, in a whisper that seemed to swell menacingly like the first 5 whisper of a rising wind. 'The horror! the horror!'

" 'His last word—to live with,' she insisted. 'Don't you understand I loved him—I loved him—I loved him!'

"I pulled myself together and spoke slowly.

" 'The last word he pronounced was—your name.'

"I heard a light sigh and then my heart stood still, stopped dead short by an exulting and terrible cry, by the cry of inconceivable triumph and of unspeakable pain. 'I knew it—I was sure!' . . . She knew. She was sure. I heard her weeping; she had hidden her face in her hands. It seemed to me that the 15 house would collapse before I could escape, that the heavens would fall upon my head. But nothing happened. The heavens do not fall for such a trifle. Would they have fallen, I wonder, if I had rendered Kurtz that justice which was his due? Hadn't he said he wanted only justice? But I couldn't. I could not tell her. It would have been too dark—too dark altogether. . . ."

Marlow ceased, and sat apart, indistinct and silent, in the pose of a meditating Buddha. Nobody moved for a time. "We have lost the first of the ebb," said the Director, suddenly. I raised my head. The offing was barred by a black bank of 25 clouds, and the tranquil waterway leading to the uttermost ends of the earth flowed sombre under an overcast sky— seemed to lead into the heart of an immense darkness.

TYPHOON

Chapter One

Captain MacWhirr, of the steamer *Nan-Shan*, had a physiognomy that, in the order of material appearances, was the exact counterpart of his mind: it presented no marked characteristics of firmness or stupidity; it had no pronounced characteristics whatever; it was simply ordinary, irresponsive, and unruffled.   5

The only thing his aspect might have been said to suggest, at times, was bashfulness; because he would sit, in business offices ashore, sunburnt and smiling faintly, with downcast eyes. When he raised them, they were perceived to be direct in their glance and of blue colour. His hair was fair and extremely fine, clasping from temple to temple the bald dome of his skull in a clamp as of fluffy silk. The hair of his face, on the contrary, carroty and flaming, resembled a growth of copper wire clipped short to the line of the lip; while, no matter how close he shaved, fiery metallic gleams passed, when he moved his head,   15 over the surface of his cheeks. He was rather below the medium height, a bit round-shouldered, and so sturdy of limb that his clothes always looked a shade too tight for his arms and legs. As if unable to grasp what is due to the difference of latitudes, he wore a brown bowler hat, a complete suit of a brownish hue, and clumsy black boots. These harbour togs gave to his thick

figure an air of stiff and uncouth smartness. A thin silver
watch-chain looped his waistcoat, and he never left his ship for
the shore without clutching in his powerful, hairy fist an ele-
gant umbrella of the very best quality, but generally unrolled.
Young Jukes, the chief mate, attending his commander to the
gangway, would sometimes venture to say, with the greatest
gentleness, "Allow me, sir"—and possessing himself of the umbrella deferentially, would elevate the ferrule, shake the folds,
twirl a neat furl in a jiffy, and hand it back; going through the
performance with a face of such portentous gravity, that Mr.
Solomon Rout, the chief engineer, smoking his morning cigar
over the skylight, would turn away his head in order to hide a
smile. "Oh! aye! The blessed gamp. . . . Thank 'ee, Jukes,
thank 'ee," would mutter Captain MacWhirr, heartily, without
looking up.

Having just enough imagination to carry him through each
successive day, and no more, he was tranquilly sure of himself;
and from the very same cause he was not in the least conceited.
It is your imaginative superior who is touchy, over-bearing, and
difficult to please; but every ship Captain MacWhirr commanded was the floating abode of harmony and peace. It was,
in truth, as impossible for him to take a flight of fancy as it
would be for a watchmaker to put together a chronometer with
nothing except a two-pound hammer and a whipsaw in the way
of tools. Yet the uninteresting lives of men so entirely given to
the actuality of the bare existence have their mysterious side. It
was impossible in Captain MacWhirr's case, for instance, to
understand what under heaven could have induced that perfectly satisfactory son of a petty grocer in Belfast to run away to
sea. And yet he had done that very thing at the age of fifteen.
It was enough, when you thought it over, to give you the idea
of an immense, potent, and invisible hand thrust into the ant-
heap of the earth, laying hold of shoulders, knocking heads together, and setting the unconscious faces of the multitude
towards inconceivable goals and in undreamt-of directions.

His father never really forgave him for this undutiful

stupidity. "We could have got on without him," he used to say later on, "but there's the business. And he an only son, too!" His mother wept very much after his disappearance. As it had never occurred to him to leave word behind, he was mourned over for dead till, after eight months, his first letter arrived 5 from Talcahuano. It was short, and contained the statement: "We had very fine weather on our passage out." But evidently, in the writer's mind, the only important intelligence was to the effect that his captain had, on the very day of writing, entered him regularly on the ship's articles as Ordinary Seaman. "Because I can do the work," he explained. The mother again wept copiously, while the remark, "Tom's an ass," expressed the emotions of the father. He was a corpulent man, with a gift for sly chaffing, which to the end of his life he exercised in his intercourse with his son, a little pityingly, as if upon a half-witted 15 person.

MacWhirr's visits to his home were necessarily rare, and in the course of years he despatched other letters to his parents, informing them of his successive promotions and of his movements upon the vast earth. In these missives could be found sentences like this: "The heat here is very great." Or: "On Christmas day at 4 P.M. we fell in with some icebergs." The old people ultimately became acquainted with a good many names of ships, and with the names of the skippers who commanded them—with the names of Scots and English shipown- 25 ers—with the names of seas, oceans, straits, promontories— with outlandish names of lumber-ports, of rice-ports, of cotton-ports—with the names of islands—with the name of their son's young woman. She was called Lucy. It did not suggest itself to him to mention whether he thought the name pretty. And then they died.

The great day of MacWhirr's marriage came in due course, following shortly upon the great day when he got his first command.

All these events had taken place many years before the 35 morning when, in the chart-room of the steamer *Nan-Shan*, he

stood confronted by the fall of a barometer he had no reason
to distrust. The fall—taking into account the excellence of the
instrument, the time of the year, and the ship's position on the
terrestrial globe—was of a nature ominously prophetic; but
the red face of the man betrayed no sort of inward disturbance.
Omens were as nothing to him, and he was unable to discover
the message of a prophecy till the fulfilment had brought it
home to his very door. "That's a fall, and no mistake," he
thought. "There must be some uncommonly dirty weather
knocking about."

The *Nan-Shan* was on her way from the southward to the
treaty port of Fu-chau, with some cargo in her lower holds, and
two hundred Chinese coolies returning to their village homes
in the province of Fo-kien, after a few years of work in various
tropical colonies. The morning was fine, the oily sea heaved
without a sparkle, and there was a queer white misty patch in
the sky like a halo of the sun. The fore-deck, packed with Chinamen, was full of sombre clothing, yellow faces, and pigtails,
sprinkled over with a good many naked shoulders, for there was
no wind, and the heat was close. The coolies lounged, talked,
smoked, or stared over the rail; some, drawing water over the
side, sluiced each other; a few slept on hatches, while several
small parties of six sat on their heels surrounding iron trays
with plates of rice and tiny teacups; and every single Celestial
of them was carrying with him all he had in the world—a
wooden chest with a ringing lock and brass on the corners, containing the savings of his labours: some clothes of ceremony,
sticks of incense, a little opium maybe, bits of nameless rubbish
of conventional value, and a small hoard of silver dollars, toiled
for in coal lighters, won in gambling-houses or in petty trading,
grubbed out of earth, sweated out in mines, on railway lines,
in deadly jungle, under heavy burdens—amassed patiently,
guarded with care, cherished fiercely.

A cross swell had set in from the direction of Formosa Channel about ten o'clock, without disturbing these passengers
much, because the *Nan-Shan*, with her flat bottom, rolling

chocks on bilges, and great breadth of beam, had the
reputation of an exceptionally steady ship in a seaway. Mr.
Jukes, in moments of expansion on shore, would proclaim
loudly that the "old girl was as good as she was pretty." It
would never have occurred to Captain MacWhirr to express his 5
favourable opinion so loud or in terms so fanciful.

She was a good ship, undoubtedly, and not old either. She
had been built in Dumbarton less than three years before, to
the order of a firm of merchants in Siam—Messrs. Sigg and
Son. When she lay afloat, finished in every detail and ready to
take up the work of her life, the builders contemplated her
with pride.

"Sigg has asked us for a reliable skipper to take her out," remarked one of the partners; and the other, after reflecting for a
while, said: "I think MacWhirr is ashore just at present." "Is 15
he? Then wire him at once. He's the very man," declared the
senior, without a moment's hesitation.

Next morning MacWhirr stood before them unperturbed,
having travelled from London by the midnight express after a
sudden but undemonstrative parting with his wife. She was the
daughter of a superior couple who had seen better days.

"We had better be going together over the ship, Captain,"
said the senior partner; and the three men started to view the
perfections of the *Nan-Shan* from stem to stern, and from her
keelson to the trucks of her two stumpy pole-masts. 25

Captain MacWhirr had begun by taking off his coat, which
he hung on the end of a steam windlass embodying all the latest improvements.

"My uncle wrote of you favourably by yesterday's mail to our
good friends—Messrs. Sigg, you know—and doubtless they'll
continue you out there in command," said the junior partner.
"You'll be able to boast of being in charge of the handiest boat
of her size on the coast of China, Captain," he added.

"Have you? Thank 'ee," mumbled vaguely MacWhirr, to
whom the view of a distant eventuality could appeal no more 35
than the beauty of a wide landscape to a purblind tourist; and

his eyes happening at the moment to be at rest upon the lock of the cabin door, he walked up to it, full of purpose, and began to rattle the handle vigorously, while he observed, in his low, earnest voice, "You can't trust the workmen nowadays. A
5 brand-new lock, and it won't act at all. Stuck fast. See? See?"

As soon as they found themselves alone in their office across the yard: "You praised that fellow up to Sigg. What is it you see in him?" asked the nephew, with faint contempt.

"I admit he has nothing of your fancy skipper about him, if that's what you mean," said the elder man, curtly. "Is the foreman of the joiners on the *Nan-Shan* outside? . . . Come in, Bates. How is it that you let Tait's people put us off with a defective lock on the cabin door? The Captain could see directly he set eye on it. Have it replaced at once. The little straws,
15 Bates . . . the little straws. . . ."

The lock was replaced accordingly, and a few days afterwards the *Nan-Shan* steamed out to the East, without MacWhirr having offered any further remark as to her fittings, or having been heard to utter a single word hinting at pride in his ship, gratitude for his appointment, or satisfaction at his prospects.

With a temperament neither loquacious nor taciturn he found very little occasion to talk. There were matters of duty, of course—directions, orders, and so on; but the past being to his mind done with, and the future not there yet, the more
25 general actualities of the day require no comment—because facts can speak for themselves with overwhelming precision.

Old Mr. Sigg liked a man of few words, and one that "you could be sure would not try to improve upon his instructions." MacWhirr, satisfying these requirements, was continued in command of the *Nan-Shan*, and applied himself to the careful navigation of his ship in the China seas. She had come out on a British register, but after some time Messrs. Sigg judged it expedient to transfer her to the Siamese flag.

At the news of the contemplated transfer Jukes grew restless,
35 as if under a sense of personal affront. He went about grumbling to himself, and uttering short scornful laughs. "Fancy

having a ridiculous Noah's Ark elephant in the ensign of one's
ship," he said once at the engine-room door. "Dash me if I can
stand it: I'll throw up the billet. Don't it make *you* sick, Mr.
Rout?" The chief engineer only cleared his throat with the air
of a man who knows the value of a good billet.   5

The first morning the new flag floated over the stern of the
Nan-Shan Jukes stood looking at it bitterly from the bridge. He
struggled with his feelings for a while, and then remarked,
"Queer flag for a man to sail under, sir."

"What's the matter with the flag?" inquired Captain
MacWhirr. "Seems all right to me." And he walked across to
the end of the bridge to have a good look.

"Well, it looks queer to me," burst out Jukes, greatly exasperated, and flung off the bridge.

Captain MacWhirr was amazed at these manners. After a   15
while he stepped quietly into the chart-room, and opened his
International Signal Code-book at the plate where the flags of
all the nations are correctly figured in gaudy rows. He ran his
finger over them, and when he came to Siam he contemplated
with great attention the red field and the white elephant.
Nothing could be more simple; but to make sure he brought
the book out on the bridge for the purpose of comparing the
coloured drawing with the real thing at the flag-staff astern.
When next Jukes, who was carrying on the duty that day with
a sort of suppressed fierceness, happened on the bridge, his   25
commander observed:

"There's nothing amiss with that flag."

"Isn't there?" mumbled Jukes, falling on his knees before a
deck-locker and jerking therefrom viciously a spare lead-line.

"No. I looked up the book. Length twice the breadth and
the elephant exactly in the middle. I thought the people ashore
would know how to make the local flag. Stands to reason. You
were wrong, Jukes. . . ."

"Well sir," began Jukes, getting up excitedly, "all I can say
——" He fumbled for the end of the coil of line with trembling   35
hands.

"That's all right." Captain MacWhirr soothed him, sitting heavily on a little canvas folding-stool he greatly affected. "All you have to do is to take care they don't hoist the elephant upside-down before they get quite used to it."

5   Jukes flung the new lead-line over on the fore-deck with a loud "Here you are, boss'n—don't forget to wet it thoroughly," and turned with immense resolution towards his commander; but Captain MacWhirr spread his elbows on the bridge-rail comfortably.

"Because it would be, I suppose, understood as a signal of distress," he went on. "What do you think? That elephant there, I take it, stands for something in the nature of the Union Jack in the flag. . . ."

"Does it!" yelled Jukes, so that every head on the *Nan-*
15 *Shan's* decks looked towards the bridge. Then he sighed, and with sudden resignation: "It would certainly be a dam' distressful sight," he said, meekly.

Later in the day he accosted the chief engineer with a confidential, "Here, let me tell you the old man's latest."

Mr. Solomon Rout (frequently alluded to as Long Sol, Old Sol, or Father Rout), from finding himself almost invariably the tallest man on board every ship he joined, had acquired the habit of a stooping, leisurely condescension. His hair was scant and sandy, his flat cheeks were pale, his bony wrists and long
25 scholarly hands were pale, too, as though he had lived all his life in the shade.

He smiled from on high at Jukes, and went on smoking and glancing about quietly, in the manner of a kind uncle lending an ear to the tale of an excited school-boy. Then, greatly amused but impassive, he asked:

"And did you throw up the billet?"

"No," cried Jukes, raising a weary, discouraged voice above the harsh buzz of the *Nan-Shan's* friction winches. All of them were hard at work, snatching slings of cargo, high up, to the
35 end of long derricks, only, as it seemed, to let them rip down recklessly by the run. The cargo chains groaned in the gins,

clinked on coamings, rattled over the side; and the whole ship quivered, with her long gray flanks smoking in wreaths of steam. "No," cried Jukes, "I didn't. What's the good? I might just as well fling my resignation at this bulkhead. I don't believe you can make a man like that understand anything. He 5 simply knocks me over."

At that moment Captain MacWhirr, back from the shore, crossed the deck, umbrella in hand, escorted by a mournful, self-possessed Chinaman, walking behind in paper-soled silk shoes, and who also carried an umbrella.

The master of the *Nan-Shan*, speaking just audibly and gazing at his boots as his manner was, remarked that it would be necessary to call at Fu-chau this trip, and desired Mr. Rout to have steam up to-morrow afternoon at one o'clock sharp. He pushed back his hat to wipe his forehead, observing at the same 15 time that he hated going ashore anyhow; while overtopping him Mr. Rout, without deigning a word, smoked austerely, nursing his right elbow in the palm of his left hand. Then Jukes was directed in the same subdued voice to keep the forward 'tween-deck clear of cargo. Two hundred coolies were going to be put down there. The Bun Hin Company were sending that lot home. Twenty-five bags of rice would be coming off in a sampan directly, for stores. All seven-years'-men they were, said Captain MacWhirr, with a camphor-wood chest to every man. The carpenter should be set to work nailing 25 three-inch battens along the deck below, fore and aft, to keep these boxes from shifting in a sea-way. Jukes had better look to it at once. "D'ye hear, Jukes?" This Chinaman here was coming with the ship as far as Fu-chau—a sort of interpreter he would be. Bun Hin's clerk he was, and wanted to have a look at the space. Jukes had better take him forward. "D'ye hear, Jukes?"

Jukes took care to punctuate these instructions in proper places with the obligatory "Yes, sir," ejaculated without enthusiasm. His brusque "Come along, John; make look see" set the 35 Chinaman in motion at his heels.

"Wanchee look see, all same look see can do," said Jukes, who having no talent for foreign languages mangled the very pidgin-English cruelly. He pointed at the open hatch. "Catchee number one piecie place to sleep in. Eh?"

5   He was gruff, as became his racial superiority, but not unfriendly. The Chinaman, gazing sad and speechless into the darkness of the hatchway, seemed to stand at the head of a yawning grave.

"No catchee rain down there—savee?" pointed out Jukes. "Suppose all'ee same fine weather, one piecie coolie-man come top-side," he pursued, warming up imaginatively. "Make so— Phooooo!" He expanded his chest and blew out his cheeks. "Savee, John? Breathe—fresh air. Good. Eh? Washee him piecie pants, chow-chow top-side—see, John?"

15   With his mouth and hands he made exuberant motions of eating rice and washing clothes; and the Chinaman, who concealed his distrust of this pantomime under a collected demeanour tinged by a gentle and refined melancholy, glanced out of his almond eyes from Jukes to the hatch and back again. "Velly good," he murmured, in a disconsolate undertone, and hastened smoothly along the decks, dodging obstacles in his course. He disappeared, ducking low under a sling of ten dirty gunny-bags full of some costly merchandise and exhaling a repulsive smell.

25   Captain MacWhirr meantime had gone on the bridge, and into the chart-room, where a letter, commenced two days before, awaited termination. These long letters began with the words, "My darling wife," and the steward, between the scrubbing of the floors and the dusting of chronometer-boxes, snatched at every opportunity to read them. They interested him much more than they possibly could the woman for whose eye they were intended; and this for the reason that they related in minute detail each successive trip of the *Nan-Shan*.

Her master, faithful to facts, which alone his consciousness
35   reflected, would set them down with painstaking care upon many pages. The house in a northern suburb to which these

pages were addressed had a bit of garden before the bow-windows, a deep porch of good appearance, coloured glass with imitation lead frame in the front door. He paid five-and-forty pounds a year for it, and did not think the rent too high, because Mrs. MacWhirr (a pretentious person with a scraggy neck and a disdainful manner) was admittedly ladylike, and in the neighbourhood considered as "quite superior." The only secret of her life was her abject terror of the time when her husband would come home to stay for good. Under the same roof there dwelt also a daughter called Lydia and a son, Tom. These two were but slightly acquainted with their father. Mainly, they knew him as a rare but privileged visitor, who of an evening smoked his pipe in the dining-room and slept in the house. The lanky girl, upon the whole, was rather ashamed of him; the boy was frankly and utterly indifferent in a straightforward, delightful, unaffected way manly boys have.

And Captain MacWhirr wrote home from the coast of China twelve times every year, desiring quaintly to be "remembered to the children," and subscribing himself "your loving husband," as calmly as if the words so long used by so many men were, apart from their shape, worn-out things, and of a faded meaning.

The China seas north and south are narrow seas. They are seas full of every-day, eloquent facts, such as islands, sandbanks, reefs, swift and changeable currents—tangled facts that nevertheless speak to a seaman in clear and definite language. Their speech appealed to Captain MacWhirr's sense of realities so forcibly that he had given up his state-room below and practically lived all his days on the bridge of his ship, often having his meals sent up, and sleeping at night in the chart-room. And he indited there his home letters. Each of them, without exception, contained the phrase, "The weather has been very fine this trip," or some other form of a statement to that effect. And this statement, too, in its wonderful persistence, was of the same perfect accuracy as all the others they contained.

Mr. Rout likewise wrote letters; only no one on board knew

how chatty he could be pen in hand, because the chief engineer had enough imagination to keep his desk locked. His wife relished his style greatly. They were a childless couple, and Mrs. Rout, a big, high-bosomed, jolly woman of forty, shared with Mr. Rout's toothless and venerable mother a little cottage near Teddington. She would run over her correspondence, at breakfast, with lively eyes, and scream out interesting passages in a joyous voice at the deaf old lady, prefacing each extract by the warning shout, "Solomon says!" She had the trick of firing off Solomon's utterances also upon strangers, astonishing them easily by the unfamiliar text and the unexpectedly jocular vein of these quotations. On the day the new curate called for the first time at the cottage, she found occasion to remark, "As Solomon says: 'the engineers that go down to the sea in ships behold the wonders of sailor nature' "; when a change in the visitor's countenance made her stop and stare.

"Solomon. . . . Oh! . . . Mrs. Rout," stuttered the young man, very red in the face, "I must say . . . I don't. . . ."

"He's my husband," she announced in a great shout, throwing herself back in the chair. Perceiving the joke, she laughed immoderately with a handkerchief to her eyes, while he sat wearing a forced smile, and, from his inexperience of jolly women, fully persuaded that she must be deplorably insane. They were excellent friends afterwards; for, absolving her from irreverent intention, he came to think she was a very worthy person indeed; and he learned in time to receive without flinching other scraps of Solomon's wisdom.

"For my part," Solomon was reported by his wife to have said once, "give me the dullest ass for a skipper before a rogue. There is a way to take a fool; but a rogue is smart and slippery." This was an airy generalization drawn from the particular case of Captain MacWhirr's honesty, which, in itself, had the heavy obviousness of a lump of clay. On the other hand, Mr. Jukes, unable to generalize, unmarried, and unengaged, was in the habit of opening his heart after another fashion to an old chum and former shipmate, actually serving as second officer on board an Atlantic liner.

First of all he would insist upon the advantages of the Eastern trade, hinting at its superiority to the Western ocean service. He extolled the sky, the seas, the ships, and the easy life of the Far East. The *Nan-Shan*, he affirmed, was second to none as a sea-boat.

"We have no brass-bound uniforms, but then we are like brothers here," he wrote. "We all mess together and live like fighting-cocks. . . . All the chaps of the black-squad are as decent as they make that kind, and old Sol, the Chief, is a dry stick. We are good friends. As to our old man, you could not find a quieter skipper. Sometimes you would think he hadn't sense enough to see anything wrong. And yet it isn't that. Can't be. He has been in command for a good few years now. He doesn't do anything actually foolish, and gets his ship along all right without worrying anybody. I believe he hasn't brains enough to enjoy kicking up a row. I don't take advantage of him. I would scorn it. Outside the routine of duty he doesn't seem to understand more than half of what you tell him. We get a laugh out of this at times; but it is dull, too, to be with a man like this—in the long-run. Old Sol says he hasn't much conversation. Conversation! O Lord! He never talks. The other day I had been yarning under the bridge with one of the engineers, and he must have heard us. When I came up to take my watch, he steps out of the chart-room and has a good look all round, peeps over at the sidelights, glances at the compass, squints upwards at the stars. That's his regular performance. By-and-by he says: 'Was that you talking just now in the port alleyway?' 'Yes, sir.' 'With the third engineer?' 'Yes, sir.' He walks off to starboard, and sits under the dodger on a little camp-stool of his, and for half an hour perhaps he makes no sound, except that I heard him sneeze once. Then after a while I hear him getting up over there, and he strolls across to port, where I was. 'I can't understand what you can find to talk about,' says he. 'Two solid hours. I am not blaming you. I see people ashore at it all day long, and then in the evening they sit down and keep at it over the drinks. Must be saying the same things over and over again. I can't understand.'

5   "Did you ever hear anything like that? And he was so patient about it. It made me quite sorry for him. But he is exasperating, too, sometimes. Of course one would not do anything to vex him even if it were worth while. But it isn't. He's so jolly innocent that if you were to put your thumb to your nose and wave your fingers at him he would only wonder gravely to himself what got into you. He told me once quite simply that he found it very difficult to make out what made people always act so queerly. He's too dense to trouble about, and that's the truth."

15   Thus wrote Mr. Jukes to his chum in the Western ocean trade, out of the fulness of his heart and the liveliness of his fancy.

He had expressed his honest opinion. It was not worth while trying to impress a man of that sort. If the world had been full of such men, life would have probably appeared to Jukes an unentertaining and unprofitable business. He was not alone in his opinion. The sea itself, as if sharing Mr. Jukes' good-natured forbearance, had never put itself out to startle the silent man, who seldom looked up, and wandered innocently over the wa-

25   ters with the only visible purpose of getting food, raiment, and house-room for three people ashore. Dirty weather he had known, of course. He had been made wet, uncomfortable, tired in the usual way, felt at the time and presently forgotten. So that upon the whole he had been justified in reporting fine weather at home. But he had never been given a glimpse of immeasurable strength and of immoderate wrath, the wrath that passes exhausted but never appeased—the wrath and fury of the passionate sea. He knew it existed, as we know that crime and abominations exist; he had heard of it as a peaceable citi-

35   zen in a town hears of battles, famines, and floods, and yet knows nothing of what these things mean—though, indeed, he

may have been mixed up in a street row, have gone without his dinner once, or been soaked to the skin in a shower. Captain MacWhirr had sailed over the surface of the oceans as some men go skimming over the years of existence to sink gently into a placid grave, ignorant of life to the last, without ever having 5 been made to see all it may contain of perfidy, of violence, and of terror. There are on sea and land such men thus fortunate— or thus disdained by destiny or by the sea.

Chapter Two

Observing the steady fall of the barometer, Captain MacWhirr thought, "There's some dirty weather knocking about." This is precisely what he thought. He had had an experience of moderately dirty weather—the term dirty as applied to the weather implying only moderate discomfort to the seaman. Had he been informed by an indisputable authority that the end of the world was to be finally accomplished by 15 a catastrophic disturbance of the atmosphere, he would have assimilated the information under the simple idea of dirty weather, and no other, because he had no experience of cataclysms, and belief does not necessarily imply comprehension. The wisdom of his country had pronounced by means of an Act of Parliament that before he could be considered as fit to take charge of a ship he should be able to answer certain simple questions on the subject of circular storms such as hurricanes, cyclones, typhoons; and apparently he had answered them, since he was now in command of the *Nan-Shan* in the 25 China seas during the season of typhoons. But if he had answered he remembered nothing of it. He was, however, conscious of being made uncomfortable by the clammy heat.

He came out on the bridge, and found no relief to this oppression. The air seemed thick. He gasped like a fish, and began to believe himself greatly out of sorts.

The *Nan-Shan* was ploughing a vanishing furrow upon the circle of the sea that had the surface and the shimmer of an undulating piece of gray silk. The sun, pale and without rays, poured down leaden heat in a strangely indecisive light, and the Chinamen were lying prostrate about the decks. Their bloodless, pinched, yellow faces were like the faces of bilious invalids. Captain MacWhirr noticed two of them especially, stretched out on their backs below the bridge. As soon as they had closed their eyes they seemed dead. Three others, however, were quarrelling barbarously away forward; and one big fellow, half naked, with herculean shoulders, was hanging limply over a winch; another, sitting on the deck, his knees up and his head drooping sideways in a girlish attitude, was plaiting his pigtail with infinite languor depicted in his whole person and in the very movement of his fingers. The smoke struggled with difficulty out of the funnel, and instead of streaming away spread itself out like an infernal sort of cloud, smelling of sulphur and raining soot all over the decks.

"What the devil are you doing there, Mr. Jukes?" asked Captain MacWhirr.

This unusual form of address, though mumbled rather than spoken, caused the body of Mr. Jukes to start as though it had been prodded under the fifth rib. He had had a low bench brought on the bridge, and sitting on it, with a length of rope curled about his feet and a piece of canvas stretched over his knees, was pushing a sail-needle vigorously. He looked up, and his surprise gave to his eyes an expression of innocence and candour.

"I was only roping some of that new set of bags we made last trip for whipping up coals," he remonstrated gently. "We shall want them for the next coaling, sir."

"What became of the others?"

"Why, worn out of course, sir."

Captain MacWhirr, after glaring down irresolutely at his chief mate, disclosed the gloomy and cynical conviction that more than half of them had been lost overboard, "if only the truth was known," and retired to the other end of the bridge. Jukes, exasperated by this unprovoked attack, broke the needle   5
at the second stitch, and dropping his work got up and cursed the heat in a violent undertone.

The propeller thumped, the three Chinamen forward had given up squabbling very suddenly, and the one who had been plaiting his tail clasped his legs and stared dejectedly over his knees. The lurid sunshine cast faint and sickly shadows. The swell ran higher and swifter every moment, and the ship lurched heavily in the smooth, deep hollows of the sea.

"I wonder where that beastly swell comes from," said Jukes aloud, recovering himself after a stagger.   15

"North-east," grunted the literal MacWhirr, from his side of the bridge. "There's some dirty weather knocking about. Go and look at the glass."

When Jukes came out of the chart-room, the cast of his countenance had changed to thoughtfulness and concern. He caught hold of the bridge-rail and stared ahead.

The temperature in the engine-room had gone up to a hundred and seventeen degrees. Irritated voices were ascending through the skylight, and through the fiddle of the stokehold in a harsh and resonant uproar, mingled with angry clangs and   25
scrapes of metal, as if men with limbs of iron and throats of bronze had been quarrelling down there. The second engineer was falling foul of the stokers for letting the steam go down. He was a man with arms like a blacksmith, and generally feared; but that afternoon the stokers were answering him back recklessly, and slammed the furnace doors with the fury of despair. Then the noise ceased suddenly, and the second engineer appeared, emerging out of the stokehold streaked with grime and soaking wet like a chimney-sweep coming out of a well. As soon as his head was clear of the fiddle he began to scold Jukes   35
for not trimming properly the stokehold ventilators; and in an-

swer Jukes made with his hands deprecatory soothing signs
meaning: "No wind—can't be helped—you can see for yourself." But the other wouldn't hear reason. His teeth flashed
angrily in his dirty face. He didn't mind, he said, the trouble of
5　punching their blanked heads down there, blank his soul, but
did the condemned sailors think you could keep steam up in
the God-forsaken boilers simply by knocking the blanked stokers about? No, by George! You had to get some draught, too—
may he be everlastingly blanked for a swab-headed deck-hand if
you didn't! And the chief, too, rampaging before the steam-
gauge and carrying on like a lunatic up and down the engine-
room ever since noon. What did Jukes think he was stuck up
there for, if he couldn't get one of his decayed, good-for-
nothing deck-cripples to turn the ventilators to the wind?
15　　　The relations of the "engine-room" and the "deck" of the
Nan-Shan were, as is known, of a brotherly nature; therefore
Jukes leaned over and begged the other in a restrained tone not
to make a disgusting ass of himself; the skipper was on the
other side of the bridge. But the second declared mutinously
that he didn't care a rap who was on the other side of the
bridge, and Jukes, passing in a flash from lofty disapproval into
a state of exaltation, invited him in unflattering terms to come
up and twist the beastly things to please himself, and catch
such wind as a donkey of his sort could find. The second
25　rushed up to the fray. He flung himself at the port ventilator as
though he meant to tear it out bodily and toss it overboard. All
he did was to move the cowl round a few inches, with an enormous expenditure of force, and seemed spent in the effort. He
leaned against the back of the wheelhouse, and Jukes walked
up to him.
　　　"Oh, Heavens!" ejaculated the engineer in a feeble voice. He
lifted his eyes to the sky, and then let his glassy stare descend
to meet the horizon that, tilting up to an angle of forty degrees, seemed to hang on a slant for a while and settled down
35　slowly. "Heavens! Phew! What's up, anyhow?"

Jukes, straddling his long legs like a pair of compasses, put on an air of superiority. "We're going to catch it this time," he said. "The barometer is tumbling down like anything, Harry. And you trying to kick up that silly row. . . ."

The word "barometer" seemed to revive the second engineer's mad animosity. Collecting afresh all his energies, he directed Jukes in a low and brutal tone to shove the unmentionable instrument down his gory throat. Who cared for his crimson barometer? It was the steam—the steam—that was going down; and what between the fireman going faint and the chief going silly, it was worse than a dog's life for him; he didn't care a tinker's curse how soon the whole show was blown out of the water. He seemed on the point of having a cry, but after regaining his breath he muttered darkly, "I'll faint them," and dashed off. He stopped upon the fiddle long enough to shake his fist at the unnatural daylight, and dropped into the dark hole with a whoop.

When Jukes turned, his eyes fell upon the rounded back and the big red ears of Captain MacWhirr, who had come across. He did not look at his chief officer, but said at once, "That's a very violent man, that second engineer."

"Jolly good second, anyhow," grunted Jukes. "They can't keep up steam," he added, rapidly, and made a grab at the rail against the coming lurch.

Captain MacWhirr, unprepared, took a run and brought himself up with a jerk by an awning stanchion.

"A profane man," he said, obstinately. "If this goes on, I'll have to get rid of him the first chance."

"It's the heat," said Jukes. "The weather's awful. It would make a saint swear. Even up here I feel exactly as if I had my head tied up in a woollen blanket."

Captain MacWhirr looked up. "D'ye mean to say, Mr. Jukes, you ever had your head tied up in a blanket? What was that for?"

"It's a manner of speaking, sir," said Jukes, stolidly.

"Some of you fellows do go on! What's that about saints swearing? I wish you wouldn't talk so wild. What sort of saint would that be that would swear? No more saint than yourself, I expect. And what's a blanket got to do with it—or the weather either. . . . The heat does not make me swear—does it? It's filthy bad temper. That's what it is. And what's the good of your talking like this?"

Thus Captain MacWhirr expostulated against the use of images in speech, and at the end electrified Jukes by a contemptuous snort, followed by words of passion and resentment: "Damme! I'll fire him out of the ship if he don't look out."

And Jukes, incorrigible, thought: "Goodness me! Somebody's put a new inside to my old man. Here's temper, if you like. Of course it's the weather; what else? It would make an angel quarrelsome—let alone a saint."

All the Chinamen on deck appeared at their last gasp.

At its setting the sun had a diminished diameter and an expiring brown, rayless glow, as if millions of centuries elapsing since the morning had brought it near its end. A dense bank of cloud became visible to the northward; it had a sinister dark olive tint, and lay low and motionless upon the sea, resembling a solid obstacle in the path of the ship. She went floundering towards it like an exhausted creature driven to its death. The coppery twilight retired slowly, and the darkness brought out overhead a swarm of unsteady, big stars, that, as if blown upon, flickered exceedingly and seemed to hang very near the earth. At eight o'clock Jukes went into the chart-room to write up the ship's log.

He copied neatly out of the rough-book the number of miles, the course of the ship, and in the column for "wind" scrawled the word "calm" from top to bottom of the eight hours since noon. He was exasperated by the continuous, monotonous rolling of the ship. The heavy inkstand would slide away in a manner that suggested perverse intelligence in dodging the pen. Having written in the large space under the head of "Remarks"

"Heat very oppressive," he stuck the end of the penholder in his teeth, pipe fashion, and mopped his face carefully.

"Ship rolling heavily in a high cross swell," he began again, and commented to himself, "Heavily is no word for it." Then he wrote: "Sunset threatening, with a low bank of clouds to N. 5 and E. Sky clear overhead."

Sprawling over the table with arrested pen, he glanced out of the door, and in that frame of his vision he saw all the stars flying upwards between the teak-wood jambs on a black sky. The whole lot took flight together and disappeared, leaving only a blackness flecked with white flashes, for the sea was as black as the sky and speckled with foam afar. The stars that had flown to the roll came back on the return swing of the ship, rushing downwards in their glittering multitude, not of fiery points, but enlarged to tiny discs brilliant with a clear wet 15 sheen.

Jukes watched the flying big stars for a moment, and then wrote: "8 p.m. Swell increasing. Ship labouring and taking water on her decks. Battened down the coolies for the night. Barometer still falling." He paused, and thought to himself, "Perhaps nothing whatever'll come of it." And then he closed resolutely his entries: "Every appearance of a typhoon coming on."

On going out he had to stand aside, and Captain MacWhirr strode over the doorstep without saying a word or making a 25 sign.

"Shut the door, Mr. Jukes, will you?" he cried from within.

Jukes turned back to do so, muttering ironically: "Afraid to catch cold, I suppose." It was his watch below, but he yearned for communion with his kind; and he remarked cheerily to the second mate: "Doesn't look so bad, after all—does it?"

The second mate was marching to and fro on the bridge, tripping down with small steps one moment, and the next climbing with difficulty the shifting slope of the deck. At the sound of Jukes' voice he stood still, facing forward, but made 35 no reply.

"Hallo! That's a heavy one," said Jukes, swaying to meet the long roll till his lowered hand touched the planks. This time the second mate made in his throat a noise of an unfriendly nature.

5   He was an oldish, shabby little fellow, with bad teeth and no hair on his face. He had been shipped in a hurry in Shanghai, that trip when the second officer brought from home had delayed the ship three hours in port by contriving (in some manner Captain MacWhirr could never understand) to fall overboard into an empty coal-lighter lying alongside, and had to be sent ashore to the hospital with concussion of the brain and a broken limb or two.

Jukes was not discouraged by the unsympathetic sound. "The Chinamen must be having a lovely time of it down
15   there," he said. "It's lucky for them the old girl has the easiest roll of any ship I've ever been in. There now! This one wasn't so bad."

"You wait," snarled the second mate.

With his sharp nose, red at the tip, and his thin pinched lips, he always looked as though he were raging inwardly; and he was concise in his speech to the point of rudeness. All his time off duty he spent in his cabin with the door shut, keeping so still in there that he was supposed to fall asleep as soon as he had disappeared; but the man who came in to wake him for his
25   watch on deck would invariably find him with his eyes wide open, flat on his back in the bunk, and glaring irritably from a soiled pillow. He never wrote any letters, did not seem to hope for news from anywhere; and though he had been heard once to mention West Hartlepool, it was with extreme bitterness, and only in connection with the extortionate charges of a boarding-house. He was one of those men who are picked up at need in the ports of the world. They are competent enough, appear hopelessly hard up, show no evidence of any sort of vice, and carry about them all the signs of manifest failure. They
35   come aboard on an emergency, care for no ship afloat, live in

their own atmosphere of casual connection amongst their shipmates who know nothing of them, and make up their minds to
leave at inconvenient times. They clear out with no words of
leave-taking in some God-forsaken port other men would fear
to be stranded in, and go ashore in company of a shabby sea-
chest, corded like a treasure-box, and with an air of shaking the
ship's dust off their feet.

"You wait," he repeated, balanced in great swings with his
back to Jukes, motionless and implacable.

"Do you mean to say we are going to catch it hot?" asked
Jukes with boyish interest.

"Say? . . . I say nothing. You don't catch me," snapped the
little second mate, with a mixture of pride, scorn, and cunning,
as if Jukes' question had been a trap cleverly detected. "Oh,
no! None of you here shall make a fool of me if I know it," he
mumbled to himself.

Jukes reflected rapidly that this second mate was a mean little beast, and in his heart he wished poor Jack Allen had never
smashed himself up in the coal-lighter. The far-off blackness
ahead of the ship was like another night seen through the
starry night of the earth—the starless night of the immensities
beyond the created universe, revealed in its appalling stillness
through a low fissure in the glittering sphere of which the earth
is the kernel.

"Whatever there might be about," said Jukes, "we are steaming straight into it."

"You've said it," caught up the second mate, always with his
back to Jukes. "You've said it, mind—not I."

"Oh, go to Jericho!" said Jukes, frankly; and the other emitted a triumphant little chuckle.

"You've said it," he repeated.

"And what of that?"

"I've known some real good men get into trouble with their
skippers for saying a dam' sight less," answered the second
mate feverishly. "Oh, no! You don't catch me."

"You seem deucedly anxious not to give yourself away," said Jukes, completely soured by such absurdity. "I wouldn't be afraid to say what I think."

"Aye, to me! That's no great trick. I am nobody, and well I know it."

The ship, after a pause of comparative steadiness, started upon a series of rolls, one worse than the other, and for a time Jukes, preserving his equilibrium, was too busy to open his mouth. As soon as the violent swinging had quieted down somewhat, he said: "This is a bit too much of a good thing. Whether anything is coming or not I think she ought to be put head on to that swell. The old man is just gone in to lie down. Hang me if I don't speak to him."

But when he opened the door of the chart-room he saw his captain reading a book. Captain MacWhirr was not lying down: he was standing up with one hand grasping the edge of the bookshelf and the other holding open before his face a thick volume. The lamp wriggled in the gimbals, the loosened books toppled from side to side on the shelf, the long barometer swung in jerky circles, the table altered its slant every moment. In the midst of all this stir and movement Captain MacWhirr, holding on, showed his eyes above the upper edge, and asked, "What's the matter?"

"Swell getting worse, sir."

"Noticed that in here," muttered Captain MacWhirr. "Anything wrong?"

Jukes, inwardly disconcerted by the seriousness of the eyes looking at him over the top of the book, produced an embarrassed grin.

"Rolling like old boots," he said, sheepishly.

"Aye! Very heavy—very heavy. What do you want?"

At this Jukes lost his footing and began to flounder.

"I was thinking of our passengers," he said, in the manner of a man clutching at a straw.

"Passengers?" wondered the Captain, gravely. "What passengers?"

"Why, the Chinamen, sir," explained Jukes, very sick of this conversation.

"The Chinamen! Why don't you speak plainly? Couldn't tell what you meant. Never heard a lot of coolies spoken of as passengers before. Passengers, indeed! What's come to you?"

Captain MacWhirr, closing the book on his forefinger, lowered his arm and looked completely mystified. "Why are you thinking of the Chinamen, Mr. Jukes?" he inquired.

Jukes took a plunge, like a man driven to it. "She's rolling her decks full of water, sir. Thought you might put her head on perhaps—for a while. Till this goes down a bit—very soon, I daresay. Head to the eastward. I never knew a ship roll like this."

He held on in the doorway, and Captain MacWhirr, feeling his grip on the shelf inadequate, made up his mind to let go in a hurry, and fell heavily on the couch.

"Head to the eastward?" he said, struggling to sit up. "That's more than four points off her course."

"Yes, sir. Fifty degrees. . . . Would just bring her head far enough round to meet this. . . ."

Captain MacWhirr was now sitting up. He had not dropped the book, and he had not lost his place.

"To the eastward?" he repeated, with dawning astonishment. "To the . . . Where do you think we are bound to? You want me to haul a full-powered steamship four points off her course to make the Chinamen comfortable! Now, I've heard more than enough of mad things done in the world—but this. . . . If I didn't know you, Jukes, I would think you were in liquor. Steer four points off. . . . And what afterwards? Steer four points over the other way, I suppose, to make the course good. What put it into your head that I would start to tack a steamer as if she were a sailing-ship?"

"Jolly good thing she isn't," threw in Jukes, with bitter readiness. "She would have rolled every blessed stick out of her this afternoon."

"Aye! And you just would have had to stand and see them

go," said Captain MacWhirr, showing a certain animation. "It's a dead calm, isn't it?"

"It is, sir. But there's something out of the common coming, for sure."

5 "Maybe. I suppose you have a notion I should be getting out of the way of that dirt," said Captain MacWhirr, speaking with the utmost simplicity of manner and tone, and fixing the oil-cloth on the floor with a heavy stare. Thus he noticed neither Jukes' discomfiture nor the mixture of vexation and astonished respect on his face.

"Now, here's this book," he continued with deliberation, slapping his thigh with the closed volume. "I've been reading the chapter on the storms there."

This was true. He had been reading the chapter on the
15 storms. When he had entered the chart-room, it was with no in-tention of taking the book down. Some influence in the air—the same influence, probably, that caused the steward to bring without orders the Captain's sea-boots and oilskin coat up to the chart-room—had as it were guided his hand to the shelf; and without taking the time to sit down he had waded with a conscious effort into the terminology of the subject. He lost himself amongst advancing semi-circles, left- and right-hand quadrants, the curves of the tracks, the probable bearing of the centre, the shifts of wind and the readings of barometer. He
25 tried to bring all these things into a definite relation to himself, and ended by becoming contemptuously angry with such a lot of words and with so much advice, all headwork and supposi-tion, without a glimmer of certitude.

"It's the damnedest thing, Jukes," he said. "If a fellow was to believe all that's in here, he would be running most of his time all over the sea trying to get behind the weather."

Again he slapped his leg with the book; and Jukes opened his mouth, but said nothing.

"Running to get behind the weather! Do you understand
35 that, Mr. Jukes? It's the maddest thing!" ejaculated Captain MacWhirr, with pauses, gazing at the floor profoundly. "You

would think an old woman had been writing this. It passes me.
If that thing means anything useful, then it means that I
should at once alter the course away, away to the devil somewhere, and come booming down on Fu-chau from the northward at the tail of this dirty weather that's supposed to be
knocking about in our way. From the north! Do you understand, Mr. Jukes? Three hundred extra miles to the distance,
and a pretty coal bill to show. I couldn't bring myself to do
that if every word in there was gospel truth, Mr. Jukes. Don't
you expect me. . . ."

And Jukes, silent, marvelled at this display of feeling and lo-
quacity.

"But the truth is that you don't know if the fellow is right,
anyhow. How can you tell what a gale is made of till you get it?
He isn't aboard here, is he? Very well. Here he says that the
centre of them things bears eight points off the wind; but we
haven't got any wind, for all the barometer falling. Where's his
centre now?"

"We will get the wind presently," mumbled Jukes.

"Let it come, then," said Captain MacWhirr, with dignified
indignation. "It's only to let you see, Mr. Jukes, that you don't
find everything in books. All these rules for dodging breezes
and circumventing the winds of heaven, Mr. Jukes, seem to me
the maddest thing, when you come to look at it sensibly."

He raised his eyes, saw Jukes gazing at him dubiously, and
tried to illustrate his meaning.

"About as queer as your extraordinary notion of dodging the
ship head to sea, for I don't know how long, to make the Chinamen comfortable; whereas all we've got to do is to take them
to Fu-chau, being timed to get there before noon on Friday. If
the weather delays me—very well. There's your log-book to talk
straight about the weather. But suppose I went swinging off
my course and came in two days late, and they asked me:
'Where have you been all that time, Captain?' What could I
say to that? 'Went around to dodge the bad weather,' I would
say. 'It must've been dam' bad,' they would say. 'Don't know,'

I would have to say; 'I've dodged clear of it.' See that, Jukes? I have been thinking it all out this afternoon."

He looked up again in his unseeing, unimaginative way. No one had ever heard him say so much at one time. Jukes, with his arms open in the doorway, was like a man invited to behold a miracle. Unbounded wonder was the intellectual meaning of his eye, while incredulity was seated in his whole countenance.

"A gale is a gale, Mr. Jukes," resumed the Captain, "and a full-powered steamship has got to face it. There's just so much dirty weather knocking about the world, and the proper thing is to go through it with none of what old Captain Wilson of the *Melita* calls 'storm strategy.' The other day ashore I heard him hold forth about it to a lot of shipmasters who came in and sat at a table next to mine. It seemed to me the greatest nonsense. He was telling them how he out-manœuvred, I think he said, a terrific gale, so that it never came nearer than fifty miles to him. A neat piece of head-work he called it. How he knew there was a terrific gale fifty miles off beats me altogether. It was like listening to a crazy man. I would have thought Captain Wilson was old enough to know better."

Captain MacWhirr ceased for a moment, then said, "It's your watch below, Mr. Jukes?"

Jukes came to himself with a start. "Yes, sir."

"Leave orders to call me at the slightest change," said the Captain. He reached up to put the book away, and tucked his legs upon the couch. "Shut the door so that it don't fly open, will you? I can't stand a door banging. They've put a lot of rubbishy locks into this ship, I must say."

Captain MacWhirr closed his eyes.

He did so to rest himself. He was tired, and he experienced that state of mental vacuity which comes at the end of an exhaustive discussion that has liberated some belief matured in the course of meditative years. He had indeed been making his confession of faith, had he only known it; and its effect was to make Jukes, on the other side of the door, stand scratching his head for a good while.

Captain MacWhirr opened his eyes.

He thought he must have been asleep. What was that loud noise? Wind? Why had he not been called? The lamp wriggled in its gimbals, the barometer swung in circles, the table altered its slant every moment; a pair of limp sea-boots with collapsed tops went sliding past the couch. He put out his hand instantly, and captured one.

Jukes' face appeared in a crack of the door; only his face, very red, with staring eyes. The flame of the lamp leaped, a piece of paper flew up, a rush of air enveloped Captain MacWhirr. Beginning to draw on the boot, he directed an expectant gaze at Jukes' swollen, excited features.

"Came on like this," shouted Jukes, "five minutes ago . . . all of a sudden."

The head disappeared with a bang, and a heavy splash and patter of drops swept past the closed door as if a pailful of melted lead had been flung against the house. A whistling could be heard now upon the deep vibrating noise outside. The stuffy chart-room seemed as full of draughts as a shed. Captain MacWhirr collared the other sea-boot on its violent passage along the floor. He was not flustered, but he could not find at once the opening for inserting his foot. The shoes he had flung off were scurrying from end to end of the cabin, gambolling playfully over each other like puppies. As soon as he stood up he kicked at them viciously, but without effect.

He threw himself into the attitude of a lunging fencer, to reach after his oilskin coat; and afterwards he staggered all over the confined space while he jerked himself into it. Very grave, straddling his legs far apart, and stretching his neck, he started to tie deliberately the strings of his sou'-wester under his chin, with thick fingers that trembled slightly. He went through all the movements of a woman putting on her bonnet before a glass, with a strained, listening attention, as though he had expected every moment to hear the shout of his name in the confused clamour that had suddenly beset his ship. Its increase filled his ears while he was getting ready to go out and confront whatever it might mean. It was tumultuous and very loud—made up of the rush of the wind, the crashes of the sea, with that prolonged deep vibration of the air, like the roll of an immense and remote drum beating the charge of the gale.

5   He stood for a moment in the light of the lamp, thick, clumsy, shapeless in his panoply of combat, vigilant and red-faced.

"There's a lot of weight in this," he muttered.

As soon as he attempted to open the door the wind caught it. Clinging to the handle, he was dragged out over the doorstep, and at once found himself engaged with the wind in a sort of personal scuffle whose object was the shutting of that door. At the last moment a tongue of air scurried in and licked out the flame of the lamp.

15   Ahead of the ship he perceived a great darkness lying upon a multitude of white flashes; on the starboard beam a few amazing stars drooped, dim and fitful, above an immense waste of broken seas, as if seen through a mad drift of smoke.

On the bridge a knot of men, indistinct and toiling, were making great efforts in the light of the wheelhouse windows that shone mistily on their heads and backs. Suddenly darkness closed upon one pane, then on another. The voices of the lost group reached him after the manner of men's voices in a gale, in shreds and fragments of forlorn shouting snatched past the

25   ear. All at once Jukes appeared at his side, yelling, with his head down.

"Watch—put in—wheelhouse shutters—glass—afraid—blow in."

Jukes heard his commander upbraiding.

"This—come—anything—warning—call me."

He tried to explain, with the uproar pressing on his lips.

"Light   air—remained—bridge—sudden—northeast—could turn—thought—you—sure—hear."

They had gained the shelter of the weather-cloth, and could

35   converse with raised voices, as people quarrel.

"I got the hands along to cover up all the ventilators. Good job I had remained on deck. I didn't think you would be asleep, and so . . . What did you say, sir? What?"

"Nothing," cried Captain MacWhirr. "I said—all right."

"By all the powers! We've got it this time," observed Jukes in a howl.   5

"You haven't altered her course?" inquired Captain Mac-Whirr, straining his voice.

"No, sir. Certainly not. Wind came out right ahead. And here comes the head sea."

A plunge of the ship ended in a shock as if she had landed her forefoot upon something solid. After a moment of stillness a lofty flight of sprays drove hard with the wind upon their faces.

"Keep her at it as long as we can," shouted Captain MacWhirr.   15

Before Jukes had squeezed the salt water out of his eyes all the stars had disappeared.

Chapter Three

Jukes was as ready a man as any half-dozen young mates that may be caught by casting a net upon the waters; and though he had been somewhat taken aback by the startling viciousness of the first squall, he had pulled himself together on the instant, had called out the hands and had rushed them along to secure such openings about the deck as had not been already battened down earlier in the evening. Shouting in his fresh, stentorian voice, "Jump, boys, and bear a hand!" he led in the work, tell-   25 ing himself the while that he had "just expected this."

But at the same time he was growing aware that this was rather more than he had expected. From the first stir of the air felt on his cheek the gale seemed to take upon itself the accumulated impetus of an avalanche. Heavy sprays enveloped the *Nan-Shan* from stem to stern, and instantly in the midst of her regular rolling she began to jerk and plunge as though she had gone mad with fright.

Jukes thought, "This is no joke." While he was exchanging explanatory yells with his captain, a sudden lowering of the darkness came upon the night, falling before their vision like something palpable. It was as if the masked lights of the world had been turned down. Jukes was uncritically glad to have his captain at hand. It relieved him as though that man had, by simply coming on deck, taken most of the gale's weight upon his shoulders. Such is the prestige, the privilege, and the burden of command.

Captain MacWhirr could expect no relief of that sort from any one on earth. Such is the loneliness of command. He was trying to see, with that watchful manner of a seaman who stares into the wind's eye as if into the eye of an adversary, to penetrate the hidden intention and guess the aim and force of the thrust. The strong wind swept at him out of a vast obscurity; he felt under his feet the uneasiness of his ship, and he could not even discern the shadow of her shape. He wished it were not so; and very still he waited, feeling stricken by a blind man's helplessness.

To be silent was natural to him, dark or shine. Jukes, at his elbow, made himself heard yelling cheerily in the gusts, "We must have got the worst of it at once, sir." A faint burst of lightning quivered all round, as if flashed into a cavern—into a black and secret chamber of the sea, with a floor of foaming crests.

It unveiled for a sinister, fluttering moment a ragged mass of clouds hanging low, the lurch of the long outlines of the ship, the black figures of men caught on the bridge, heads forward, as if petrified in the act of butting. The darkness palpitated down upon all this, and then the real thing came at last.

It was something formidable and swift, like the sudden smashing of a vial of wrath. It seemed to explode all round the ship with an overpowering concussion and a rush of great waters, as if an immense dam had been blown up to windward. In an instant the men lost touch of each other. This is the disintegrating power of a great wind: it isolates one from one's kind. An earthquake, a landslip, an avalanche, overtake a man incidentally, as it were—without passion. A furious gale attacks him like a personal enemy, tries to grasp his limbs, fastens upon his mind, seeks to rout his very spirit out of him.

Jukes was driven away from his commander. He fancied himself whirled a great distance through the air. Everything disappeared—even, for a moment, his power of thinking; but his hand had found one of the rail-stanchions. His distress was by no means alleviated by an inclination to disbelieve the reality of this experience. Though young, he had seen some bad weather, and had never doubted his ability to imagine the worst; but this was so much beyond his powers of fancy that it appeared incompatible with the existence of any ship whatever. He would have been incredulous about himself in the same way, perhaps, had he not been so harassed by the necessity of exerting a wrestling effort against a force trying to tear him away from his hold. Moreover, the conviction of not being utterly destroyed returned to him through the sensations of being half-drowned, bestially shaken, and partly choked.

It seemed to him he remained there precariously alone with the stanchion for a long, long time. The rain poured on him, flowed, drove in sheets. He breathed in gasps; and sometimes the water he swallowed was fresh and sometimes it was salt. For the most part he kept his eyes shut tight, as if suspecting his sight might be destroyed in the immense flurry of the elements. When he ventured to blink hastily, he derived some moral support from the green gleam of the starboard light shining feebly upon the flight of rain and sprays. He was actually looking at it when its ray fell upon the uprearing sea which put it out. He saw the head of the wave topple over, adding the mite of its crash to the tremendous uproar raging around him, and almost at the same instant the stanchion was wrenched

away from his embracing arms. After a crushing thump on his
back he found himself suddenly afloat and borne upwards. His
first irresistible notion was that the whole China Sea had
climbed on the bridge. Then, more sanely, he concluded him-
5   self gone overboard. All the time he was being tossed, flung,
and rolled in great volumes of water, he kept on repeating mentally, with the utmost precipitation, the words: "My God! My
God! My God! My God!"

All at once, in a revolt of misery and despair, he formed the
crazy resolution to get out of that. And he began to thresh
about with his arms and legs. But as soon as he commenced his
wretched struggles he discovered that he had become somehow
mixed up with a face, an oilskin coat, somebody's boots. He
clawed ferociously all these things in turn, lost them, found
15 them again, lost them once more, and finally was himself
caught in the firm clasp of a pair of stout arms. He returned
the embrace closely round a thick solid body. He had found his
captain.

They tumbled over and over, tightening their hug. Suddenly
the water let them down with a brutal bang; and, stranded
against the side of the wheelhouse, out of breath and bruised,
they were left to stagger up in the wind and hold on where
they could.

Jukes came out of it rather horrified, as though he had es-
25 caped some unparalleled outrage directed at his feelings. It
weakened his faith in himself. He started shouting aimlessly to
the man he could feel near him in that fiendish blackness, "Is
it you, sir? Is it you, sir?" till his temples seemed ready to burst.
And he heard in answer a voice, as if crying far away, as if
screaming to him fretfully from a very great distance, the one
word "Yes!" Other seas swept again over the bridge. He received them defencelessly right over his bare head, with both
his hands engaged in holding.

The motion of the ship was extravagant. Her lurches had an
35 appalling helplessness: she pitched as if taking a header into a
void, and seemed to find a wall to hit every time. When she

rolled she fell on her side headlong, and she would be righted
back by such a demolishing blow that Jukes felt her reeling as a
clubbed man reels before he collapses. The gale howled and
scuffled about gigantically in the darkness, as though the entire
world were one black gully. At certain moments the air   5
streamed against the ship as if sucked through a tunnel with a
concentrated solid force of impact that seemed to lift her clean
out of the water and keep her up for an instant with only a
quiver running through her from end to end. And then she
would begin her tumbling again as if dropped back into a boiling cauldron. Jukes tried hard to compose his mind and judge
things coolly.

The sea, flattened down in the heavier gusts, would uprise
and overwhelm both ends of the *Nan-Shan* in snowy rushes of
foam, expanding wide, beyond both rails, into the night. And   15
on this dazzling sheet, spread under the blackness of the clouds
and emitting a bluish glow, Captain MacWhirr could catch a
desolate glimpse of a few tiny specks black as ebony, the tops
of the hatches, the battened companions, the heads of the covered winches, the foot of a mast. This was all he could see of
his ship. Her middle structure, covered by the bridge which
bore him, his mate, the closed wheelhouse where a man was
steering shut up with the fear of being swept overboard
together with the whole thing in one great crash—her middle
structure was like a half-tide rock awash upon a coast. It was   25
like an outlying rock with the water boiling up, streaming over,
pouring off, beating round—like a rock in the surf to which
shipwrecked people cling before they let go—only it rose, it
sank, it rolled continuously, without respite and rest, like a
rock that should have miraculously struck adrift from a coast
and gone wallowing upon the sea.

The *Nan-Shan* was being looted by the storm with a senseless, destructive fury: trysails torn out of the extra gaskets,
double-lashed awnings blown away, bridge swept clean,
weather-cloths burst, rails twisted, light-screens smashed—and   35
two of the boats had gone already. They had gone unheard and

unseen, melting, as it were, in the shock and smother of the wave. It was only later, when upon the white flash of another high sea hurling itself amidships, Jukes had a vision of two pairs of davits leaping black and empty out of the solid black-
5   ness, with one overhauled fall flying and an iron-bound block capering in the air, that he became aware of what had happened within about three yards of his back.

He poked his head forward, groping for the ear of his commander. His lips touched it—big, fleshy, very wet. He cried in an agitated tone, "Our boats are going now, sir."

And again he heard that voice, forced and ringing feebly, but with a penetrating effect of quietness in the enormous discord of noises, as if sent out from some remote spot of peace beyond the black wastes of the gale; again he heard a man's voice
15   —the frail and indomitable sound that can be made to carry an infinity of thought, resolution and purpose, that shall be pronouncing confident words on the last day, when heavens fall, and justice is done—again he heard it, and it was crying to him, as if from very, very far—"All right."

He thought he had not managed to make himself understood. "Our boats—I say boats—the boats, sir! Two gone!"

The same voice, within a foot of him and yet so remote, yelled sensibly, "Can't be helped."

Captain MacWhirr had never turned his face, but Jukes
25   caught some more words on the wind.

"What can—expect—when hammering through—such—— Bound to leave—something behind—stands to reason."

Watchfully Jukes listened for more. No more came. This was all Captain MacWhirr had to say; and Jukes could picture to himself rather than see the broad squat back before him. An impenetrable obscurity pressed down upon the ghostly glimmers of the sea. A dull conviction seized upon Jukes that there was nothing to be done.

If the steering-gear did not give way, if the immense volumes
35   of water did not burst the deck in or smash one of the hatches, if the engines did not give up, if way could be kept on the ship

against this terrific wind, and she did not bury herself in one of these awful seas, of whose white crests alone, topping high above her bows, he could now and then get a sickening glimpse —then there was a chance of her coming out of it. Something within him seemed to turn over, bringing uppermost the feeling that the *Nan-Shan* was lost.

"She's done for," he said to himself, with a surprising mental agitation, as though he had discovered an unexpected meaning in this thought. One of these things was bound to happen. Nothing could be prevented now, and nothing could be remedied. The men on board did not count, and the ship could not last. This weather was too impossible.

Jukes felt an arm thrown heavily over his shoulders; and to this overture he responded with great intelligence by catching hold of his captain round the waist.

They stood clasped thus in the blind night, bracing each other against the wind, cheek to cheek and lip to ear, in the manner of two hulks lashed stem to stern together.

And Jukes heard the voice of his commander hardly any louder than before, but nearer, as though, starting to march athwart the prodigious rush of the hurricane, it had approached him, bearing that strange effect of quietness like the serene glow of a halo.

"D'ye know where the hands got to?" it asked, vigorous and evanescent at the same time, overcoming the strength of the wind, and swept away from Jukes instantly.

Jukes didn't know. They were all on the bridge when the real force of the hurricane struck the ship. He had no idea where they had crawled to. Under the circumstances they were nowhere, for all the use that could be made of them. Somehow the Captain's wish to know distressed Jukes.

"Want the hands, sir?" he cried, apprehensively.

"Ought to know," asserted Captain MacWhirr. "Hold hard."

They held hard. An outburst of unchained fury, a vicious rush of the wind absolutely steadied the ship; she rocked only, quick and light like a child's cradle, for a terrific moment of suspense, while the whole atmosphere, as it seemed, streamed furiously past her, roaring away from the tenebrous earth.

It suffocated them, and with eyes shut they tightened their grasp. What from the magnitude of the shock might have been a column of water running upright in the dark, butted against the ship, broke short, and fell on her bridge, crushingly, from on high, with a dead burying weight.

A flying fragment of that collapse, a mere splash, enveloped them in one swirl from their feet over their heads, filling violently their ears, mouths and nostrils with salt water. It knocked out their legs, wrenched in haste at their arms, seethed away swiftly under their chins; and opening their eyes, they saw the piled-up masses of foam dashing to and fro amongst what looked like the fragments of a ship. She had given way as if driven straight in. Their panting hearts yielded, too, before the tremendous blow; and all at once she sprang up again to her desperate plunging, as if trying to scramble out from under the ruins.

The seas in the dark seemed to rush from all sides to keep her back where she might perish. There was hate in the way she was handled, and a ferocity in the blows that fell. She was like a living creature thrown to the rage of a mob: hustled terribly, struck at, borne up, flung down, leaped upon. Captain MacWhirr and Jukes kept hold of each other, deafened by the noise, gagged by the wind; and the great physical tumult beating about their bodies, brought, like an unbridled display of passion, a profound trouble to their souls. One of those wild and appalling shrieks that are heard at times passing mysteriously overhead in the steady roar of a hurricane, swooped, as if borne on wings, upon the ship, and Jukes tried to outscream it.

"Will she live through this?"

The cry was wrenched out of his breast. It was as unintentional as the birth of a thought in the head, and he heard nothing of it himself. It all became extinct at once—thought, intention, effort—and of his cry the inaudible vibration added to the tempest waves of the air.

He expected nothing from it. Nothing at all. For indeed what answer could be made? But after a while he heard with amazement the frail and resisting voice in his ear, the dwarf sound, unconquered in the giant tumult.

"She may!" 5

It was a dull yell, more difficult to seize than a whisper. And presently the voice returned again, half submerged in the vast crashes, like a ship battling against the waves of an ocean.

"Let's hope so!" it cried—small, lonely and unmoved, a stranger to the visions of hope or fear; and it flickered into disconnected words: "Ship. . . . This. . . . Never—Anyhow . . . for the best." Jukes gave it up.

Then, as if it had come suddenly upon the one thing fit to withstand the power of a storm, it seemed to gain force and firmness for the last broken shouts: 15

"Keep on hammering . . . Builders . . . Good men. . . . And chance it . . . engines. . . . Rout . . . good man."

Captain MacWhirr removed his arm from Jukes' shoulders, and thereby ceased to exist for his mate, so dark it was; Jukes, after a tense stiffening of every muscle, would let himself go limp all over. The gnawing of profound discomfort existed side by side with an incredible disposition to somnolence, as though he had been buffeted and worried into drowsiness. The wind would get hold of his head and try to shake it off his shoulders; his clothes, full of water, were as heavy as lead, cold and drip- 25 ping like an armour of melting ice: he shivered—it lasted a long time; and with his hands closed hard on his hold, he was letting himself sink slowly into the depths of bodily misery. His mind became concentrated upon himself in an aimless, idle way, and when something pushed lightly at the back of his knees he nearly, as the saying is, jumped out of his skin.

In the start forward he bumped the back of Captain MacWhirr, who didn't move; and then a hand gripped his thigh. A lull had come, a menacing lull of the wind, the hold-ing of a stormy breath—and he felt himself pawed all over. It 35 was the boatswain. Jukes recognized these hands, so thick and enormous that they seemed to belong to some new species of man.

The boatswain had arrived on the bridge, crawling on all fours against the wind, and had found the chief mate's legs
5   with the top of his head. Immediately he crouched and began to explore Jukes' person upwards with prudent, apologetic touches, as became an inferior.

He was an ill-favoured, undersized, gruff sailor of fifty, coarsely hairy, short-legged, long-armed, resembling an elderly ape. His strength was immense; and in his great lumpy paws, bulging like brown boxing-gloves on the end of furry forearms, the heaviest objects were handled like playthings. Apart from the grizzled pelt on his chest, the menacing demeanour and the hoarse voice, he had none of the classical attributes of his rat-
15   ing. His good nature almost amounted to imbecility: the men did what they liked with him, and he had not an ounce of ini- tiative in his character, which was easy-going and talkative. For these reasons Jukes disliked him; but Captain MacWhirr, to Jukes' scornful disgust, seemed to regard him as a first-rate petty officer.

He pulled himself up by Jukes' coat, taking that liberty with the greatest moderation, and only so far as it was forced upon him by the hurricane.

"What is it, boss'n, what is it?" yelled Jukes, impatiently.
25   What could that fraud of a boss'n want on the bridge? The ty- phoon had got on Jukes' nerves. The husky bellowings of the other, though unintelligible, seemed to suggest a state of lively satisfaction. There could be no mistake. The old fool was pleased with something.

The boatswain's other hand had found some other body, for in a changed tone he began to inquire: "Is it you, sir? Is it you, sir?" The wind strangled his howls.

"Yes!" cried Captain MacWhirr.

Chapter Four

All that the boatswain, out of a superabundance of yells, could make clear to Captain MacWhirr was the bizarre intelligence that "All them Chinamen in the fore 'tween-deck have fetched away, sir."

Jukes to leeward could hear these two shouting within six inches of his face, as you may hear on a still night half a mile away two men conversing across a field. He heard Captain MacWhirr's exasperated "What? What?" and the strained pitch of the other's hoarseness. "In a lump . . . seen them myself. . . . Awful sight, sir . . . thought . . . tell you."

Jukes remained indifferent, as if rendered irresponsible by the force of the hurricane, which made the very thought of action utterly vain. Besides, being very young, he had found the occupation of keeping his heart completely steeled against the worst so engrossing that he had come to feel an overpowering dislike towards any other form of activity whatever. He was not scared; he knew this because, firmly believing he would never see another sunrise, he remained calm in that belief.

These are the moments of do-nothing heroics to which even good men surrender at times. Many officers of ships can no doubt recall a case in their experience when just such a trance of confounded stoicism would come all at once over a whole ship's company. Jukes, however, had no wide experience of men or storms. He conceived himself to be calm—inexorably calm; but as a matter of fact he was daunted; not abjectly, but only so far as a decent man may, without becoming loathsome to himself.

It was rather like a forced-on numbness of spirit. The long, long stress of a gale does it; the suspense of the interminably culminating catastrophe; and there is a bodily fatigue in the mere holding on to existence within the excessive tumult; a searching and insidious fatigue that penetrates deep into a man's breast to cast down and sadden his heart, which is incorrigible, and of all the gifts of the earth—even before life itself—aspires to peace.

5　　Jukes was benumbed much more than he supposed. He held on—very wet, very cold, stiff in every limb; and in a momentary hallucination of swift visions (it is said that a drowning man thus reviews all his life) he beheld all sorts of memories altogether unconnected with his present situation. He remembered his father, for instance: a worthy business man, who at an unfortunate crisis in his affairs went quietly to bed and died forthwith in a state of resignation. Jukes did not recall these circumstances, of course, but remaining otherwise unconcerned he seemed to see distinctly the poor man's face; a certain game of
15　　nap played when quite a boy in Table Bay on board a ship, since lost with all hands; the thick eyebrows of his first skipper; and without any emotion, as he might years ago have walked listlessly into her room and found her sitting there with a book, he remembered his mother—dead, too, now—the resolute woman, left badly off, who had been very firm in his bringing up.

It could not have lasted more than a second, perhaps not so much. A heavy arm had fallen about his shoulders; Captain MacWhirr's voice was speaking his name into his ear.

25　　"Jukes! Jukes!"

He detected the tone of deep concern. The wind had thrown its weight on the ship, trying to pin her down amongst the seas. They made a clean breach over her, as over a deep-swimming log; and the gathered weight of crashes menaced monstrously from afar. The breakers flung out of the night with a ghostly light on their crests—the light of sea-foam that in a ferocious, boiling-up pale flash showed upon the slender body of the ship the toppling rush, the downfall, and the seething mad scurry of each wave. Never for a moment could
35　　she shake herself clear of the water; Jukes, rigid, perceived in her motion the ominous sign of haphazard floundering. She

was no longer struggling intelligently. It was the beginning of
the end; and the note of busy concern in Captain MacWhirr's
voice sickened him like an exhibition of blind and pernicious
folly.

The spell of the storm had fallen upon Jukes. He was pene- 5
trated by it, absorbed by it; he was rooted in it with a rigour of
dumb attention. Captain MacWhirr persisted in his cries, but
the wind got between them like a solid wedge. He hung round
Jukes' neck as heavy as a millstone, and suddenly the sides of
their heads knocked together.

"Jukes! Mr. Jukes, I say!"

He had to answer that voice that would not be silenced. He
answered in the customary manner: ". . . Yes, sir."

And directly, his heart, corrupted by the storm that breeds a
craving for peace, rebelled against the tyranny of training and 15
command.

Captain MacWhirr had his mate's head fixed firm in the
crook of his elbow, and pressed it to his yelling lips mysteriously. Sometimes Jukes would break in, admonishing hastily:
"Look out, sir!" or Captain MacWhirr would bawl an earnest
exhortation to "Hold hard, there!" and the whole black
universe seemed to reel together with the ship. They paused.
She floated yet. And Captain MacWhirr would resume his
shouts. ". . . Says . . . whole lot . . . fetched away. . . .
Ought to see . . . what's the matter." 25

Directly the full force of the hurricane had struck the ship,
every part of her deck became untenable; and the sailors, dazed
and dismayed, took shelter in the port alleyway under the
bridge. It had a door aft, which they shut; it was very black,
cold, and dismal. At each heavy fling of the ship they would
groan all together in the dark, and tons of water could be heard
scuttling about as if trying to get at them from above. The
boatswain had been keeping up a gruff talk, but a more unrea-
sonable lot of men, he said afterwards, he had never been with.
They were snug enough there, out of harm's way, and not 35
wanted to do anything, either; and yet they did nothing but

grumble and complain peevishly like so many sick kids. Finally, one of them said that if there had been at least some light to see each other's noses by, it wouldn't be so bad. It was making him crazy, he declared, to lie there in the dark waiting
5   for the blamed hooker to sink.

"Why don't you step outside, then, and be done with it at once?" the boatswain turned on him.

This called up a shout of execration. The boatswain found himself overwhelmed with reproaches of all sorts. They seemed to take it ill that a lamp was not instantly created for them out of nothing. They would whine after a light to get drowned by —anyhow! And though the unreason of their revilings was patent—since no one could hope to reach the lamp-room, which was forward—he became greatly distressed. He did not think it
15   was decent of them to be nagging at him like this. He told them so, and was met by general contumely. He sought refuge, therefore, in an embittered silence. At the same time their grumbling and sighing and muttering worried him greatly, but by-and-by it occurred to him that there were six globe lamps hung in the 'tween-deck, and that there could be no harm in depriving the coolies of one of them.

The *Nan-Shan* had an athwartship coal-bunker, which, being at times used as cargo space, communicated by an iron door with the fore 'tween-deck. It was empty then, and its manhole
25   was the foremost one in the alleyway. The boatswain could get in, therefore, without coming out on deck at all; but to his great surprise he found he could induce no one to help him in taking off the manhole cover. He groped for it all the same, but one of the crew lying in his way refused to budge.

"Why, I only want to get you that blamed light you are crying for," he expostulated, almost pitifully.

Somebody told him to go and put his head in a bag. He regretted he could not recognize the voice, and that it was too dark to see, otherwise, as he said, he would have put a head on
35   *that* son of a sea-cook, anyway, sink or swim. Nevertheless, he

had made up his mind to show them he could get a light, if he
were to die for it.

Through the violence of the ship's rolling, every movement
was dangerous. To be lying down seemed labour enough. He
nearly broke his neck dropping into the bunker. He fell on his   5
back, and was sent shooting helplessly from side to side in the
dangerous company of a heavy iron bar—a coal-trimmer's slice
probably—left down there by somebody. This thing made him
as nervous as though it had been a wild beast. He could not see
it, the inside of the bunker coated with coal-dust being perfectly and impenetrably black; but he heard it sliding and clat-
tering, and striking here and there, always in the neighbourhood of his head. It seemed to make an extraordinary noise,
too—to give heavy thumps as though it had been as big as a
bridge girder. This was remarkable enough for him to notice   15
while he was flung from port to starboard and back again, and
clawing desperately the smooth sides of the bunker in the endeavour to stop himself. The door into the 'tween-deck not
fitting quite true, he saw a thread of dim light at the bottom.

Being a sailor, and a still active man, he did not want much
of a chance to regain his feet; and as luck would have it, in
scrambling up he put his hand on the iron slice, picking it up
as he rose. Otherwise he would have been afraid of the thing
breaking his legs, or at least knocking him down again. At first
he stood still. He felt unsafe in this darkness that seemed to   25
make the ship's motion unfamiliar, unforeseen, and difficult to
counteract. He felt so much shaken for a moment that he
dared not move for fear of "taking charge again." He had no
mind to get battered to pieces in that bunker.

He had struck his head twice; he was dazed a little. He
seemed to hear yet so plainly the clatter and bangs of the iron
slice flying about his ears that he tightened his grip to prove to
himself he had it there safely in his hand. He was vaguely
amazed at the plainness with which down there he could hear
the gale raging. Its howls and shrieks seemed to take on, in the   35

emptiness of the bunker, something of the human character, of
human rage and pain—being not vast but infinitely poignant.
And there were, with every roll, thumps, too—profound, ponderous thumps, as if a bulky object of five-ton weight or so had
5 got play in the hold. But there was no such thing in the cargo.
Something on deck? Impossible. Or alongside? Couldn't be.

He thought all this quickly, clearly, competently, like a seaman, and in the end remained puzzled. This noise, though,
came deadened from outside, together with the washing and
pouring of water on deck above his head. Was it the wind?
Must be. It made down there a row like the shouting of a big
lot of crazed men. And he discovered in himself a desire for a
light, too—if only to get drowned by—and a nervous anxiety to
get out of that bunker as quickly as possible.

15 He pulled back the bolt: the heavy iron plate turned on its
hinges; and it was as though he had opened the door to the
sounds of the tempest. A gust of hoarse yelling met him: the
air was still; and the rushing of water overhead was covered by a
tumult of strangled, throaty shrieks that produced an effect of
desperate confusion. He straddled his legs the whole width of
the doorway and stretched his neck. And at first he perceived
only what he had come to seek: six small yellow flames swinging violently on the great body of the dusk.

It was stayed like the gallery of a mine, with a row of stan-
25 chions in the middle, and cross-beams overhead, penetrating
into the gloom ahead—indefinitely. And to port there loomed,
like the caving in of one of the sides, a bulky mass with a slanting outline. The whole place, with the shadows and the shapes,
moved all the time. The boatswain glared: the ship lurched to
starboard, and a great howl came from that mass that had the
slant of fallen earth.

Pieces of wood whizzed past. Planks, he thought, inexpressi-
bly startled, and flinging back his head. At his feet a man went
sliding over, open-eyed, on his back, straining with uplifted
35 arms for nothing: and another came bounding like a detached
stone with his head between his legs and his hands clenched.

His pigtail whipped in the air; he made a grab at the boatswain's legs, and from his opened hand a bright white disc rolled against the boatswain's foot. He recognized a silver dollar, and yelled at it with astonishment. With a precipitated sound of trampling and shuffling of bare feet, and with guttural cries, the mound of writhing bodies piled up to port detached itself from the ship's side and sliding, inert and struggling, shifted to starboard, with a dull, brutal thump. The cries ceased. The boatswain heard a long moan through the roar and whistling of the wind; he saw an inextricable confusion of heads and shoulders, naked soles kicking upwards, fists raised, tumbling backs, legs, pigtails, faces.

"Good Lord!" he cried, horrified, and banged-to the iron door upon this vision.

This was what he had come on the bridge to tell. He could not keep it to himself; and on board ship there is only one man to whom it is worth while to unburden yourself. On his passage back the hands in the alleyway swore at him for a fool. Why didn't he bring that lamp? What the devil did the coolies matter to anybody? And when he came out, the extremity of the ship made what went on inside of her appear of little moment.

At first he thought he had left the alleyway in the very moment of her sinking. The bridge ladders had been washed away, but an enormous sea filling the after-deck floated him up. After that he had to lie on his stomach for some time, holding to a ring-bolt, getting his breath now and then, and swallowing salt water. He struggled farther on his hands and knees, too frightened and distracted to turn back. In this way he reached the after-part of the wheelhouse. In that comparatively sheltered spot he found the second mate. The boatswain was pleasantly surprised—his impression being that everybody on deck must have been washed away a long time ago. He asked eagerly where the Captain was.

The second mate was lying low, like a malignant little animal under a hedge.

"Captain? Gone overboard, after getting us into this mess."

The mate, too, for all he knew or cared. Another fool. Didn't matter. Everybody was going by-and-by.

The boatswain crawled out again into the strength of the wind; not because he much expected to find anybody, he said, but just to get away from "that man." He crawled out as outcasts go to face an inclement world. Hence his great joy at finding Jukes and the Captain. But what was going on in the 'tween-deck was to him a minor matter by that time. Besides, it was difficult to make yourself heard. But he managed to convey the idea that the Chinamen had broken adrift together with their boxes, and that he had come up on purpose to report this. As to the hands, they were all right. Then, appeased, he subsided on the deck in a sitting posture, hugging with his arms and legs the stand of the engine-room telegraph—an iron casting as thick as a post. When that went, why, he expected he would go, too. He gave no more thought to the coolies.

Captain MacWhirr had made Jukes understand that he wanted him to go down below—to see.

"What am I to do then, sir?" And the trembling of his whole wet body caused Jukes' voice to sound like bleating.

"See first . . . Boss'n . . . says . . . adrift."

"That boss'n is a confounded fool," howled Jukes, shakily.

The absurdity of the demand made upon him revolted Jukes. He was as unwilling to go as if the moment he had left the deck the ship were sure to sink.

"I must know . . . can't leave. . . ."

"They'll settle, sir."

"Fight . . . boss'n says they fight. . . . Why? Can't have . . . fighting . . . board ship. . . . Much rather keep you here . . . case. . . . I should . . . washed overboard myself. . . . Stop it . . . some way. You see and tell me . . . through engine-room tube. Don't want you . . . come up here . . . too often. Dangerous . . . moving about . . . deck."

Jukes, held with his head in chancery, had to listen to what seemed horrible suggestions.

"Don't want . . . you get lost . . . so long . . . ship isn't.
. . . Rout . . . Good man . . . Ship . . . may . . . through this
. . . all right yet."

All at once Jukes understood he would have to go.

"Do you think she may?" he screamed.

But the wind devoured the reply, out of which Jukes heard
only the one word, pronounced with great energy " . . . Always. . . ."

Captain MacWhirr released Jukes, and bending over the
boatswain, yelled, "Get back with the mate." Jukes only knew
that the arm was gone off his shoulders. He was dismissed with
his orders—to do what? He was exasperated into letting go his
hold carelessly, and on the instant was blown away. It seemed
to him that nothing could stop him from being blown right
over the stern. He flung himself down hastily, and the boatswain, who was following, fell on him.

"Don't you get up yet, sir," cried the boatswain. "No hurry!"

A sea swept over. Jukes understood the boatswain to splutter
that the bridge ladders were gone. "I'll lower you down, sir, by
your hands," he screamed. He shouted also something about
the smoke-stack being as likely to go overboard as not. Jukes
thought it very possible, and imagined the fires out, the ship
helpless. . . . The boatswain by his side kept on yelling.
"What? What is it?" Jukes cried distressfully; and the other repeated, "What would my old woman say if she saw me now?"

In the alleyway, where a lot of water had got in and splashed
in the dark, the men were still as death, till Jukes stumbled
against one of them and cursed him savagely for being in the
way. Two or three voices then asked, eager and weak, "Any
chance for us, sir?"

"What's the matter with you fools?" he said brutally. He felt
as though he could throw himself down amongst them and
never move any more. But they seemed cheered; and in the
midst of obsequious warnings, "Look out! Mind that manhole
lid, sir," they lowered him into the bunker. The boatswain
tumbled down after him, and as soon as he had picked himself

up he remarked, "She would say, 'Serve you right, you old fool, for going to sea.'"

The boatswain had some means, and made a point of alluding to them frequently. His wife—a fat woman—and two grown-up daughters kept a greengrocer's shop in the East End of London.

In the dark, Jukes, unsteady on his legs, listened to a faint thunderous patter. A deadened screaming went on steadily at his elbow, as it were; and from above the louder tumult of the storm descended upon these near sounds. His head swam. To him, too, in that bunker, the motion of the ship seemed novel and menacing, sapping his resolution as though he had never been afloat before.

He had half a mind to scramble out again; but the remembrance of Captain MacWhirr's voice made this impossible. His orders were to go and see. What was the good of it, he wanted to know. Enraged, he told himself he would see—of course. But the boatswain, staggering clumsily, warned him to be careful how he opened that door; there was a blamed fight going on. And Jukes, as if in great bodily pain, desired irritably to know what the devil they were fighting for.

"Dollars! Dollars, sir. All their rotten chests got burst open. Blamed money skipping all over the place, and they are tumbling after it head over heels—tearing and biting like anything. A regular little hell in there."

Jukes convulsively opened the door. The short boatswain peered under his arm.

One of the lamps had gone out, broken perhaps. Rancorous, guttural cries burst out loudly on their ears, and a strange panting sound, the working of all these straining breasts. A hard blow hit the side of the ship: water fell above with a stunning shock, and in the forefront of the gloom, where the air was reddish and thick, Jukes saw a head bang the deck violently, two thick calves waving on high, muscular arms twined round a naked body, a yellow-face, open-mouthed and with a set wild stare, look up and slide away. An empty chest clattered turning over; a man fell head first with a jump, as if lifted by a kick; and farther off, indistinct, others streamed like a mass of rolling stones down a bank, thumping the deck with their feet and flourishing their arms wildly. The hatchway ladder was loaded with coolies swarming on it like bees on a branch. They hung on the steps in a crawling, stirring cluster, beating madly with their fists the underside of the battened hatch, and the headlong rush of the water above was heard in the intervals of their yelling. The ship heeled over more, and they began to drop off: first one, then two, then all the rest went away together, falling straight off with a great cry.

Jukes was confounded. The boatswain, with gruff anxiety, begged him, "Don't you go in there, sir."

The whole place seemed to twist upon itself, jumping incessantly the while; and when the ship rose to a sea Jukes fancied that all these men would be shot upon him in a body. He backed out, swung the door to, and with trembling hands pushed at the bolt. . . .

As soon as his mate had gone Captain MacWhirr, left alone on the bridge, sidled and staggered as far as the wheelhouse. Its door being hinged forward, he had to fight the gale for admittance, and when at last he managed to enter, it was with an instantaneous clatter and a bang, as though he had been fired through the wood. He stood within, holding on to the handle.

The steering-gear leaked steam, and in the confined space the glass of the binnacle made a shiny oval of light in a thin white fog. The wind howled, hummed, whistled, with sudden booming gusts that rattled the doors and shutters in the vicious patter of sprays. Two coils of lead-line and a small canvas bag hung on a long lanyard, swung wide off, and came back clinging to the bulkheads. The gratings underfoot were nearly afloat; with every sweeping blow of a sea, water squirted violently through the cracks all round the door, and the man at the helm had flung down his cap, his coat, and stood propped against the gear-casing in a striped cotton shirt open on his breast. The little brass wheel in his hands had the appearance

of a bright and fragile toy. The cords of his neck stood hard
and lean, a dark patch lay in the hollow of his throat, and his
face was still and sunken as in death.

Captain MacWhirr wiped his eyes. The sea that had nearly
taken him overboard had, to his great annoyance, washed his
sou'wester hat off his bald head. The fluffy, fair hair, soaked
and darkened, resembled a mean skein of cotton threads fes-
tooned round his bare skull. His face, glistening with sea-water,
had been made crimson with the wind, with the sting of sprays.
He looked as though he had come off sweating from before a
furnace.

"You here?" he muttered, heavily.

The second mate had found his way into the wheelhouse
some time before. He had fixed himself in a corner with his
knees up, a fist pressed against each temple; and this attitude
suggested rage, sorrow, resignation, surrender, with a sort of
concentrated unforgiveness. He said mournfully and defiantly,
"Well, it's my watch below now: ain't it?"

The steam gear clattered, stopped, clattered again; and the
helmsman's eyeballs seemed to project out of a hungry face as
if the compass-card behind the binnacle glass had been meat.
God knows how long he had been left there to steer, as if forgotten by all his shipmates. The bells had not been struck;
there had been no reliefs; the ship's routine had gone down
wind; but he was trying to keep her head north-northeast. The
rudder might have been gone for all he knew, the fires out, the
engines broken down, the ship ready to roll over like a corpse.
He was anxious not to get muddled and lose control of her
head, because the compass-card swung far both ways, wriggling
on the pivot, and sometimes seemed to whirl right round. He
suffered from mental stress. He was horribly afraid, also, of the
wheelhouse going. Mountains of water kept on tumbling
against it. When the ship took one of her desperate dives the
corners of his lips twitched.

Captain MacWhirr looked up at the wheelhouse clock.
Screwed to the bulkhead, it had a white face on which the

black hands appeared to stand quite still. It was half-past one in the morning.

"Another day," he muttered to himself.

The second mate heard him, and lifting his head as one grieving amongst ruins, "You won't see it break," he exclaimed. His wrists and his knees could be seen to shake violently. "No, by God! You won't. . . ."

He took his face again between his fists.

The body of the helmsman had moved slightly, but his head didn't budge on his neck—like a stone head fixed to look one way from a column. During a roll that all but took his booted legs from under him, and in the very stagger to save himself, Captain MacWhirr said austerely, "Don't you pay any attention to what that man says." And then, with an indefinable change of tone, very grave, he added, "He isn't on duty."

The sailor said nothing.

The hurricane boomed, shaking the little place, which seemed air-tight; and the light of the binnacle flickered all the time.

"You haven't been relieved," Captain MacWhirr went on, looking down. "I want you to stick to the helm, though, as long as you can. You've got the hang of her. Another man coming here might make a mess of it. Wouldn't do. No child's play. And the hands are probably busy with a job down below. . . . Think you can?"

The steering-gear leaped into an abrupt short clatter, stopped smouldering like an ember; and the still man, with a motionless gaze, burst out, as if all the passion in him had gone into his lips: "By Heavens, sir! I can steer for ever if nobody talks to me."

"Oh! aye! All right. . . ." The Captain lifted his eyes for the first time to the man, ". . . Hackett."

And he seemed to dismiss this matter from his mind. He stooped to the engine-room speaking-tube, blew in, and bent his head. Mr. Rout below answered, and at once Captain MacWhirr put his lips to the mouthpiece.

With the uproar of the gale around him he applied alternately his lips and his ear, and the engineer's voice mounted to him, harsh and as if out of the heat of an engagement. One of the stokers was disabled, the others had given in, the second
5   engineer and the donkey-man were firing-up. The third engineer was standing by the steam-valve. The engines were being tended by hand. How was it above?

"Bad enough. It mostly rests with you," said Captain MacWhirr. Was the mate down there yet? No? Well, he would be presently. Would Mr. Rout let him talk through the speaking-tube?—through the deck speaking-tube, because he— the Captain—was going out again on the bridge directly. There was some trouble amongst the Chinamen. They were fighting, it seemed. Couldn't allow fighting anyhow. . . .
15 Mr. Rout had gone away, and Captain MacWhirr could feel against his ear the pulsation of the engines, like the beat of the ship's heart. Mr. Rout's voice down there shouted something distantly. The ship pitched headlong, the pulsation leaped with a hissing tumult, and stopped dead. Captain MacWhirr's face was impassive, and his eyes were fixed aimlessly on the crouching shape of the second mate. Again Mr. Rout's voice cried out in the depths, and the pulsating beats recommenced, with slow strokes—growing swifter.

Mr. Rout had returned to the tube. "It don't matter much
25 what they do," he said, hastily; and then, with irritation, "She takes these dives as if she never meant to come up again."

"Awful sea," said the Captain's voice from above.

"Don't let me drive her under," barked Solomon Rout up the pipe.

"Dark and rain. Can't see what's coming," uttered the voice. "Must—keep—her—moving—enough to steer—and chance it," it went on to state distinctly.

"I am doing as much as I dare."

"We are—getting—smashed up—a good deal up here," pro-
35 ceeded the voice mildly. "Doing—fairly well—though. Of course, if the wheelhouse should go. . . ."

Mr. Rout, bending an attentive ear, muttered peevishly something under his breath.

But the deliberate voice up there became animated to ask: "Jukes turned up yet?" Then, after a short wait, "I wish he would bear a hand. I want him to be done and come up here in case of anything. To look after the ship. I am all alone. The second mate's lost. . . ."

"What?" shouted Mr. Rout into the engine-room, taking his head away. Then up the tube he cried, "Gone overboard?" and clapped his ear to.

"Lost his nerve," the voice from above continued in a matter-of-fact tone. "Damned awkward circumstance."

Mr. Rout, listening with bowed neck, opened his eyes wide at this. However, he heard something like the sounds of a scuffle and broken exclamations coming down to him. He strained his hearing; and all the time Beale, the third engineer, with his arms uplifted, held between the palms of his hands the rim of a little black wheel projecting at the side of a big copper pipe. He seemed to be poising it above his head, as though it were a correct attitude in some sort of game.

To steady himself, he pressed his shoulder against the white bulkhead, one knee bent, and a sweat-rag tucked in his belt hanging on his hip. His smooth cheek was begrimed and flushed, and the coal dust on his eyelids, like the black pencil-ing of a make-up, enhanced the liquid brilliance of the whites, giving to his youthful face something of a feminine, exotic and fascinating aspect. When the ship pitched he would with hasty movements of his hands screw hard at the little wheel.

"Gone crazy," began the Captain's voice suddenly in the tube. "Rushed at me. . . . Just now. Had to knock him down. . . . This minute. You heard, Mr. Rout?"

"The devil!" muttered Mr. Rout. "Look out, Beale!"

His shout rang out like the blast of a warning trumpet, be-tween the iron walls of the engine-room. Painted white, they rose high into the dusk of the skylight, sloping like a roof; and the whole lofty space resembled the interior of a monument, divided by floors of iron grating, with lights flickering at different levels, and a mass of gloom lingering in the middle, within the columnar stir of machinery under the motionless swelling of the cylinders. A loud and wild resonance, made up of all the noises of the hurricane, dwelt in the still warmth of the air. There was in it the smell of hot metal, of oil, and a slight mist of steam. The blows of the sea seemed to traverse it in an unringing, stunning shock, from side to side.

Gleams, like pale long flames, trembled upon the polish of metal; from the flooring below the enormous crankheads emerged in their turns with a flash of brass and steel—going over; while the connecting-rods, big-jointed, like skeleton limbs, seemed to thrust them down and pull them up again with an irresistible precision. And deep in the half-light other rods dodged deliberately to and fro, crossheads nodded, discs of metal rubbed smoothly against each other, slow and gentle, in a commingling of shadows and gleams.

Sometimes all those powerful and unerring movements would slow down simultaneously, as if they had been the functions of a living organism, stricken suddenly by the blight of languor; and Mr. Rout's eyes would blaze darker in his long sallow face. He was fighting this fight in a pair of carpet slippers. A short shiny jacket barely covered his loins, and his white wrists protruded far out of the tight sleeves, as though the emergency had added to his stature, had lengthened his limbs, augmented his pallor, hollowed his eyes.

He moved, climbing high up, disappearing low down, with a restless, purposeful industry, and when he stood still, holding the guard-rail in front of the starting-gear, he would keep glancing to the right at the steam-gauge, at the water-gauge, fixed upon the white wall in the light of a swaying lamp. The mouths of two speaking-tubes gaped stupidly at his elbow, and the dial of the engine-room telegraph resembled a clock of large diameter, bearing on its face curt words instead of figures. The grouped letters stood out heavily black, around the pivot-head of the indicator, emphatically symbolic of loud exclamations:

AHEAD, ASTERN, SLOW, HALF, STAND BY; and the fat black hand
pointed downwards to the word FULL, which, thus singled out,
captured the eye as a sharp cry secures attention.

The wood-encased bulk of the low-pressure cylinder, frown-
ing portly from above, emitted a faint wheeze at every thrust, 5
and except for that low hiss the engines worked their steel
limbs headlong or slow with a silent, determined smoothness.
And all this, the white walls, the moving steel, the floor plates
under Solomon Rout's feet, the floors of iron grating above his
head, the dusk and the gleams, uprose and sank continuously,
with one accord, upon the harsh wash of the waves against the
ship's side. The whole loftiness of the place, booming hollow
to the great voice of the wind, swayed at the top like a tree,
would go over bodily, as if borne down this way and that by
the tremendous blasts. 15

"You've got to hurry up," shouted Mr. Rout, as soon as he
saw Jukes appear in the stokehold doorway.

Jukes' glance was wandering and tipsy; his red face was
puffy, as though he had overslept himself. He had had an arduous road, and had travelled over it with immense vivacity, the
agitation of his mind corresponding to the exertions of his
body. He had rushed up out of the bunker, stumbling in the
dark alleyway amongst a lot of bewildered men who, trod
upon, asked "What's up, sir?" in awed mutters all round him
—down the stokehold ladder, missing many iron rungs in his 25
hurry, down into a place deep as a well, black as Tophet, tip-
ping over back and forth like a see-saw. The water in the bilges
thundered at each roll, and lumps of coal skipped to and fro,
from end to end, rattling like an avalanche of pebbles on a
slope of iron.

Somebody in there moaned with pain, and somebody else
could be seen crouching over what seemed the prone body of a
dead man; a lusty voice blasphemed; and the glow under each
fire-door was like a pool of flaming blood radiating quietly in a
velvety blackness. 35

A gust of wind struck upon the nape of Jukes' neck and next

moment he felt it streaming about his wet ankles. The stoke-hold ventilators hummed: in front of the six fire-doors two wild figures, stripped to the waist, staggered and stooped, wrestling with two shovels.

5   "Hallo! Plenty of draught now," yelled the second engineer at once, as though he had been all the time looking out for Jukes. The donkey-man, a dapper little chap with a dazzling fair skin and a tiny, gingery moustache, worked in a sort of mute transport. They were keeping a full head of steam, and a profound rumbling, as of an empty furniture van trotting over a bridge, made a sustained bass to all the other noises of the place.

"Blowing off all the time," went on yelling the second. With a sound as of a hundred scoured saucepans, the orifice of a ven-
15   tilator spat upon his shoulders a sudden gush of salt water, and he volleyed a stream of curses upon all things on earth includ-ing his own soul, ripping and raving, and all the time attending to his business. With a sharp clash of metal the ardent pale glare of the fire opened upon his bullet head, showing his splut-tering lips, his insolent face, and with another clang closed like the white-hot wink of an iron eye.

"Where's the blooming ship? Can you tell me? Blast my eyes! Under water—or what? It's coming down here in tons. Are the condemned cowls gone to Hades? Hey? Don't you know any-
25   thing—you jolly sailor-man you . . . ?"

Jukes, after a bewildered moment, had been helped by a roll to dart through; and as soon as his eyes took in the compara-tive vastness, peace and brilliance of the engine-room, the ship, setting her stern heavily in the water, sent him charging head down upon Mr. Rout.

The chief's arm, long like a tentacle, and straightening as if worked by a spring, went out to meet him, and deflected his rush into a spin towards the speaking-tubes. At the same time Mr. Rout repeated earnestly:

35   "You've got to hurry up, whatever it is."

Jukes yelled "Are you there, sir?" and listened. Nothing. Suddenly the roar of the wind fell straight into his ear, but presently a small voice shoved aside the shouting hurricane quietly.

"You, Jukes?—Well?"

Jukes was ready to talk; it was only time that seemed to be wanting. It was easy enough to account for everything. He could perfectly imagine the coolies battened down in the reeking 'tween-deck, lying sick and scared between the rows of chests. Then one of these chests—or perhaps several at once—breaking loose in a roll, knocking out others, sides splitting, lids flying open, and all these clumsy Chinamen rising up in a body to save their property. Afterwards every fling of the ship would hurl that tramping, yelling mob here and there, from side to side, in a whirl of smashed wood, torn clothing, rolling dollars. A struggle once started, they would be unable to stop themselves. Nothing could stop them now except main force. It was a disaster. He had seen it, and that was all he could say. Some of them must be dead, he believed. The rest would go on fighting. . . .

He sent up his words, tripping over each other, crowding the narrow tube. They mounted as if into a silence of an enlightened comprehension dwelling alone up there with a storm. And Jukes wanted to be dismissed from the face of that odious trouble intruding on the great need of the ship.

Chapter Five

He waited. Before his eyes the engines turned with slow labour, that in the moment of going off into a mad fling would stop dead at Mr. Rout's shout, "Look out, Beale!" They paused in an intelligent immobility, stilled in midstroke, a heavy crank arrested on the cant, as if conscious of danger and the passage of time. Then, with a "Now, then!" from the chief, and the sound of a breath expelled through clenched teeth, they would accomplish the interrupted revolution and begin another.

There was the prudent sagacity of wisdom and the delibera-tion of enormous strength in their movements. This was their
5 work—this patient coaxing of a distracted ship over the fury of the waves and into the very eye of the wind. At times Mr. Rout's chin would sink on his breast, and he watched them with knitted eyebrows as if lost in thought.

The voice that kept the hurricane out of Jukes' ear began: "Take the hands with you . . . ," and left off unexpectedly.

"What could I do with them, sir?"

A harsh, abrupt, imperious clang exploded suddenly. The three pairs of eyes flew up to the telegraph dial to see the hand jump from FULL to STOP, as if snatched by a devil. And then
15 these three men in the engine-room had the intimate sensation of a check upon the ship, of a strange shrinking, as if she had gathered herself for a desperate leap.

"Stop her!" bellowed Mr. Rout.

Nobody—not even Captain MacWhirr, who alone on deck had caught sight of a white line of foam coming on at such a height that he couldn't believe his eyes—nobody was to know the steepness of that sea and the awful depth of the hollow the hurricane had scooped out behind the running wall of water.

It raced to meet the ship, and, with a pause, as of girding the
25 loins, the Nan-Shan lifted her bows and leaped. The flames in all the lamps sank, darkening the engine-room. One went out. With a tearing crash and a swirling, raving tumult, tons of water fell upon the deck, as though the ship had darted under the foot of a cataract.

Down there they looked at each other, stunned.

"Swept from end to end, by God!" bawled Jukes.

She dipped into the hollow straight down, as if going over the edge of the world. The engine-room toppled forward men-acingly, like the inside of a tower nodding in an earthquake.
35 An awful racket, of iron things falling, came from the stoke-

hold. She hung on this appalling slant long enough for Beale to drop on his hands and knees and begin to crawl as if he meant to fly on all fours out of the engine-room, and for Mr. Rout to turn his head slowly, rigid, cavernous, with the lower jaw dropping. Jukes had shut his eyes, and his face in a moment became hopelessly blank and gentle, like the face of a blind man.

At last she rose slowly, staggering, as if she had to lift a mountain with her bows.

Mr. Rout shut his mouth; Jukes blinked; and little Beale stood up hastily.

"Another one like this, and that's the last of her," cried the chief.

He and Jukes looked at each other, and the same thought came into their heads. The Captain! Everything must have been swept away. Steering-gear gone—ship like a log. All over directly.

"Rush!" ejaculated Mr. Rout thickly, glaring with enlarged, doubtful eyes at Jukes, who answered him by an irresolute glance.

The clang of the telegraph gong soothed them instantly. The black hand dropped in a flash from STOP to FULL.

"Now then, Beale!" cried Mr. Rout.

The steam hissed low. The piston-rods slid in and out. Jukes put his ear to the tube. The voice was ready for him. It said: "Pick up all the money. Bear a hand now. I'll want you up here." And that was all.

"Sir?" called up Jukes. There was no answer.

He staggered away like a defeated man from the field of battle. He had got, in some way or other, a cut above his left eyebrow—a cut to the bone. He was not aware of it in the least: quantities of the China Sea, large enough to break his neck for him, had gone over his head, had cleaned, washed, and salted that wound. It did not bleed, but only gaped red; and this gash over the eye, his dishevelled hair, the disorder of his clothes, gave him the aspect of a man worsted in a fight with fists.

"Got to pick up the dollars." He appealed to Mr. Rout, smiling pitifully at random.

"What's that?" asked Mr. Rout, wildly. "Pick up . . . ? I don't care. . . ." Then, quivering in every muscle, but with an exaggeration of paternal tone, "Go away now, for God's sake. You deck people'll drive me silly. There's that second mate been going for the old man. Don't you know? You fellows are going wrong for want of something to do. . . ."

At these words Jukes discovered in himself the beginnings of anger. Want of something to do—indeed. . . . Full of hot scorn against the chief, he turned to go the way he had come. In the stokehold the plump donkey-man toiled with his shovel mutely, as if his tongue had been cut out; but the second was carrying on like a noisy, undaunted maniac, who had preserved his skill in the art of stoking under a marine boiler.

"Hallo, you wandering officer! Hey! Can't you get some of your slush-slingers to wind up a few of them ashes? I am getting choked with them here. Curse it! Hallo! Hey! Remember the articles: *Sailors and firemen to assist each other*. Hey! D'ye hear?"

Jukes was climbing out frantically, and the other, lifting up his face after him, howled, "Can't you speak? What are you poking about here for? What's your game, anyhow?"

A frenzy possessed Jukes. By the time he was back amongst the men in the darkness of the alleyway, he felt ready to wring all their necks at the slightest sign of hanging back. The very thought of it exasperated him. *He* couldn't hang back. They shouldn't.

The impetuosity with which he came amongst them carried them along. They had already been excited and startled at all his comings and goings—by the fierceness and rapidity of his movements; and more felt than seen in his rushes, he appeared formidable—busied with matters of life and death that brooked no delay. At his first word he heard them drop into the bunker one after another obediently, with heavy thumps.

They were not clear as to what would have to be done.

"What is it? What is it?" they were asking each other. The boatswain tried to explain; the sounds of a great scuffle surprised them: and the mighty shocks, reverberating awfully in the black bunker, kept them in mind of their danger. When the boatswain threw open the door it seemed that an eddy of the 5 hurricane, stealing through the iron sides of the ship, had set all these bodies whirling like dust: there came to them a confused uproar, a tempestuous tumult, a fierce mutter, gusts of screams dying away, and the tramping of feet mingling with the blows of the sea.

For a moment they glared amazed, blocking the doorway. Jukes pushed through them brutally. He said nothing, and simply darted in. Another lot of coolies on the ladder, struggling suicidally to break through the battened hatch to a swamped deck, fell off as before, and he disappeared under them like a 15 man overtaken by a landslide.

The boatswain yelled excitedly: "Come along. Get the mate out. He'll be trampled to death. Come on."

They charged in, stamping on breasts, on fingers, on faces, catching their feet in heaps of clothing, kicking broken wood; but before they could get hold of him Jukes emerged waist deep in a multitude of clawing hands. In the instant he had been lost to view, all the buttons of his jacket had gone, its back had got split up to the collar, his waistcoat had been torn open. The central struggling mass of Chinamen went over to 25 the roll, dark, indistinct, helpless, with a wild gleam of many eyes in the dim light of the lamps.

"Leave me alone—damn you. I am all right," screeched Jukes. "Drive them forward. Watch your chance when she pitches. Forward with 'em. Drive them against the bulkhead. Jam 'em up."

The rush of the sailors into the seething 'tween-deck was like a splash of cold water into a boiling cauldron. The commotion sank for a moment.

The bulk of Chinamen were locked in such a compact scrim- 35 mage that, linking their arms and aided by an appalling dive of the ship, the seamen sent it forward in one great shove, like a solid block. Behind their backs small clusters and loose bodies tumbled from side to side.

The boatswain performed prodigious feats of strength. With his long arms open, and each great paw clutching at a stanchion, he stopped the rush of seven entwined Chinamen rolling like a boulder. His joints cracked; he said, "Ha!" and they flew apart. But the carpenter showed the greater intelligence. Without saying a word to anybody he went back into the alleyway to fetch several coils of cargo gear he had seen there— chain and rope. With these life-lines were rigged.

There was really no resistance. The struggle, however it began, had turned into a scramble of blind panic. If the coolies had started up after their scattered dollars they were by that time fighting only for their footing. They took each other by the throat merely to save themselves from being hurled about. Whoever got a hold anywhere would kick at the others who caught at his legs and hung on, till a roll sent them flying together across the deck.

The coming of the white devils was a terror. Had they come to kill? The individuals torn out of the ruck became very limp in the seamen's hands: some, dragged aside by the heels, were passive, like dead bodies, with open, fixed eyes. Here and there a coolie would fall on his knees as if begging for mercy; several, whom the excess of fear made unruly, were hit with hard fists between the eyes, and cowered; while those who were hurt submitted to rough handling, blinking rapidly without a plaint. Faces streamed with blood; there were raw places on the shaven heads, scratches, bruises, torn wounds, gashes. The broken porcelain out of the chests was mostly responsible for the latter. Here and there a Chinaman, wild-eyed, with his tail unplaited, nursed a bleeding sole.

They had been ranged closely, after having been shaken into submission, cuffed a little to allay excitement, addressed in gruff words of encouragement that sounded like promises of

evil. They sat on the deck in ghastly, drooping rows, and at the
end the carpenter, with two hands to help him, moved busily
from place to place, setting taut and hitching the life-lines. The
boatswain, with one leg and one arm embracing a stanchion,
struggled with a lamp pressed to his breast, trying to get a light,   5
and growling all the time like an industrious gorilla. The figures
of seamen stooped repeatedly, with the movements of gleaners,
and everything was being flung into the bunker: clothing,
smashed wood, broken china, and the dollars, too, gathered up
in men's jackets. Now and then a sailor would stagger towards
the doorway with his arms full of rubbish; and dolorous, slanting eyes followed his movements.

   With every roll of the ship the long rows of sitting Celestials
would sway forward brokenly, and her headlong dives knocked
together the line of shaven polls from end to end. When the   15
wash of water rolling on the deck died away for a moment, it
seemed to Jukes, yet quivering from his exertions, that in his
mad struggle down there he had overcome the wind somehow:
that a silence had fallen upon the ship, a silence in which the
sea struck thunderously at her sides.

   Everything had been cleared out of the 'tween-deck—all the
wreckage, as the men said. They stood erect and tottering
above the level of heads and drooping shoulders. Here and
there a coolie sobbed for his breath. Where the high light fell,
Jukes could see the salient ribs of one, the yellow, wistful face   25
of another; bowed necks; or would meet a dull stare directed at
his face. He was amazed that there had been no corpses; but
the lot of them seemed at their last gasp, and they appeared to
him more pitiful than if they had been all dead.

   Suddenly one of the coolies began to speak. The light came
and went on his lean, straining face; he threw his head up like
a baying hound. From the bunker came the sounds of knocking
and the tinkle of some dollars rolling loose; he stretched out his
arm, his mouth yawned black, and the incomprehensible guttural hooting sounds, that did not seem to belong to a human   35

language, penetrated Jukes with a strange emotion as if a brute had tried to be eloquent.

Two more started mouthing what seemed to Jukes fierce denunciations; the others stirred with grunts and growls. Jukes ordered the hands out of the 'tween-deck hurriedly. He left last himself, backing through the door, while the grunts rose to a loud murmur and hands were extended after him as after a malefactor. The boatswain shot the bolt, and remarked uneasily, "Seems as if the wind had dropped, sir."

The seamen were glad to get back into the alleyway. Secretly each of them thought that at the last moment he could rush out on deck—and that was a comfort. There is something horribly repugnant in the idea of being drowned under a deck. Now they had done with the Chinamen, they again became conscious of the ship's position.

Jukes on coming out of the alleyway found himself up to the neck in the noisy water. He gained the bridge, and discovered he could detect obscure shapes as if his sight had become preternaturally acute. He saw faint outlines. They recalled not the familiar aspect of the *Nan-Shan*, but something remembered—an old dismantled steamer he had seen years ago rotting on a mudbank. She recalled that wreck.

There was no wind, not a breath, except the faint currents created by the lurches of the ship. The smoke tossed out of the funnel was settling down upon her deck. He breathed it as he passed forward. He felt the deliberate throb of the engines, and heard small sounds that seemed to have survived the great uproar: the knocking of broken fittings, the rapid tumbling of some piece of wreckage on the bridge. He perceived dimly the squat shape of his captain holding on to a twisted bridge-rail, motionless and swaying as if rooted to the planks. The unexpected stillness of the air oppressed Jukes.

"We have done it, sir," he gasped.

"Thought you would," said Captain MacWhirr.

"Did you?" murmured Jukes to himself.

"Wind fell all at once," went on the Captain.

Jukes burst out: "If you think it was an easy job———"

But his captain, clinging to the rail, paid no attention. "According to the books the worst is not over yet."

"If most of them hadn't been half dead with sea-sickness and fright, not one of us would have come out of that 'tween-deck alive," said Jukes.

"Had to do what's fair by them," mumbled MacWhirr, stolidly. "You don't find everything in books."

"Why, I believe they would have risen on us if I hadn't ordered the hands out of that pretty quick," continued Jukes with warmth.

After the whisper of their shouts, their ordinary tones, so distinct, rang out very loud to their ears in the amazing stillness of the air. It seemed to them they were talking in a dark and echoing vault.

Through a jagged aperture in the dome of clouds the light of a few stars fell upon the black sea, rising and falling confusedly. Sometimes the head of a watery cone would topple on board and mingle with the rolling flurry of foam on the swamped deck; and the *Nan-Shan* wallowed heavily at the bottom of a circular cistern of clouds. This ring of dense vapours, gyrating madly round the calm of the centre, encompassed the ship like a motionless and unbroken wall of an aspect inconceivably sinister. Within, the sea, as if agitated by an internal commotion, leaped in peaked mounds that jostled each other, slapping heavily against her sides; and a low moaning sound, the infinite plaint of the storm's fury, came from beyond the limits of the menacing calm. Captain MacWhirr remained silent, and Jukes' ready ear caught suddenly the faint, long-drawn roar of some immense wave rushing unseen under that thick blackness, which made the appalling boundary of his vision.

"Of course," he started resentfully, "they thought we had caught at the chance to plunder them. Of course! You said—pick up the money. Easier said than done. They couldn't tell what was in our heads. We came in, smash—right into the middle of them. Had to do it by a rush."

"As long as it's done . . . ," mumbled the Captain, without attempting to look at Jukes. "Had to do what's fair."

"We shall find yet there's the devil to pay when this is over," said Jukes, feeling very sore. "Let them only recover a bit, and you'll see. They will fly at our throats, sir. Don't forget, sir, she isn't a British ship now. These brutes know it well, too. The damned Siamese flag."

"We are on board, all the same," remarked Captain Mac-Whirr.

"The trouble's not over yet," insisted Jukes, prophetically, reeling and catching on. "She's a wreck," he added, faintly.

"The trouble's not over yet," assented Captain MacWhirr, half aloud. . . . "Look out for her a minute."

"Are you going off the deck, sir?" asked Jukes, hurriedly, as if the storm were sure to pounce upon him as soon as he had been left alone with the ship.

He watched her, battered and solitary, labouring heavily in a wild scene of mountainous black waters lit by the gleams of distant worlds. She moved slowly, breathing into the still core of the hurricane the excess of her strength in a white cloud of steam—and the deep-toned vibration of the escape was like the defiant trumpeting of a living creature of the sea impatient for the renewal of the contest. It ceased suddenly. The still air moaned. Above Jukes' head a few stars shone into a pit of black vapours. The inky edge of the cloud-disc frowned upon the ship under the patch of glittering sky. The stars, too, seemed to look at her intently, as if for the last time, and the cluster of their splendour sat like a diadem on a lowering brow.

Captain MacWhirr had gone into the chart-room. There was no light there; but he could feel the disorder of that place where he used to live tidily. His armchair was upset. The books had tumbled out on the floor: he scrunched a piece of glass under his boot. He groped for the matches, and found a box on a shelf with a deep ledge. He struck one, and puckering the corners of his eyes, held out the little flame towards the barometer whose glittering top of glass and metal nodded at him continuously.

It stood very low—incredibly low, so low that Captain MacWhirr grunted. The match went out, and hurriedly he extracted another, with thick, stiff fingers.

Again a little flame flared up before the nodding glass and metal of the top. His eyes looked at it, narrowed with attention,   5
as if expecting an imperceptible sign. With his grave face he resembled a booted and misshapen pagan burning incense before the oracle of a Joss. There was no mistake. It was the lowest reading he had ever seen in his life.

Captain MacWhirr emitted a low whistle. He forgot himself till the flame diminished to a blue spark, burnt his fingers and vanished. Perhaps something had gone wrong with the thing!

There was an aneroid glass screwed above the couch. He turned that way, struck another match, and discovered the white face of the other instrument looking at him from the   15
bulkhead, meaningly, not to be gainsaid, as though the wisdom of men were made unerring by the indifference of matter. There was no room for doubt now. Captain MacWhirr pshawed at it, and threw the match down.

The worst was to come, then—and if the books were right this worst would be very bad. The experience of the last six hours had enlarged his conception of what heavy weather could be like. "It'll be terrific," he pronounced, mentally. He had not consciously looked at anything by the light of the matches except at the barometer; and yet somehow he had seen that his   25
waterbottle and the two tumblers had been flung out of their stand. It seemed to give him a more intimate knowledge of the tossing the ship had gone through. "I wouldn't have believed it," he thought. And his table had been cleared, too; his rulers, his pencils, the inkstand—all the things that had their safe appointed places—they were gone, as if a mischievous hand had plucked them out one by one and flung them on the wet floor. The hurricane had broken in upon the orderly arrangements of his privacy. This had never happened before, and the feeling of dismay reached the very seat of his composure. And the worst   35
was to come yet! He was glad the trouble in the 'tween-deck had been discovered in time. If the ship had to go after all,

then, at least, she wouldn't be going to the bottom with a lot of people in her fighting teeth and claw. That would have been odious. And in that feeling there was a humane intention and a vague sense of the fitness of things.

5   These instantaneous thoughts were yet in their essence heavy and slow, partaking of the nature of the man. He extended his hand to put back the matchbox in its corner of the shelf. There were always matches there—by his order. The steward had his instructions impressed upon him long before. "A box . . . just there, see? Not so very full . . . where I can put my hand on it, steward. Might want a light in a hurry. Can't tell on board ship *what* you might want in a hurry. Mind, now."

And of course on his side he would be careful to put it back
15   in its place scrupulously. He did so now, but before he removed his hand it occurred to him that perhaps he would never have occasion to use that box any more. The vividness of the thought checked him and for an infinitesimal fraction of a second his fingers closed again on the small object as though it had been the symbol of all these little habits that chain us to the weary round of life. He released it at last, and letting himself fall on the settee, listened for the first sounds of returning wind.

Not yet. He heard only the wash of water, the heavy
25   splashes, the dull shocks of the confused seas boarding his ship from all sides. She would never have a chance to clear her decks.

But the quietude of the air was startlingly tense and unsafe, like a slender hair holding a sword suspended over his head. By this awful pause the storm penetrated the defences of the man and unsealed his lips. He spoke out in the solitude and the pitch darkness of the cabin, as if addressing another being awakened within his breast.

"I shouldn't like to lose her," he said half aloud.

35   He sat unseen, apart from the sea, from his ship, isolated, as if withdrawn from the very current of his own existence, where

such freaks as talking to himself surely had no place. His palms reposed on his knees, he bowed his short neck and puffed heavily, surrendering to a strange sensation of weariness he was not enlightened enough to recognize for the fatigue of mental stress.

From where he sat he could reach the door of a washstand locker. There should have been a towel there. There was. Good. . . . He took it out, wiped his face, and afterwards went on rubbing his wet head. He towelled himself with energy in the dark, and then remained motionless with the towel on his knees. A moment passed, of a stillness so profound that no one could have guessed there was a man sitting in that cabin. Then a murmur arose.

"She may come out of it yet."

When Captain MacWhirr came out on deck, which he did brusquely, as though he had suddenly become conscious of having stayed away too long, the calm had lasted already more than fifteen minutes—long enough to make itself intolerable even to his imagination. Jukes, motionless on the forepart of the bridge, began to speak at once. His voice, blank and forced as though he were talking through hard-set teeth, seemed to flow away on all sides into the darkness, deepening again upon the sea.

"I had the wheel relieved. Hackett began to sing out that he was done. He's lying in there alongside the steering-gear with a face like death. At first I couldn't get anybody to crawl out and relieve the poor devil. That boss'n's worse than no good, I always said. Thought I would have had to go myself and haul out one of them by the neck."

"Ah, well," muttered the Captain. He stood watchful by Jukes' side.

"The second mate's in there, too, holding his head. Is he hurt, sir?"

"No—crazy," said Captain MacWhirr, curtly.

"Looks as if he had a tumble, though."

"I had to give him a push," explained the Captain.

Jukes gave an impatient sigh.

"It will come very sudden," said Captain MacWhirr, "and from over there, I fancy. God only knows though. These books are only good to muddle your head and make you jumpy. It will be bad, and there's an end. If we only can steam her round in time to meet it. . . ."

A minute passed. Some of the stars winked rapidly and vanished.

"You left them pretty safe?" began the Captain abruptly, as though the silence were unbearable.

"Are you thinking of the coolies, sir? I rigged life-lines all ways across that 'tween-deck."

"Did you? Good idea, Mr. Jukes."

"I didn't . . . think you cared to . . . know," said Jukes—the lurching of the ship cut his speech as though somebody had been jerking him around while he talked—"how I got on with . . . that infernal job. We did it. And it may not matter in the end."

"Had to do what's fair, for all—they are only Chinamen. Give them the same chance with ourselves—hang it all. She isn't lost yet. Bad enough to be shut up below in a gale——"

"That's what I thought when you gave me the job, sir," interjected Jukes, moodily.

"——without being battered to pieces," pursued Captain MacWhirr with rising vehemence. "Couldn't let that go on in my ship, if I knew she hadn't five minutes to live. Couldn't bear it, Mr. Jukes."

A hollow echoing noise, like that of a shout rolling in a rocky chasm, approached the ship and went away again. The last star, blurred, enlarged, as if returning to the fiery mist of its beginning, struggled with the colossal depth of blackness hanging over the ship—and went out.

"Now for it!" muttered Captain MacWhirr. "Mr. Jukes."

"Here, sir."

The two men were growing indistinct to each other.

"We must trust her to go through it and come out on the

other side. That's plain and straight. There's no room for Captain Wilson's storm-strategy here."

"No, sir."

"She will be smothered and swept again for hours," mumbled the Captain. "There's not much left by this time above 5 deck for the sea to take away—unless you or me."

"Both, sir," whispered Jukes, breathlessly.

"You are always meeting trouble half way, Jukes," Captain MacWhirr remonstrated quaintly. "Though it's a fact that the second mate is no good. D'ye hear, Mr. Jukes? You would be left alone if . . ."

Captain MacWhirr interrupted himself, and Jukes, glancing on all sides, remained silent.

"Don't you be put out by anything," the Captain continued, mumbling rather fast. "Keep her facing it. They may say what 15 they like, but the heaviest seas run with the wind. Facing it— always facing it—that's the way to get through. You are a young sailor. Face it. That's enough for any man. Keep a cool head."

"Yes, sir," said Jukes, with a flutter of the heart.

In the next few seconds the Captain spoke to the engine-room and got an answer.

For some reason Jukes experienced an access of confidence, a sensation that came from outside like a warm breath, and made him feel equal to every demand. The distant muttering of the 25 darkness stole into his ears. He noted it unmoved, out of that sudden belief in himself, as a man safe in a shirt of mail would watch a point.

The ship laboured without intermission amongst the black hills of water, paying with this hard tumbling the price of her life. She rumbled in her depths, shaking a white plummet of steam into the night, and Jukes' thought skimmed like a bird through the engine-room, where Mr. Rout—good man—was ready. When the rumbling ceased it seemed to him that there was a pause of every sound, a dead pause in which Captain 35 MacWhirr's voice rang out startlingly.

"What's that? A puff of wind?"—it spoke much louder than Jukes had ever heard it before—"On the bow. That's right. She may come out of it yet."

The mutter of the winds drew near apace. In the forefront could be distinguished a drowsy waking plaint passing on, and far off the growth of a multiple clamour, marching and expanding. There was the throb as of many drums in it, a vicious rushing note, and like the chant of a tramping multitude.

Jukes could no longer see his captain distinctly. The darkness was absolutely piling itself upon the ship. At most he made out movements, a hint of elbows spread out, of a head thrown up.

Captain MacWhirr was trying to do up the top button of his oilskin coat with unwonted haste. The hurricane, with its power to madden the seas, to sink ships, to uproot trees, to overturn strong walls and dash the very birds of the air to the ground, had found this taciturn man in its path, and, doing its utmost, had managed to wring out a few words. Before the renewed wrath of winds swooped on his ship, Captain MacWhirr was moved to declare, in a tone of vexation, as it were: "I wouldn't like to lose her."

He was spared that annoyance.

Chapter Six

On a bright sunshiny day, with the breeze chasing her smoke far ahead, the *Nan-Shan* came into Fu-chau. Her arrival was at once noticed on shore, and the seamen in harbour said: "Look! Look at that steamer. What's that? Siamese—isn't she? Just look at her!"

She seemed, indeed, to have been used as a running target for the secondary batteries of a cruiser. A hail of minor shells could not have given her upper works a more broken, torn, and devastated aspect: and she had about her the worn, weary air of ships coming from the far ends of the world—and indeed with truth, for in her short passage she had been very far; sighting, verily, even the coast of the Great Beyond, whence no ship ever returns to give up her crew to the dust of the earth. She 5 was incrusted and gray with salt to the trucks of her masts and to the top of her funnel; as though (as some facetious seaman said) "the crowd on board had fished her out somewhere from the bottom of the sea and brought her in here for salvage." And further, excited by the felicity of his own wit, he offered to give five pounds for her—"as she stands."

Before she had been quite an hour at rest, a meagre little man, with a red-tipped nose and a face cast in an angry mould, landed from a sampan on the quay of the Foreign Concession, and incontinently turned to shake his fist at her. 15

A tall individual, with legs much too thin for a rotund stomach, and with watery eyes, strolled up and remarked, "Just left her—eh? Quick work."

He wore a soiled suit of blue flannel with a pair of dirty cricketing shoes; a dingy gray moustache drooped from his lip, and daylight could be seen in two places between the rim and the crown of his hat.

"Hallo! what are you doing here?" asked the ex-second mate of the *Nan-Shan*, shaking hands hurriedly.

"Standing by for a job—chance worth taking—got a quiet 25 hint," explained the man with the broken hat, in jerky, apathetic wheezes.

The second shook his fist again at the *Nan-Shan*. "There's a fellow there that ain't fit to have the command of a scow," he declared, quivering with passion, while the other looked about listlessly.

"Is there?"

But he caught sight on the quay of a heavy seaman's chest, painted brown under a fringed sailcloth cover, and lashed with new manila line. He eyed it with awakened interest. 35

"I would talk and raise trouble if it wasn't for that damned

Siamese flag. Nobody to go to—or I would make it hot for him.
The fraud! Told his chief engineer—that's another fraud for
you—I had lost my nerve. The greatest lot of ignorant fools
that ever sailed the seas. No! You can't think. . . ."

5   "Got your money all right?" inquired his seedy acquaintance
suddenly.

"Yes. Paid me off on board," raged the second mate. " 'Get
your breakfast on shore,' says he."

"Mean skunk!" commented the tall man, vaguely, and
passed his tongue on his lips. "What about having a drink of
some sort?"

"He struck me," hissed the second mate.

"No! Struck! You don't say?" The man in blue began to bus-
tle about sympathetically. "Can't possibly talk here. I want to
15   know all about it. Struck—eh? Let's get a fellow to carry your
chest. I know a quiet place where they have some bottled
beer. . . ."

Mr. Jukes, who had been scanning the shore through a pair
of glasses, informed the chief engineer afterwards that "our late
second mate hasn't been long in finding a friend. A chap looking uncommonly like a bummer. I saw them walk away together from the quay."

The hammering and banging of the needful repairs did not
disturb Captain MacWhirr. The steward found in the letter he
25   wrote, in a tidy chart-room, passages of such absorbing interest
that twice he was nearly caught in the act. But Mrs. MacWhirr,
in the drawing-room of the forty-pound house, stifled a yawn—
perhaps out of self-respect—for she was alone.

She reclined in a plush-bottomed and gilt hammock-chair
near a tiled fireplace, with Japanese fans on the mantel and a
glow of coals in the grate. Lifting her hands, she glanced wearily here and there into the many pages. It was not her fault
they were so prosy, so completely uninteresting—from "My
darling wife" at the beginning, to "Your loving husband" at
35   the end. She couldn't be really expected to understand all

these ship affairs. She was glad, of course, to hear from him, but she had never asked herself why, precisely.

". . . They are called typhoons . . . The mate did not seem to like it . . . Not in books . . . Couldn't think of letting it go on. . . ."

The paper rustled sharply. ". . . A calm that lasted more than twenty minutes," she read perfunctorily; and the next words her thoughtless eyes caught, on the top of another page, were: "see you and the children again. . . ." She had a movement of impatience. He was always thinking of coming home. He had never had such a good salary before. What was the matter now?

It did not occur to her to turn back overleaf to look. She would have found it recorded there that between 4 and 6 A.M. on December 25th, Captain MacWhirr did actually think that his ship could not possibly live another hour in such a sea, and that he would never see his wife and children again. Nobody was to know this (his letters got mislaid so quickly)—nobody whatever but the steward, who had been greatly impressed by that disclosure. So much so, that he tried to give the cook some idea of the "narrow squeak we all had" by saying solemnly, "The old man himself had a dam' poor opinion of our chance."

"How do you know?" asked, contemptuously, the cook, an old soldier. "He hasn't told you, maybe?"

"Well, he did give me a hint to that effect," the steward brazened it out.

"Get along with you! He will be coming to tell *me* next," jeered the old cook, over his shoulder.

Mrs. MacWhirr glanced farther, on the alert. ". . . Do what's fair. . . . Miserable objects. . . . Only three, with a broken leg each, and one . . . Thought had better keep the matter quiet . . . hope to have done the fair thing. . . ."

She let fall her hands. No: there was nothing more about coming home. Must have been merely expressing a pious wish. Mrs. MacWhirr's mind was set at ease, and a black marble clock,

5

15

25

35

priced by the local jeweller at £3 18s. 6d., had a discreet stealthy tick.

The door flew open, and a girl in the long-legged, short-frocked period of existence, flung into the room. A lot of colourless, rather lanky hair was scattered over her shoulders. Seeing her mother, she stood still, and directed her pale prying eyes upon the letter.

"From father," murmured Mrs. MacWhirr. "What have you done with your ribbon?"

The girl put her hands up to her head and pouted.

"He's well," continued Mrs. MacWhirr, languidly. "At least I think so. He never says." She had a little laugh. The girl's face expressed a wandering indifference, and Mrs. MacWhirr surveyed her with fond pride.

"Go and get your hat," she said after a while. "I am going out to do some shopping. There is a sale at Linom's."

"Oh, how jolly!" uttered the child, impressively, in unexpectedly grave vibrating tones, and bounded out of the room.

It was a fine afternoon, with a gray sky and dry sidewalks. Outside the draper's Mrs. MacWhirr smiled upon a woman in a black mantle of generous proportions armoured in jet and crowned with flowers blooming falsely above a bilious matronly countenance. They broke into a swift little babble of greetings and exclamations both together, very hurried, as if the street were ready to yawn open and swallow all that pleasure before it could be expressed.

Behind them the high glass doors were kept on the swing. People couldn't pass, men stood aside waiting patiently, and Lydia was absorbed in poking the end of her parasol between the stone flags. Mrs. MacWhirr talked rapidly.

"Thank you very much. He's not coming home yet. Of course it's very sad to have him away, but it's such a comfort to know he keeps so well." Mrs. MacWhirr drew breath. "The climate there agrees with him," she added, beamingly, as if poor MacWhirr had been away touring in China for the sake of his health.

Neither was the chief engineer coming home yet. Mr. Rout knew too well the value of a good billet.

"Solomon says wonders will never cease," cried Mrs. Rout joyously at the old lady in her armchair by the fire. Mr. Rout's mother moved slightly, her withered hands lying in black half- 5 mittens on her lap.

The eyes of the engineer's wife fairly danced on the paper. "That captain of the ship he is in—a rather simple man, you remember, mother?—has done something rather clever, Solomon says."

"Yes, my dear," said the old woman meekly, sitting with bowed silvery head, and that air of inward stillness characteristic of very old people who seem lost in watching the last flickers of life. "I think I remember."

Solomon Rout, Old Sol, Father Sol, the Chief, "Rout, good 15 man"—Mr. Rout, the condescending and paternal friend of youth, had been the baby of her many children—all dead by this time. And she remembered him best as a boy of ten—long before he went away to serve his apprenticeship in some great engineering works in the North. She had seen so little of him since, she had gone through so many years, that she had now to retrace her steps very far back to recognize him plainly in the mist of time. Sometimes it seemed that her daughter-in-law was talking of some strange man.

Mrs. Rout junior was disappointed. "H'm. H'm." She turned 25 the page. "How provoking! He doesn't say what it is. Says I couldn't understand how much there was in it. Fancy! What could it be so very clever? What a wretched man not to tell us!"

She read on without further remark soberly, and at last sat looking into the fire. The chief wrote just a word or two of the typhoon; but something had moved him to express an increased longing for the companionship of the jolly woman. "If it hadn't been that mother must be looked after, I would send you your passage-money to-day. You could set up a small house out here. I would have a chance to see you sometimes then. We 35 are not growing younger. . . ."

"He's well, mother," sighed Mrs. Rout, rousing herself.

"He always was a strong healthy boy," said the old woman, placidly.

But Mr. Jukes' account was really animated and very full. His friend in the Western Ocean trade imparted it freely to the other officers of his liner. "A chap I know writes to me about an extraordinary affair that happened on board his ship in that typhoon—you know—that we read of in the papers two months ago. It's the funniest thing! Just see for yourself what he says. I'll show you his letter."

There were phrases in it calculated to give the impression of lighthearted, indomitable resolution. Jukes had written them in good faith, for he felt thus when he wrote. He described w'th lurid effect the scenes in the 'tween-deck. ". . . It struck me ir a flash that those confounded Chinamen couldn't tell w weren't a desperate kind of robbers. 'Tisn't good to part tne Chinaman from his money if he is the stronger party. We need have been desperate indeed to go thieving in such weather, but what could these beggars know of us? So, without thinking of it twice, I got the hands away in a jiffy. Our work was done— that the old man had set his heart on. We cleared out without staying to inquire how they felt. I am convinced that if they had not been so unmercifully shaken, and afraid—each individual one of them—to stand up, we would have been torn to pieces. Oh! It was pretty complete, I can tell you; and you may run to and fro across the Pond to the end of time before you find yourself with such a job on your hands."

After this he alluded professionally to the damage done to the ship, and went on thus:

"It was when the weather quieted down that the situation became confoundedly delicate. It wasn't made any better by us having been lately transferred to the Siamese flag; though the skipper can't see that it makes any difference—'as long as we are on board'—he says. There are feelings that this man simply hasn't got—and there's an end of it. You might just as well try to make a bedpost understand. But apart from this it is an in-

fernally lonely state for a ship to be going about the China seas
with no proper consuls, not even a gunboat of her own anywhere, nor a body to go to in case of some trouble.

"My notion was to keep these Johnnies under hatches for
another fifteen hours or so; as we weren't much farther than 5
that from Fu-chau. We would find there, most likely, some sort
of a man-of-war, and once under her guns we were safe enough;
for surely any skipper of a man-of-war—English, French or
Dutch—would see white men through as far as row on board
goes. We could get rid of them and their money afterwards by
delivering them to their Mandarin or Taotai, or whatever they
call these chaps in goggles you see being carried about in
sedan-chairs through their stinking streets.

"The old man wouldn't see it somehow. He wanted to keep
the matter quiet. He got that notion into his head, and a 15
steam windlass couldn't drag it out of him. He wanted as little
fuss made as possible, for the sake of the ship's name and for
the sake of the owners—'for the sake of all concerned,' says he,
looking at me very hard. It made me angry hot. Of course you
couldn't keep a thing like that quiet; but the chests had been
secured in the usual manner and were safe enough for any
earthly gale, while this had been an altogether fiendish business
I couldn't give you even an idea of.

"Meantime, I could hardly keep on my feet. None of us had
a spell of any sort for nearly thirty hours, and there the old 25
man sat rubbing his chin, rubbing the top of his head, and so
bothered he didn't even think of pulling his long boots off.

" 'I hope, sir,' says I, 'you won't be letting them out on deck
before we make ready for them in some shape or other.' Not,
mind you, that I felt very sanguine about controlling these
beggars if they meant to take charge. A trouble with a cargo of
Chinamen is no child's play. I was dam' tired, too. 'I wish,'
said I, 'you would let us throw the whole lot of these dollars
down to them and leave them to fight it out amongst themselves, while we get a rest.' 35

" 'Now you talk wild, Jukes,' says he, looking up in his slow way that makes you ache all over, somehow. 'We must plan out something that would be fair to all parties.'

"I had no end of work on hand, as you may imagine, so I set the hands going, and then I thought I would turn in a bit. I hadn't been asleep in my bunk ten minutes when in rushes the steward and begins to pull at my leg.

" 'For God's sake, Mr. Jukes, come out! Come on deck quick, sir. Oh, do come out!'

"The fellow scared all the sense out of me. I didn't know what had happened: another hurricane—or what. Could hear no wind.

" 'The Captain's letting them out. Oh, he is letting them out! Jump on deck, sir, and save us. The chief engineer has just run below for his revolver.'

"That's what I understood the fool to say. However, Father Rout swears he went in there only to get a clean pocket-handkerchief. Anyhow, I made one jump into my trousers and flew on deck aft. There was certainly a good deal of noise going on forward of the bridge. Four of the hands with the boss'n were at work abaft. I passed up to them some of the rifles all the ships on the China coast carry in the cabin, and led them on the bridge. On the way I ran against Old Sol, looking startled and sucking at an unlighted cigar.

" 'Come along,' I shouted to him.

"We charged, the seven of us, up to the chart-room. All was over. There stood the old man with his sea-boots still drawn up to the hips and in shirt-sleeves—got warm thinking it out, I suppose. Bun Hin's dandy clerk at his elbow, as dirty as a sweep, was still green in the face. I could see directly I was in for something.

" 'What the devil are these monkey tricks, Mr. Jukes?' asks the old man, as angry as ever he could be. I tell you frankly it made me lose my tongue. 'For God's sake, Mr. Jukes,' says he, 'do take away these rifles from the men. Somebody's sure to get hurt before long if you don't. Damme, if this ship isn't worse than Bedlam! Look sharp now. I want you up here to help me and Bun Hin's Chinaman to count that money. You wouldn't mind lending a hand, too, Mr. Rout, now you are here. The more of us the better.'

"He had settled it all in his mind while I was having a snooze. Had we been an English ship, or only going to land our cargo of coolies in an English port, like Hong-Kong, for instance, there would have been no end of inquiries and bother, claims for damages and so on. But these Chinamen know their officials better than we do.

"The hatches had been taken off already, and they were all on deck after a night and a day down below. It made you feel queer to see so many gaunt, wild faces together. The beggars stared about at the sky, at the sea, at the ship, as though they had expected the whole thing to have been blown to pieces. And no wonder! They had had a doing that would have shaken the soul out of a white man. But then they say a Chinaman has no soul. He has, though, something about him that is deuced tough. There was a fellow (amongst others of the badly hurt) who had had his eye all but knocked out. It stood out of his head the size of half a hen's egg. This would have laid out a white man on his back for a month: and yet there was that chap elbowing here and there in the crowd and talking to the others as if nothing had been the matter. They made a great hubbub amongst themselves, and whenever the old man showed his bald head on the foreside of the bridge, they would all leave off jawing and look at him from below.

"It seems that after he had done his thinking he made that Bun Hin's fellow go down and explain to them the only way they could get their money back. He told me afterwards that, all the coolies having worked in the same place and for the same length of time, he reckoned he would be doing the fair thing by them as near as possible if he shared all the cash we had picked up equally among the lot. You couldn't tell one man's dollars from another's, he said, and if you asked each man how much money he brought on board he was afraid they would lie, and he would find himself a long way short. I think he was right there. As to giving up the money to any Chinese official he could scare up in Fu-chau, he said he might just as well put the lot in his own pocket at once for all the good it would be to them. I suppose they thought so, too.

5   "We finished the distribution before dark. It was rather a sight: the sea running high, the ship a wreck to look at, these Chinamen staggering up on the bridge one by one for their share, and the old man still booted, and in his shirt-sleeves, busy paying out at the chart-room door, perspiring like anything, and now and then coming down sharp on myself or Father Rout about one thing or another not quite to his mind. He took the share of those who were disabled himself to them on the No. 2 hatch. There were three dollars left over, and these went to the three most damaged coolies, one to each. We

15   turned-to afterwards, and shovelled out on deck heaps of wet rags, all sorts of fragments of things without shape, and that you couldn't give a name to, and let them settle the ownership themselves.

"This certainly is coming as near as can be to keeping the thing quiet for the benefit of all concerned. What's your opinion, you pampered mailboat swell? The old chief says that this was plainly the only thing that could be done. The skipper remarked to me the other day, 'There are things you find nothing about in books.' I think that he got out of it very well for such

25   a stupid man."

THE SECRET SHARER

One

On my right hand there were lines of fishing stakes resembling a mysterious system of half-submerged bamboo fences, incomprehensible in its division of the domain of tropical fishes, and crazy of aspect as if abandoned forever by some nomad tribe of fishermen now gone to the other end of the ocean; for there was no sign of human habitation as far as the eye could reach. To the left a group of barren islets, suggesting ruins of stone walls, towers, and blockhouses, had its foundations set in a blue sea that itself looked solid, so still and stable did it lie below my feet; even the track of light from the westering sun shone smoothly, without that animated glitter which tells of an imperceptible ripple. And when I turned my head to take a parting glance at the tug which had just left us anchored outside the bar, I saw the straight line of the flat shore joined to the stable sea, edge to edge, with a perfect and unmarked closeness, in one leveled floor half brown, half blue under the enormous dome of the sky. Corresponding in their insignificance to the islets of the sea, two small clumps of trees, one on each side of the only fault in the impeccable joint, marked the mouth of the river Meinam we had just left on the first preparatory stage of our homeward journey; and, far back on the inland level, a larger and loftier mass, the grove surrounding the

221

great Paknam pagoda, was the only thing on which the eye could rest from the vain task of exploring the monotonous sweep of the horizon. Here and there gleams as of a few scattered pieces of silver marked the windings of the great river; and on the nearest of them, just within the bar, the tug steaming right into the land became lost to my sight, hull and funnel and masts, as though the impassive earth had swallowed her up without an effort, without a tremor. My eye followed the light cloud of her smoke, now here, now there, above the plain, according to the devious curves of the stream, but always fainter and farther away, till I lost it at last behind the miter-shaped hill of the great pagoda. And then I was left alone with my ship, anchored at the head of the Gulf of Siam.

She floated at the starting point of a long journey, very still in an immense stillness, the shadows of her spars flung far to the eastward by the setting sun. At that moment I was alone on her decks. There was not a sound in her—and around us nothing moved, nothing lived, not a canoe on the water, not a bird in the air, not a cloud in the sky. In this breathless pause at the threshold of a long passage we seemed to be measuring our fitness for a long and arduous enterprise, the appointed task of both our existences to be carried out, far from all human eyes, with only sky and sea for spectators and for judges.

There must have been some glare in the air to interfere with one's sight, because it was only just before the sun left us that my roaming eyes made out beyond the highest ridges of the principal islet of the group something which did away with the solemnity of perfect solitude. The tide of darkness flowed on swiftly; and with tropical suddenness a swarm of stars came out above the shadowy earth, while I lingered yet, my hand resting lightly on my ship's rail as if on the shoulder of a trusted friend. But, with all that multitude of celestial bodies staring down at one, the comfort of quiet communion with her was gone for good. And there were also disturbing sounds by this time— voices, footsteps forward; the steward flitted along the main-deck, a busily ministering spirit; a hand bell tinkled urgently under the poop deck. . . .

I found my two officers waiting for me near the supper table, in the lighted cuddy. We sat down at once, and as I helped the chief mate, I said:

"Are you aware that there is a ship anchored inside the islands? I saw her mastheads above the ridge as the sun went 5 down."

He raised sharply his simple face, overcharged by a terrible growth of whisker, and emitted his usual ejaculations: "Bless my soul, sir! You don't say so!"

My second mate was a round-cheeked, silent young man, grave beyond his years, I thought; but as our eyes happened to meet I detected a slight quiver on his lips. I looked down at once. It was not my part to encourage sneering on board my ship. It must be said, too, that I knew very little of my officers. In consequence of certain events of no particular significance, 15 except to myself, I had been appointed to the command only a fortnight before. Neither did I know much of the hands forward. All these people had been together for eighteen months or so, and my position was that of the only stranger on board. I mention this because it has some bearing on what is to follow. But what I felt most was my being a stranger to the ship; and if all the truth must be told, I was somewhat of a stranger to myself. The youngest man on board (barring the second mate), and untried as yet by a position of the fullest responsibility, I was willing to take the adequacy of the others for granted. They 25 had simply to be equal to their tasks; but I wondered how far I should turn out faithful to that ideal conception of one's own personality every man sets up for himself secretly.

Meantime the chief mate, with an almost visible effect of collaboration on the part of his round eyes and frightful whiskers, was trying to evolve a theory of the anchored ship. His dominant trait was to take all things into earnest consideration. He was of a painstaking turn of mind. As he used to say, he "liked to account to himself" for practically everything that came in his way, down to a miserable scorpion he had found in 35 his cabin a week before. The why and the wherefore of that

scorpion—how it got on board and came to select his room rather than the pantry (which was a dark place and more what a scorpion would be partial to), and how on earth it managed to drown itself in the inkwell of his writing desk—had exercised
5   him infinitely. The ship within the islands was much more easily accounted for; and just as we were about to rise from table he made his pronouncement. She was, he doubted not, a ship from home lately arrived. Probably she drew too much water to cross the bar except at the top of spring tides. Therefore she went into that natural harbor to wait for a few days in preference to remaining in an open roadstead.

"That's so," confirmed the second mate, suddenly, in his slightly hoarse voice. "She draws over twenty feet. She's the Liverpool ship *Sephora* with a cargo of coal. Hundred and
15   twenty-three days from Cardiff."

We looked at him in surprise.

"The tugboat skipper told me when he came on board for your letters, sir," explained the young man. "He expects to take her up the river the day after tomorrow."

After thus overwhelming us with the extent of his information he slipped out of the cabin. The mate observed regretfully that he "could not account for that young fellow's whims." What prevented him telling us all about it at once, he wanted to know.

25   I detained him as he was making a move. For the last two days the crew had had plenty of hard work, and the night before they had very little sleep. I felt painfully that I—a stranger—was doing something unusual when I directed him to let all hands turn in without setting an anchor watch. I proposed to keep on deck myself till one o'clock or thereabouts. I would get the second mate to relieve me at that hour.

"He will turn out the cook and the steward at four," I concluded, "and then give you a call. Of course at the slightest sign of any sort of wind we'll have the hands up and make a
35   start at once."

He concealed his astonishment. "Very well, sir." Outside the cuddy he put his head in the second mate's door to inform him of my unheard-of caprice to take a five hours' anchor watch on myself. I heard the other raise his voice incredulously—"What? The Captain himself?" Then a few more murmurs, a door closed, then another. A few moments later I went on deck.   5

My strangeness, which had made me sleepless, had prompted that unconventional arrangement, as if I had expected in those solitary hours of the night to get on terms with the ship of which I knew nothing, manned by men of whom I knew very little more. Fast alongside a wharf, littered like any ship in port with a tangle of unrelated things, invaded by unrelated shore people, I had hardly seen her yet properly. Now, as she lay cleared for sea, the stretch of her main-deck seemed to me very fine under the stars. Very fine, very roomy for her size, and very inviting. I descended the poop and paced the waist, my mind   15 picturing to myself the coming passage through the Malay Archipelago, down the Indian Ocean, and up the Atlantic. All its phases were familiar enough to me, every characteristic, all the alternatives which were likely to face me on the high seas— everything! . . . except the novel responsibility of command. But I took heart from the reasonable thought that the ship was like other ships, the men like other men, and that the sea was not likely to keep any special surprises expressly for my discomfiture.

Arrived at that comforting conclusion, I bethought myself of   25 a cigar and went below to get it. All was still down there. Everybody at the after end of the ship was sleeping profoundly. I came out again on the quarterdeck, agreeably at ease in my sleeping suit on that warm breathless night, barefooted, a glowing cigar in my teeth, and, going forward, I was met by the profound silence of the fore end of the ship. Only as I passed the door of the forecastle I heard a deep, quiet, trustful sigh of some sleeper inside. And suddenly I rejoiced in the great security of the sea as compared with the unrest of the land, in my choice of that untempted life presenting no disquieting prob-   35 lems, invested with an elementary moral beauty by the absolute straightforwardness of its appeal and by the singleness of its purpose.

The riding light in the forerigging burned with a clear, untroubled, as if symbolic, flame, confident and bright in the mysterious shades of the night. Passing on my way aft along the other side of the ship, I observed that the rope side ladder, put over, no doubt, for the master of the tug when he came to fetch away our letters, had not been hauled in as it should have been. I became annoyed at this, for exactitude in some small matters is the very soul of discipline. Then I reflected that I had myself peremptorily dismissed my officers from duty, and by my own act had prevented the anchor watch being formally set and things properly attended to. I asked myself whether it was wise ever to interfere with the established routine of duties even from the kindest of motives. My action might have made me appear eccentric. Goodness only knew how that absurdly whiskered mate would "account" for my conduct, and what the whole ship thought of that informality of their new captain. I was vexed with myself.

Not from compunction certainly, but, as it were mechanically, I proceeded to get the ladder in myself. Now a side ladder of that sort is a light affair and comes in easily, yet my vigorous tug, which should have brought it flying on board, merely recoiled upon my body in a totally unexpected jerk. What the devil! . . . I was so astounded by the immovableness of that ladder that I remained stockstill, trying to account for it to myself like that imbecile mate of mine. In the end, of course, I put my head over the rail.

The side of the ship made an opaque belt of shadow on the darkling glassy shimmer of the sea. But I saw at once something elongated and pale floating very close to the ladder. Before I could form a guess a faint flash of phosphorescent light, which seemed to issue suddenly from the naked body of a man, flickered in the sleeping water with the elusive, silent play of summer lightning in a night sky. With a gasp I saw revealed to my stare a pair of feet, the long legs, a broad livid back im-

mersed right up to the neck in a greenish cadaverous glow. One
hand, awash, clutched the bottom rung of the ladder. He was
complete but for the head. A headless corpse! The cigar
dropped out of my gaping mouth with a tiny plop and a short
hiss quite audible in the absolute stillness of all things under   5
heaven. At that I suppose he raised up his face, a dimly pale
oval in the shadow of the ship's side. But even then I could
only barely make out down there the shape of his black-haired
head. However, it was enough for the horrid, frost-bound sensation which had gripped me about the chest to pass off. The
moment of vain exclamations was past, too. I only climbed
on the spare spar and leaned over the rail as far as I could, to
bring my eyes nearer to that mystery floating alongside.

As he hung by the ladder, like a resting swimmer, the sea
lightning played about his limbs at every stir; and he appeared   15
in it ghastly, silvery, fishlike. He remained as mute as a fish, too.
He made no motion to get out of the water, either. It was inconceivable that he should not attempt to come on board, and
strangely troubling to suspect that perhaps he did not want to.
And my first words were prompted by just that troubled incerti-
tude.

"What's the matter?" I asked in my ordinary tone, speaking
down to the face upturned exactly under mine.

"Cramp," it answered, no louder. Then slightly anxious, "I
say, no need to call anyone."   25

"I was not going to," I said.

"Are you alone on deck?"

"Yes."

I had somehow the impression that he was on the point of
letting go the ladder to swim away beyond my ken—mysterious
as he came. But, for the moment, this being appearing as if he
had risen from the bottom of the sea (it was certainly the nearest land to the ship) wanted only to know the time. I told him.
And he, down there, tentatively:

"I suppose your captain's turned in?"   35

"I am sure he isn't," I said.

He seemed to struggle with himself, for I heard something like the low, bitter murmur of doubt. "What's the good?" His next words came out with a hesitating effort.

"Look here, my man. Could you call him out quietly?"

5   I thought the time had come to declare myself.

"I am the captain."

1 heard a "By Jove!" whispered at the level of the water. The phosphorescence flashed in the swirl of the water all about his limbs, his other hand seized the ladder.

"My name's Leggatt."

The voice was calm and resolute. A good voice. The self-possession of that man had somehow induced a corresponding state in myself. It was very quietly that I remarked:

"You must be a good swimmer."

15   "Yes. I've been in the water practically since nine o'clock. The question for me now is whether I am to let go this ladder and go on swimming till I sink from exhaustion, or—to come on board here."

I felt this was no mere formula of desperate speech, but a real alternative in the view of a strong soul. I should have gathered from this that he was young; indeed, it is only the young who are ever confronted by such clear issues. But at the time it was pure intuition on my part. A mysterious communication was established already between us two—in the face of that si-

25   lent, darkened tropical sea. I was young, too; young enough to make no comment. The man in the water began suddenly to climb up the ladder, and I hastened away from the rail to fetch some clothes.

Before entering the cabin I stood still, listening in the lobby at the foot of the stairs. A faint snore came through the closed door of the chief mate's room. The second mate's door was on the hook, but the darkness in there was absolutely soundless. He, too, was young and could sleep like a stone. Remained the steward, but he was not likely to wake up before he was called.

35   I got a sleeping suit out of my room and, coming back on deck, saw the naked man from the sea sitting on the main hatch,

glimmering white in the darkness, his elbows on his knees and his head in his hands. In a moment he had concealed his damp body in a sleeping suit of the same gray-stripe pattern as the one I was wearing and followed me like my double on the poop. Together we moved right aft, barefooted, silent. 5

"What is it?" I asked in a deadened voice, taking the lighted lamp out of the binnacle, and raising it to his face.

"An ugly business."

He had rather regular features; a good mouth; light eyes under somewhat heavy, dark eyebrows; a smooth, square forehead; no growth on his cheeks; a small, brown mustache, and a well-shaped, round chin. His expression was concentrated, meditative, under the inspecting light of the lamp I held up to his face; such as a man thinking hard in solitude might wear. My sleeping suit was just right for his size. A well-knit young fellow 15 of twenty-five at most. He caught his lower lip with the edge of white, even teeth.

"Yes," I said, replacing the lamp in the binnacle. The warm, heavy tropical night closed upon his head again.

"There's a ship over there," he murmured.

"Yes, I know. The *Sephora*. Did you know of us?"

"Hadn't the slightest idea. I am the mate of her——" He paused and corrected himself. "I should say I *was*."

"Aha! Something wrong?"

"Yes. Very wrong indeed. I've killed a man." 25

"What do you mean? Just now?"

"No, on the passage. Weeks ago. Thirty-nine south. When I say a man——"

"Fit of temper," I suggested, confidently.

The shadowy, dark head, like mine, seemed to nod imperceptibly above the ghostly gray of my sleeping suit. It was, in the night, as though I had been faced by my own reflection in the depths of a somber and immense mirror.

"A pretty thing to have to own up to for a Conway boy," murmured my double, distinctly. 35

"You're a Conway boy?"

"I am," he said, as if startled. Then, slowly . . . "Perhaps you too———"

It was so; but being a couple of years older I had left before he joined. After a quick interchange of dates a silence fell; and I thought suddenly of my absurd mate with his terrific whiskers and the "Bless my soul—you don't say so" type of intellect. My double gave me an inkling of his thoughts by saying: "My father's a parson in Norfolk. Do you see me before a judge and jury on that charge? For myself I can't see the necessity. There are fellows that an angel from heaven—— And I am not that. He was one of those creatures that are just simmering all the time with a silly sort of wickedness. Miserable devils that have no business to live at all. He wouldn't do his duty and wouldn't let anybody else do theirs. But what's the good of talking! You know well enough the sort of ill-conditioned snarling cur———"

He appealed to me as if our experiences had been as identical as our clothes. And I knew well enough the pestiferous danger of such a character where there are no means of legal repression. And I knew well enough also that my double there was no homicidal ruffian. I did not think of asking him for details, and he told me the story roughly in brusque, disconnected sentences. I needed no more. I saw it all going on as though I were myself inside that other sleeping suit.

"It happened while we were setting a reefed foresail, at dusk. Reefed foresail! You understand the sort of weather. The only sail we had left to keep the ship running; so you may guess what it had been like for days. Anxious sort of job, that. He gave me some of his cursed insolence at the sheet. I tell you I was overdone with this terrific weather that seemed to have no end to it. Terrific, I tell you—and a deep ship. I believe the fellow himself was half crazed with funk. It was no time for gentlemanly reproof, so I turned round and felled him like an ox. He up and at me. We closed just as an awful sea made for the ship. All hands saw it coming and took to the rigging, but I had him by the throat, and went on shaking him like a rat, the men above us yelling, 'Look out! look out!' Then a crash as if

the sky had fallen on my head. They say that for over ten minutes hardly anything was to be seen of the ship—just the three
masts and a bit of the forecastle head and of the poop all
awash driving along in a smother of foam. It was a miracle that
they found us, jammed together behind the forebitts. It's
clear that I meant business, because I was holding him by the
throat still when they picked us up. He was black in the face.
It was too much for them. It seems they rushed us aft together,
gripped as we were, screaming 'Murder!' like a lot of lunatics,
and broke into the cuddy. And the ship running for her life,
touch and go all the time, any minute her last in a sea fit to
turn your hair gray only a-looking at it. I understand that the
skipper, too, started raving like the rest of them. The man had
been deprived of sleep for more than a week, and to have this
sprung on him at the height of a furious gale nearly drove him
out of his mind. I wonder they didn't fling me overboard after
getting the carcass of their precious shipmate out of my fingers. They had rather a job to separate us, I've been told. A sufficiently fierce story to make an old judge and a respectable jury
sit up a bit. The first thing I heard when I came to myself was
the maddening howling of that endless gale, and on that the
voice of the old man. He was hanging on to my bunk, staring
into my face out of his sou'wester.

" 'Mr. Leggatt, you have killed a man. You can act no longer
as chief mate of this ship.' "

His care to subdue his voice made it sound monotonous.
He rested a hand on the end of the skylight to steady himself
with, and all that time did not stir a limb, so far as I could see.
"Nice little tale for a quiet tea party," he concluded in the
same tone.

One of my hands, too, rested on the end of the skylight;
neither did I stir a limb, so far as I knew. We stood less than a
foot from each other. It occurred to me that if old "Bless my
soul—you don't say so" were to put his head up the companion
and catch sight of us, he would think he was seeing double, or
imagine himself come upon a scene of weird witchcraft; the

strange captain having a quiet confabulation by the wheel with
his own gray ghost. I became very much concerned to prevent
anything of the sort. I heard the other's soothing undertone.

"My father's a parson in Norfolk," it said. Evidently he had
5   forgotten he had told me this important fact before. Truly a
nice little tale.

"You had better slip down into my stateroom now," I said,
moving off stealthily. My double followed my movements; our
bare feet made no sound; I let him in, closed the door with
care, and, after giving a call to the second mate, returned on
deck for my relief.

"Not much sign of any wind yet," I remarked when he approached.

"No, sir. Not much," he assented, sleepily, in his hoarse voice,
15   with just enough deference, no more, and barely suppressing a
yawn.

"Well, that's all you have to look out for. You have got your
orders."

"Yes, sir."

I paced a turn or two on the poop and saw him take up his
position face forward with his elbow in the ratlines of the miz-
zen rigging before I went below. The mate's faint snoring was
still going on peacefully. The cuddy lamp was burning over the
table on which stood a vase with flowers, a polite attention
25   from the ship's provision merchant—the last flowers we should
see for the next three months at the very least. Two bunches of
bananas hung from the beam symmetrically, one on each side
of the rudder casing. Everything was as before in the ship—
except that two of her captain's sleeping suits were simultaneously in use, one motionless in the cuddy, the other keeping
very still in the captain's stateroom.

It must be explained here that my cabin had the form of the
capital letter L, the door being within the angle and opening
into the short part of the letter. A couch was to the left, the bed
35   place to the right; my writing desk and the chronometers' table
faced the door. But anyone opening it, unless he stepped right

inside, had no view of what I call the long (or vertical) part of the letter. It contained some lockers surmounted by a bookcase; and a few clothes, a thick jacket or two, caps, oilskin coat, and such like, hung on hooks. There was at the bottom of that part a door opening into my bathroom, which could be entered also directly from the saloon. But that way was never used.

The mysterious arrival had discovered the advantage of this particular shape. Entering my room, lighted strongly by a big bulkhead lamp swung on gimbals above my writing desk, I did not see him anywhere till he stepped out quietly from behind the coats hung in the recessed part.

"I heard somebody moving about, and went in there at once," he whispered.

I, too, spoke under my breath.

"Nobody is likely to come in here without knocking and getting permission."

He nodded. His face was thin and the sunburn faded, as though he had been ill. And no wonder. He had been, I heard presently, kept under arrest in his cabin for nearly seven weeks. But there was nothing sickly in his eyes or in his expression. He was not a bit like me, really; yet, as we stood leaning over my bed place, whispering side by side, with our dark heads together and our backs to the door, anybody bold enough to open it stealthily would have been treated to the uncanny sight of a double captain busy talking in whispers with his other self.

"But all this doesn't tell me how you came to hang on to our side ladder," I inquired, in the hardly audible murmurs we used, after he had told me something more of the proceedings on board the *Sephora* once the bad weather was over.

"When we sighted Java Head I had had time to think all those matters out several times over. I had six weeks of doing nothing else, and with only an hour or so every evening for a tramp on the quarter-deck."

He whispered, his arms folded on the side of my bed place, staring through the open port. And I could imagine perfectly the manner of this thinking out—a stubborn if not a steadfast operation; something of which I should have been perfectly incapable.

5   "I reckoned it would be dark before we closed with the land," he continued, so low that I had to strain my hearing near as we were to each other, shoulder touching shoulder almost. "So I asked to speak to the old man. He always seemed very sick when he came to see me—as if he could not look me in the face. You know, that foresail saved the ship. She was too deep to have run long under bare poles. And it was I that managed to set it for him. Anyway, he came. When I had him in my cabin—he stood by the door looking at me as if I had the halter round my neck already—I asked him right away to leave my cabin door unlocked at night while the ship was going through
15   Sunda Straits. There would be the Java coast within two or three miles, off Angier Point. I wanted nothing more. I've had a prize for swimming my second year in the Conway."

"I can believe it," I breathed out.

"God only knows why they locked me in every night. To see some of their faces you'd have thought they were afraid I'd go about at night strangling people. Am I a murdering brute? Do I look it? By Jove! If I had been he wouldn't have trusted himself like that into my room. You'll say I might have chucked him aside and bolted out, there and then—it was dark already.
25   Well, no. And for the same reason I wouldn't think of trying to smash the door. There would have been a rush to stop me at the noise, and I did not mean to get into a confounded scrimmage. Somebody else might have got killed—for I would not have broken out only to get chucked back, and I did not want any more of that work. He refused, looking more sick than ever. He was afraid of the men, and also of that old second mate of his who had been sailing with him for years—a gray-headed old humbug; and his steward, too, had been with him devil knows how long—seventeen years or more—a dog-
35   matic sort of loafer who hated me like poison, just because I was the chief mate. No chief mate ever made more than one voyage in the *Sephora*, you know. Those two old chaps ran the

ship. Devil only knows what the skipper wasn't afraid of (all his nerve went to pieces altogether in that hellish spell of bad weather we had)—of what the law would do to him—of his wife, perhaps. Oh, yes! she's on board. Though I don't think she would have meddled. She would have been only too glad to have me out of the ship in any way. The 'brand of Cain' business, don't you see. That's all right. I was ready enough to go off wandering on the face of the earth—and that was price enough to pay for an Abel of that sort. Anyhow, he wouldn't listen to me. 'This thing must take its course. I represent the law here.' He was shaking like a leaf. 'So you won't?' 'No!' 'Then I hope you will be able to sleep on that,' I said, and turned my back on him. 'I wonder that *you* can,' cries he, and locks the door.

"Well after that, I couldn't. Not very well. That was three weeks ago. We have had a slow passage through the Java Sea; drifted about Carimata for ten days. When we anchored here they thought, I suppose, it was all right. The nearest land (and that's five miles) is the ship's destination; the consul would soon set about catching me; and there would have been no object in bolting to these islets there. I don't suppose there's a drop of water on them. I don't know how it was, but tonight that steward, after bringing me my supper, went out to let me eat it, and left the door unlocked. And I ate it—all there was, too. After I had finished I strolled out on the quarterdeck. I don't know that I meant to do anything. A breath of fresh air was all I wanted, I believe. Then a sudden temptation came over me. I kicked off my slippers and was in the water before I had made up my mind fairly. Somebody heard the splash and they raised an awful hullabaloo. 'He's gone! Lower the boats! He's committed suicide! No, he's swimming.' Certainly I was swimming. It's not so easy for a swimmer like me to commit suicide by drowning. I landed on the nearest islet before the boat left the ship's side. I heard them pulling about in the dark, hailing, and so on, but after a bit they gave up. Everything quieted down and the anchorage became as still as death. I sat down on a stone and began to think. I felt certain they would start searching for me at daylight. There was no place to hide on those stony things—and if there had been, what would have been the good? But now I was clear of that ship, I was not going back. So after a while I took off all my clothes, tied them up in a bundle with a stone inside, and dropped them in the deep water on the outer side of that islet. That was suicide enough for me. Let them think what they liked, but I didn't mean to drown myself. I meant to swim till I sank—but that's not the same thing. I struck out for another of these little islands, and it was from that one that I first saw your riding light. Something to swim for. I went on easily, and on the way I came upon a flat rock a foot or two above water. In the daytime, I dare say, you might make it out with a glass from your poop. I scrambled up on it and rested myself for a bit. Then I made another start. That last spell must have been over a mile."

His whisper was getting fainter and fainter, and all the time he stared straight out through the porthole, in which there was not even a star to be seen. I had not interrupted him. There was something that made comment impossible in his narrative, or perhaps in himself; a sort of feeling, a quality, which I can't find a name for. And when he ceased, all I found was a futile whisper: "So you swam for our light?"

"Yes—straight for it. It was something to swim for. I couldn't see any stars low down because the coast was in the way, and I couldn't see the land, either. The water was like glass. One might have been swimming in a confounded thousand-feet-deep cistern with no place for scrambling out anywhere; but what I didn't like was the notion of swimming round and round like a crazed bullock before I gave out; and as I didn't mean to go back . . . No. Do you see me being hauled back, stark naked, off one of these little islands by the scruff of the neck and fighting like a wild beast? Somebody would have got killed for certain, and I did not want any of that. So I went on. Then your ladder——"

"Why didn't you hail the ship?" I asked, a little louder.

He touched my shoulder lightly. Lazy footsteps came right over our heads and stopped. The second mate had crossed from the other side of the poop and might have been hanging over the rail for all we knew.

"He couldn't hear us talking—could he?" My double   5
breathed into my very ear, anxiously.

His anxiety was an answer, a sufficient answer, to the question I had put to him. An answer containing all the difficulty of that situation. I closed the porthole quietly, to make sure. A louder word might have been overheard.

"Who's that?" he whispered then.

"My second mate. But I don't know much more of the fellow than you do."

And I told him a little about myself. I had been appointed to take charge while I least expected anything of the sort,   15
not quite a fortnight ago. I didn't know either the ship or the people. Hadn't had the time in port to look about me or size anybody up. And as to the crew, all they knew was that I was appointed to take the ship home. For the rest, I was almost as much of a stranger on board as himself, I said. And at the moment I felt it most acutely. I felt that it would take very little to make me a suspect person in the eyes of the ship's company.

He had turned about meantime; and we, the two strangers in the ship, faced each other in identical attitudes.   25

"Your ladder——" he murmured, after a silence. "Who'd have thought of finding a ladder hanging over at night in a ship anchored out here! I felt just then a very unpleasant faintness. After the life I've been leading for nine weeks, anybody would have got out of condition. I wasn't capable of swimming round as far as your rudder chains. And, lo and behold! there was a ladder to get hold of. After I gripped it I said to myself, 'What's the good?' When I saw a man's head looking over I thought I would swim away presently and leave him shouting—in whatever language it was. I didn't mind being   35
looked at. I—I liked it. And then you speaking to me so qui-

etly—as if you had expected me—made me hold on a little
longer. It had been a confounded lonely time—I don't mean
while swimming. I was glad to talk a little to somebody that
didn't belong to the *Sephora*. As to asking for the captain, that
5 was a mere impulse. It could have been no use, with all the ship
knowing about me and the other people pretty certain to be
round here in the morning. I don't know—I wanted to be seen,
to talk with somebody, before I went on. I don't know what I
would have said. . . . 'Fine night, isn't it?' or something of the
sort."

"Do you think they will be round here presently?" I asked
with some incredulity.

"Quite likely," he said, faintly.

He looked extremely haggard all of a sudden. His head rolled
15 on his shoulders.

"H'm. We shall see then. Meantime get into that bed," I
whispered. "Want help? There."

It was a rather high bed place with a set of drawers underneath. This amazing swimmer really needed the lift I gave
him by seizing his leg. He tumbled in, rolled over on his back,
and flung one arm across his eyes. And then, with his face
nearly hidden, he must have looked exactly as I used to look
in that bed. I gazed upon my other self for a while before drawing across carefully the two green serge curtains which ran on a
25 brass rod. I thought for a moment of pinning them together
for greater safety, but I sat down on the couch, and once there
I felt unwilling to rise and hunt for a pin. I would do it in a
moment. I was extremely tired, in a peculiarly intimate way
by the strain of stealthiness, by the effort of whispering and the
general secrecy of this excitement. It was three o'clock by now
and I had been on my feet since nine, but I was not sleepy; I
could not have gone to sleep. I sat there, fagged out, looking
at the curtains, trying to clear my mind of the confused sensation of being in two places at once, and greatly bothered by an
35 exasperating knocking in my head. It was a relief to discover
suddenly that it was not in my head at all, but on the outside

of the door. Before I could collect myself the words "Come in" were out of my mouth, and the steward entered with a tray, bringing in my morning coffee. I had slept, after all, and I was so frightened that I shouted, "This way! I am here, steward," as though he had been miles away. He put down the tray on the table next the couch and only then said, very quietly, "I can see you are here, sir." I felt him give me a keen look, but I dared not meet his eyes just then. He must have wondered why I had drawn the curtains of my bed before going to sleep on the couch. He went out, hooking the door open as usual.

I heard the crew washing decks above me. I knew I would have been told at once if there had been any wind. Calm, I thought, and I was doubly vexed. Indeed, I felt dual more than ever. The steward reappeared suddenly in the doorway. I jumped up from the couch so quickly that he gave a start.

"What do you want here?"

"Close your port, sir—they are washing decks."

"It is closed," I said, reddening.

"Very well, sir." But he did not move from the doorway and returned my stare in an extraordinary, equivocal manner for a time. Then his eyes wavered, all his expression changed, and in a voice unusually gentle, almost coaxingly:

"May I come in to take the empty cup away, sir?"

"Of course!" I turned my back on him while he popped in and out. Then I unhooked and closed the door and even pushed the bolt. This sort of thing could not go on very long. The cabin was as hot as an oven, too. I took a peep at my double, and discovered that he had not moved, his arm was still over his eyes; but his chest heaved; his hair was wet; his chin glistened with perspiration. I reached over him and opened the port.

"I must show myself on deck," I reflected.

Of course, theoretically, I could do what I liked, with no one to say nay to me within the whole circle of the horizon; but to lock my cabin door and take the key away I did not dare. Directly I put my head out of the companion I saw the group of my two officers, the second mate barefooted, the chief mate in long India-rubber boots, near the break of the poop, and the steward halfway down the poop ladder talking to them eagerly. He happened to catch sight of me and dived, the second ran down on the main-deck shouting some order or other, and the chief mate came to meet me, touching his cap.

There was a sort of curiosity in his eye that I did not like. I don't know whether the steward had told them that I was "queer" only, or downright drunk, but I know the man meant to have a good look at me. I watched him coming with a smile which, as he got into point-blank range, took effect and froze his very whiskers. I did not give him time to open his lips.

"Square the yards by lifts and braces before the hands go to breakfast."

It was the first particular order I had given on board that ship; and I stayed on deck to see it executed, too. I had felt the need of asserting myself without loss of time. That sneering young cub got taken down a peg or two on that occasion, and I also seized the opportunity of having a good look at the face of every foremast man as they filed past me to go to the after braces. At breakfast time, eating nothing myself, I presided with such frigid dignity that the two mates were only too glad to escape from the cabin as soon as decency permitted; and all the time the dual working of my mind distracted me almost to the point of insanity. I was constantly watching myself, my secret self, as dependent on my actions as my own personality, sleeping in that bed, behind that door which faced me as I sat at the head of the table. It was very much like being mad, only it was worse because one was aware of it.

I had to shake him for a solid minute, but when at last he opened his eyes it was in the full possession of his senses, with an inquiring look.

"All's well so far," I whispered. "Now you must vanish into the bathroom."

He did so, as noiseless as a ghost, and then I rang for the steward, and facing him boldly, directed him to tidy up my stateroom while I was having my bath—"and be quick about it." As my tone admitted of no excuses, he said, "Yes, sir," and ran off to fetch his dustpan and brushes. I took a bath and did most of my dressing, splashing, and whistling softly for the steward's edification, while the secret sharer of my life stood drawn up bolt upright in that little space, his face looking very sunken in daylight, his eyelids lowered under the stern, dark line of his eyebrows drawn together by a slight frown.

When I left him there to go back to my room the steward was finishing dusting. I sent for the mate and engaged him in some insignificant conversation. It was, as it were, trifling with the terrific character of his whiskers; but my object was to give him an opportunity for a good look at my cabin. And then I could at last shut, with a clear conscience, the door of my stateroom and get my double back into the recessed part. There was nothing else for it. He had to sit still on a small folding stool, half smothered by the heavy coats hanging there. We listened to the steward going into the bathroom out of the saloon, filling the water bottles there, scrubbing the bath, setting things to rights, whisk, bang, clatter—out again into the saloon—turn the key—click. Such was my scheme for keeping my second self invisible. Nothing better could be contrived under the circumstances. And there we sat; I at my writing desk ready to appear busy with some papers, he behind me out of sight of the door. It would not have been prudent to talk in daytime; and I could not have stood the excitement of that queer sense of whispering to myself. Now and then, glancing over my shoulder, I saw him far back there, sitting rigidly on the low stool, his bare feet close together, his arms folded, his head hanging on his breast—and perfectly still. Anybody would have taken him for me.

I was fascinated by it myself. Every moment I had to glance over my shoulder. I was looking at him when a voice outside the door said:

"Beg pardon, sir."

"Well!" . . . I kept my eyes on him, and so when the voice

outside the door announced, "There's a ship's boat coming our way, sir," I saw him give a start—the first movement he had made for hours. But he did not raise his bowed head.

"All right. Get the ladder over."

5   I hesitated. Should I whisper something to him? But what? His immobility seemed to have been never disturbed. What could I tell him he did not know already? . . . Finally I went on deck.

Two

The skipper of the *Sephora* had a thin red whisker all round his face, and the sort of complexion that goes with hair of that color; also the particular, rather smeary shade of blue in the eyes. He was not exactly a showy figure; his shoulders were high, his stature but middling—one leg slightly more bandy than the other. He shook hands, looking vaguely around. A spir-
15   itless tenacity was his main characteristic, I judged. I behaved with a politeness which seemed to disconcert him. Perhaps he was shy. He mumbled to me as if he were ashamed of what he was saying; gave his name (it was something like Archbold— but at this distance of years I hardly am sure), his ship's name, and a few other particulars of that sort, in the manner of a criminal making a reluctant and doleful confession. He had had terrible weather on the passage out—terrible—terrible—wife aboard, too.

By this time we were seated in the cabin and the steward
25   brought in a tray with a bottle and glasses. "Thanks! No." Never took liquor. Would have some water, though. He drank two tumblerfuls. Terrible thirsty work. Ever since daylight had been exploring the islands round his ship.

"What was that for—fun?" I asked, with an appearance of polite interest.

"No!" He sighed. "Painful duty."

As he persisted in his mumbling and I wanted my double to hear every word, I hit upon the notion of informing him that I regretted to say I was hard of hearing.

"Such a young man, too!" he nodded, keeping his smeary blue, unintelligent eyes fastened upon me. "What was the cause of it—some disease?" he inquired, without the least sympathy and as if he thought that, if so, I'd got no more than I deserved.

"Yes; disease," I admitted in a cheerful tone which seemed to shock him. But my point was gained, because he had to raise his voice to give me his tale. It is not worth while to record that version. It was just over two months since all this had happened, and he had thought so much about it that he seemed completely muddled as to its bearings, but still immensely impressed.

"What would you think of such a thing happening on board your own ship? I've had the *Sephora* for these fifteen years. I am a well-known shipmaster."

He was densely distressed—and perhaps I should have sympathized with him if I had been able to detach my mental vision from the unsuspected sharer of my cabin as though he were my second self. There he was on the other side of the bulkhead, four or five feet from us, no more, as we sat in the saloon. I looked politely at Captain Archbold (if that was his name), but it was the other I saw, in a gray sleeping suit, seated on a low stool, his bare feet close together, his arms folded, and every word said between us falling into the ears of his dark head bowed on his chest.

"I have been at sea now, man and boy, for seven-and-thirty years, and I've never heard of such a thing happening in an English ship. And that it should be my ship. Wife on board, too."

I was hardly listening to him.

"Don't you think," I said, "that the heavy sea which, you told me, came aboard just then might have killed the man? I have seen the sheer weight of a sea kill a man very neatly, by simply breaking his neck."

"Good God!" he uttered, impressively, fixing his smeary blue eyes on me. "The sea! No man killed by the sea ever
5 looked like that." He seemed positively scandalized at my suggestion. And as I gazed at him certainly not prepared for anything original on his part, he advanced his head close to mine and thrust his tongue out at me so suddenly that I couldn't help starting back.

After scoring over my calmness in this graphic way he nodded wisely. If I had seen the sight, he assured me, I would never forget it as long as I lived. The weather was too bad to give the corpse a proper sea burial. So next day at dawn they took it up on the poop, covering its face with a bit of bunting; he read
15 a short prayer, and then, just as it was, in its oilskins and long boots, they launched it amongst those mountainous seas that seemed ready every moment to swallow up the ship herself and the terrified lives on board of her.

"That reefed foresail saved you," I threw in.

"Under God—it did," he exclaimed fervently. "It was by a special mercy, I firmly believe, that it stood some of those hurricane squalls."

"It was the setting of that sail which——" I began.

"God's own hand in it," he interrupted me. "Nothing less
25 could have done it. I don't mind telling you that I hardly dared give the order. It seemed impossible that we could touch anything without losing it, and then our last hope would have been gone."

The terror of that gale was on him yet. I let him go on for a bit, then said, casually—as if returning to a minor subject:

"You were very anxious to give up your mate to the shore people, I believe?"

He was. To the law. His obscure tenacity on that point had in it something incomprehensible and a little awful; some-
35 thing, as it were, mystical, quite apart from his anxiety that he should not be suspected of "countenancing any doings of that sort." Seven-and-thirty virtuous years at sea, of which over

twenty of immaculate command, and the last fifteen in the *Sephora*, seemed to have laid him under some pitiless obligation.

"And you know," he went on, groping shame-facedly amongst his feelings, "I did not engage that young fellow. His people had some interest with my owners. I was in a way forced to take him on. He looked very smart, very gentlemanly, and all that. But do you know—I never liked him, somehow I am a plain man. You see, he wasn't exactly the sort for the chief mate of a ship like the *Sephora*."

I had become so connected in thoughts and impressions with the secret sharer of my cabin that I felt as if I, personally, were being given to understand that I, too, was not the sort that would have done for the chief mate of a ship like the *Sephora*. I had no doubt of it in my mind.

"Not at all the style of man. You understand," he insisted, superfluously, looking hard at me.

I smiled urbanely. He seemed at a loss for a while.

"I suppose I must report a suicide."

"Beg pardon?"

"Sui-cide! That's what I'll have to write to my owners directly I get in."

"Unless you manage to recover him before tomorrow," I assented, dispassionately. . . . "I mean, alive."

He mumbled something which I really did not catch, and I turned my ear to him in a puzzled manner. He fairly bawled:

"The land—I say, the mainland is at least seven miles off my anchorage."

"About that."

My lack of excitement, of curiosity, of surprise, of any sort of pronounced interest, began to arouse his distrust. But except for the felicitous pretense of deafness I had not tried to pretend anything. I had felt utterly incapable of playing the part of ignorance properly, and therefore was afraid to try. It is also certain that he had brought some ready-made suspicions with him, and that he viewed my politeness as a strange and unnatural phenomenon. And yet how else could I have

received him? Not heartily! That was impossible for psychological reasons, which I need not state here. My only object was
to keep off his inquiries. Surlily? Yes, but surliness might have
provoked a point-blank question. From its novelty to him and
5   from its nature, punctilious courtesy was the manner best calculated to restrain the man. But there was the danger of his
breaking through my defense bluntly. I could not, I think,
have met him by a direct lie, also for psychological (not moral)
reasons. If he had only known how afraid I was of his putting
my feeling of identity with the other to the test! But,
strangely enough—(I thought of it only afterwards)—I believe that he was not a little disconcerted by the reverse side
of that weird situation, by something in me that reminded
him of the man he was seeking—suggested a mysterious simili-
15   tude to the young fellow he had distrusted and disliked from
the first.

However that might have been, the silence was not very
prolonged. He took another oblique step.

"I reckon I had no more than a two-mile pull to your ship.
Not a bit more."

"And quite enough, too, in this awful heat," I said.

Another pause full of mistrust followed. Necessity, they say,
is mother of invention, but fear, too, is not barren of ingenious
suggestions. And I was afraid he would ask me point-blank for
25   news of my other self.

"Nice little saloon, isn't it?" I remarked, as if noticing for
the first time the way his eyes roamed from one closed door to
the other. "And very well fitted out, too. Here, for instance,"
I continued, reaching over the back of my seat negligently and
flinging the door open, "is my bathroom."

He made an eager movement, but hardly gave it a glance. I
got up, shut the door of the bathroom, and invited him to
have a look round, as if I were very proud of my accommoda-
tion. He had to rise and be shown round, but he went through
35   the business without any raptures whatever.

"And now we'll have a look at my stateroom," I declared,

in a voice as loud as I dared to make it, crossing the cabin to the starboard side with purposely heavy steps.

He followed me in and gazed around. My intelligent double had vanished. I played my part.

"Very convenient—isn't it?"   5

"Very nice. Very comf . . ." He didn't finish and went out brusquely as if to escape from some unrighteous wiles of mine. But it was not to be. I had been too frightened not to feel vengeful; I felt I had him on the run, and I meant to keep him on the run. My polite insistence must have had something menacing in it, because he gave in suddenly. And I did not let him off a single item; mate's room, pantry, storerooms, the very sail locker which was also under the poop—he had to look into them all. When at last I showed him out on the quarter-deck he drew a long, spiritless sigh, and mumbled dismally that he   15 must really be going back to his ship now. I desired my mate, who had joined us, to see to the captain's boat.

The man of whiskers gave a blast on the whistle which he used to wear hanging round his neck, and yelled, "*Sephora's* away!" My double down there in my cabin must have heard, and certainly could not feel more relieved than I. Four fellows came running out from somewhere forward and went over the side, while my own men, appearing on deck too, lined the rail. I escorted my visitor to the gangway ceremoniously, and nearly overdid it. He was a tenacious beast. On the very ladder he   25 lingered, and in that unique, guiltily conscientious manner of sticking to the point:

"I say . . . you . . . you don't think that——"

I covered his voice loudly:

"Certainly not. . . . I am delighted. Good-by."

I had an idea of what he meant to say, and just saved myself by the privilege of defective hearing. He was too shaken generally to insist, but my mate, close witness of that parting, looked mystified and his face took on a thoughtful cast. As I did not want to appear as if I wished to avoid all communica-   35 tion with my officers, he had the opportunity to address me.

"Seems a very nice man. His boat's crew told our chaps a very extraordinary story, if what I am told by the steward is true. I suppose you had it from the captain, sir?"

"Yes. I had a story from the captain."

5   "A very horrible affair—isn't it, sir?"

"It is."

"Beats all these tales we hear about murders in Yankee ships."

"I don't think it beats them. I don't think it resembles them in the least."

"Bless my soul—you don't say so! But of course I've no acquaintance whatever with American ships, not I, so I couldn't go against your knowledge. It's horrible enough for me. . . . But the queerest part is that those fellows seemed to have some

15   idea the man was hidden aboard here. They had really. Did you ever hear of such a thing?"

"Preposterous—isn't it?"

We were walking to and fro athwart the quarter-deck. No one of the crew forward could be seen (the day was Sunday), and the mate pursued:

"There was some little dispute about it. Our chaps took offense. 'As if we would harbor a thing like that,' they said. 'Wouldn't you like to look for him in our coalhole?' Quite a tiff. But they made it up in the end. I suppose he did drown

25   himself. Don't you, sir?"

"I don't suppose anything."

"You have no doubt in the matter, sir?"

"None whatever."

I left him suddenly. I felt I was producing a bad impression, but with my double down there it was most trying to be on deck. And it was almost as trying to be below. Altogether a nerve-trying situation. But on the whole I felt less torn in two when I was with him. There was no one in the whole ship whom I dared take into my confidence. Since the hands had

35   got to know his story, it would have been impossible to pass him off for anyone else, and an accidental discovery was to be dreaded now more than ever. . . .

The steward being engaged in laying the table for dinner, we could talk only with our eyes when I first went down. Later in the afternoon we had a cautious try at whispering. The Sunday quietness of the ship was against us; the stillness of air and water around her was against us; the elements, the men 5 were against us—everything was against us in our secret partnership; time itself—for this could not go on forever. The very trust in Providence was, I suppose, denied to his guilt. Shall I confess that this thought cast me down very much? And as to the chapter of accidents which counts for so much in the book of success, I could only hope that it was closed. For what favorable accident could be expected?

"Did you hear everything?" were my first words as soon as we took up our position side by side, leaning over my bed place.

He had. And the proof of it was his earnest whisper, "The 15 man told you he hardly dared to give the order."

I understood the reference to be to that saving foresai.

"Yes. He was afraid of it being lost in the setting."

"I assure you he never gave the order. He may think he did, but he never gave it. He stood there with me on the break of the poop after the main topsail blew away, and whimpered about our last hope—positively whimpered about it and nothing else—and the night coming on! To hear one's skipper go on like that in such weather was enough to drive any fellow out of his mind. It worked me up into a sort of desperation. I 25 just took it into my own hands and went away from him, boiling, and—— But what's the use telling you? You know! . . . Do you think that if I had not been pretty fierce with them I should have got the men to do anything? Not I! The bo's'n perhaps? Perhaps! It wasn't a heavy sea—it was a sea gone mad! I suppose the end of the world will be something like that; and a man may have the heart to see it coming once and be done with it—but to have to face it day after day—— I don't blame anybody. I was precious little better than the rest. Only—I was an officer of that old coal wagon, anyhow——" 35

"I quite understand," I conveyed that sincere assurance into his ear. He was out of breath with whispering; I could hear him pant slightly. It was all very simple. The same strung-up force which had given twenty-four men a chance, at least, for their lives, had, in a sort of recoil, crushed an unworthy mutinous existence.

5   But I had no leisure to weigh the merits of the matter— footsteps in the saloon, a heavy knock. "There's enough wind to get under way with, sir." Here was the call of a new claim upon my thoughts and even upon my feelings.

"Turn the hands up," I cried through the door. "I'll be on deck directly."

I was going out to make the acquaintance of my ship. Before I left the cabin our eyes met—the eyes of the only two strangers on board. I pointed to the recessed part where the little campstool awaited him and laid my finger on my lips. He

15   made a gesture—somewhat vague—a little mysterious, accompanied by a faint smile, as if of regret.

This is not the place to enlarge upon the sensations of a man who feels for the first time a ship move under his feet to his own independent word. In my case they were not unalloyed. I was not wholly alone with my command; for there was that stranger in my cabin. Or rather, I was not completely and wholly with her. Part of me was absent. That mental feeling of being in two places at once affected me physically as if the mood of secrecy had penetrated my very soul. Before an hour

25   had elapsed since the ship had begun to move, having occasion to ask the mate (he stood by my side) to take a compass bearing of the pagoda, I caught myself reaching up to his ear in whispers. I say I caught myself, but enough had escaped to startle the man. I can't describe it otherwise than by saying that he shied. A grave, preoccupied manner, as though he were in possession of some perplexing intelligence, did not leave him henceforth. A little later I moved away from the rail to look at the compass with such a stealthy gait that the helmsman noticed it—and I could not help noticing the unusual roundness

35   of his eyes. These are trifling instances, though it's to no commander's advantage to be suspected of ludicrous eccentric-

ities. But I was also more seriously affected. There are to a
seaman certain words, gestures, that should in given conditions
come as naturally, as instinctively as the winking of a menaced
eye. A certain order should spring on to his lips without thinking; a certain sign should get itself made, so to speak, without   5
reflection. But all unconscious alertness had abandoned me. I
had to make an effort of will to recall myself back (from the
cabin) to the conditions of the moment. I felt that I was
appearing an irresolute commander to those people who were
watching me more or less critically.

And, besides, there were the scares. On the second day out,
for instance, coming off the deck in the afternoon (I had straw
slippers on my bare feet) I stopped at the open pantry door
and spoke to the steward. He was doing something there with
his back to me. At the sound of my voice he nearly jumped out   15
of his skin, as the saying is, and incidentally broke a cup.

"What on earth's the matter with you?" I asked, astonished.

He was extremely confused. "Beg your pardon, sir. I made
sure you were in your cabin."

"You see I wasn't."

"No, sir. I could have sworn I had heard you moving in there
not a moment ago. It's most extraordinary . . . very sorry,
sir."

I passed on with an inward shudder. I was so identified with
my secret double that I did not even mention the fact in those   25
scanty, fearful whispers we exchanged. I suppose he had made
some slight noise of some kind or other. It would have been
miraculous if he hadn't at one time or another. And yet,
haggard as he appeared, he looked always perfectly self-con-
trolled, more than calm—almost invulnerable. On my suggestion he remained almost entirely in the bathroom, which, upon
the whole, was the safest place. There could be really no shadow
of an excuse for anyone ever wanting to go in there, once the
steward had done with it. It was a very tiny place. Sometimes
he reclined on the floor, his legs bent, his head sustained on   35
one elbow. At others I would find him on the campstool, sit-

ting in his gray sleeping suit and with his cropped dark hair like
a patient, unmoved convict. At night I would smuggle him
into my bed place, and we would whisper together, with the
regular footfalls of the officer of the watch passing and repass-
5   ing over our heads. It was an infinitely miserable time. It was
lucky that some tins of fine preserves were stowed in a locker
in my stateroom; hard bread I could always get hold of; and so
he lived on stewed chicken, *pâté de foie gras*, asparagus,
cooked oysters, sardines—on all sorts of abominable sham deli-
cacies out of tins. My early-morning coffee he always drank;
and it was all I dared do for him in that respect.

Every day there was the horrible maneuvering to go through
so that my room and then the bathroom should be done in
the usual way. I came to hate the sight of the steward, to ab-
15   hor the voice of that harmless man. I felt that it was he who
would bring on the disaster of discovery. It hung like a sword
over our heads.

The fourth day out, I think (we were then working down
the east side of the Gulf of Siam, tack for tack, in light winds
and smooth water)—the fourth day, I say, of this miserable
juggling with the unavoidable, as we sat at our evening meal,
that man, whose slightest movement I dreaded, after putting
down the dishes ran up on deck busily. This could not be dangerous. Presently he came down again; and then it appeared
25   that he had remembered a coat of mine which I had thrown
over a rail to dry after having been wetted in a shower which
had passed over the ship in the afternoon. Sitting stolidly at
the head of the table I became terrified at the sight of the gar-
ment on his arm. Of course he made for my door. There was no
time to lose.

"Steward," I thundered. My nerves were so shaken that
I could not govern my voice and conceal my agitation. This
was the sort of thing that made my terrifically whiskered mate
tap his forehead with his forefinger. I had detected him using
35   that gesture while talking on deck with a confidential air to the

carpenter. It was too far to hear a word, but I had no doubt that this pantomime could only refer to the strange new captain.

"Yes, sir," the pale-faced steward turned resignedly to me. It was this maddening course of being shouted at, checked without rhyme or reason, arbitrarily chased out of my cabin, suddenly called into it, sent flying out of his pantry on incomprehensible errands, that accounted for the growing wretchedness of his expression.

"Where are you going with that coat?"

"To your room, sir."

"Is there another shower coming?"

"I'm sure I don't know, sir. Shall I go up again and see, sir?"

"No! never mind."

My object was attained, as of course my other self in there would have heard everything that passed. During this interlude my two officers never raised their eyes off their respective plates; but the lip of that confounded cub, the second mate, quivered visibly.

I expected the steward to hook my coat on and come out at once. He was very slow about it; but I dominated my nervousness sufficiently not to shout after him. Suddenly I became aware (it could be heard plainly enough) that the fellow for some reason or other was opening the door of the bathroom. It was the end. The place was literally not big enough to swing a cat in. My voice died in my throat and I went stony all over. I expected to hear a yell of surprise and terror, and made a movement, but had not the strength to get on my legs. Everything remained still. Had my second self taken the poor wretch by the throat? I don't know what I could have done next moment if I had not seen the steward come out of my room, close the door, and then stand quietly by the sideboard.

"Saved," I thought. "But, no! Lost! Gone! He was gone!"

I laid my knife and fork down and leaned back in my chair. My head swam. After a while, when sufficiently recovered to speak in a steady voice, I instructed my mate to put the ship round at eight o'clock himself.

"I won't come on deck," I went on. "I think I'll turn in, and unless the wind shifts I don't want to be disturbed before mid-
5   night. I feel a bit seedy."

"You did look middling bad a little while ago," the chief mate remarked without showing any great concern.

They both went out, and I stared at the steward clearing the table. There was nothing to be read on that wretched man's face. But why did he avoid my eyes, I asked myself. Then I thought I should like to hear the sound of his voice.

"Steward!"

"Sir!" Startled as usual.

"Where did you hang up that coat?"
15   "In the bathroom, sir." The usual anxious tone. "It's not quite dry yet, sir."

For some time longer I sat in the cuddy. Had my double vanished as he had come? But of his coming there was an ex-planation, whereas his disappearance would be inexplicable.
. . . I went slowly into my dark room, shut the door, lighted the lamp, and for a time dared not turn round. When at last I did I saw him standing bolt-upright in the narrow recessed part. It would not be true to say I had a shock, but an irresist-ible doubt of his bodily existence flitted through my mind.
25   Can it be, I asked myself, that he is not visible to other eyes than mine? It was like being haunted. Motionless, with a grave face, he raised his hands slightly at me in a gesture which meant clearly, "Heavens! what a narrow escape!" Narrow indeed. I think I had come creeping quietly as near insanity as any man who has not actually gone over the border. That gesture restrained me, so to speak.

The mate with the terrific whiskers was now putting the ship on the other tack. In the moment of profound silence which follows upon the hands going to their stations I heard
35   on the poop his raised voice: "Hard alee!" and the distant shout of the order repeated on the main-deck. The sails, in that

light breeze, made but a faint fluttering noise. It ceased. The
ship was coming round slowly: I held my breath in the renewed
stillness of expectation; one wouldn't have thought that there
was a single living soul on her decks. A sudden brisk shout,
"Mainsail haul!" broke the spell, and in the noisy cries and
rush overhead of the men running away with the main brace
we two, down in my cabin, came together in our usual position
by the bed place.

He did not wait for my question. "I heard him fumbling
here and just managed to squat myself down in the bath," he
whispered to me. "The fellow only opened the door and put
his arm in to hang the coat up. All the same——"

"I never thought of that," I whispered back, even more appalled than before at the closeness of the shave, and marveling
at that something unyielding in his character which was carrying him through so finely. There was no agitation in his whisper. Whoever was being driven distracted, it was not he. He
was sane. And the proof of his sanity was continued when he
took up the whispering again.

"It would never do for me to come to life again."

It was something that a ghost might have said. But what
he was alluding to was his old captain's reluctant admission of
the theory of suicide. It would obviously serve his turn—if I
had understood at all the view which seemed to govern the unalterable purpose of his action.

"You must maroon me as soon as ever you can get amongst
these islands off the Cambodge shore," he went on.

"Maroon you! We are not living in a boy's adventure tale," I
protested. His scornful whispering took me up.

"We aren't indeed! There's nothing of a boy's tale in this.
But there's nothing else for it. I want no more. You don't suppose I am afraid of what can be done to me? Prison or gallows
or whatever they may please. But you don't see me coming
back to explain such things to an old fellow in a wig and twelve
respectable tradesmen, do you? What can they know whether
I am guilty or not—or of *what* I am guilty, either? That's my

affair. What does the Bible say? 'Driven off the face of the earth.' Very well, I am off the face of the earth now. As I came at night so I shall go."

"Impossible!" I murmured. "You can't."

5 "Can't? . . . Not naked like a soul on the Day of Judgment. I shall freeze on to this sleeping suit. The Last Day is not yet—and . . . you have understood thoroughly. Didn't you?"

I felt suddenly ashamed of myself. I may say truly that I understood—and my hesitation in letting that man swim away from my ship's side had been a mere sham sentiment, a sort of cowardice.

"It can't be done now till next night," I breathed out. "The ship is on the off-shore tack and the wind may fail us."

15 "As long as I know that you understand," he whispered. "But of course you do. It's a great satisfaction to have got somebody to understand. You seem to have been there on purpose." And in the same whisper, as if we two whenever we talked had to say things to each other which were not fit for the world to hear, he added, "It's very wonderful."

We remained side by side talking in our secret way—but sometimes silent or just exchanging a whispered word or two at long intervals. And as usual he stared through the port. A breath of wind came now and again into our faces. The 25 ship might have been moored in dock, so gently and on an even keel she slipped through the water, that did not murmur even at our passage, shadowy and silent like a phantom sea.

At midnight I went on deck, and to my mate's great surprise put the ship round on the other tack. His terrible whiskers flitted round me in silent criticism. I certainly should not have done it if it had been only a question of getting out of that sleepy gulf as quickly as possible. I believe he told the second mate, who relieved him, that it was a great want of judgment. The other only yawned. That intolerable cub shuffled 35 about so sleepily and lolled against the rails in such a slack, improper fashion that I came down on him sharply.

"Aren't you properly awake yet?"

"Yes, sir! I am awake."

"Well, then, be good enough to hold yourself as if you were. And keep a lookout. If there's any current we'll be closing with some islands before daylight." 5

The east side of the gulf is fringed with islands, some solitary, others in groups. On the blue background of the high coast they seem to float, on silvery patches of calm water, arid and gray, or dark green and rounded like clumps of evergreen bushes, with the larger ones, a mile or two long, showing the outlines of ridges, ribs of gray rock under the dank mantle of matted leafage. Unknown to trade, to travel, almost to geography, the manner of life they harbor is an unsolved secret. There must be villages—settlements of fishermen at least—on the largest of them, and some communication with the world is 15 probably kept up by native craft. But all that forenoon, as we headed for them, fanned along by the faintest of breezes, I saw no sign of man or canoe in the field of the telescope I kept on pointing at the scattered group.

At noon I gave no orders for a change of course, and the mate's whiskers became much concerned and seemed to be offering themselves unduly to my notice. At last I said:

"I am going to stand right in. Quite in—as far as I can take her."

The stare of extreme surprise imparted an air of ferocity also 25 to his eyes, and he looked truly terrific for a moment.

"We're not doing well in the middle of the gulf," I continued, casually. "I am going to look for the land breezes tonight."

"Bless my soul! Do you mean, sir, in the dark amongst the lot of all them islands and reefs and shoals?"

"Well—if there are any regular land breezes at all on this coast one must get close inshore to find them, mustn't one?"

"Bless my soul!" he exclaimed again under his breath. All that afternoon he wore a dreamy, contemplative appearance 35 which in him was a mark of perplexity. After dinner I went into

my stateroom as if I meant to take some rest. There we two
bent our dark heads over a half-unrolled chart lying on my
bed.

"There," I said. "It's got to be Koh-ring. I've been looking
5   at it ever since sunrise. It has got two hills and a low point. It
must be inhabited. And on the coast opposite there is what
looks like the mouth of a biggish river—with some towns, no
doubt, not far up. It's the best chance for you that I can see."

"Anything. Koh-ring let it be."

He looked thoughtfully at the chart as if surveying chances
and distances from a lofty height—and following with his
eyes his own figure wandering on the blank land of Cochin-
China, and then passing off that piece of paper clean out of
sight into uncharted regions. And it was as if the ship had two
15   captains to plan her course for her. I had been so worried and
restless running up and down that I had not had the patience
to dress that day. I had remained in my sleeping suit, with
straw slippers and a soft floppy hat. The closeness of the heat
in the gulf had been most oppressive, and the crew were used
to seeing me wandering in that airy attire.

"She will clear the south point as she heads now," I whispered into his ear. "Goodness only knows when, though, but
certainly after dark. I'll edge her in to half a mile, as far as I
may be able to judge in the dark——"

25   "Be careful," he murmured, warningly—and I realized suddenly that all my future, the only future for which I was fit,
would perhaps go irretrievably to pieces in any mishap to my
first command.

I could not stop a moment longer in the room. I motioned
him to get out of sight and made my way on the poop. That
unplayful cub had the watch. I walked up and down for a
while thinking things out, then beckoned him over.

"Send a couple of hands to open the two quarter-deck
ports," I said, mildly.

35   He actually had the impudence, or else so forgot himself in
his wonder at such an incomprehensible order, as to repeat:

"Open the quarter-deck ports! What for, sir?"

"The only reason you need concern yourself about is because I tell you to do so. Have them open wide and fastened properly."

He reddened and went off, but I believe made some jeering remark to the carpenter as to the sensible practice of ventilating a ship's quarter-deck. I know he popped into the mate's cabin to impart the fact to him because the whiskers came on deck, as it were by chance, and stole glances at me from below —for signs of lunacy or drunkenness, I suppose.

A little before supper, feeling more restless than ever, I rejoined, for a moment, my second self. And to find him sitting so quietly was surprising, like something against nature, inhuman.

I developed my plan in a hurried whisper.

"I shall stand in as close as I dare and then put her round. I will presently find means to smuggle you out of here into the sail locker, which communicates with the lobby. But there is an opening, a sort of square for hauling the sails out, which gives straight on the quarter-deck and which is never closed in fine weather, so as to give air to the sails. When the ship's way is deadened in stays and all the hands are aft at the main braces, you will have a clear road to slip out and get overboard through the open quarter-deck port. I've had them both fastened up. Use a rope's end to lower yourself into the water so as to avoid a splash—you know. It could be heard and cause some beastly complication."

He kept silent for a while, then whispered, "I understand."

"I won't be there to see you go," I began with an effort. "The rest . . . I only hope I have understood, too."

"You have. From first to last"—and for the first time there seemed to be a faltering, something strained in his whisper. He caught hold of my arm, but the ringing of the supper bell made me start. He didn't though; he only released his grip.

After supper I didn't come below again till well past eight o'clock. The faint, steady breeze was loaded with dew; and the

wet, darkened sails held all there was of propelling power in it. The night, clear and starry, sparkled darkly, and the opaque, lightless patches shifting slowly against the low stars were the drifting islets. On the port bow there was a big one more dis-
5   tant and shadowily imposing by the great space of sky it eclipsed.

On opening the door I had a back view of my very own self looking at a chart. He had come out of the recess and was standing near the table.

"Quite dark enough," I whispered.

He stepped back and leaned against my bed with a level, quiet glance. I sat on the couch. We had nothing to say to each other. Over our heads the officer of the watch moved here and there. Then I heard him move quickly. I knew what that
15   meant. He was making for the companion; and presently his voice was outside my door.

"We are drawing in pretty fast, sir. Land looks rather close."

"Very well," I answered. "I am coming on deck directly."

I waited till he was gone out of the cuddy, then rose. My double moved too. The time had come to exchange our last whispers, for neither of us was ever to hear each other's natural voice.

"Look here!" I opened a drawer and took out three sovereigns. "Take this anyhow. I've got six and I'd give you the lot,
25   only I must keep a little money to buy some fruit and vegetables for the crew from native boats as we go through Sunda Straits."

He shook his head.

"Take it," I urged him, whispering desperately. "No one can tell what——"

He smiled and slapped meaningly the only pocket of the sleeping jacket. It was not safe, certainly. But I produced a large old silk handkerchief of mine, and tying the three pieces of gold in a corner, pressed it on him. He was touched, I sup-
35   pose, because he took it at last and tied it quickly round his waist under the jacket, on his bare skin.

Our eyes met; several seconds elapsed, till, our glances still mingled I extended my hand and turned the lamp out. Then I passed through the cuddy, leaving the door of my room wide open. . . . "Steward!"

He was still lingering in the pantry in the greatness of his zeal, giving a rub-up to a plated cruet stand the last thing before going to bed. Being careful not to wake up the mate, whose room was opposite, I spoke in an undertone.

He looked round anxiously. "Sir!"

"Can you get me a little hot water from the galley?"

"I am afraid, sir, the galley fire's been out for some time now."

"Go and see."

He flew up the stairs.

"Now," I whispered, loudly, into the saloon—too loudly, perhaps, but I was afraid I couldn't make a sound. He was by my side in an instant—the double captain slipped past the stairs—through a tiny dark passage . . . a sliding door. We were in the sail locker, scrambling on our knees over the sails. A sudden thought struck me. I saw myself wandering barefooted, bareheaded, the sun beating on my dark poll. I snatched off my floppy hat and tried hurriedly in the dark to ram it on my other self. He dodged and fended off silently. I wonder what he thought had come to me before he understood and suddenly desisted. Our hands met gropingly, lingered united in a steady, motionless clasp for a second. . . . No word was breathed by either of us when they separated.

I was standing quietly by the pantry door when the steward returned.

"Sorry, sir. Kettle barely warm. Shall I light the spirit lamp?"

"Never mind."

I came out on deck slowly. It was now a matter of conscience to shave the land as close as possible—for now he must go overboard whenever the ship was put in stays. Must! There could be no going back for him. After a moment I walked over to leeward and my heart flew into my mouth at the nearness of the land on the bow. Under any other circumstances I would not have held on a minute longer. The second mate had followed me anxiously.

I looked on till I felt I could command my voice.

5   "She will weather," I said then in a quiet tone.

"Are you going to try that, sir?" he stammered out incredulously.

I took no notice of him and raised my tone just enough to be heard by the helmsman.

"Keep her good full."

"Good full, sir."

The wind fanned my cheek, the sails slept, the world was silent. The strain of watching the dark loom of the land grow bigger and denser was too much for me. I had shut my eyes—

15   because the ship must go closer. She must! The stillness was intolerable. Were we standing still?

When I opened my eyes the second view started my heart with a thump. The black southern hill of Koh-ring seemed to hang right over the ship like a towering fragment of the everlasting night. On that enormous mass of blackness there was not a gleam to be seen, not a sound to be heard. It was gliding irresistibly towards us and yet seemed already within reach of the hand. I saw the vague figures of the watch grouped in the waist, gazing in awed silence.

25   "Are you going on, sir?" inquired an unsteady voice at my elbow.

I ignored it. I had to go on.

"Keep her full. Don't check her way. That won't do now," I said, warningly.

"I can't see the sails very well," the helmsman answered me, in strange, quavering tones.

Was she close enough? Already she was, I won't say in the shadow of the land, but in the very blackness of it, already swallowed up as it were, gone too close to be recalled, gone

35   from me altogether.

"Give the mate a call," I said to the young man who stood at my elbow as still as death. "And turn all hands up."

My tone had a borrowed loudness reverberated from the height of the land. Several voices cried out together: "We are all on deck, sir."

Then stillness again, with the great shadow gliding closer, towering higher, without a light, without a sound. Such a hush had fallen on the ship that she might have been a bark of the dead floating in slowly under the very gate of Erebus.

"My God! Where are we?"

It was the mate moaning at my elbow. He was thunderstruck, and as it were deprived of the moral support of his whiskers. He clapped his hands and absolutely cried out, "Lost!"

"Be quiet," I said, sternly.

He lowered his tone, but I saw the shadowy gesture of his despair. "What are we doing here?"

"Looking for the land wind."

He made as if to tear his hair, and addressed me recklessly.

"She will never get out. You have done it, sir. I knew it'd end in something like this. She will never weather, and you are too close now to stay. She'll drift ashore before she's round. O my God!"

I caught his arm as he was raising it to batter his poor devoted head, and shook it violently.

"She's ashore already," he wailed, trying to tear himself away.

"Is she? . . . Keep good full there!"

"Good full, sir," cried the helmsman in a frightened, thin, childlike voice.

I hadn't let go the mate's arm and went on shaking it. "Ready about, do you hear? You go forward"—shake—"and stop there"—shake—"and hold your noise"—shake—"and see these head-sheets properly overhauled"—shake, shake—shake.

And all the time I dared not look towards the land lest my heart should fail me. I released my grip at last and he ran forward as if fleeing for dear life.

I wondered what my double there in the sail locker thought of this commotion. He was able to hear everything—and per-

haps he was able to understand why, on my conscience, it had
to be thus close—no less. My first order "Hard alee!" re-echoed
ominously under the towering shadow of Koh-ring as if I had
shouted in a mountain gorge. And then I watched the land
5 intently. In that smooth water and light wind it was impossible
to feel the ship coming-to. No! I could not feel her. And my
second self was making now ready to ship out and lower himself overboard. Perhaps he was gone already . . . ?

The great black mass brooding over our very mastheads began to pivot away from the ship's side silently. And now I forgot the secret stranger ready to depart, and remembered only
that I was a total stranger to the ship. I did not know her.
Would she do it? How was she to be handled?

I swung the mainyard and waited helplessly. She was per-
15 haps stopped, and her very fate hung in the balance, with the
black mass of Koh-ring like the gate of the everlasting night
towering over her taffrail. What would she do now? Had she
way on her yet? I stepped to the side swiftly, and on the shadowy water I could see nothing except a faint phosphorescent
flash revealing the glassy smoothness of the sleeping surface. It
was impossible to tell—and I had not learned yet the feel of
my ship. Was she moving? What I needed was something easily
seen, a piece of paper, which I could throw overboard and
watch. I had nothing on me. To run down for it I didn't dare.
25 There was no time. All at once my strained, yearning stare distinguished a white object floating within a yard of the ship's
side. White on the black water. A phosphorescent flash passed
under it. What was that thing? . . . I recognized my own
floppy hat. It must have fallen off his head . . . and he didn't
bother. Now I had what I wanted—the saving mark for my
eyes. But I hardly thought of my other self, now gone from
the ship, to be hidden forever from all friendly faces, to be a
fugitive and a vagabond on the earth, with no brand of the
curse on his sane forehead to stay a slaying hand . . . too
35 proud to explain.

And I watched the hat—the expression of my sudden pity

for his mere flesh. It had been meant to save his homeless head from the dangers of the sun. And now—behold—it was saving the ship, by serving me for a mark to help out the ignorance of my strangeness. Ha! It was drifting forward, warning me just in time that the ship had gathered sternway.   5

"Shift the helm," I said in a low voice to the seaman standing still like a statue.

The man's eyes glistened wildly in the binnacle light as he jumped round to the other side and spun round the wheel.

I walked to the break of the poop. On the overshadowed deck all hands stood by the forebraces waiting for my order. The stars ahead seemed to be gliding from right to left. And all was so still in the world that I heard the quiet remark, "She's round," passed in a tone of intense relief between two seamen.

"Let go and haul."   15

The foreyards ran round with a great noise, amidst cheery cries. And now the frightful whiskers made themselves heard giving various orders. Already the ship was drawing ahead. And I was alone with her. Nothing! no one in the world should stand now between us, throwing a shadow on the way of silent knowledge and mute affection, the perfect communion of a seaman with his first command.

Walking to the taffrail, I was in time to make out, on the very edge of a darkness thrown by a towering black mass like the very gateway of Erebus—yes, I was in time to catch an   25
evanescent glimpse of my white hat left behind to mark the spot where the secret sharer of my cabin and of my thoughts, as though he were my second self, had lowered himself into the water to take his punishment: a free man, a proud swimmer striking out for a new destiny.

READER'S GUIDE

Julie Stern

Teacher of English
Newtown High School
New York City

READER'S GUIDE CONTENTS

INTRODUCTION   271

QUESTIONS

Youth   279

Heart of Darkness
    Introductory Note   284
    Unit I (Pages 37 to 53)   285
    Unit II (Pages 53 to 74)   291
    Unit III (Pages 74 to 90)   300
    Unit IV (Pages 90 to 105)   308
    Unit V (Pages 105 to 121)   315
    Unit VI (Pages 121 to 135)   322

Typhoon
    Unit I (Chapter One)   328
    Unit II (Chapter Two)   334
    Unit III (Chapter Three)   338
    Unit IV (Chapter Four)   342
    Unit V (Chapter Five)   347
    Unit VI (Chapter Six)   351

The Secret Sharer
    Unit I (Chapter One)   356
    Unit II (Chapter Two)   362

INTRODUCTION

Of the four short novels in this volume, three of them, *Youth*, *Typhoon*, and *The Secret Sharer*, take place aboard British freighters, and the fourth, *Heart of Darkness*, follows a British riverboat on a journey up the Congo. The author's choice of these settings is understandable because when seventeen-year-old Jozef Teodor Konrad Korzeniowski ran away from Poland to Marseilles in 1874, he got involved in smuggling guns for a band of Spanish exiles. He then began a twenty-year career at sea, mostly as an officer in the British merchant marine.

Joseph Conrad's true life adventures on the seas and in the jungles of Africa and Southeast Asia provided ideal subject matter. He had first-hand experience with the violence of both nature and man. In the course of his many voyages he met the people around whom he would later create his stories—Malay princes and Chinese coolies, carefree adventurers and haunted men running from their own private nightmares.

What is remarkable, though, is that this Polish emigrant, who taught himself English from newspapers so that he could pass the exam to become a third mate, went on to become one of the foremost prose stylists in the English language, and a psychological novelist whose explorations of the human mind laid the groundwork for much of modern literature.

While the works of Joseph Conrad can be found in many shipboard libraries where sailors enjoy them for their authenticity, these books are more than just the autobiographical recollections of a retired sea captain. Like the ocean itself, they are very deep. Beneath the surface adventure lies a complex vision of human nature.

In his tales of lonely men faced with a difficult and dangerous job, Conrad worked and reworked the themes which most fascinated him—the nature of human strength and weakness, the idealism of youth and the subsequent rude awakening experience can bring, the testing of the self in the face of savage elements, the strange and sometimes comical workings of fate.

271

The material in the *Reader's Guide* which follows is designed to aid you in reading Conrad on a mature level. The exercises are meant to focus your attention and pinpoint significant passages so that you become aware of what the author is saying and doing. If you follow them care fully, you should find these four short novels a memorable reading ex perience, one which will leave you thinking for a long time afterward.

For purposes of study, the four novels have been divided into fifteen units. The first unit covers the story *Youth*, which can be read in one sitting. *Heart of Darkness*, the most ambitious and difficult story, has been divided into six short units. The other units correspond to the individual chapters of the remaining novels. In each unit, questions will be grouped around each of these topics:

> Action and Adventure
> Psychology of the Characters
> Reading in Depth
> Vocabulary for Enrichment

Before beginning your reading of the text and your work with the *Reader's Guide*, read the following explanatory comments.

ACTION AND ADVENTURE

During the nineteenth century the exotic and mysterious regions of Asia and Africa were gradually being explored, subjugated, and colonized. Popular opinion justified the exploitation of the darker races because the highly technological European culture indicated that the Europeans were "more civilized"—higher up on the scale of human perfection. By im posing their rule and institutions upon the "backward" colonial peoples, the Europeans were serving the cause of "progress."

At bottom, however, this was largely a selfish business, financed by large trading companies, which saw in imperialism the chance to collect raw materials and precious resources for ridiculously low prices, while European soldiers protected them against any rebellious natives.

But there were also many Europeans who joined the imperialist venture for purposes other than making their own personal fortunes. A few were the kind of idealists who today might be found in the Peace Corps or some other organization serving humanity. Others were professional men, sailors and engineers, who wanted a chance at adventure and the oppor tunity to test their own resourcefulness.

To Conrad there was an ironic but unbreakable link between the two worlds of the trader and the adventurer, two groups with such different values. The trader's fortune often depended on the heroism and sacrifice of men who had no interest in the money involved, who stood little chance of getting any of it anyhow, and who might not even have been able to say why they endured such hardships except that it was part of their job.

It is this second group, men who shared, as he put it, "the fellowship of the craft," with whom Conrad identifies. He shows them to us in action—on the Indian Ocean, trapped aboard a ship with a fire smoldering ominously in its hold; setting off upriver toward the farthest jungle outpost of an ivory trading station in search of a mysterious godlike white man and his native kingdom; caught in a typhoon of such unbelievable force that they give up all hope of survival.

The questions in this part of the *Guide* are meant to help you share in the adventure by visualizing the struggle of these ordinary human beings against the destructive forces of nature around them and against fear and weakness within.

PSYCHOLOGY OF THE CHARACTERS

A psychological novelist probes deeply into the thoughts and feelings of his characters. Even when he is telling a story full of action, he studies the character's mental responses, providing a picture of the inner workings of the person's mind, a picture that is as real and vivid as the outward physical events. Furthermore, of all the things that happen to the main characters, what the author means us to remember and think about the most are mental events, the sudden insights and new realizations that come as a result of their experiences.

Psychological themes are central to all of Conrad's writing. Inner conflicts and explorations of the mind take place amidst violent and stormy adventures at sea. A few of his basic themes are:

The Search for Identity: A major character, usually a young man beginning his profession, is innocent and untested. He worries over it, torn between a desire to be very fine and special and the fear that he will never amount to much. In particular, he would like to show the people around him that he is better than they seem to think. In the course of some profound experience, he discovers the extent of his strength as well as the nature of his limitations. He is then able to face the world knowing a little more about who he is and what role he is meant to play.

The Conflict Between Ideals and Reality: Nearly everyone starts out with ideals of some kind—images of ourselves, the people we most admire, the role we mean to play in the world. If we didn't have these ideals to inspire us, we might be too cynical and depressed ever to do anything. Yet it often happens that when ideals are put to the test, they turn out to be only illusions. We believe that we want to know the truth, but sometimes the truth can be shattering.

The Dark Side of the Heart: As civilized people we have absorbed many of the values and ethics of our culture. These take the form of deeply ingrained feelings of right and wrong, a sense of decency. If we violate these beliefs we feel guilty and ashamed.

However, there is in everyone a dark, primitive side from which spring all of our violent, irrational impulses. Given the proper conditions, in spite of all our civilized values and beliefs, we are all capable of giving in to these impulses. The person who believes he is incapable of losing control of himself in a burst of rage or moment of panic is merely ignorant. He may learn the truth only when it is too late and he has committed some unforgivable offense.

More fortunate is the bystander who recognizes his own kinship to the criminal and suddenly understands that he too could have done the same thing. While this knowledge may be terrifying, it can be turned into strength. Once we know about our inner weak spots, we can guard against them.

The questions in this section are designed to point up Conrad's psychological observations and character portrayals.

READING IN DEPTH

The skillful writer is very careful in the way he structures his work, the language he uses, and the method by which he develops his ideas and unfolds his information. It will add to your enjoyment of Conrad if you understand some of these techniques.

The Use of a Frame: The first two stories in this volume have identical openings—a group of old friends are sitting together and Marlow decides to recount a youthful experience of his. At the end of each, an unnamed narrator brings us back to the present once more. This framing of the story enables us to see both the young Marlow in the midst of earlier experience and the mature Marlow who has been unalterably shaped by that experience but who can still look back on it and see it in perspective.

The nature of reality is ambiguous—so much of it depends upon the person who perceives it. So the facts in all of these stories are given to us by specific characters. Marlow strives to remember exactly how it was and to convey this accurately to his audience; in *Typhoon* we are given the conflicting testimony of the letters written by the captain and his officers. The stories are filtered through time, through the multiple perspectives of the people who were involved and those who were merely onlookers.

Charlie Marlow, who appears in many of Conrad's works, is a semi-autobiographical figure whose adventures correspond closely to the author's own. Very often Marlow or some similar character is moved by some incident to philosophize about life in general. The resultant passage has a place in the story but could easily be removed and taken by itself. Here the author is inviting us to listen to his opinions and consider them. You may not necessarily agree with all of Conrad's philosophy, but the questions in this part of the *Guide* are aimed at making you see what his ideas are, so that you can make up your own mind.

Irony serves many purposes and takes many forms. It can be used for humorous reasons, but it can also be very serious. In general, there are three types of irony you should be able to recognize.

The first, *simple irony*, is very much like sarcasm. In a light vein a student reporter may describe the "gourmet delights" to be found in the school lunchroom, when he is really complaining about the terrible food. Students who have eaten there will appreciate the incongruity between his words and the reality.

More seriously, irony can be a quiet but effective form of protest or criticism. You will see instances of this in *Heart of Darkness* where Conrad describes the brutality of the Europeans toward the Africans and then refers to imperialism as the "noble cause" and the "exalted enterprise." Again the pointed discrepancy between the high-sounding words and the ugly reality indicates the author's personal attitude toward what he is describing.

Dramatic irony is a matter of one character's ignorance of what is happening or about to happen, while the audience or the reader can see the true situation. A character may make a remark that is ironic in the light of what is really going on. Thus Julius Caesar might say, "Brutus, I know you're the one person I can always count on as a friend," on the very day Brutus has agreed to join a conspiracy to assassinate him.

Cosmic irony suggests that chance events are somehow related to our own personal hopes and fears and fate. No matter how hard we try to avoid something, it happens in spite of us; if destiny is smiling at the moment, some chance action becomes the means to our salvation. Cosmic irony can be illustrated by Nathaniel Hawthorne's short story, "The Ambitious Guest," about the family that insisted on living directly in the path of an enormous boulder precariously perched near the top of a mountain. One evening they heard rumblings. Realizing the boulder had been jarred loose, they all ran outside to get out of its way. They were all killed by the rockslide which came with the boulder. Only the empty house remained untouched.

Literal, Figurative, and Symbolic Imagery: All of Conrad's writing is intensely visual. Each story contains a succession of vivid word pictures ranging from the calm and peaceful beauty of a great river at sunset to strikingly etched portraits to the wild destructive violence of a raging storm. In addition to these literal descriptions, Conrad also uses language *figuratively.*

In the story *Youth,* a central image is the fire in the hold, which eventually blazes out of control and destroys the ship. As Marlow recalls the final conflagration, he turns it into a *metaphor:*

> Oh, the glamour of youth! Oh, the fire of it, more dazzling than the flames of the burning ship, throwing a magic light on the wide earth, leaping audaciously to the sky, presently to be quenched by time, more cruel, more pitiless, more bitter than the sea—and like the flames of the burning ship surrounded by an impenetrable night. (page 24, lines 13-18)

As the idea of youth is described in terms of a dazzling fire, it becomes easier to understand Marlow's point that youth is both so beautiful and so fleeting.

Another form of figurative language is called *personification.* In *Heart of Darkness* Marlow recalls his first impressions of the Europeans in Africa:

> I've seen the devil of violence, and the devil of greed, and the devil of hot desire; but, by all the stars! these were strong, lusty, red-eyed devils, that swayed and drove men—men, I tell you. But as I stood on this hillside I foresaw that in the blinding sunshine of that land I would become acquainted with a flabby, pretending, weak-eyed devil of a rapacious and pitiless folly. How insidious he could be, too, I was only to find out several months later and a thousand miles farther. (page 54, lines 21-29)

Here abstract human motivations are *personified* as "devils" whose individual characteristics reflect the kinds of people driven by those motivations and the kinds of things greed and desire and folly drive people to do.

When literal physical events or objects, or metaphorical images, are used not only for their own sake but also to suggest intangible ideas, it is called *symbolism*. Again in *Heart of Darkness*, when Marlow first sets foot on the African continent to begin his journey inland, he says:

> I came upon a boiler wallowing in the grass, then found a path leading up the hill. It turned aside for the boulders, and also for an undersized railway-truck lying there on its back with its wheels in the air. One was off. The thing looked as dead as the carcass of some animal. I came upon more pieces of decaying machinery, a stack of rusty rails. To the left a clump of trees made a shady spot, where dark things seemed to stir feebly. I blinked, the path was steep. A horn tooted to the right, and I saw the black people run. A heavy and dull detonation shook the ground, a puff of smoke came out of the cliff, and that was all. No change appeared on the face of the rock. They were building a railway. The cliff was not in the way or anything; but this objectless blasting was all the work going on. (page 53, lines 9-21)

Notice how in this description the mechanical objects are made to resemble animals. The image of the dead machines is a metaphor which adds vivid detail to the scene. However, the image also holds deeper implications for the entire novel. The dead pieces of machinery are *symbols* of European technology which has somehow run aground in trying to conquer the jungle. The picture of the equipment that will never be used and the account of the meaningless blasting that frightens the natives but accomplishes nothing real are representative of the futility of the European efforts.

Another form of symbolism is a device known as the *doppelganger*, or double. A character in a story becomes closely involved with another person who in many ways is so similar he could be the man's double. Sensing their common heritage, the character feels almost mystically drawn to this other person. Yet this double has certain violent or otherwise unacceptable tendencies which the character himself has never shown. In one sense the two figures are really separate halves of a complete personality. The character must recognize in himself, and come to terms with, the qualities symbolized by his double.

The questions in the *Guide* which deal with language are designed to help clarify the images and to bring out the purpose for which the images are employed.

VOCABULARY FOR ENRICHMENT

Every fine writer has an excellent vocabulary which he uses with precision. One of the desirable outcomes for the reader who studies any well-written book is that his own vocabulary is enriched. To some degree, the reader will absorb some of this vocabulary simply through his contact with the words used in meaningful context. This learning will be reinforced in the *Guide* through appropriate exercises based on selected words.

QUESTIONS

Youth

ACTION AND ADVENTURE

1. "You fight, work, sweat, nearly kill yourself, sometimes do kill yourself, trying to accomplish something—and you can't . . . not even marry an old maid, or get a wretched 600-ton cargo of coal to its port of destination." (page 2, lines 6–11) Give some examples of events in the story of the *Judea* that illustrate Marlow's thought.

2. "It was one of the happiest days of my life," recalls Marlow, speaking of the day he signed on the *Judea*. "Fancy! Second mate for the first time—a really responsible officer!" (page 2, lines 34–36) From your reading of the story, what were the responsibilities of the second mate on this type of ship? How did Marlow handle them?

3. In the series of disasters which befell the *Judea*, the men's lives were continually placed in jeopardy and their day-to-day existence was generally miserable. Give some illustrations.

PSYCHOLOGY OF THE CHARACTERS

4. As we read the story, we sense that Marlow is quite unlike the other characters in the story. Specifically in what ways is he different? Which of these differences is most important?

5. *Youth* differs from many other accounts of trouble and shipwreck at sea in that while the experiences described are by turns frustrating, frightening, and painful, the main character's response to them is so cheerful that if you don't read carefully you can easily miss how bad things actually are.

    a. Why is it that Marlow remains so cheerful?

b. Being so pleased with his heroic self-image, Marlow has a tendency to show off. Cite incidents from the story to illustrate this, and explain what the results are.

c. How do the attitudes of Captain Beard and Mr. Mahon compare to Marlow's?

6. What is Marlow's attitude toward the captain and Mahon? How would you explain it?

READING IN DEPTH

7. "You fellows know there are those voyages that seem ordered for the illustration of life, that might stand for a symbol of existence," says Marlow at the opening of his tale. Reread this passage. (page 2, lines 4-11)

a. Interpret the passage in the light of the story. That is, how does this voyage stand for a symbol of existence?

b. A tale whose main incidents involve mishap, futility, and frustration may be told in two entirely different ways—as comedy or as tragedy. In your opinion, how is this tale told? Does it leave you with a comic feeling or a tragic one? Explain your answer.

8. "Then, on a fine moonlight night, all the rats left the ship." (page 13, line 1) Marlow and Mahon stand and discuss this phenomenon. What is ironic about their discussion and how is this same irony repeated at other points in the story?

9. Nemesis was a Greek goddess of justice and retribution. Marlow refers to the "lands of brown nations, where a stealthy Nemesis lies in wait, pursues, overtakes so many of the conquering race, who are proud of their wisdom, of their knowledge, of their strength." (page 34, lines 17-20)

a. What is Marlow saying here?

b. What connection does this idea have to the central idea of *Youth*?

c. How is this idea supported by having Marlow tell his story twenty-two years later? What effect is achieved?

10. Reread the last paragraph in the story. The speaker (not Marlow!) tells now of "something" they have all looked for out of life and which has passed them all by, which is now gone ". . . together with the youth, with the strength, with the romance of illusions." (page 35, lines 12-13) *a.* What is that "something" he refers to?

b. What are both men saying about what life has to offer? To what extent is this a pessimistic philosophy?

11. You have undoubtedly been impressed by Conrad's genius for creating sharply etched, striking word images. One good example is the description of the captain on page 2:

> He was sixty if a day; a little man, with a broad, not very straight back, with bowed shoulders and one leg more bandy than the other, he had that queer twisted-about appearance you see so often in men who work in the fields. He had a nutcracker face—chin and nose trying to come together over a sunken mouth—and it was framed in iron-gray fluffy hair, that looked like a chin-strap of cotton-wool sprinkled with coal-dust. And he had blue eyes in that old face of his, which were amazingly like a boy's, with that candid expression some quite common men preserve to the end of their days by a rare internal gift of simplicity of heart and rectitude of soul. (page 2, lines 14–25)

a. Mention some of the words and phrases that contribute to the sharp, strong quality of this description.

b. From elsewhere in the story, select a favorite example of your own of Conrad's genius for word pictures.

VOCABULARY FOR ENRICHMENT

Each of the following ten words is first given in the context of the sentence in which it appears in the book (A), then in a second sentence (B) whose context gives specific help as to the meaning of the word. Read the two sentences; then select the best definition of the word from the four choices given.

1. *doleful* (page 6, line 13)

    A. "A *doleful* voice arose hailing somewhere in the middle of the dock, '*Judea* ahoy!'"

    B. As the old man spoke in *doleful* tones, we realized how bad things had been for him lately.

       a. mysterious   *c.* sorrowful
       b. angry   *d.* comical

2. *indomitable* (page 12, line 29)

    A. "He had grog-blossoms all over his face, an *indomitable* energy, and was a jolly soul."

    B. Only the *indomitable* spirit of the pioneers kept them from surrendering to the hardships of cruel weather, poor crops, and loneliness.

      a. limited   *c.* nervous
      b. unusual   *d.* unconquerable

3. *affably* (page 13, line 3)

    A. "They had destroyed our sails, consumed more stores than the crews, *affably* shared our beds and our dangers, and now, when the ship was made seaworthy, concluded to clear out."

    B. They were a friendly outgoing couple, mixing *affably* with everyone in the neighborhood.

      a. rudely   *c.* secretly
      b. boldly   *d.* sociably

4. *negligently* (page 14, line 26)

    A. "I answered *negligently*, 'It's good for the health, they say,' and walked aft."

    B. The man tossed away a match *negligently* and started the forest fire.

      a. carelessly   *c.* thoughtfully
      b. honestly   *d.* proudly

5. *pellucid* (page 16, line 8)

    A. "The sea was polished, was blue, was *pellucid* . . . ."

    B. Through the *pellucid* waters he could see the flashing colors of tropical fish.

      a. translucent   *c.* dazzling
      b. alive   *d.* muddy

6. *audaciously* (page 24, line 15)

    A. "Oh, the fire of it . . . leaping *audaciously* to the sky, presently to be quenched by time. . . ."

    B. He climbed to the very top of the church steeple and dangled *audaciously* by his feet.

a. brightly   c. angrily
b. loudly   d. daringly

7. *deferentially* (page 24, line 33)

   A. "We said 'Ay, ay, sir,' *deferentially*, and on the quiet let the things slip overboard."

   B. The waiter stood by *deferentially* while the guest of honor tasted the wine.

   a. sarcastically   c. respectfully
   b. reluctantly   d. dishonestly

8. *commune* (page 27, line 25)

   A. "The skipper lingered disconsolately, and we left him to *commune* alone for a while with his first command."

   B. Occasionally it's relaxing to camp out and *commune* with nature.

   a. die   c. debate
   b. work   d. confer

9. *impalpable* (page 30, line 24)

   A. "It was *impalpable* and enslaving, like a charm, like a whispered promise of mysterious delight."

   B. There were no obvious clues or evidence, but something *impalpable* led the detective to suspect foul play.

   a. intangible   c. magical
   b. unavoidable   d. unbelievable

10. *resplendent* (page 33, line 28)

   A. "This was the East of the ancient navigators, so old, so mysterious, *resplendent* and sombre, living and unchanged, full of danger and promise."

   B. The marching band turned out in their *resplendent* dress uniforms, full of gold braid and shining medals.

   a. brilliant   c. dangerous
   b. modest   d. famous

Heart of Darkness

INTRODUCTORY NOTE

In 1885 the European nations met in Berlin to decide how the various parts of Africa should be divided among them, so that they need not fight over territory. One result of this conference was that the Congo was recognized as the private personal estate of King Leopold II of Belgium.

Leopold had set his sights on this goal long before, when he spoke of "the need to open to civilization the only part of our globe where Christianity has not penetrated, and to pierce the darkness which envelops the entire population." As Chief of State of the Congo, he explained:

> The mission which the agents of the State have to accomplish in the Congo is a noble one.... Placed face to face with primitive barbarism, grappling with bloody customs that date back thousands of years, they are obliged to reduce these gradually. They must accustom the population to general laws, of which the most needful and the most salutary is assuredly that of work.

Thus he deposed all native tribal chiefs and divided his new territory into fifteen districts, appointing a commissioner for each one. These commissioners had the job of administering Belgian rule and collecting taxes due the new mother country. In lieu of payment of taxes, the commissioners could force the natives to work for the trading companies that were granted exclusive rights to each district. Any natives who refused were then considered criminals.

It was for one of these companies, the Société du Haut Congo, that Joseph Conrad commanded the steamer *Roi des Belges* in 1890, travelling upriver to the Société's ivory trading stations. Nine years later Conrad would describe that African adventure in a three-part serialized novel, *Heart of Darkness*.

In the novel the main character has become Charlie Marlow, hero of the earlier story *Youth*. Now a middle-aged man with sunken cheeks and an ascetic air, Marlow, in the midst of a pleasure cruise with old friends, is suddenly prompted to recall his Congo journey, saying, ". . . You ought to know how I got out there, what I saw, how I went up that river to the place where I first met the poor chap." (page 42, lines 33–35)

The "poor chap" is the legendary Mr. Kurtz, the man everyone predicted was destined for so much greatness. Marlow's encounter with Kurtz affects him so profoundly that it becomes the focal point of the story. It was, he says,

> . . . the culminating point of my experience. It seemed somehow to throw a kind of light on everything about me—and into my thoughts. It was sombre enough, too—and pitiful—not extraordinary in any way—not very clear either. No, not very clear. And yet it seemed to throw a kind of light. (page 42, line 36–page 43, line 4)

As Marlow tells his story, he tries to do it in such a way as to show not only what happened, but what it meant—the "light" which his experience cast on everything else. As you read *Heart of Darkness* you will see that the terms "darkness" and "light" take on a variety of meanings—that Marlow's journey was not merely an account of the white man's abuse of the dark continent, but an investigation of the dark side of the heart as well.

Heart of Darkness: Unit I

Pages 37 to 53

ACTION AND ADVENTURE

1. As the yawl *Nellie* lies at anchor amidst the bustling traffic and evening lights of the Thames, Marlow remarks to his friends, "And this also . . . has been one of the dark places of the earth." (page 39, lines 35–36)

a. What does Marlow mean when he says this? (Review pages 39–42.)

b. In addition to physical discomforts, disease, and bad weather, what further pitfall does Marlow suggest awaited the young Roman who ventured out to Britain?

c. What parallel is Marlow drawing between the Roman conquerors of Caesar's time and himself and his friends?

2. Read the opening description of the river and shoreline as the day gradually turns into night. (pages 37–39) Notice the mood of stability and permanence that continues as the sky grows darker and the lights begin to appear along the shore.

a. What train of thought does this start in the narrator?

b. What idea is conveyed by the last paragraph on page 38?

c. While the narrator is prompted by the immediate setting to muse upon the majesty of empire, Marlow's mind is working in quite a different way, musing upon how even in the midst of this very civilized setting they are still frighteningly close to a world that is totally savage and primitive.

In his opening words he compares that here-and-now setting with both the past—which he refers to as being "just the other day"—and those parts of the earth, in this case Africa, where his countrymen are engaged in conquest and colonization.

What implication can we draw from Marlow's remarks about civilization and darkness? How does his view differ from the narrator's?

3. It sometimes happens that a twist of fate determines a person's destiny, that the truly important experience in his life can be traced back to some chance coincidence or accident which caused him to embark on a particular course of action; and he did not realize how great the consequences of that action were going to be.

Marlow's trip to Africa was the result of a combination of such accidents and coincidences. Explain how this is true.

4. Marlow's first contact with the African environment comes when he journeys out to reach his post, first travelling on the French steamer which cruises along the coast of French Equatorial Africa, then changing to another ship which could take him thirty miles upriver to his Company's first trading station. He recalls, "Nowhere did we stop long enough to get a particularized impression, but the general sense of vague and oppressive wonder grew upon me. It was like a weary pilgrimage amongst hints for nightmares." (page 52, lines 8–11)

a. What are some of the details which convey the nightmarish quality of his journey?

b. In his description on page 51 of the man-of-war, Marlow ridicules the idea of the natives constituting a real threat, although someone on board the ship refers to them as "enemies." If the Europeans do in fact have a real enemy to face, who, or *what*, is it going to be? If there is to be any real conflict, between what two forces will the conflict occur? (Remember Marlow's earlier comments about the Romans in Britain.)

PSYCHOLOGY OF THE CHARACTERS

5. The point is made in the Introduction to this *Guide* that people became involved in imperialistic activity for various and often dissimilar reasons. In his account of "how I got out there," Marlow explains his own motivations. He also indicates, through his encounters with the Belgians and the meeting with his aunt, their attitudes toward African development.

a. Compare Marlow with his aunt and the Company personnel in terms of the kind of appeal Africa has for each of them.

b. To what extent do Marlow, his aunt, and the Belgians recognize and understand the differences in their attitudes?

c. Faced with the idealism of his aunt on the one hand, and the materialism of the Company on the other, to what extent does Marlow identify with either? Why?

6. Reread the account of Marlow's visit with his aunt before he leaves. (page 49)

a. How does he explain her idealism in terms of feminine psychology?

b. How would you explain this attitude?

7. The Company doctor who examines Marlow says he is an alienist, that is, a psychiatrist, and that he has a theory which he hopes to prove with the help of "you Messieurs who go out there." He doesn't say what the theory is, but it has to do with changes that take place "inside" after the men have been overseas.

The theme of people who change after they go "out there" recurs several times in this part of the novel. What instances can you cite of people mentioned in the story whose personality or behavior undergoes radical change? What seems to be the cause?

READING IN DEPTH

8. The original narrator of the story points out on page 40 that Marlow is not a typical seaman. In what way is he different from others who "follow the sea"? What significance might this have for the novel?

9. Marlow takes a long time to develop his story, saying that in order for his friends to appreciate the meaning of his experience, he must first tell the events that led up to it. He does so in a very roundabout fashion so that by the end of this segment of the novel the only concrete facts we have are that, with the aid of his aunt, Marlow was posted to Africa to command a river steamer, and, according to the one-sentence plot summary at the bottom of page 42, he went out there, he saw something, he went up the river, and he met a "poor chap."

However, the alert reader will have caught the feeling of ominous foreboding that pervades Marlow's satirical account of his first dealings with the Company and his subsequent journey to Africa. One way by which Conrad achieves this effect is by the interjection into this seemingly cheerful part of the narrative of unexpectedly eerie and morbid images and incidents, suggesting desolation, insanity, and death.

Read over pages 45-53.

   a. What supporting examples can you find?

   b. How does Conrad's use of color contribute to the effect?

10. From his title onward, Conrad is ambiguous in his use of the terms "light" and "darkness." As you read through the text you will see these words figure in a great many images. As the story progresses, the meaning he attaches to the words changes from the narrator's literal descriptive usage to Marlow's more suggestive metaphors.

   a. How many different meanings for the word "darkness" can you find in this part of the book? What are the implications of each?

   b. On page 40, line 30, Marlow speaks of "light" coming out of the river. Again, on page 49, line 18, Marlow says his aunt expected him to be an "emissary of light."

   Given the meanings of *darkness*, what does Conrad mean by "light"? To what extent is light considered good and darkness evil?

11. "The conquest of the earth, which mostly means the taking it away from those who have a different complexion or slightly flatter noses than ourselves, is not a pretty thing when you look into it too much. What redeems it is the idea only. An idea at the back of it; not a sentimental pretence but an idea; and an unselfish belief in the idea—something you can set up, and bow down before, and offer a sacrifice to. . . ." (page 42, lines 12-18)

   a. What kind of idea is Marlow talking about? How does it redeem the act of taking the earth away from people with different complexions?

   b. Of all the people encountered in this section of *Heart of Darkness*, is there anyone who can be described as a representative of, or believer in, "the idea"?

VOCABULARY FOR ENRICHMENT

Each of the following ten words is first given in the context of the sentence in which it appears in the book (A), then in a second sentence (B) whose context gives specific help as to the meaning of the word. Read the two sentences; then select the best definition of the word from the four choices given.

1. *immutability* (page 40, line 8)

   A. "In the *immutability* of their surroundings the foreign shores, the foreign faces, the changing immensity of life, glide past. . . ."

   B. With his stubborn *immutability*, he would never change his mind once he said he'd sell the farm, so there was no use in trying to persuade him.

a. beauty	*c.* foreignness
b. mystery	*d.* fixedness

2. *spectral* (page 40, line 23)

   A. ". . . A glow brings out a haze, in the likeness of one of these misty halos that sometimes are made visible by the *spectral* illumination of moonshine."

   B. As he walked through the cemetery at midnight the boy dared not look behind him lest he spy some *spectral* figure following in pursuit.

a. gruesome	*c.* ghostly
b. evil	*d.* vengeful

3. *sepulchre* (page 45, line 32)

   A. "In a very few hours I arrived in a city that always makes me think of a whited *sepulchre*."

   B. The coffin was laid to rest in the family *sepulchre* [or *sepulcher*].

a. estate	*c.* angel
b. tomb	*d.* tradition

4. *somnambulist* (page 46, line 11)

   A. "The slim one got up and walked straight at me . . . and only just as I began to think of getting out of her way, as you would for a *somnambulist*, stood still, and looked up."

B. His college roommate was a *somnambulist* who one night, in the midst of a dream, almost fell out of a fourth floor window.

   a. lunatic   *c.* sleepwalker
   b. imbecile   *d.* medical student

5. *imperturbably* (page 48, line 27)

   A. " 'Every doctor should be—a little,' answered that original, *imperturbably*."

   B. He climbed the ladder *imperturbably*, evidently unruffled by the prospect of diving a hundred feet into a tiny tank of water.

   a. foolishly   *c.* angrily
   b. calmly   *d.* hopelessly

6. *emissary* (page 49, line 18)

   A. "Something like an *emissary* of light, something like a lower sort of apostle."

   B. The emperor did not attend the talks in person, but sent his *emissary* instead.

   a. diplomat   *c.* kind
   b. representative   *d.* wife

7. *enigma* (page 50, line 13)

   A. "Watching a coast as it slips by the ship is like thinking about an *enigma*."

   B. The answer to why and how the crew disappeared from the ship remains an *enigma* to this day.

   a. dream   *c.* heaven
   b. map   *d.* mystery

8. *lugubrious* (page 51, line 30)

   A. "There was a touch of insanity in the proceeding, a sense of *lugubrious* drollery in the sight...."

   B. Even when he is happy, the bloodhound's *lugubrious* expression makes him look as if he had just lost his best friend.

   a. mournful   *c.* humorous
   b. merry   *d.* angry

9. *dissipated* (page 51, line 31)

   A. "... And it was not *dissipated* by somebody on board assuring me earnestly there was a camp of natives—he called them enemies! —hidden out of sight somewhere."

   B. Her fears were *dissipated* when the footsteps behind her turned out to be those of the policeman on the beat.

a. dispelled	*c*. excited
b. improved	*d*. exaggerated

10. *morose* (page 52, line 19)

   A. "He was a young man, lean, fair, and *morose*, with lanky hair and a shuffling gait."

   B. He was so *morose*, sulking off in a corner, that even the prospect of a birthday party failed to cheer him up.

a. stupid	*c*. strong
b. intelligent	*d*. gloomy

Heart of Darkness: Unit II

Pages 53 to 74

ACTION AND ADVENTURE

1. As he leaves the steamer and starts up the slope toward the station, Marlow receives a severe jolt. "For a moment I stood appalled, as though by a warning," (page 54, lines 29-30) he says, resolving not to climb any further until the men chained together have passed out of sight. But as he goes instead to wait in a shady grove of trees, he says, "No sooner within than it seemed to me I had stepped into the gloomy circle of some Inferno." (page 55, lines 6-7)

   a. What is the purpose of the chain gang? Why is it unfair?

   b. "Behind this raw matter one of the reclaimed, the product of the new forces at work, strolled despondently...." Marlow is being ironic here as he describes the native guard watching over the prisoners. What does he mean by "raw matter"? In what sense is the guard "reclaimed"? What are the "new forces at work"?

c. As he hastens to get out of the way of the chain gang, Marlow stumbles upon another group of Africans of whom he says, "These moribund shapes were as free as air—and nearly as thin." (page 55, lines 27-28) What does Marlow mean by this remark? Who are these men and what has happened to them?

d. "...As I stood on this hillside I foresaw that in the blinding sunshine of that land I would become acquainted with a flabby, pretending, weak-eyed devil of a rapacious and pitiless folly." (page 54, lines 24-27) What is it about the whole spectacle which most enrages and upsets Marlow?

2. After a ten-day wait at the Company's Coastal Station where he was deposited by the Swedish captain, Marlow sets out to walk the 200 miles upriver to the Central Station where the general manager has his headquarters and where Marlow's riverboat is awaiting his command.

a. How do Marlow's experiences during this leg of the journey serve to reinforce his initial impressions of Africa?

b. Marlow remembers the old Belgian doctor and his remark, "It would be interesting for science to watch the mental changes of individuals, on the spot." Marlow comments, "I felt I was becoming scientifically interesting." (page 60, line 13) What was making Marlow "scientifically interesting"?

3. The Central Station to which Marlow must report is the headquarters for all the small trading posts strung out along a thousand-mile stretch of the Congo River. Each of these substations is manned by one or two white men who deal with the tribes in their immediate area, exchanging cheap trade goods for the precious ivory. The only avenue of transportation for getting the trade goods, the ivory, and the traders back and forth between the Central Station with its storage depots and the remote outer stations, is the treacherous river itself. One small steamer plies back and forth, replenishing men and supplies, and it is this boat which Marlow will command.

But when, after a fifteen-day, two-hundred-mile march, Marlow reaches the Central Station, he discovers that somebody had tried taking off without him a few days earlier and had managed to wreck the boat in the process. Now it lies at the bottom of the river.

a. According to the station manager, why was it so urgent for them to leave that they couldn't wait two more days for Marlow to get there?

b. The excitable man with the black moustaches assures Marlow that "everybody had behaved splendidly! splendidly!" at the occasion of the sinking of the steamer. But the same man makes an identical comment when they are all fighting a fire in a storage shed. What does this reveal about this man's judgment? What light does it shed on the sinking of the steamer?

c. On the other hand, looking at the event in retrospect as he recounts the story to his companions, Marlow says,

> I did not see the real significance of that wreck at once. I fancy I see it now, but I am not sure—not at all. Certainly the affair was too stupid—when I think of it—to be altogether natural. Still . . . . (page 60, lines 31-34)

Later when Marlow angrily tells the manager that now it may take several months to get the boat repaired the manager says, "Some months. . . . Well, let us say three months before we can make a start. Yes. That ought to do the affair." (page 63, lines 8-9) Afterward Marlow is impressed by how accurate the manager's estimate turns out to be.

If it wasn't sheer stupidity which caused the loss of the steamer, what other explanation is Marlow hinting at here? What motive could there be?

d. Reread Marlow's conversation with the brickmaker on pages 70-71. When Marlow demands rivets and says that one letter to the coast could obtain them, the brickmaker, who actually serves as the manager's secretary, cries, "My dear sir, . . . I write from dictation." How would the confusion over the rivets support the argument that the three month delay is a deliberate one?

4. The chief accountant back at the Coastal Station told Marlow that he preferred not to write to Mr. Kurtz because he suspected that his letters might be intercepted and read at the Central Station.

a. Who would want to intercept his letters and why?

b. How is the brickmaker laboring under a misunderstanding concerning Marlow?

5. "I would not have gone so far as to fight for Kurtz, but I went for him near enough to a lie." (page 68, lines 27-29)

a. Does Marlow actually tell a lie? If not, what does he do and how can this be of any help to Kurtz?

o. What is the threat implicit in the brickmaker's warning to Marlow, "No man—you apprehend me?—no man here bears a charmed life"? How does this tie in with the manager's apparent lack of "entrails"?

6. Three weeks after Marlow's exchange with the brickmaker, the rivets still haven't come but the Eldorado Exploring Expedition has. What is its purpose and what is its connection with the trading company?

PSYCHOLOGY OF THE CHARACTERS

7. The first person Marlow meets at the Coastal Station is the chief accountant—"a sort of vision" in starched collar and cuffs, clean white trousers, and polished shoes, even though he has been out there for three years already. Of this man Marlow says:

> His appearance was certainly that of a hairdresser's dummy; but in the great demoralization of the land he kept up his appearance. That's backbone. His starched collars and got-up shirt-fronts were achievements of character. (page 56, line 36—page 57, line 4)

a. What quality in the accountant makes Marlow respect him as a man of "character"? That is, what enables the accountant to keep up his appearance? How else does this quality manifest itself?

b. While he describes the man as having backbone and showing character, Marlow also shows a much less favorable aspect of the accountant, indicating that while he may be a man admirable for his self-control, he is lacking in common humanity. What evidence can you find in the text to support this?

8. "Once when various tropical diseases had laid low almost every 'agent' in the station," the general manager was heard to say, "'Men who come out here should have no entrails.'" (page 62, lines 7-9) In what ways is this a key to the manager's character? How has it led to his success?

9. You may have observed that whereas all the people Marlow meets are known to us only by their occupations—for example, the accountant or the brickmaker—or possibly their physical characteristics—for example, the man with the moustaches—we are told the name of only one man, Mr. Kurtz, a man Marlow has never seen. The picture we get of Mr. Kurtz emerges from the various things the other characters say about him, their opinions of his ability and his motivations, their personal feelings regarding him.

a. These feelings seem to combine respect, fear, envy, and scorn. What is it about Kurtz that arouses such mixed emotions in the others? In what ways is he different from the other people involved in the ivory trade?

b. Evidently Kurtz means to combine the roles of missionary and ivory trader. In what ways might his activity as an ivory trader improve his chances of success as "an emissary of pity, and science, and progress . . . "? How does it distinguish him from the other people in Europe who preach the idea of spreading progress?

c. The brickmaker is thought by the other "pilgrims" to be the manager's spy on the rest of them. Certainly he has taken on the job of personal secretary and confidant of the manager. However, when he invites Marlow to his room and begins to pump him about Marlow's connections in Europe, the brickmaker is in a way double-crossing his friend. Explain how this is so. What is he trying to accomplish? Why is the brickmaker so interested in Marlow?

10. During this section of the novel Marlow undergoes a considerable change in his attitude toward Kurtz, moving from a kind of scorn and disinterest to a sense of faith in and allegiance to this man he has never met.

a. Why, when he first hears Kurtz's name mentioned by the accountant and later by the manager, is Marlow less than enthusiastic? What reasons cause him to change his mind?

b. The brickmaker says to Marlow, "You are of the new gang—the gang of virtue," meaning that Marlow, like Kurtz, is a believer in the humanitarian purpose of the Company, and has visions of helping the backward natives. Up till now Marlow has vigorously disclaimed such a notion, insisting that he was interested only in the technical side of his job. Yet he doesn't say this to the brickmaker or deny the man's description of him. To what extent *does* Marlow belong to the "gang of virtue" despite his denials? Why doesn't he argue the point with the brickmaker?

11. Marlow soon develops a deep affection for the wrecked steamer which he jokingly calls his most influential friend. Why does it mean so much to him? What solace does it provide?

READING IN DEPTH

12. On page 56 when Marlow comes upon the dying natives in the grove, he notices that one of them has tied a bit of white thread around his neck. Reread the description in the first paragraph on that page. What is the ironic symbolism suggested in that image?

13. Read the descriptions of the station's inhabitants on pages 63 and 65.

a. Marlow sarcastically calls them "pilgrims" because with their long staves or walking sticks they resemble the religious pilgrims of the Middle Ages who went on long treks to the Holy Land. How is this comparison meant to be ironic?

b. In both the above-mentioned descriptions Marlow stresses the idea of the unreality of it all, and he does so throughout this portion of the novel. In what ways is it unreal?

14. In reference to the pilgrims, Marlow says, "By heavens! there is something after all in the world allowing one man to steal a horse while another must not look at a halter." (page 65, lines 20-22) Read this entire passage, beginning on line 20.

a. What does Marlow mean? What is the difference between the two actions?

b. How does this relate to Marlow's remarks about "the devil of violence" on page 54, lines 21-27? What is Marlow saying about the kinds of crimes different people commit?

15. "And outside, the silent wilderness . . . struck me as something great and invincible, like evil or truth, waiting patiently for the passing away of this fantastic invasion." (page 63, lines 26-30) Marlow *personifies* the wilderness, speaking of it as if it were some living entity, with human motivations. He repeats this idea several times in the next ten pages.

a. What other instances can you find where Marlow personifies the jungle or the wilderness?

b. As Marlow characterizes the wilderness, what seems to be the relationship between the wilderness and the Europeans? How are the white men deluded?

c. In this conflict between the Europeans and the jungle, what weapons does Nature have at her disposal? That is, with what destructive forces or conditions do the Europeans have to contend? Which of these are they readily aware of? Which other ones might be called more *insidious*?

16. Marlow describes a painting done by Kurtz before he left to go up-river. It was "a woman, draped and blindfolded, carrying a lighted torch. The background was sombre—almost black. The movement of the woman was stately, and the effect of the torch-light on the face was sinister." (page 66, lines 6-9)

a. What does Conrad mean this picture to represent? What relation might it have to the title of the novel?

b. What is the implication of the sinister effect of the torchlight on her face?

17. On one level this novel can be seen as a descent into and a journey through Hell. What indications can you find to support this interpretation? (Remember that these might include physical conditions, characters encountered, and figures of speech.)

VOCABULARY FOR ENRICHMENT

1. *wallowing* (page 53, line 9)

A. "I came upon a boiler *wallowing* in the grass, then found a path leading up the hill."

B. We saw a hippopotamus *wallowing* in the thick mire at the edge of the river.

a. eating	*c.* rusting
b. lying heavily	*d.* backing up slowly

2. *detonation* (page 53, line 17)

A. "A heavy and dull *detonation* shook the ground, a puff of smoke came out of the cliff, and that was all."

B. Windows were broken for miles around by the *detonation* of the gas tank.

a. filling	*c.* music
b. explosion	*d.* sound

3. *meagre* (page 53, line 36)

A. "All their *meagre* breasts panted together, the violently dilated nostrils quivered, the eyes stared stonily up-hill."

B. The *meagre* |or *meager*| garments of the beggar afforded him no protection against the chill winds.

a. muscular   *c.* unusual
b. anxious   *d.* thin

4. *rapacious* (page 54, line 27)

A. "... I would become acquainted with a flabby, pretending, weak-eyed devil of a *rapacious* and pitiless folly."

B. The *rapacious* mine owners were perfectly willing to scar the countryside with open mines so long as it would bring in quick profits.

a. speedy   *c.* criminal
b. grasping   *d.* pointless

5. *insidious* (page 54, line 27)

A. "How *insidious* he could be, too, I was only to find out several months later and a thousand miles farther."

B. This stretch of the river is particularly *insidious* because it is full of hidden snags and you don't realize how fast the current is pushing you toward them.

a. busy   *c.* stupid
b. clever   *d.* treacherous

6. *moribund* (page 55, line 27)

A. "These *moribund* shapes were free as air—and nearly as thin."

B. Our geranium was so badly neglected this summer that it is *moribund* and I doubt if even your expert attentions can save it now.

a. dying   *c.* mortal
b. delicate   *d.* chained

7. *languidly* (page 60, line 21)

A. "White men with long staves in their hands appeared *languidly* from amongst the buildings, strolling up to take a look at me, and then retired out of sight somewhere."

B. Still weak from the long illness, she would get up in the morning, *languidly* make an attempt to tidy up the apartment, and then sink down on the couch and fall asleep.

a. suddenly	*c.* listlessly
b. stealthily	*d.* excitedly

8. *volubility* (page 60, line 25)

A. "One of them ... informed me with great *volubility* and many digressions ... that my steamer was at the bottom of the river."

B. Judging by his *volubility* you'd think he was an expert on horses, but underneath all those words there really isn't much knowledge of the subject.

a. speed	*c.* size
b. wordiness	*d.* readiness

9. *trenchant* (page 61, line 14)

A. "His eyes, of the usual blue, were perhaps remarkably cold, and he certainly could make his glance fall on one as *trenchant* and heavy as an axe."

B. She had the *trenchant* mind of a true scientist, getting down to the crux of the issue immediately so that she could find the best method of dealing with it.

a. unpleasant	*c.* absent
b. dangerous	*d.* incisive

10. *prodigy* (page 66, line 19)

A. " 'He is a *prodigy*,' he said at last."

B. Mozart was a child *prodigy* who began to compose at the age of four.

a. rebel	*c.* idealist
b. wonder	*d.* mistake

Heart of Darkness: Unit III

Pages 74 to 90

ACTION AND ADVENTURE

1. Marlow finds himself inadvertently eavesdropping on the manager and his uncle.   Realizing that they are discussing Kurtz, he begins to listen more closely.

   a. From this conversation, what new details does Marlow, and thus the reader, learn about Kurtz's gradual isolation?

   b. What reasons does Marlow have for being concerned about Kurtz's well-being?

   c. Marlow hears the manager answering a question with the words, "No one, as far as I know, unless a species of wandering trader. . . ." (page 76, lines 1-2) We are not told the question to which this is obviously an answer, but, given the context of the conversation, what had the manager's uncle probably asked?

   d. Why are the manager and his uncle both so emphatic in declaring that this person ought to be hanged? How is their attitude ironic in view of the uncle's motive in coming to Africa himself?

2. How does this conversation serve to reinforce Marlow's earlier suspicions about the manager's intriguing? Cite specific statements to support your answer.

3. Marlow notes that "In a few days the Eldorado Expedition went into the patient wilderness. . . . Long afterwards the news came that all the donkeys were dead. I know nothing as to the fate of the less valuable animals." (page 77, lines 13-16) What were the "less valuable animals" and why does Marlow use that label? What probably happened to them?

4. To convey an idea of the magnitude of their journey and the painfully slow pace at which they inch along, Marlow compares the steamer to "a sluggish beetle, crawling on the floor of a lofty portico." Travelling from dawn to dusk, seven days a week, how long does the little boat take to get from the Central Station to Kurtz's outpost?

5. As captain, Marlow is kept constantly busy by his many duties and responsibilities, and only his skill and judgment can prevent the ever-present dangers from turning into disasters. Support this statement with concrete details.

6. In addition to Marlow and the manager, "three or four" pilgrims and twenty cannibals are crammed on board the little steamer.

a. How do the pilgrims compare with the cannibals in terms of their usefulness to the expedition?

b. How does the Company reward the cannibals for their services?

7. We read that one native who has been "improved," that is, taught to fire up a vertical boiler, "sweated and fired up and watched the glass fearfully (with an impromptu charm, made of rags, tied to his arm. . .)." (page 82, lines 2-4) What is the reason for both his fear and his charm? To what extent do the cannibals understand the workings of the engine?

8. The expedition comes upon the remains of a camp, fifty miles below the Inner Station. Here there is a woodpile with a note urging them to "hurry up. Approach cautiously."

a. This message is vague and the signature illegible (though the name is definitely *not* Kurtz's). Who apparently has left this note? What possibilities does its warning suggest?

b. We might expect the manager to be grateful to this unknown Samaritan who made the effort to warn them as well as leave them a supply of wood. Instead, he is quite angry and has only dark words and malevolent looks. How can his attitude be explained?

9. The boat is anchored for the night at a point just eight miles below the Inner Station, and the group wakes up the next morning to find themselves caught in a fog which drops down around them like a "white shutter." Momentarily the mist lifts and they begin to pull up anchor, "and then the white shutter came down again." Marlow orders the anchor played back out, when suddenly they hear the hair-raising scream, culminating in a "hurried outbreak of almost intolerably excessive shrieking." (page 85, lines 24-25)

a. What varied reactions does this provoke in the pilgrims, the cannibals, and Marlow?

b. When the pilgrims demand that Marlow move the boat on, why does he refuse?

PSYCHOLOGY OF THE CHARACTERS

10. In the conversation between the manager and his uncle, the image of Kurtz as an idealist with powerful connections is reinforced. This is a man who believes that every trading station "should be like a beacon on the road towards better things . . . humanizing, improving, instructing." (page 76, lines 17–19) But in the story of Kurtz's dismissal of his assistant and his strange last-minute decision to send the ivory on downriver and return to his post alone, we see a new side of the man. What might these incidents indicate about Kurtz's frame of mind? What change of heart might he have undergone?

11. In this portion of the novel, Marlow's feelings of identification with Kurtz are heightened, and he becomes increasingly preoccupied with the man.

a. Support the above statement with passages from the text.

b. How would you explain this intensity of feeling on Marlow's part? What does he see in Kurtz?

c. Why has the conversation Marlow overheard made him especially anxious to reach Kurtz soon?

12. Marlow reflects that, judging by the appearance of the surrounding landscape, he and his companions might well have been the first men on the planet; and then, suddenly,

> . . . As we struggled round a bend, there would be a glimpse of rush walls, of peaked grass-roofs, a burst of yells, a whirl of black limbs, a mass of hands clapping, of feet stamping, of bodies swaying, of eyes rolling, under the droop of heavy and motionless foliage. (page 80, lines 8–12)

These savages are primitive not only in that they lack technology and live in grass huts. What does Marlow mean when he says that he and his companions were "travelling in the night of first ages"? Why is the behavior of these savages so incomprehensible to him?

13. A few lines later, Marlow reconsiders: ". . . If you were man enough you would admit to yourself that there was in you just the faintest trace of a response to the terrible frankness of that noise. . . . The mind of man is capable of anything—because everything is in it, all the past as well as all the future." (page 80, line 31–page 81, line 2) What new insight does Marlow suddenly gain into savagery?

14. You may notice that the mysterious figure of Kurtz and the primitive savages along the riverbank represent totally opposite poles of social development. Yet each plays an important part in Marlow's search for his own identity. How can this be explained?

15. Marlow's speculations regarding the savages and his own sense of kinship with them may be somewhat difficult for the reader to follow. Remember, he is trying to convey to his friends on the barge, twenty years later, the essence of what for him was a traumatic discovery. He alternates between reliving his experience, completely absorbed in it, and being jolted back to the present by the light remarks of his companions who are a little embarrassed by Marlow's emotional outbursts. This creates the occasional interruptions in the narrative where one of Marlow's listeners is prompted to warn him to "be civil" or to tease him about whether Marlow should have given in and gone ashore for "a howl and a dance" himself. What do emerge in this part of the narrative are the key elements in Marlow's analysis of human nature and behavior—a savage core, the human capacity to believe in someone or something, and the "inborn strength" which it takes to act on one's beliefs.

a. How does this "inborn strength" work to keep men from succumbing to the temptations of savagery?

b. What Marlow says here about "belief" sheds some light on his earlier remark (page 42) about the conquest of the earth being redeemed only by the idea in back of it. Reread that passage (lines 3-18) and explain how it applies to imperialism as practiced by both the pilgrims and Kurtz. Is Marlow saying that imperialism is justified?

c. How would Marlow's theory explain the fact that even when they are desperate from hunger, the cannibals refrain from attacking and eating the Europeans?

16. Marlow discovers the book *An Inquiry into Some Points of Seamanship.* This is a highly technical subject, and as Marlow says, "The matter looked dreary reading enough, with illustrative diagrams and repulsive tables of figures." (page 83, lines 2-3) Yet he handles it "tenderly" and finally decides to take it away with him because "to leave off reading was like tearing myself away from the shelter of an old and solid friendship." (page 83, lines 26-27)

a. Marlow is deeply touched both by the book itself and by the loving way its last owner treated it. What is it about these that he finds so moving? How is this especially meaningful to Marlow here in the jungle?

b. How is this response to the book consistent with Marlow's character? What is his own attitude toward work?

17. How does Marlow's attitude toward work provide him with inner strength?

18. Marlow says of the manager: "He was just the kind of man who would wish to preserve appearances. That was his restraint." (page 89, lines 4–5) What does Marlow mean by this? To what extent is the manager sincere in saying he "would be desolated if anything should happen to Mr. Kurtz before we came up"?

READING IN DEPTH

19. Marlow often speaks of "truth" but he makes a distinction between what he calls "reality" and what he calls "surface truth." For example, read the passages on page 78, lines 6–22, and page 81, lines 16–22.

a. What does Marlow mean by "surface truth"? In contrast, what does he mean by "reality"?

b. Marlow says that when you are preoccupied with surface truth, the reality fades and "the truth is hidden—luckily, luckily." Why is this so? Why does Marlow consider it a good thing that the truth is hidden?

20. Marlow depicts the wilderness as something basically hostile to both himself and the pilgrims, resenting what Marlow calls their "fantastic invasion."

a. Consider how, as Marlow says, "We are accustomed to look upon the shackled form of a conquered monster, but there—there you could look at a thing monstrous and free." (page 80, lines 22–24) What does he mean by the phrase "a conquered monster"? In what sense is it shackled? Why would the wilderness be hostile to Europeans?

b. Would the wilderness be equally hostile to the tribes Marlow encounters along the riverbank? Explain.

21. Marlow makes several references to the stillness of the wilderness, which he says is not in any way peaceful.

a. Why does the stillness seem to make him uneasy?

b. Marlow speaks of "the playful paw-strokes of the wilderness." What is he referring to *literally*? Why is this an effective image? What does it suggest may happen eventually?

22. Marlow annoys one of his listeners with his remark about the mysterious stillness "watching me at my monkey tricks, just as it watches you fellows performing on your respective tight-ropes for—what is it? half-a-crown a tumble—" (page 78, lines 19–21) This is the mature Marlow's cynicism coming through, and it is also a variation on a theme which has been stated many times throughout literature. When Marlow speaks of his own "monkey tricks" and refers to his friends "performing on your respective tight-ropes," he is saying that life is a circus. But while a circus is ordinarily thought of as being the epitome of fun and excitement, Marlow's analogy is unflattering and gloomy.

a. In what way does Marlow suggest that he and his friends are like circus performers? Why is this disparaging?

b. In Marlow's interpretation of life, what are the actual rewards for which he and his friends perform? That is, what might he and his friends be working for?

c. What does Marlow mean when he says on page 78 that "heartache" makes up the rest of the price? How does this change the tone of his interpretation of the human condition and make that interpretation more sympathetic?

23. "Going up that river was like travelling back to the earliest beginnings of the world." (page 77, lines 22–23) We have noted that *Heart of Darkness* could be seen on an allegorical level as a descent into and journey through Hell. Now another theme is presented—that of the journey backward into time.

a. What aspects of the journey upriver would make Marlow feel as if he were going backward in time?

b. Assuming that Kurtz has deliberately chosen to go back in time to the past, what would be his apparent purpose? Describe this in terms of light and darkness.

c. Look back over the opening chapter of *Heart of Darkness*. What situation is described there to parallel Marlow's journey up the Congo?

24. Marlow is journeying deep into the heart of primitive and uncharted territory. So far we have mentioned two possible allegorical interpretations of his voyage—the descent into Hell and the trip backward in time. If we take *Heart of Darkness* strictly on a psychological level, what third interpretation can we place on his voyage? What other territory could Marlow be exploring?

VOCABULARY FOR ENRICHMENT

1. *sagacious* (page 76, line 25)

   A. ". . . His *sagacious* relative lifted his head."

   B. The *sagacious* old chief understood the ways of men and could always be relied on for good advice.

a. elderly	*c*. kindly
b. foolish	*d*. wise

2. *edifying* (page 81, line 25)

   A. "He was there below me, and, upon my word, to look at him was as *edifying* as seeing a dog in a parody of breeches. . . ."

   B. It was very *edifying* to the coach to see how much those boys could accomplish with the right guidance and encouragement.

a. startling	*c*. ridiculous
b. instructive	*d*. unpleasant

3. *thrall* (page 81, line 33)

   A. ". . . He was hard at work, a *thrall* to strange witchcraft, full of improving knowledge."

   B. Once he accepted that first bribe he discovered he had made himself a *thrall* to the corrupt elements who controlled much of the town, and they could now ask of him whatever they wanted.

a. victim	*c*. believer
b. slave	*d*. dance

4. *futility* (page 84, line 12)

   A. ". . . It occurred to me that my speech or my silence, indeed any action of mine, would be a mere *futility*."

   B. Recognizing at last the *futility* of trying to change his ways, she gave up and broke their engagement.

a. fiction	*c*. uselessness
b. attempt	*d*. trouble

5. *pensive* (page 86, line 28)

   A. "'Eat 'im!' he said, curtly, and, leaning his elbow on the rail, looked out into the fog in a dignified and profoundly *pensive* attitude."

B. The boy watched the airplane silent and *pensive*, wondering if the day would come when he too would be able to fly like that.

a. thoughtful   c. fearful
b. proud   d. angry

6. *farcical* (page 87, line 1)

A. ". . . As long as there was a piece of paper written over in accordance with some *farcical* law or other made down the river, it didn't enter anybody's head to trouble how they would live."

B. He always gave some *farcical* excuse to explain his lateness, such as that he had been kidnapped by Martians, or a wicked witch had placed him in a pumpkin.

a. ridiculous   c. ancient
b. military   d. unjust

7. *recondite* (page 87, line 17)

A. ". . . The director . . . didn't want to stop the steamer for some more or less *recondite* reason."

B. He must have had some *recondite* reason for appointing such a man as ambassador, but nobody could figure what that reason could be.

a. cruel   c. formal
b. secret   d. imaginary

8. *inexorable* (page 88, line 14)

A. "Yes; I looked at them as you would on any human being, with a curiosity of their impulses, motives, capacities, weaknesses, when brought to the test of an *inexorable* physical necessity."

B. The wide-open spaces were gradually fenced in and built up, victims of the *inexorable* forward march of progress.

a. primitive   c. inescapable
b. psychological   d. invigorating

9. *scruple* (page 88, line 26)

A. "And these chaps, too, had no earthly reason for any kind of *scruple*."

B. A man without a single *scruple*, he would betray his own brother if it paid well enough.

  a. principle   *c.* fear
  b. intelligence   *d.* question

10. *boding* (page 90, line 1)

  A. "They had not the fierce character *boding* immediate hostile intention."

  B. The skies were dark and overcast, *boding* trouble to come.

   a. threatening   *c.* causing
   b. lacking   *d.* embodying

Heart of Darkness: Unit IV
Pages 90 to 105

ACTION AND ADVENTURE

1. Reread page 90, lines 10–23.

a. What is the pilgrims' reaction to Marlow's decision to stay where they are until the fog lifts?

b. To what extent is Marlow's judgment correct? What does he mean when he says, in lines 18–19, that "what we afterwards alluded to as an attack was really an attempt at repulse"?

2. About a mile and a half below Kurtz's station, the party reaches a point where the river divides to flow around an island and they must choose either the east branch or the west. Which side does Marlow choose, and why? How does his choice help to bring on the "attack"?

3. Marlow observes "I was looking down at the sounding-pole. . . ." (page 92, line 4) Why is he annoyed by the fact that each time he looks, a little more of the pole sticks out? What are the implications of this phenomenon?

4. Suddenly the poleman drops flat on the deck and the fireman sits down and ducks his head. How do you explain their behavior? What are the little sticks?

5. Read the description of the layout of the steamer on page 91 in lines 17–26, and try to visualize the position of the pilothouse constructed on the roof which shades the deck below. If you like, draw a picture or diagram based on Marlow's description. This should help you to clarify the action that takes place there.

a. What does Marlow attempt to do in order to protect his helmsman? How does this lead him to see the face in the bush?

b. As Marlow stands in the pilothouse trying to calm his terrified helmsman, he notices a V-shaped ripple in the water ahead. The steamer is headed for another snag! How is his attempt to cope with this problem frustrated by the behavior of the pilgrims?

c. To what extent does the gunfire serve any useful purpose? (See also page 101.)

6. If Marlow succeeded in closing the shutter once, how does it come to be opened again? How is the helmsman killed? (A Martini-Henry is a large rifle.) What is the "long cane"?

7. What finally puts an end to the attack, and why?

8. Why does Marlow throw his "perfectly good" shoes overboard?

9. Why does Marlow feel so "desolate" at this point? What conclusion does he draw from the "attack"?

10. At this point Conrad suddenly departs from the linear time-sequence of Marlow's narrative and gives us a five-page digression (95-100) in which he jumps forward into the future and tells what really did happen to Kurtz, giving hints about Kurtz's relationship with the natives and the fact that his "let us say—nerves, went wrong. . . ." We also learn that Kurtz was writing a report for the International Society for the Suppression of Savage Customs.

a. Why would Kurtz have been "intrusted" to make this report? What kind of organization must the Society have been? What was to be the purpose of the report?

b. According to the report, what was Kurtz's primary recommendation on how to get the natives to adopt civilized behavior? How could Europeans "exert a power for good practically unbounded"?

c. According to Marlow, sometime after Kurtz wrote this report his "nerves went wrong." What does Marlow mean by this? To what extent did Kurtz follow his own recommendation and in what way did he depart from it?

d. What role did the ivory play in Kurtz's new view of things? How is this contrary to what Marlow had imagined?

11. Marlow makes several references to "a girl" and again, to Kurtz's "Intended." What is the meaning of the phrase "My Intended"? Who must the girl be?

12. Returning to the point in the story where the helmsman has just been killed, Marlow describes how he threw the man's corpse overboard. (pages 100–101) How do the pilgrims react to this deed? Why does Marlow do it?

13. Now that the attack is over, how do the pilgrims view it in retrospect? Why are they so indignant toward Marlow?

14. What are the manager's plans regarding continuing the rescue mission? What does he want Marlow to do? What does Marlow see which prevents him from carrying out the manager's order?

15. "Armed to the teeth," the manager and the pilgrims set off to investigate the station house, leaving Marlow alone with the stranger, who has come on board the steamer for a chat. "I don't like this," Marlow remarks. What is he worried about? What reassurance does the stranger offer?

16. What small mystery is solved when Marlow learns the identity of the stranger?

17. What does Marlow learn about the real purpose of the "attack"?

PSYCHOLOGY OF THE CHARACTERS

18. On page 100, lines 26–27, Marlow says of the dead helmsman, he "had no restraint." This is a subject he has touched on in earlier parts of the story. What does he mean by it? In what way did the helmsman demonstrate a lack of restraint?

19. How do Marlow's feelings toward the helmsman change after the man's death? How does he explain this change?

20. Note Marlow's comment about the helmsman that "he had done something, he had steered." How is this remark in keeping with Marlow's character and values? How does it relate to other reactions he has had to characters earlier in the novel?

21. Marlow says, concerning Kurtz, "I never imagined him as doing, you know, but as discoursing." How is this a departure from his usual view, as of the helmsman?

22. "You should have heard him say, 'My ivory.' Oh yes, I heard him. 'My Intended, my ivory, my station, my river, my—'" (page 97, lines 24-26) What does this reveal to us about Kurtz's illness? What has happened to him?

23. What is the significance of the postscriptum to his report, "Exterminate all the brutes"? What does this indicate?

24. Read back over the first ten lines of page 104, in which Marlow and the Russian first become acquainted. Be careful to follow, by the quotation marks, which one of them is saying what. What made the Russian come to this area in the first place? What made him decide to stay on? (Note the exchange in lines 9-10, "'Here!' I interrupted. 'You never can tell! Here I met Mr. Kurtz.'")

READING IN DEPTH

25. On page 95 Marlow is expressing his own feelings of sorrow and desolation at the prospect of never getting to meet Kurtz, when one of his listeners interrupts, accusing Marlow of being "absurd." At this point Marlow breaks the train of the narrative to jump ahead in time, revealing to us the startling truth of what he will actually find when he reaches the Inner Station.

   a. What ironic effect does Conrad achieve by suddenly giving us a glimpse of the truth about Kurtz?

   b. How does this lend an important extra dimension to the subsequent pages of the story? That is, knowing the truth as we do, what are we able to see about the other characters in the story? For example, how does this affect the reader's reaction to the Russian?

26. Read closely from page 96 to the bottom of page 98. On page 96, Marlow reminds his friends that they each have two good addresses, a butcher and a policeman. Again, at the bottom of page 97 and over on to 98 he speaks of neighbors, butchers, and policemen.

   a. According to Marlow, what important function do all of these serve? What do they protect us from and how?

   b. According to Marlow, what happens when the external restraints of society are removed? What must a person then have to prevent him from acting out his impulses?

27. How is the allegorical interpretation of *Heart of Darkness* as a journey through Hell borne out in this section of the novel?

28. Reread carefully page 98. Marlow makes the point that fools are rarely assaulted by the powers of Darkness, but that ordinary men frequently are. He describes this assault in terms of "dead hippo." You may remember that dead hippo meat was brought along for food by the cannibals, but that the pilgrims threw it overboard because the stench was so awful that, as Marlow says, to have to breathe it continually would make you lose your grip on existence. However, as Marlow uses the phrase now, "dead hippo" stands for more than just the rotten meat brought on board by the natives.

a. On a more symbolic level, what exactly does "dead hippo" stand for, and why would its existence constitute an assault on us by the powers of Darkness?

b. What does Marlow mean by saying that a man's strength is dependent on "faith in his ability for the digging of unostentatious holes to bury the stuff in"? (page 98, lines 24–25) What does he feel we must do, when faced with the phenomenon of dead hippo?

c. On the surface Marlow is speaking only of physical decay and corruption. Can a further analogy be drawn between this and moral corruption and decay? How would this be appropriate for *Heart of Darkness*?

d. Why would fools and exalted creatures be exempted from confronting moral corruption? Whom is Marlow referring to when he speaks of "exalted creatures"?

VOCABULARY FOR ENRICHMENT

Each of the following ten words is first given in the context of the sentence in which it appears in the book (A), then in a second sentence (B) whose context gives specific help as to the meaning of the word. Select the best definition of the word from the four choices given.

1. *revile* (page 90, line 10)

A. "They had no heart to grin or even to *revile* me. . . ."

B. You may scream and *revile* me all you like but I have my orders and you will not be admitted without a written pass.

    a. hit   *c.* amuse
    b. curse   *d.* anger

2. *dubious* (page 95, line 4)

A. "He looked very *dubious;* but I made a grab at his arm, and he understood at once I meant him to steer whether or no."

B. The chances of their winning the championship are rather *dubious* at this point unless their batters pull out of their slump.

a. frightened   c. doubtful
b. stupid   d. unhappy

3. *inestimable* (page 96, line 24)

A. "I was cut to the quick at the idea of having lost the *inestimable* privilege of listening to the gifted Kurtz."

B. He is a person of *inestimable* value to our country, a man we simply cannot afford to lose.

a. honorable   c. small
b. unfortunate   d. immeasurable

4. *sordid* (page 96, line 31)

A. ". . . The memory of that time itself lingers around me, impalpable, like a dying vibration of one immense jabber, silly, atrocious, *sordid*, savage, or simply mean, without any kind of sense."

B. In her work as a crime reporter she soon became acquainted with the more *sordid* details of life.

a. ugly   c. musical
b. assorted   d. foreign

5. *disinterred* (page 97, line 3)

A. "You should have heard the *disinterred* body of Mr. Kurtz saying 'My Intended.' "

B. On Halloween, ghosts and *disinterred* corpses are said to wander freely away from their graves.

a. dissatisfied   c. unhealthy
b. disturbed   d. unburied

6. *disparagingly* (page 97, line 17)

A. " 'Mostly fossil,' the manager had remarked, *disparagingly*."

B. They spoke so *disparagingly* of the hotel that I really wondered why they always stayed there.

    a. proudly   *c.* slightingly
    b. hopefully   *d.* sadly

7. *exalted* (page 98, line 16)

    A. "Or you may be such a thunderingly *exalted* creature as to be altogether deaf and blind to anything but heavenly sights and sounds."

    B. In former days, kings were *exalted* creatures, whose powers were regarded as being of divine origin.

        a. glorified   *c.* innocent
        b. stupid   *d.* busy

8. *wraith* (page 98, line 29)

    A. "This initiated *wraith* from the back of Nowhere honoured me with its amazing confidence before it vanished altogether."

    B. The *wraith* appeared before the king for a few moments, sighed, and then disappeared in smoke.

        a. anger   *c.* traveller
        b. genius   *d.* spirit

9. *peroration* (page 99, line 19)

    A. "The *peroration* was magnificent, though difficult to remember, you know."

    B. After a rousing *peroration*, the speaker sat down.

        a. style   *c.* conclusion
        b. introduction   *d.* subject

10. *cipher* (page 104, line 34)

    A. " 'I thought they were written in *cipher*,' I said."

    B. It was a very simple kind of *cipher*—the kind two schoolboys might invent to send secret messages to each other.

        a. language   *c.* code
        b. Greek   *d.* jest

Heart of Darkness: Unit V

Pages 105 to 121

ACTION AND ADVENTURE

1. In the course of his conversation with the Russian, Marlow learns more about what Kurtz has been doing in the past year.

a. Exactly how has Kurtz been carrying on his ivory trading? What use has he made of the natives?

b. Why did Kurtz at one point threaten to shoot the Russian?

c. What is the significance of the "ornamental knobs" atop the "fence-posts" which surround Kurtz's house? What did Marlow think they were at first? What are they in fact?

2. The Russian explains to Marlow how, when he first met Kurtz, the two of them stayed up all night talking, and that experience made such an impression on him that he has stayed on in the jungle ever since, just to be near Kurtz. Yet when Marlow asks if they have been together all this time, the Russian tells him no. What was the nature of the Russian's relationship with Kurtz? Why was it so difficult?

3. How does the Russian justify Kurtz's behavior? Why does he urge Marlow, "You take Kurtz away quick--quick--I tell you"? (page 105, line 16)

4. The pilgrims have Kurtz brought out of his house on a stretcher so that he can be taken on board the steamer. At this point the Russian remarks to Marlow, "Now, if he does not say the right thing to them we are all done for." (page 111, lines 24–25)

a. Who does he mean by "them"? Why are Marlow and company in danger?

b. How in fact does Kurtz react to the situation?

5. Once Kurtz has been carried on board, what are his reactions to Marlow and the pilgrims? To what extent does he seem to have assumed his old personality?

315

6. Why does the Russian decide to leave at this point?

7. Before leaving, however, the Russian tells Marlow that he trusts him as a brother seaman and knows that Marlow won't betray Kurtz or spoil Kurtz's reputation by repeating what he is about to tell him. He then proceeds to tell a secret.

a. What information does he reveal?

b. What is the warning inherent in this new information? If it is true, what must Marlow be prepared to expect?

8. How is this warning fulfilled? How does Kurtz escape? Where does he try to go?

9. Rather than awaken any of the pilgrims, Marlow decides to deal with this situation himself, following Kurtz's trail through the tall grass of the clearing.

a. Why is what Marlow is doing dangerous?

b. How does Marlow convince Kurtz to turn around and come back with him? What does Marlow mean when he says, "You will be lost"? (page 120, line 1)

PSYCHOLOGY OF THE CHARACTERS

10. The young Russian seems to be continually taking extraordinary risks and enduring terrible hardships. As Marlow says, "For months—for years—his life hadn't been worth a day's purchase; and there he was gallantly, thoughtlessly alive, to all appearance indestructible solely by the virtue of his few years and of his unreflecting audacity." (page 105, lines 19-22)

a. What does Marlow mean when, speaking of the Russian's love for adventure, he says, "Glamour urged him on, glamour kept him unscathed"? What does he mean by "glamour" and how does it play a part in the Russian's life?

b. What exactly are the young man's feelings about Kurtz? How has this relationship affected his life?

c. Think back to Marlow's early expectations regarding Kurtz. To what extent is the Russian similar in nature to Marlow? Where do they differ, and why?

11. Kurtz first got the natives to "adore him" and then was able to use them to carry out his tyrannical program. How did he win their adoration?

12. What does Marlow mean when he says, "Some of the pilgrims behind the stretcher carried his arms—two shot-guns, a heavy rifle, and a light revolver-carbine—the thunderbolts of that pitiful Jupiter"? (page 112, lines 17-19)

13. After Marlow has realized the significance of the ornamented poles, he says that the wilderness has taken vengeance on Kurtz for the fantastic invasion and "had whispered to him things about himself which he did not know, things of which he had no conception till he took counsel with this great solitude." (page 109, lines 32-34) This is of course personification; the wilderness didn't actually speak to Kurtz, but certain ideas did enter his mind after he had been alone there for some time.

a. What sorts of things did the wilderness whisper?

b. How did the suggestions of the wilderness fit in with the personal moral code which Kurtz had espoused all his life?

14. Once the primitive personality of Kurtz emerged, what happened to the other one? Under what circumstances would it reappear? When it did reappear, how did he behave?

15. When Kurtz is in a normal state of mind, to what extent is he aware of what he has been doing in his bad periods?

16. What is the manager's attitude toward what has happened? What does he plan to do about it? What does he mean when he tells Marlow, "The time was not ripe for vigorous action"? (page 115, line 3)

17. What is Marlow's reaction to the manager? To what extent does any real communication take place between him and the manager? Why is there a communication gap?

18. What does Marlow mean when he says, "Ah! but it was something to have a choice of nightmares." How has the entire African experience been nightmarish for him? In what sense does he now, and for the first time, have a choice?

19. "I did not betray Mr. Kurtz—it was ordered I should never betray him—it was written I should be loyal to the nightmare of my choice." (page 118, lines 21-23)

a. What does being loyal to the nightmare of his choice consist of?

b. Why does Marlow use the expressions "it was written" and "it was ordered"? To what extent is he in control of what he does on these occasions? To what extent is it a matter of fate?

20. In the midst of Marlow's confrontation with Kurtz, Marlow says that it is here at this very moment that "the foundations of our intimacy were being laid." What does he mean by this? Why would such a confrontation be the basis of any subsequent intimacy between them?

21. Why does Kurtz go back to the jungle after he has allowed himself to be taken on board the steamer?

22. Why is the experience so terrifying for Marlow? What does he mean when he says Kurtz had "kicked himself loose of the earth"? What does such an act make Kurtz?

READING IN DEPTH

23. The Russian recounts his all-night discussion with Kurtz, ending with the exclamation, "He made me see things—things." Just as the Russian says that Kurtz made him see things in the middle of the forest, Marlow looks around and realizes that "never before, did this land, this river, this jungle, the very arch of this blazing sky, appear to me so hopeless and so dark, so impenetrable to human thought, so pitiless to human weakness." (page 106, lines 24-27)

What is the irony in placing these two paragraphs next to each other?

24. Marlow says of Kurtz that the whisper of the wilderness proved irresistibly fascinating to Kurtz, and "It echoed loudly within him because he was hollow at the core." (page 109, lines 35-36) Read this carefully. The use of the word echo is really a metaphor. What is Conrad saying about the inner nature of man in relation to the force of nature in general? What common relationship do they both share with civilization?

25. The magnificent "gorgeous apparition of a woman" comes out of the jungle, walks up to the steamer, throws her arms to the sky and then retreats back into the bushes. Who is this woman? On a more symbolic level what might she represent?

26. All throughout *Heart of Darkness* much emphasis is placed upon Kurtz's voice. The pilgrims keep saying, "You should hear him!" Marlow looks forward to hearing him. The Russian tells Marlow of how marvelous an experience it is to hear the man talk. Then Marlow remarks that "there was something wanting in him—some small matter which, when the pressing need arose, could not be found under his magnificent eloquence." (page 109, lines 25-28)

What is the danger which is always involved in the use of oratory, a danger of which Kurtz is an example? What point is Marlow making about the "magnificent eloquence"?

27. On page 110 the Russian has just explained to Marlow that the heads on stakes are those of rebels. Marlow says, "I shocked him excessively by laughing. Rebels! What would be the next definition I was to hear? There had been enemies, criminals, workers—and these were rebels." (lines 25-27)

Who were the "enemies, criminals, workers"? Why is Marlow laughing?

28. We have traced the allegorical interpretation of Marlow's journey as a voyage through Hell.

a. What new instances of this can you find in this section of the novel?

b. How does the Russian fit into this interpretation? Why is he able to come to this place without getting trapped? Why is he able to leave without any trouble?

29. While the main allegory of *Heart of Darkness* is that of the trip through Hell, the story can be interpreted, to a lesser degree, as a trip backward in time to the dark ages of Man, and a descent through the civilized layers of consciousness into the depths of the human psyche. At this point the careful reader should be able to sort out and recognize all three of these themes and also discover how they can be tied together. In order to do this let us first consider some of the various connotations of the word Hell.

In the Greek sense, Hades is the land of the dead, and a place where the gods provided appropriate punishments to anyone who defied them. In the Christian sense, Hell is the kingdom of evil or the Devil. It is also characterized by the complete absence of goodness or of God, and it is where human souls are punished for the sins of their former life. In a broader sense, Hell is a place or condition from which there is no escape and in which the one thing a person hates or dreads most will happen to him.

a. To what extent do the above connotations apply to *Heart of Darkness*?

b. What does Conrad seem to be saying about good and evil? How do light and darkness fit in to Conrad's ideas on good and evil?

c. What is the connection between the themes of the journey through

Hell, the journey backward to the dawn of Man, and the inward journey into the psyche? As he goes on all three of these trips, what does Marlow discover?

VOCABULARY FOR ENRICHMENT

1. *privation* (page 105, line 27)

   A. "His need was to exist, and to move onwards at the greatest possible risk, and with a maximum of *privation*."

   B. After years of *privation*, doing without a winter coat, washing dishes to pay for supplies, he suddenly found himself a wealthy and successful artist.

   a. privilege   *c*. privacy
   b. hardship   *d*. gain

2. *aspirations* (page 108, line 25)

   A. "Evidently the appetite for more ivory had got the better of the—what shall I say?—less material *aspirations*."

   B. He married the president's daughter, took over the business, and forgot all his former *aspirations* to become a composer.

   a. colonialists   *c*. ambitions
   b. spirits   *d*. things

3. *brusque* (page 108, line 32)

   A. "And then I made a *brusque* movement, and one of the remaining posts of that vanished fence leaped up in the field of my glass."

   B. Pardon me for having been so *brusque* over the phone, but my boss walked in unexpectedly and I had to hang up.

   a. careless   *c*. tricky
   b. surprise   *d*. abrupt

4. *ascendancy* (page 110, line 7)

   A. "His *ascendancy* was extraordinary."

   B. He gained *ascendancy* over the other boys in the third grade by being able to wiggle his ears and by beating them at marbles.

   a. inheritance   *c*. ancestry
   b. dominance   *d*. temper

5. *veriest* (page 110, line 23)

   A. "If it had come to crawling before Mr. Kurtz, he crawled as the *veriest* savage of them all."

   B. Even the *veriest* beggar in the streets looks in better shape than you.

   a. truest   *c.* wildest
   b. happiest   *d.* bravest

6. *fecund* (page 113, line 27)

   A. ". . . The colossal body of the *fecund* and mysterious life seemed to look at her. . . ."

   B. They soon discovered that all manner of fruits and vegetables could thrive beautifully in the *fecund* California soil.

   a. secret   *c.* fertile
   b. poor   *d.* evil

7. *formidable* (page 114, line 10)

   A. "A *formidable* silence hung over the scene."

   B. Dinner with her parents is as *formidable* as sharing a picnic with a grizzly bear.

   a. mysterious   *c.* fortunate
   b. fearsome   *d.* peaceful

8. *deplorable* (page 115, line 5)

   A. "The district is closed to us for a time. *Deplorable*!"

   B. It is truly *deplorable* the way we have allowed our rivers and air to become so polluted.

   a. marvelous   *c.* impossible
   b. shameful   *d.* amusing

9. *obtruded* (page 118, line 33)

   A. "The knitting old woman with the cat *obtruded* herself upon my memory as a most improper person to be sitting at the other end of such an affair."

   B. Although nobody invited him and none of us liked him, he always *obtruded* himself into our group when we went out Saturday nights.

   a. invited   *c.* erased
   b. forced   *d.* invented

10. *beguiled* (page 120, line 22)

   A. ". . . This alone had *beguiled* his unlawful soul beyond the bounds of permitted aspirations."

   B. The child *beguiled* the baby sitter into letting him stay up past midnight.

      a. permitted   *c.* changed
      b. enticed   *d.* damaged

Heart of Darkness: Unit VI

Pages 121 to 135

ACTION AND ADVENTURE

1. What is the "fierce river-demon" Marlow refers to on page 121, line 29? What are the three men in red trying to do?

2. Marlow begins to pull the string, sounding the whistle repeatedly. Why does he do it? Why don't the pilgrims want him to do it?

3. Why does Kurtz hand his private papers over to Marlow?

4. In the course of the return trip, the engine breaks down, forcing them to stop a long time for repairs. Marlow says, "I toiled wearily in a wretched scrap-heap—unless I had the shakes too bad to stand." (page 124, lines 26–27) What is the matter with him? How serious do these "shakes" become?

5. After Marlow has been nursed back to health again in Brussels, under the care of his aunt, he receives a series of visitors. Each man comes looking for something in particular. What is each one looking for? How does Marlow deal with each and why?

6. Why does Marlow go to visit Kurtz's fiancée?

7. When Marlow finds the girl, she is still in mourning, even though it is more than a year since she learned of Kurtz's death. Almost immediately she makes a mistaken assumption about Marlow. What does she presume his feelings about Kurtz to be? Why?

8. Why does she ask Marlow to tell her Kurtz's last words? Why does he lie to her?

PSYCHOLOGY OF THE CHARACTERS

9. In the last few pages of the story, Marlow reveals certain information about Kurtz's life before he went out to Africa, as told to him by his various visitors. In some ways this information supports the idea of what an extraordinary person Kurtz was, and accentuates the tragedy of what had happened to him.

We learn that Kurtz was indeed a multitalented genius, that he could have been a great success in politics, that his goodness served as an example and an inspiration to all those who knew him. At the same time, however, we are given certain clues into the character of the man which might explain his downfall. What things do we learn about Kurtz's personality which, while not necessarily bad in themselves, might have precipitated what happened to him?

10. Reread closely pages 123-125. What does Marlow mean when he says, "The shade of the original Kurtz frequented the bedside of the hollow sham. . . . But both the diabolic love and the unearthly hate of the mysteries it had penetrated fought for the possession of that soul satiatea with primitive emotions, avid of lying fame . . ."? (page 123, lines 19-24)

11. What is the final event in Kurtz's life? His last words are "The horror! The horror!" What happens to make him say this? What does he mean? (See page 125, lines 31-34.)

12. When the manager's boy comes out to announce that Kurtz is dead, the pilgrims rush in to see, but Marlow goes on eating his dinner, causing the pilgrims to accuse him of being brutally callous. How do you explain his behavior?

13. Shortly after Kurtz's death, Marlow becomes critically ill himself, and for weeks he lies on the brink of death. He describes this state on pages 125-126.

a. What are his predominant emotions at this point?

b. What is the big difference that Marlow believes exists between himself in his extremity and Kurtz in his?

c. Why does this make Kurtz remarkable, in Marlow's opinion? Why does it constitute a kind of victory?

14. Marlow returns to Belgium and eventually recovers. During the period of his convalescence he feels very critical of the Belgians, by turns resenting them and restraining a desire to burst out laughing at them. What is it about the Belgians that so disturbs Marlow? How is this attitude the result of his own recent experience?

15. Marlow goes to meet the girl, acknowledging a sense of panic as she ushers him into her house. Marlow realizes that "for her he had died only yesterday. And, by Jove! the impression was so powerful that for me, too, he seemed to have died only yesterday . . . ." (page 131, lines 25–27)

Why is Marlow so disturbed at this? Why is the difference between her image of Kurtz's death and his own so important?

16. Why is the girl so anxious to speak with Marlow?

17. Marlow listens to the girl talk and then confides to his listeners that he is not even sure Kurtz had given him the right bundle of letters. What is the point of this remark? Why does it add to Marlow's growing unease?

18. Check Marlow's previous references to the girl on pages 97, 100, and 127. Notice the constant emphasis on her purity and unselfishness. Is she portrayed as a believable human being, or is this portrait a romanticized view of Woman, as conceived by a male writer who doesn't really understand female psychology, and imagines women to be generically different from men? Explain your answer.

READING IN DEPTH

19. Notice how on page 134, lines 10–17, Marlow juxtaposes the images of the two women. What do they have in common? How does each one represent a single side of Kurtz? To what extent could either one comprehend the existence of the other?

20. Notice Conrad's use of darkness in the final scene of Marlow's tale when he confronts the girl. Why does it keep getting darker in the room during the course of their conversation?

21. Observe how Marlow makes it seem as if the girl is the one source of light in the room. (pages 131–133)

a. In what metaphorical sense is she giving off light?

b. To explore this metaphor further, why does Marlow say that to have rendered Kurtz the justice which was his due would have made it too dark altogether?

c. In general, what is Conrad saying about illusions and their place in our lives? Does everyone need them? What happens if they are destroyed?

22. Read the final paragraph of the story. In terms of light and dark, what subtle change has been effected in the description of the river? What does this indicate about the effect which the story has had upon Marlow's audience? (Check back to the opening pages of the story.)

23. Marlow has a sudden intense vision of Kurtz, of whom he says, "He lived then before me; he lived as much as he had ever lived—a shadow insatiable of splendid appearances, of frightful realities." (page 130, lines 6–8) Consider the possible meanings which this phrase evokes. How can it be taken as a central image of *Heart of Darkness*? How does it apply to the whole phenomenon of imperialism?

VOCABULARY FOR ENRICHMENT

1. *tenebrous* (page 123, line 9)

   A. "It is strange how I accepted the unforeseen partnership, this choice of nightmares forced upon me in the *tenebrous* land invaded by those mean and greedy phantoms."

   B. Those supernatural creatures dwell in that *tenebrous* region that lies between night and day, between life and death.

      a. beautiful   *c.* shadowy
      b. hot   *d.* green

2. *avid* (page 123, line 24)

   A. "But both the diabolic love and the unearthly hate of the mysteries it had penetrated fought for the possession of that soul satiated with primitive emotions, *avid* of lying fame. . . ."

   B. She was an *avid* reader, devouring all the new books as they came into the library and still waiting impatiently for more.

      a. tired   *c.* scornful
      b. indifferent   *d.* greedy

3. *candour* (page 126, line 16)

   A. ". . . It had *candour*, it had conviction, it had a vibrating note of revolt in its whisper. . . ."

B. He spoke with complete *candour* [or *candor*], admitting to his prison record and subsequent difficulties with the law.

a. sweetness   c. frankness
b. criminality   d. pride

4. *evanescence* (page 126, line 21)

A. "And it is not my own extremity I remember best—a vision of grayness without form filled with physical pain, and a careless contempt for the *evanescence* of all things. . . ."

B. Like the *evanescence* of the sunset her beauty was short-lived.

a. fleetingness   c. ugliness
b. mystery   d. substance

5. *circuitous* (page 127, line 31)

A. "A clean-shaved man . . . called on me one day and made inquiries, at first *circuitous*, afterwards suavely pressing, about what he was pleased to *denominate* certain 'documents.' "

B. As the crow flies the two towns are only seven miles apart but the road is so *circuitous* it takes nearly an hour to drive there.

a. crude   c. roundabout
b. open   d. bumpy

6. *denominate* (page 127, line 32)

A. See 5A.

B. If you wish to *denominate* him leader, you may do so, but then you will have to obey him.

a. name   c. desire
b. sell   d. demand

7. *oblivion* (page 129, line 28)

A. ". . . I wanted to give that up, too, to the past, in a way—to surrender personally all that remained of him with me to that *oblivion* which is the last word of our common fate."

B. After a few years of glory the star lost his touch and finally was consigned to *oblivion* along with so many other has-beens.

a. state of forgiveness   c. state of glory
b. state of innocence   d. state of being forgotten

8. *abject* (page 130, line 22)

   A. "I remembered his *abject* pleading, his abject threats, the colossal scale of his vile desires, the meanness, the torment, the tempestuous anguish of his soul."

   B. The old beggar turned up both hands in an *abject* gesture of despair.

   a. servile   *c*. evil
   b. proud   *d*. insane

9. *sarcophagus* (page 131, line 6)

   A. "A grand piano stood massively in a corner; with dark gleams on the flat surfaces like a sombre and polished *sarcophagus*."

   B. The archaeologists ventured into the opened tomb in an attempt to decipher the hieroglyphics on the *sarcophagus* of the pharoah.

   a. sculpture   *c*. idol
   b. coffin   *d*. altar

10. *infernal* (page 134, line 17)

   A. ". . . I shall see her, too, a tragic and familiar Shade, . . . stretching bare brown arms over the glitter of the *infernal* stream, the stream of darkness."

   B. Few people have ever managed to descend to the *infernal* regions and then escape, still in possession of their souls.

   a. endless   *c*. famous
   b. glittering   *d*. hellish

Typhoon: Unit I

Chapter One

ACTION AND ADVENTURE

1. The first chapter of *Typhoon* is disordered in its time sequence because it contains so many flashbacks and digressions. We are told of how MacWhirr ran off to sea at the age of fifteen, how he rose to the rank of captain and then married, how the *Nan-Shan* was commissioned and built and MacWhirr selected to be her captain, how the owners decided to change the registry, that the cargo and the coolies are taken on board destined for Fu-Chau, and how the barometer begins to fall.

Why would the *Nan-Shan*'s owners have considered it a wise move to transfer the ship from British registry to Siamese?

2. The coolies are being sent home after seven years by the Bun Hin Company, which originally hired and imported them from Fo-kien province. The Bun Hin Company clerk is sent on board to ensure that the coolies are properly accommodated.

   a. Read the speech to the clerk which Jukes makes in pidgin-English, (the dialect used by English and Orientals to communicate with each other) on page 146. What does Jukes assure the man?

   b. Where in fact are the coolies being accommodated?

3. The captain orders the ship's carpenter to nail three-inch high strips of wood along the cargo deck to secure the coolies' boxes in place should the boat start to toss on rough seas. Why are these boxes so important to the coolies?

4. Actually the last in the chronological sequence of events in Chapter One (and this is where Chapter Two will take up) is when, in the chartroom on the bridge of the steamer, Captain MacWhirr checks the barometer and notices that it has fallen.

   a. What is the significance of the drop in pressure?

   b. What other indications are there on page 140 of bad weather to come?

PSYCHOLOGY OF THE CHARACTERS

5. One dominant quality of Captain MacWhirr is his lack of "imagination," i.e., his indifference to everything but the practical and the present. As Conrad says, MacWhirr has "just enough imagination to carry him through each successive day, and no more," (page 138, lines 16–17) and, it would be "as impossible for him to take a flight of fancy as it would be for a watchmaker to put together a chronometer with nothing except a two-pound hammer and a whipsaw in the way of tools." (page 138, lines 22–25)

Viewed from another angle, MacWhirr's lack of "imagination" can be interpreted as calm objectivity, and an unwillingness to indulge in emotionalism or romantic fantasies.

    a. How do MacWhirr's lack of "imagination" and his objectivity reveal themselves in his letters home to his parents?

    b. How does MacWhirr's character affect the tenor of life on board his ship?

    c. How does MacWhirr's character affect his reaction to the falling barometer?

6. After the *Nan-Shan* is built, her builders decide that MacWhirr would be a good, reliable captain for her. Read over the account of their interview with him and MacWhirr's first inspection of the ship. (pages 141–142) Notice how MacWhirr's behavior in this situation is totally characteristic. After the interview, the two partners disagree on the desirability of having such a man as captain. How do you explain the difference in their judgment? Why is the younger partner so contemptuous? What details served to form each man's opinion?

7. We are told that MacWhirr travelled up from London after "a sudden but undemonstrative parting with his wife. She was the daughter of a superior couple who had seen better days." (page 141, lines 19–21) This is a form of ironic understatement, by means of which Conrad is filling us in on MacWhirr's relationship with his wife. What is Conrad really telling us here? What other instances can you find in the text to support this?

8. In contrast to the captain is the character of Mr. Jukes, the first mate, who has a very highly developed imagination and who is continually butting his head against the brick wall of MacWhirr's matter-of-factedness. What exactly are Jukes' feelings toward his captain? Why, when he is so annoyed over the incident of the flag, doesn't he "throw up his billet" (quit) as he had promised Mr. Rout he would?

9. Conrad says that Jukes "was gruff, as became his racial superiority, but not unfriendly." (page 146, lines 5-6)

   a. Does Conrad really mean that Jukes is racially superior, or only that he considers himself so? Explain.

   b. How does this attitude of racial conceit underlie Jukes' dislike of the new flag?

READING IN DEPTH
10. Speaking in a light vein, Conrad notes that "the uninteresting lives of men so entirely given to the actuality of the bare existence have their mysterious side." (page 138, lines 25-26) This statement is meant to be ironic.

   a. What is the one and only mystery Conrad sees in MacWhirr's history? How is this observation just another way of stressing the man's personality?

   b. What solution does Conrad offer to the mystery?

11. Again, touching on the subject of MacWhirr's literalness, the builder says to the captain, "My uncle wrote of you favourably.... You'll be able to boast of being in charge of the handiest boat of her size on the coast of China." (page 141, lines 29-33) MacWhirr mumbles an answer and Conrad observes that, to the captain, "the view of a distant eventuality could appeal no more than the beauty of a wide landscape to a purblind tourist." Explain this analogy. Why is MacWhirr unable to appreciate a distant eventuality?

12. Conrad treats MacWhirr's clashes with Jukes in a comic fashion, the humor lying in the absurdity of the captain's literal-mindedness and his complete obliviousness to the reaction he is producing in his first mate. Often MacWhirr will say or do something that drives Jukes wild, but there is really nothing Jukes can do because MacWhirr wouldn't want to understand what was bothering him. What instances can you find in the text to illustrate this?

13. In this chapter considerable emphasis is placed on MacWhirr's lack of "imagination," and some fun is had at his expense because of it. However, a careful reading of the story should reveal that in a deeper sense MacWhirr's lack of imagination is not necessarily a fault or a weakness, and that, in the author's eyes, "imagination" is not really such a valuable asset.

 a. Consider what Conrad seems to mean by the term "imagination," and explain why it might not be such a good thing in a ship's captain.

 b. In the dispute over the Siamese flag, how is Jukes' attitude the result of his imagination? Does the author mean us to side with Jukes? Explain.

14. In this chapter we see passages from the letters written by the captain, the chief mate, and the chief engineer. These serve two purposes in that they give us glimpses of shipboard life, seen from the perspective of each man, and they provide insight into the men themselves.

 a. What do we learn about each of these three men from their letters? Keep in mind the style, the content, the choice of whom to write to, and the reactions of the people who receive the letters.

 b. What is the joke involved in Mrs. Rout's encounter with the curate? (page 148)

 c. Jukes tells his friend, "All the chaps of the black-squad are as decent as they make that kind." (page 149, lines 10-11) What is the black-squad? What is the traditional relationship between the black-squad and deckhands?

15. What is the significance of the fact that *every* letter MacWhirr writes contains some comment to the effect that there has been "fine weather this trip"?

16. "Captain MacWhirr had sailed over the surface of the oceans as some men go skimming over the years of existence. . . . " (page 151, lines 2-4)

 a. What is Conrad saying about people who lead an easy, happy life? What is ambivalent about the last sentence of the chapter?

 b. Having read this first chapter, and especially these last two pages, what can we as readers assume is going to happen?

VOCABULARY FOR ENRICHMENT

1. *physiognomy* (page 137, line 1)

 A. "Captain MacWhirr, of the steamer *Nan-Shan*, had a *physiognomy* that, in the order of material appearances, was the exact counterpart of his mind. . . ."

B. From his battered *physiognomy* you could tell he'd been a professional fighter.

   a. physique   *c.* face
   b. wardrobe   *d.* brain

2. *corpulent* (page 139, line 13)

   A. "He was a *corpulent* man, with a gift for sly chaffing. . . ."

   B. In later years he grew so *corpulent* that he had to pay extra for outsized clothes.

   a. wealthy   *c.* stingy
   b. stout   *d.* humorous

3. *missives* (page 139, line 20)

   A. "In these *missives* could be found sentences like this: 'The heat here is very great.' "

   B. The *missives* my brother sent home from college consisted mainly of requests for food and money.

   a. letters   *c.* books
   b. missiles   *d* speeches

4. *loquacious* (page 142, line 21)

   A. "With a temperament neither *loquacious* nor *taciturn* he found very little occasion to talk."

   B. My sister is so *loquacious* she normally stays on the phone for at least an hour.

   a. shy   *c.* nervous
   b. talkative   *d.* intelligent

5. *taciturn* (page 142, line 21)

   A. See 4A.

   B. Normally a *taciturn* person, he outdid himself this time by saying not one word for the nine hours they were together.

   a. talkative   *c.* amusing
   b. friendly   *d.* silent

6. *affront* (page 142, line 35)

   A. "At the news of the contemplated transfer Jukes grew restless, as if under a sense of personal *affront*."

   b. mission   *d.* argument

7. *venerable* (page 148, line 5)

   A. "...Mrs. Rout, a big, high-bosomed, jolly woman of forty, shared with Mr. Rout's toothless and *venerable* mother a little cottage near Teddington."

   B. The new tenant was a *venerable* man with ragged white hair and a doddering walk, but he appeared mentally alert and lively.

   a. nagging   *c.* aged
   b. wealthy   *d.* poor

8. *forbearance* (page 150, line 23)

   A. "The sea itself, as if sharing Mr. Jukes' good-natured *forbearance*, had never put itself out to startle the silent man...."

   B. A good nurse must have the *forbearance* to put up with a difficult patient and not lose her temper.

   a. patience   *c.* indifference
   b. ancestry   *d.* hostility

9. *perfidy* (page 151, line 6)

   A. "Captain MacWhirr had sailed over the surface of the oceans ... without ever having been made to see all it may contain of *perfidy*, of violence, and of terror."

   B. He discovered too late the *perfidy* of his supposed friends who celebrated with him while he was a champion and then closed their doors on him once he lost all his money.

   a. fear   *c.* beauty
   b. perfection   *d.* falseness

10. *disdained* (page 151, line 8)

   A. "There are on sea and land such men thus fortunate—or thus *disdained* by destiny and by the sea."

   B. The elderly lady *disdained* the boy scout's offer of assistance and trotted gaily across the street without a backward glance.

   a. accepted   *c.* ignored
   b. hated   *d.* selected

Typhoon: Unit II

Chapter Two

ACTION AND ADVENTURE

1. From the opening chapter, as well as from the title of the story, we are led to expect that Captain MacWhirr and the *Nan-Shan* are going to become embroiled in a typhoon.   As Chapter Two begins, we see the first indications of the storm that is about to hit them.

a. What physical signs make it apparent that something is wrong?

b. The second engineer comes up on deck to berate Jukes for not "trimming" the ventilators, that is, turning them so they catch the wind and send air down to cool the stokehold.   Actually, why is no air coming down through the ventilators?

2. How are the men on board affected by the weather conditions?

3. Jukes looks out of the door of the chartroom and sees "all the stars flying upwards between the teak-wood jambs on a black sky.   The whole lot took flight together and disappeared. . . ." (page 157, lines 8–10)   Why do the stars "disappear"?   What is actually happening?

4. Captain MacWhirr is advised by both Jukes and the textbook on navigation to alter his course.   What reasons do they offer?   What is Mac-Whirr's reaction to that reasoning?

5. What is "storm strategy"?   Why doesn't MacWhirr believe in it?

6. MacWhirr closes his eyes, then almost immediately opens them again. (pages 164–165)   What has happened during that interval?   What changes does he notice immediately?

7. In the terrific wind it is very difficult for the men to hear each other's speech.   Hence the conversation between Jukes and MacWhirr (pages 166–167) is reproduced not as it was spoken, but as the two men heard each other, with each man catching only bits and pieces of what the other says.   Read over this passage carefully.   What are they actually saying to each other?

8. MacWhirr is instantly mollified by Jukes' explanation (page 166, lines 27-28, 32-33) and satisfied at how the mate has handled things while he was asleep. However, there is one matter still bothering him. What doesn't MacWhirr want Jukes to do?

PSYCHOLOGY OF THE CHARACTERS

9. What is MacWhirr's reaction to the second engineer's outburst? To what extent is this reaction uncharacteristic?

10. As we meet him during his conversation with Jukes, the second mate is a seedy and unpleasant character, suspicious of everything, and apparently convinced that everybody is out to get him. What details can you cite to support this statement?

11. How are Jukes' and MacWhirr's attitudes toward the plight of the coolies indicative of the difference between the two men?

12. Why is MacWhirr so contemptuous of the book on weather?

READING IN DEPTH

13. On page 154 Conrad makes a reference to Jukes' letter to his friend back in Chapter One when he says, "The relations of the 'engine-room' and the 'deck' of the *Nan-Shan* were, as is known, of a brotherly nature."

   a. Why does Conrad say this at this point? How is he being ironic?

   b. Are we to consider the quarrel between Jukes and the engineer serious? Why?

14. "Thus Captain MacWhirr expostulated against the use of images in speech." (page 156, lines 8-9) What "images" have annoyed him? Why?

15. In Chapter One we saw personification used in the description of the sea which, so far, seemed to have shared Jukes' "good-natured forbearance" and not put itself out to bother MacWhirr. Now however, as the typhoon begins, we see the first playful little touches as the wind begins to tease him, prior to attacking in earnest. What instances can you find in the text which give the feeling of intelligence behind the storm, deliberately teasing the people who are now trapped in it?

VOCABULARY FOR ENRICHMENT

1. *assimilated* (page 151, line 17)

   A. "... He would have *assimilated* the information under the simple idea of dirty weather, and no other, because he had no experience of *cataclysms*. . . ."

   B. While some American Indians continue to live on reservations, many others have become *assimilated* into the mainstream of American society.

a. believed	*c.* absorbed
b. disbelieved	*d.* acquired

2. *cataclysms* (page 151, line 20)

   A. See 1A.

   B. When news of the *cataclysm* reached the outside world, nearly every government rushed in emergency food and supplies to help the thousands of victims.

a. upheavals	*c.* prophecies
b. caves	*d.* religion

3. *deprecatory* (page 154, line 1)

   A. "... In answer Jukes made with his hands *deprecatory* soothing signs meaning: 'No wind—can't be helped—you can see for yourself.' "

   B. The manager made a polite and *deprecatory* speech, explaining that our rooms were not ready yet but that he hoped to accommodate us by three o'clock.

a. angry	*c.* apologetic
b. insulting	*d.* foolish

4. *manifest* (page 158, line 34)

   A. "They are competent enough, appear hopelessly hard up, show no evidence of any sort of vice, and carry about them all the signs of *manifest* failure."

   B. Since it is *manifest* that you like the house, I think we ought to buy it.

a. economic	*c.* human
b. social	*d.* evident

5. *implacable* (page 159, line 9)

A. " 'You wait,' he repeated, balanced in great swings with his back to Jukes, motionless and *implacable*."

B. The *implacable* demands of his creditors, who insisted on being paid before the end of the year, finally drove him into bankruptcy.

   a. unruffled   *c.* tense
   b. unyielding   *d.* unimportant

6. *terminology* (page 162, line 21)

A. "... Without taking the time to sit down he had waded with a conscious effort into the *terminology* of the subject."

B. When the doctor starts using all that medical *terminology* I understand so little of what he is saying that he might as well be speaking Greek.

   a. mathematics   *c.* science
   b. spirit   *d.* vocabulary

7. *incredulity* (page 164, line 7)

A. "Unbounded wonder was the intellectual meaning of his eye, while *incredulity* was seated in his whole countenance."

B. That look of *incredulity* on your face indicates that you don't really believe I can quit smoking.

   a. intelligence   *c.* stupidity
   b. disbelief   *d.* curiosity

8. *vacuity* (page 164, line 31)

A. "He was tired, and he experienced that state of mental *vacuity* which comes at the end of an exhaustive discussion. ..."

B. His mental *vacuity* was such that an original idea never entered his head.

   a. feeling   *c.* energy
   b. tiredness   *d.* emptiness

9. *panoply* (page 166, line 6)

A. "He stood for a moment in the light of the lamp, thick, clumsy, shapeless in his *panoply* of combat, vigilant and red-faced."

B. The knights were attired in full *panoply*—shields, chain mail, helmets, and visors.

a. array
b. desire
c. fear
d. mystery

10. *upbraiding* (page 166, line 29)

A. "Jukes heard his commander *upbraiding*."

B. Some parents always seem to be *upbraiding* their children about something—long hair, bad companions, poor grades—until the children start to feel they can't do anything right.

a. marching
b. reproaching
c. praising
d. praying

Typhoon: Unit III

Chapter Three

ACTION AND ADVENTURE

1. What is Jukes' primary responsibility and function in a situation like this one? How is it different from the captain's?

2. Things have gotten so bad that Jukes, his eyes shut tight, is clinging desperately to one of the stanchions supporting the rail which encloses the "bridge" or top deck on which he is standing. Whenever he opens his eyes momentarily he is reassured by the gleam of the starboard light. Suddenly, while he is looking at the light, it disappears.

a. What is happening? What has put out the light?

b. What does Jukes think has happened to him? Why?

3. Why, when Jukes reaches the captain, must the two men cling to each other?

4. What plan of action, if any, is MacWhirr following at this point?

5. Why does MacWhirr ask Jukes the whereabouts of the rest of the hands? (page 173)

PSYCHOLOGY OF THE CHARACTERS

6. Why does Jukes feel relieved to have the captain up on deck with him?

7. How do Jukes and MacWhirr differ in their immediate reactions to the storm?

8. Jukes looks up at the empty davits swinging back and forth and realizes that the lifeboats have been swept away. How do he and MacWhirr differ in their reactions to this fact?

9. At this point, what begins to happen to Jukes psychologically?

10. We are told that Jukes dislikes the boatswain, but that the captain considers him a first-rate petty officer. How do you explain this difference of opinion?

READING IN DEPTH

11. Conrad notes that a gale is different from other cataclysms such as an earthquake, a landslide, or an avalanche. (page 169, line 5) In what way is it different?

12. Conrad is describing a storm of such magnitude that it is utterly beyond the experience of the men caught in it, beyond the imagination of even Jukes, so that it brings to mind Conrad's earlier reference to Judgment Day itself. Part of the author's descriptive genius lies in his ability to make such a terrible storm real to his readers. What passages can you cite which make this storm so real that the reader feels he is in the midst of it himself?

13. In this chapter Conrad continues with his personification of the sea. What instances can you find of this personification?

14. Read the passage on page 172, lines 12-19. Conrad is using very heroic language to describe MacWhirr as his voice prevails over the clamor of the storm. How do MacWhirr's actual words fit in with this description? To what extent are we dealing with a "heroic" or larger-than-life figure in the character of MacWhirr?

15. How can the arrival of the boatswain be taken as a moment of comic relief?

VOCABULARY FOR ENRICHMENT

1. *stentorian* (page 167, line 24)

   A. "Shouting in his fresh, *stentorian* voice, 'Jump, boys, and bear a hand!' "

   B. Her *stentorian* voice echoed across the auditorium like an army drill sergeant's.

a. cheerful	*c.* educated
b. innocent	*d.* loud

2. *palpitated* (page 168, line 33)

   A. "The darkness *palpitated* down upon all this, and then the real thing came at last."

   B. His heart *palpitated* with a mixture of emotions as he gazed at the flag.

a. looked	*c.* listened
b. throbbed	*d.* rained

3. *formidable* (page 168, line 35)

   A. "It was something *formidable* and swift, like the sudden smashing of a vial of wrath."

   B. To an amateur like him the mountain seemed almost as *formidable* a challenge as Mount Everest.

a. awesome	*c.* easy
b. surprising	*d.* ancient

4. *alleviated* (page 169, line 13)

   A. "His distress was by no means *alleviated* by an inclination to disbelieve the reality of this experience."

   B. The old medicine man *alleviated* much of the pain of their wounds by the use of strange herbs.

a. increased	*c.* eased
b. caused	*d.* explained

5. *precipitation* (page 170, line 7)

   A. ". . . He kept on repeating mentally, with the utmost *precipitation*, the words: 'My God! My God! My God! My God!' "

B. Having overslept, he dressed and tore out of the house with such *precipitation* that he completely forgot to shave.

   a. haste   *c.* devotion
   b. dignity   *d.* seriousness

6. *prodigious* (page 173, line 21)

A. "And Jukes heard the voice of his commander hardly any louder than before, but nearer, as though, starting to march athwart the *prodigious* rush of the hurricane, it had approached him. . . ."

B. The team made one last *prodigious* effort, pulling on the rope, and won the tug-of-war.

   a. loud   *c.* stormy
   b. destructive   *d.* mighty

7. *evanescent* (page 173, line 25)

A. " 'D'ye know where the hands got to?' it asked, vigorous and *evanescent* at the same time, overcoming the strength of the wind, and swept away from Jukes instantly."

B. The *evanescent* flame of life flickered briefly and sputtered out.

   a. strong   *c.* angry
   b. brief   *d.* merry

8. *apprehensively* (page 173, line 32)

A. " 'Want the hands, sir?' he cried, *apprehensively*."

B. She waited outside the door, wringing her glove *apprehensively*, wondering whether she would be blamed for the mistake.

   a. proudly   *c.* joyfully
   b. worriedly   *d.* dutifully

9. *somnolence* (page 175, line 22)

A. "The gnawing of profound discomfort existed side by side with an incredible disposition to *somnolence*, as though he had been buffeted and worried into drowsiness."

B. He drank cup after cup of black coffee to fight off a growing sense of *somnolence*.

   a. hysteria   *c.* laughter
   b. sleepiness   *d.* fear

10. *grizzled* (page 176, line 13)

    A. "Apart from the *grizzled* pelt on his chest, the menacing demeanour and the hoarse voice, he had none of the classical attributes of his rating."

    B. The old man's hair was streaked and *grizzled* now where once it was a rich chestnut brown.

        a. tangled   *c.* bearlike
        b. black   *d.* gray

Typhoon: Unit IV

Chapter Four

ACTION AND ADVENTURE

1. At this point we get the whole of the boatswain's story. Where are all the deckhands during the period that MacWhirr and Jukes are trapped out on the bridge? What are they doing?

2. Where does the boatswain go in order to get a light? What route does he take and why is it dangerous?

3. We see the boatswain "amazed at the plainness with which down there he could hear the gale raging," even in the bunker, and it seems to him that its sounds have taken on a human quality. Then he distinguishes the sound of some bulky and heavy object—perhaps five tons in weight—thumping round in the tween deck.

    a. What is actually causing all the sounds he hears? What does he see when he finally makes his way to the connecting door and gets a look at what is going on in the coolies' section?

    b. What is the boatswain's first impulse on seeing this? What does he do?

4. By the time the boatswain has reached Jukes and MacWhirr in the scene that ended Chapter Three, he has had two severe shocks which make the matter of the coolies seem far less important to him. What has jolted him? Why is he so delighted to find Jukes and MacWhirr?

5. What does MacWhirr want Jukes to do about the problem of the coolies? Why does he tell him to report back via the engine-room speaking tube rather than return to the bridge?

6. As it turns out, what are the coolies fighting about?

7. What is Jukes' immediate reaction when he sees what is going on?

8. While Jukes is occupied down below, the captain makes his way back to the wheelhouse to see what is happening there and to be ready to receive Jukes' report over the engine-room speaking tube. What is happening in the wheelhouse?

9. MacWhirr communicates with Rout who is down in the engine room, and discusses the situation quite calmly. In the middle of their conversation (page 191, lines 14-15), Rout hears something like the sounds of a scuffle. What is causing that sound? Why does MacWhirr suddenly change his mind and ask Rout to send Jukes back up on deck after all?

10. Moments later Jukes comes tearing into the engine room with his report for the captain on the situation in the hold. What does Jukes want MacWhirr to do about the fighting?

PSYCHOLOGY OF THE CHARACTERS

11. Conrad says of Jukes that "he was daunted; not abjectly, but only so far as a decent man may, without becoming loathsome to himself." (page 177, lines 25-27) Explain this statement.

12. The psychologist Freud has described an instinct which he called the "death wish," which comes out in everyone from time to time. This is a desire not to have to cope – to escape to sleep and darkness and nothingness. This is the opposite of the survival instinct which makes people struggle against impossible odds in order to remain alive. To what extent is the death-wish operating in Jukes? What evidence can you find to support this?

13. A boatswain is a petty officer—the equivalent of a sergeant or a foreman—whose job it is to supervise the crew and transmit to them the orders of the captain and his mates.

a. What problem does this particular boatswain have with this crew? Why is it he himself who finally goes in search of a light for them?

b. When Jukes comes down to investigate the situation, he must go through the same dark alleyway, stepping over the same men. How does their treatment of him contrast with their treatment of the boatswain? Why?

14. What are Jukes' feelings as he crawls into the bunker? What forces him to go?

15. After Jukes goes below, the captain makes his way to the wheelhouse where he finds two men, the sailor, Hackett, and the second mate. In the situation in which all of these men find themselves, everyone is afraid. The important distinction lies in the way the men react to their fear, and how the fear affects their ability to function as seamen. Compare Jukes, Hackett, the boatswain, the second mate, and Rout, in terms of their attitudes and reactions. What role does the captain play?

16. What are MacWhirr's own preoccupations at this point? How are they in keeping with his overall character?

17. The last sentence of Chapter Four is, 'And Jukes wanted to be dismissed from the face of that odious trouble intruding on the great need of the ship." What does Conrad mean by this? How does Jukes view the problem of the Chinamen as opposed to the wav MacWhirr views it?

READING IN DEPTH

18. In this chapter, we see the problem of the coolies as it exists in the shadow of the larger problem of the *Nan-Shan*'s efforts to survive the typhoon. In what ways are these two problems related? How are they both tests of MacWhirr's will and skill? Of his basic values?

VOCABULARY FOR ENRICHMENT

1. *pernicious* (page 179, line 3)

A. ". . . The note of busy concern in Captain MacWhirr's voice sickened him like an exhibition of blind and *pernicious* folly."

B. The new district attorney pledged to put a stop to the *pernicious* activities of the underworld.

    a. pointless   *c.* wicked
    b. childish   *d.* helpless

2. *admonishing* (page 179, line 19)

   A. "Sometimes Jukes would break in, *admonishing* hastily: 'Look out, sir!' . . ."

   B. The traffic patrolmen spend most of their time *admonishing* old ladies about crossing against the lights.

   a. cautioning   *c.* begging
   b. whispering   *d.* punishing

3. *execration* (page 180, line 8)

   A. "This called up a shout of *execration*."

   B. The bombing of the church is an *execration* which has aroused shame and anger.

   a. pleasure   *c.* abomination
   b. anger   *d.* disbelief

4. *contumely* (page 180, line 16)

   A. "He told them so, and was met by general *contumely*."

   B. She faced down the *contumely* and derision of the mob and finished her speech.

   a. insults   *c.* respect
   b. indifference   *d.* silence

5. *inclement* (page 184, line 6)

   A. "He crawled out as outcasts go to face an *inclement* world."

   B. You need heavy clothing if you plan to go out in such *inclement* weather.

   a. forgiving   *c.* forgotten
   b. empty   *d.* harsh

6. *obsequious* (page 185, line 34)

   A. ". . . In the midst of *obsequious* warnings, 'Look out! Mind that manhole lid, sir,' they lowered him into the bunker."

   B. The salesman was too *obsequious* for my taste, full of flattery and nice words, but really just interested in making a sale.

   a. rude   *c.* fawning
   b. nervous   *d.* loud

7. *austerely* (page 189, line 13)

   A. ". . . Captain MacWhirr said *austerely*, 'Don't you pay any attention to what that man says.' "

   B. Father scolded her so *austerely* that the poor little thing burst into tears.

a. sternly	*c.* pleasantly
b. mildly	*d.* sensibly

8. *arduous* (page 193, line 19)

   A. "He had had an *arduous* road, and had travelled over it with immense vivacity, the agitation of his mind corresponding to the exertions of his body."

   B. Since you had so much trouble with math and language, perhaps you should sign up for a less *arduous* program next semester.

a. easy	*c.* difficult
b. interesting	*d.* unusual

9. *transport* (page 194, line 9)

   A. "The donkey-man, a dapper little chap with a dazzling fair skin and a tiny, gingery moustache, worked in a sort of mute *transport*."

   B. The very thought of the gaily decorated tree and piles of presents sent her into a *transport* of delight.

a. anger	*c.* movement
b. effort	*d.* ecstasy

10. *odious* (page 195, line 22)

   A. "And Jukes wanted to be dismissed from the face of that *odious* trouble intruding on the great need of the ship."

   B. The freshmen had the *odious* job of cleaning up the entire stadium after the game was over.

a. easy	*c.* strange
b. hateful	*d.* miraculous

Typhoon: Unit V

Chapter Five

ACTION AND ADVENTURE

1. How is the situation of the men in the engine room different from that of the deck crew during the storm? How does the storm make itself felt? What effect does it have on them and how do they cope with it?

2. MacWhirr speaks to Jukes through the tube, saying, "Take the hands with you . . . ," then breaks off in the middle of his sentence.

"What could I do with them, sir?" Jukes asks, but he gets no answer. Instead there is a sudden order to change the engines from Full to Stop.

What is happening? Why does MacWhirr break off speaking and flash this message down to Rout?

3. When the ship does fall, what do the men in the engine room assume has happened? Why does Rout urge Jukes to "Rush"? (page 197, line 17) Why does the clang of the telegraph, three lines later, soothe them instantly?

4. The wave interrupted MacWhirr in the middle of a sentence, leaving Jukes confused as to what his captain wants him to do. Then, the immediate danger over, MacWhirr resumes the thread of that earlier conversation without missing a word.

Find the sentence on page 197 which answers Jukes' question of "What could I do with them, sir?" What is MacWhirr in fact ordering the mate to do and why?

5. What does Jukes finally do to help the coolies? In what sense do they misunderstand his motives?

6. What does Jukes fear will happen as a result of this maneuver? Why does the fact that they are now flying the Siamese flag take on increased importance?

7. The boatswain remarks to Jukes that it "seems as if the wind had dropped, sir." (page 202, line 9) When Jukes emerges on deck, wading through water up to his neck, he finds that indeed there is *no* wind. Why is this new calm so ominous? What do the barometers in the chartroom indicate, and what does this mean?

8. What strategy, if any, does MacWhirr intend to use to get through the rest of the typhoon? Why?

9. What are the first indications that the hurricane is beginning anew?

10. What is the significance of the last line of Chapter Five?

PSYCHOLOGY OF THE CHARACTERS

11. Jukes has been ordered to go back into the hold and pick up the dollars. How do the engineers react to this fact when he announces that this ⁄nat he is going to do? What reaction in turn does this produce in ukes? That is, how does he take their response?

12. How does Jukes' newly kindled fury enable him to accomplish the task he has been given? Why is he able to get the men to respond?

13. Jukes reports to MacWhirr and tells him that the job is done. Read over this portion of the chapter. (pages 202-204) What is the captain's reaction, and why is Jukes so infuriated by it?

14. How does MacWhirr actually feel about the matter of the coolies?

15. Follow the interchange between Jukes and MacWhirr after the captain comes back out on deck (pages 207-209). Why does Jukes suddenly experience "an access of confidence"? (page 209, line 23)

READING IN DEPTH

16. The incident of the hundreds of coolies fighting down in the hold serves many purposes in this story, ranging from affording a bizarre and colorful subplot, to providing a chance for the main characters to test their values, to being the impetus to mobilize men into action. Show how this statement is true.

17. Reread pages 204-207, in which MacWhirr is alone in the chartroom. What is the significance of the matchbox?

18. MacWhirr advises Jukes on how to deal with the storm, telling him, "Face it. That's enough for any man. Keep a cool head." (page 209, lines

18-19) On what two levels can this piece of advice be taken? To what extent does MacWhirr follow it himself?

19. In addition to making *Typhoon* an adventure narrative of a small group of men battling the elements, Conrad has also made it, on a more symbolic level, a study of the struggle between man and the great blind savage forces of Nature. This can be a fit subject for tragedy, but *Typhoon* is a comic story—comic in the sense that it ends happily with the main character triumphing over great odds, and comic also in some of its droll images and ironic observations. It is fitting, therefore, that after building up for four chapters the enormity of the destructive force of the typhoon, Conrad suddenly shifts his tone and, in the last three quick sentences of the chapter, assures us that everything turned out all right. Explain the irony of the last three sentences of Chapter Five. What is the purpose of the deliberate understatement, "He was spared that annoyance"?

VOCABULARY FOR ENRICHMENT

1. *cant* (page 195, line 28)

   A. "They paused in intelligent immobility, stilled in midstroke, a heavy crank arrested on the *cant*, as if conscious of danger and the passage of time."

   B. You could tell the veterans by the jaunty *cant* of their well-soiled berets.

   a. sound   *c*. moment
   b. tilt   *d*. reason

2. *impetuosity* (page 198, line 29)

   A. "The *impetuosity* with which he came amongst them carried them along."

   B. The *impetuosity* of his temper had us all cowering in fear.

   a. modesty   *c*. humor
   b. joy   *d*. force

3. *brooked* (page 198, line 33)

   A. ". . . More felt than seen in his rushes, he appeared formidable—busied with matters of life and death that *brooked* no delay."

   B. The captain *brooked* no drinking on board his ship and any sailor rash enough to be caught drinking was quickly punished.

     a. caused   *c.* punished
     b. tolerated   *d.* broke

4. *allay* (page 200, line 34)

   A. "They had been ranged closely, after having been shaken into submission, cuffed a little to *allay* excitement. . . ."

   B. If it will *allay* your fears any, I promise I'll lock both doors to-night.

     a. worsen   *c.* ease
     b. encourage   *d.* add

5. *dolorous* (page 201, line 11)

   A. "Now and then a sailor would stagger towards the doorway with his arms full of rubbish; and *dolorous*, slanting eyes followed his movements."

   B. Having learned that her father refused to allow her to see him any more, the young man occupied himself with glancing up at her window with the *dolorous* eyes of a hound dog and thinking sad thoughts of lost love.

     a. mournful   *c.* sly
     b. mercenary   *d.* angry

6. *polls* (page 201, line 15)

   A. ". . . Her headlong dives knocked together the line of shaven *polls* from end to end."

   B. As the marine recruits doubletimed back from the barber, their shorn *polls* shone in the sun.

     a. benches   *c.* heads
     b. parrots   *d.* backs

7. *gainsaid* (page 205, line 16)

   A. "He turned that way, struck another match, and discovered the white face of the other instrument looking at him from the bulk-head, meaningly, not to be *gainsaid*. . . ."

   B. It cannot be *gainsaid* that some people are just luckier than others.

     a. increased   *c.* wrong
     b. denied   *d.* true

8. *scrupulously* (page 206, line 15)

A. "And of course on his side he would be careful to put it back in its place *scrupulously*."

B. He very *scrupulously* paid back every cent of the loan before taking a vacation.

    a. conscientiously   *c.* rudely

    b. stingily   *d.* carelessly

9. *vehemence* (page 208, line 25)

A. " '—without being battered to pieces,' pursued Captain MacWhirr with rising *vehemence*."

B. My usually placid sister spoke with such unexpected *vehemence* that I turned around in amazement to see what had gotten into her.

    a. amusement   *c.* fervor

    b. calmness   *d.* pleasure

10. *vexation* (page 210, line 20)

A. "Before the renewed wrath of winds swooped on his ship, Captain MacWhirr was moved to declare, in a tone of *vexation*, as it were: 'I wouldn't like to lose her.' "

B. She stamped her foot in *vexation* when she realized that the timetable had been changed and she had missed the train.

    a. disbelief   *c.* sadness

    b. prayer   *d.* annoyance

Typhoon: Unit VI

Chapter Six

ACTION AND ADVENTURE

1. Back home in England, Mrs. MacWhirr skims through her husband's letter without really understanding it. At one point she sees the words "Do what's fair.... Miserable objects.... Only three, with a broken leg each, and one...." (page 213, lines 29–31) What is the captain talking about here? On the basis of what Jukes tells his friend, explain the above phrases.

2. The remaining facts of how the problem of the coolies was solved are given to us in Jukes' letter.

a. Why was Jukes so anxious to reach a man-of-war? What did he envision as the only possible ending to the incident?

b. Why was MacWhirr opposed to Jukes' solution?

c. Jukes writes to his friend that he himself passed out rifles to the crew members as defense against the coolies. Like many similar "defensive actions," this is really the result of a misunderstanding. What caused Jukes to take this measure? What did he think was happening, and why?

d. What solution did MacWhirr come up with for getting the money back to the coolies? Why was this solution so effective?

PSYCHOLOGY OF THE CHARACTERS

3. Sometimes a person is so unwilling to acknowledge his own weakness that he reverses the truth in his own mind and blames other people for wrongdoing in order to avoid facing the truth about himself. How does the second mate provide an example of this type of behavior? Why is he so angry and hostile toward Captain MacWhirr?

4. What is the mate's relationship to the man he meets on shore? What does each man have to offer the other? Why is the mate more affable toward him than to any of the *Nan-Shan*'s officers, and why is this man so ready with his sympathy for the mate?

5. What is the really significant statement in MacWhirr's letter to his wife? Why is it especially important, coming as it does, from him?

6. Why was the steward the only person to know this?

7. What do we learn about Mrs. MacWhirr from her response to her husband's letter and her encounter with the woman in front of the store?

8. We are given a glimpse of what Mr. Rout wrote home to his wife. We are told that he said a few words about the typhoon, and then that "something had moved him to express an increased longing for the companionship of the jolly woman."

a. Why was Rout moved to write this?

b. MacWhirr's letter, as we have seen, was uncharacteristic. In what way is Rout's also different from his usual letters? Given the character of the man and the kind of letter he usually writes, how is this one unusual or out of character?

10. In Jukes' letter we see that "there were phrases in it calculated to give the impression of lighthearted, indomitable resolution." (page 216, lines 11-12) To what extent does Jukes' account depart from the psychological reality of the situation? Why does he so change it?

11. What motivated MacWhirr's final decision to divide up the dollars? Why was his attitude so different from that of Jukes?

READING IN DEPTH

12. In its own way, each of the three letters described in the last chapter is ironic. Consider the question of how well people are known or understood through their letters. To what extent do the people who read these letters have an accurate picture of the people who wrote them or over the events which they describe?

13. What is the irony of the last sentence of the story?

VOCABULARY FOR ENRICHMENT

1. *verily* (page 211, line 4)

   A. ". . . Sighting, *verily*, even the coast of the Great Beyond, whence no ship ever returns to give up her crew to the dust of the earth."

   B. According to the Bible, once Noah and his family were aboard the Ark safely, it began to rain, and did not stop, *verily*, for forty days.

   a. practically   *c.* truly
   b. figuratively   *d.* frequently

2. *facetious* (page 211, line 7)

   A. "She was incrusted . . . as though (as some *facetious* seaman said) 'the crowd on board had fished her out somewhere from the bottom of the sea and brought her in here for salvage.' "

   B. A *facetious* remark to the wrong person can get you in trouble because he may take you seriously and be insulted.

a. humorous   c. serious
b. angry   d. imaginative

3. *felicity* (page 211, line 10)

   A. "And further, excited by the *felicity* of his own wit, he offered to give five pounds for her—'as she stands.' "

   B. Their home was such a model of *felicity* and domestic bliss that visitors were reluctant to leave, finding it such a pleasant and inviting atmosphere.

   a. happiness   c. ferociousness
   b. stupidity   d. intelligence

4. *incontinently* (page 211, line 15)

   A. ". . . A meagre little man . . . landed from a sampan on the quay of the Foreign Concession, and *incontinently* turned to shake his fist at her."

   B. At the site of the earthquake the King wept *incontinently*, the tears streaming down his face as he grieved for his lost subjects.

   a. angrily   c. unrestrainedly
   b. quickly   d. weakly

5. *perfunctorily* (page 213, line 7)

   A. " '. . . A calm that lasted more than twenty minutes,' she read *perfunctorily*. . . ."

   B. He leafed through the pages of the report *perfunctorily* for a few minutes and then put it away, deciding he could concentrate better in the morning.

   a. joyfully   c. suspiciously
   b. carefully   d. indifferently

6. *brazened* (page 213, line 25)

   A. " 'Well, he did give me a hint to that effect,' the steward *brazened* it out."

   B. They caught him with the goods red-handed but he *brazened* his way out, saying that he was really an undercover agent for the FBI.

   a. confessed   c. fought
   b. bluffed   d. pleaded

7. *bilious* (page 214, line 22)

 A. "Outside the draper's Mrs. MacWhirr smiled upon a woman in a black mantle of generous proportions armoured in jet and crowned with flowers blooming falsely above a *bilious* matronly countenance."

 B. They called her a witch but her *bilious* expression was due more to bad digestion than to a dislike of small children.

 a. cross   *c.* beautiful
 b. pleasant   *d.* aristocratic

8. *indomitable* (page 216, line 12)

 A. "There were phrases in it calculated to give the impression of lighthearted, *indomitable* resolution."

 B. Only his *indomitable* spirit enabled him to keep going in the face of such bitter troubles.

 a. foolish   *c.* secret
 b. charming   *d.* unconquerable

9. *sanguine* (page 217, line 30)

 A. " 'Not, mind you, that I felt very *sanguine* about controlling these beggars if they meant to take charge.' "

 B. He appeared quite *sanguine* about his chances of getting the job, especially since the interview had gone well and his qualifications were satisfactory.

 a. worried   *c.* annoyed
 b. optimistic   *d.* indifferent

10. *swell* (page 220, line 21)

 A. " 'What's your opinion, you pampered mailboat *swell*?' "

 B. He was a real big city *swell*, a big spender, a flashy dresser, with fancy manners.

 a. buddy   *c.* idiot
 b. dandy   *d.* genius

The Secret Sharer: Unit I

Chapter One

ACTION AND ADVENTURE

1. As the story opens, the nameless captain-narrator is standing on the deck of his ship, gazing toward the shore, his sharp eyes picking out the Meinam River and then focusing on the grove of trees surrounding great Paknam Pagoda. At what stage of the voyage are we being introduced to this ship? Where has she come from and what is she about to do?

2. What is unusual about the circumstances of the narrator's position as captain? How does this present difficulties for him?

3. The captain directs all hands to turn in, without setting an anchor watch, and then announces that he himself will take this watch for five hours between 8 P.M. and 1 A.M. How is this an extraordinary gesture on his part? Why does he do it?

4. The captain is annoyed to see that the ship's rope ladder, which has last been used to permit the captain of the tug to come aboard and collect the mail, is still hanging over the side of the ship instead of being stowed neatly in its proper place. What is it about this ladder which first awakens the captain's curiosity and causes him to discover the man in the water?

5. In addition to being surprised at finding someone hanging onto the rope ladder, the captain is disturbed and frightened by what he thinks he sees.

    a. What is it about the stranger's position in the water which causes the captain to feel a "horrid frost-bound sensation" grip his chest? In actuality what is the man doing?

    b. What does the captain do to cause the stranger to jerk his head back up and discover that he is being watched?

6. At this point the stranger confronts the captain and identifies himself as a Mr. Leggatt. Having done so, what is the immediate choice which Leggatt must now make?

7. Leggatt explains to the captain that he is in trouble because he killed a man aboard the *Sephora*, a ship anchored in the vicinity. As he tells his story, to what extent were there mitigating circumstances to his crime?

8. When the storm receded Leggatt was summarily stripped of his position as chief mate and locked in his cabin. After about six weeks of this he requested his captain to leave the cabin door unlocked one evening. What sort of bargain was Leggatt suggesting? What was his captain's reasoning in refusing?

9. How did Leggatt come to end up at the bottom of the rope ladder?

10. When the captain resolves to take Leggatt on board and conceal him, at least temporarily, he chooses his own cabin as the best hiding place. Why is the cabin especially suited for this purpose?

11. How does the captain's decision to hide Leggatt there bring him unexpected problems almost immediately? Why does the steward become suspicious that next morning?

12. The captain has enough insight to realize that he must be prompting all sorts of suspicions in the steward's mind. The steward will report that something peculiar is going on or that perhaps the new captain is an alcoholic who gets drunk on the first night out and remains in that condition for the rest of the voyage. What steps does the captain take to dispel such suspicions?

13. What is the significance of the message which the captain receives concerning a ship's boat approaching?

PSYCHOLOGY OF THE CHARACTERS

14. The captain informs us that he feels himself a stranger on three counts—a stranger to the crew, a stranger to the ship, and a stranger to himself. What does he mean when he says, "I wondered how far I should turn out faithful to that ideal conception of one's own personality every man sets up for himself secretly"? (page 223, lines 26-28) How does he consider himself different from the others on board in this sense?

15. When the captain discovers that the rope ladder has been left dangling over the side, he becomes very annoyed, first at the crew, then at himself. Why is there this reversal in his attitude? How does this indicate both a strength and a weakness in his character?

16. Once the captain and Leggatt begin to talk to one another, the captain informs us that "a mysterious communication was established already between us two." (page 228, lines 23-25)

   a. What is the basis for such a sense of communication? What do these two men have in common that makes the captain so receptive to Leggatt?

   b. As the captain is listening to Leggatt's story, he remarks, "I knew well enough the pestiferous danger of such a character where there are no means of legal repression." (page 230, lines 17-19) What does he mean by this? Does he feel that Leggatt's behavior was justifiable?

17. As Leggatt tells it, the crew and the captain all look upon him as a vicious murderer who choked their shipmate to death in a blind rage. They feel neither pity nor sympathy for Leggatt and desire only to see him tried and hanged. Yet according to Leggatt, it was his action alone which saved the ship. How does he account for this total lack of sympathy? Why are the officers against him? Why might the crew hate him?

18. Leggatt twice mentions his father, the Norfolk parson, and makes it clear that he would rather die than have to go home and have his father see him stand trial. What does this reveal to us about Leggatt's sense of values? What is he afraid of and what is he not afraid of?

19. Throughout the first chapter, beginning on page 229, the captain makes continual references to Leggatt as his "double" and speaks of the "dualism" of his own thinking since Leggatt came on board.

   a. What instances can you find in the text to support this?

   b. On a surface level, the reason for the captain's sense of dualism, or his feeling that Leggatt is his double, comes from the coincidence that they are about the same age, the same size, and are dressed in identical outfits, so that if anyone else on board were to catch a quick glimpse of Leggatt, he would mistake him for the captain. However, there is a deeper side to his feeling of identification with the man. Consider what Leggatt has done. To what extent is this something which the captain might also have done under similar circumstances? To what extent does the captain share Leggatt's sense of isolation and estrangement from the rest of the men around him?

READING IN DEPTH

20. Note the opening description on pages 221 and 222. Note the effect of stillness that Conrad achieves so that it is as if the captain is gazing at a painting rather than the coast of Siam.

a. What details can you cite which might contribute to this effect?

b. Apart from providing an example of Conrad's visual artistry, what purpose might there be in opening the story in this way? What moral or psychological state would this physical description be likely to symbolize?

21. Consider the passage which begins with page 225, line 33 and continues through page 226, line 5.

a. What assumption is the captain making here? What does he base it on? Why would the sea be in any way morally purer than the land?

b. What is the irony in having the captain make this reflection at the point in the story where he does?

c. How is the irony continued in the captain's fancy that "the riding light in the forerigging burned with a clear, untroubled, as if symbolic, flame"? What is the light supposedly symbolic of? What was it that made Leggatt decide to swim to the ship?

22. Leggatt tells the captain that, with regard to his plan for escaping from the *Sephora*, "I was ready enough to go off wandering on the face of the earth—and that was price enough to pay for an Abel of that sort." (page 235, lines 7-9) Explain this statement. Does Leggatt feel that he does deserve to be punished, and if so, in what way? What does he mean by "an Abel of that sort"?

23. In literature the *doppelganger* is a character who appears quite unexpectedly and has a special meaning for one character in the story—usually the protagonist—because he is a kind of *alter ego*, or other self. The *doppelganger* represents or embodies a side of the person which is normally suppressed, so in many ways he is quite different from the protagonist; yet at the same time there is something inexplicably familiar about him and the protagonist feels strangely drawn to this newcomer.

Obviously the *doppelganger* is a device which an author employs to achieve a melodramatic and surrealistic effect. However, the device is also useful in portraying psychological conflicts and resolutions. By seeing what he is and isn't, a character is able to gain insight into himself and to come to terms with his own psyche.

How does all of this apply to *The Secret Sharer*? Could Leggatt be called a *doppelganger*? Explain.

VOCABULARY FOR ENRICHMENT

Each of the following ten words is first given in the context of the sentence in which it appears in the book (A), then in a second sentence (B) whose context gives specific help as to the meaning of the word. Read the two sentences; then select the best definition of the word from the four choices given.

1. *imperceptible* (page 221, line 12)

   A. "... Even the track of light from the westering sun shone smoothly, without that animated glitter which tells of an *imperceptible* ripple."

   B. If there was any change in her attitude toward the children, it was so *imperceptible* that they remained totally unaware of it.

a. undetectable	*c.* accidental
b. dangerous	*d.* natural

2. *impeccable* (page 221, line 19)

   A. "... Two small clumps of trees, one on each side of the only fault in the *impeccable* joint, marked the mouth of the river...."

   B. Anxious to make a good impression at the dinner party, he took great pains to insure that his dress was perfect and his manners *impeccable*.

a. tiny	*c.* faultless
b. distant	*d.* imperfect

3. *devious* (page 222, line 10)

   A. "My eye followed the light cloud of her smoke, now here, now there, above the plain, according to the *devious* curves of the stream...."

   B. So as not to be followed, he took a *devious* route to the post office, doubling and redoubling his steps.

a. twisting	*c.* direct
b. rolling	*d.* original

4. *caprice* (page 225, line 2)

  A. "Outside the cuddy he put his head in the second mate's door to inform him of my unheard-of *caprice* to take a five hours' anchor watch on myself."

  B. Had you been planning to send her that card all along or was it a mere *caprice* of the moment?

    a. nerve   *c.* stupidity
    b. whim   *d.* slavery

5. *exactitude* (page 226, line 9)

  A. "I became annoyed at this, for *exactitude* in some small matters is the soul of discipline."

  B. Plotting the course of the ship calls for great *exactitude*, for a mistake which seems small on paper can send you hundreds of miles off course.

    a. hardship   *c.* preciseness
    b. honesty   *d.* confidence

6. *peremptorily* (page 226, line 11)

  A. "Then I reflected that I had myself *peremptorily* dismissed my officers from duty. . . ."

  B. The big bully set himself up as unofficial group leader and very *peremptorily* began telling all the rest of us what we had to do.

    a. dictatorially   *c.* quickly
    b. foolishly   *d.* timidly

7. *compunction* (page 226, line 20)

  A. "Not from *compunction* certainly, but, as it were mechanically, I proceeded to get the ladder in myself."

  B. When I saw how hurt his feelings were, a wave of *compunction* swept over me and I vowed never to speak so harshly to a child again.

    a. anger   *c.* compulsion
    b. boredom   *d.* remorse

8. *livid* (page 226, line 36)

  A. "With a gasp I saw revealed to my stare a pair of feet, the long legs, a broad *livid* back immersed right up to the neck in a greenish cadaverous glow."

B. The blood drained from his face with fear, giving him the *livid* complexion of a corpse.

    a. rosy   *c.* vital
    b. whitish   *d.* angry

9. *tentatively* (page 227, line 34)

A. "And he, down there, *tentatively:* 'I suppose your captain's turned in?' "

B. He ventured *tentatively* out on to the ice, uncertain as to whether it would hold him.

    a. quietly   *c.* experimentally
    b. loudly   *d.* firmly

10. *edification* (page 241, line 5)

A. "I took a bath and did most of my dressing, splashing, and whistling softly for the steward's *edification*. . . ."

B. For the *edification* of the more scientific-minded members of the audience, he gave an elaborate explanation of how the synthesizer was constructed.

    a. boredom   *c.* devotion
    b. effort   *d.* instruction

The Secret Sharer: Unit II

Chapter Two

ACTION AND ADVENTURE

1. As the reader expected, the ship's boat which comes over to pay a visit is from the *Sephora*; her captain has come seeking information on the whereabouts of Leggatt, and the first part of the chapter is given over to a very frosty encounter between the two captains. Why at this time does the narrator pretend to be deaf?

2. As the narrator continues to show little enthusiasm for Captain Archbold's manhunt, Archbold begins to grow suspicious. He doesn't make any direct accusations but he does drop certain meaningful hints. What does he suggest without saying so directly?

3. Archbold is a persistent fellow, driven by what the narrator calls a "spiritless tenacity." The narrator soon realizes that if Archbold does not get an answer to his inquiry, he will simply rephrase it in far less diplomatic terms. How does the narrator act to forestall this possibility?

4. The narrator notes, "I escorted my visitor to the gangway ceremoniously, and nearly overdid it." (page 247, lines 24-25) What does he mean by this? In the last few moments as the two captains are standing together, what thought suddenly occurs to Archbold? How does the captain cope with this emergency?

5. Once Archbold is gone, the captain still has his own crew to contend with. Now that they know the story of the *Sephora*, it is more important than ever that Leggatt not be discovered because his identity would be obvious. However, a plan which seems foolproof is rarely as perfect as it first seems, a lesson which the captain soon learns to his own dismay. Where does the greatest danger of discovery lie? How is this something which he can't completely control?

6. Not only is it difficult for the captain to keep hiding Leggatt, but it would also be difficult for him to allow Leggatt to escape without its being noticed. Explain. Why will it be even more difficult for Leggatt to get off the ship than it was for him to get there in the first place?

7. In order to solve this problem the captain finds himself forced to take a number of steps which are designed to help Leggatt but which only serve to increase the captain's reputation among the crew as an oddball and perhaps a dangerous one at that. Explain this statement with references to the text.

8. On page 258, line 25, Leggatt murmurs to the captain warningly, "Be careful." What is this a warning about? For whom is Leggatt concerned here, and why?

9. What is the captain's exact plan in skirting the Koh-ring coast? Why is it so dangerous?

10. What is the importance of the white hat? How does it miraculously appear in time to save them?

PSYCHOLOGY OF THE CHARACTERS

11. As we see him through the narrator's eyes on pages 242-247, the captain of the *Sephora* comes off as a singularly unappealing character. What are the qualities which make him so unattractive?

12. There is a humorous expression which goes, "Any enemy of yours is a sure friend of mine." Consider how this applies to the feelings of the captain toward Archbold; the narrator's feeling of closeness with Leggatt is heightened by his sense of alienation from Archbold.

   a. What is the implication of Archbold's comment about Leggatt, " 'You see, he wasn't exactly the sort for the chief mate of a ship like the *Sephora'* "? Why did Archbold dislike Leggatt?

   b. To what extent might Archbold see in the narrator the same qualities which he resented in Leggatt? How does he react?

13. Realizing his own dangerous position, the captain decides that the best thing to do would be to adopt a pose which keeps Archbold confused and at arm's distance, so that Archbold is too flustered to ask a direct question. He explains that he might have chosen to appear surly and unapproachable but rejected that in favor of treating Archbold with "punctilious courtesy." Why does he choose this method? Why would being surly not have worked?

14. Why does the mate's face take on a "thoughtful cast"? (page 247, line 34)

15. Reread the section on pages 249–250 in which the captain confers with Leggatt after Archbold has gone. What does the captain mean when he says, " 'I quite understand' "? What does he understand? What is Leggatt trying to convey to him?

16. After Archbold leaves, the captain becomes extremely preoccupied with secrecy, to the degree that his behavior becomes very suspicious.

   a. What instances of this can you cite from the text?

   b. In addition to arousing the curiosity and suspicion of the crew, this preoccupation with the stranger in his cabin has a more serious effect on the captain's ability to perform his duties. Explain. How does the crew interpret his behavior?

17. Despite the close call occasioned by the steward's hanging the captain's wet coat in the bathroom, note Leggatt's extraordinary calmness. How does this compare to the captain's demeanor? What does it reveal about the difference between them?

18. In what other ways has this basic difference between the two men been borne out in the story? How has it affected their reasoning and their actions?

19. Explain Leggatt's desire to be marooned. How does he see this as an appropriate fate for himself?

20. What is the captain's reaction to this? Explain what he means when he says that his "hesitation in letting that man swim away from my ship's side had been a mere sham sentiment, a sort of cowardice." (page 256, lines 10-12)

21. Leggatt whispers to the captain, "As long as I know that you understand. . . . You seem to have been there on purpose. . . . It's very wonderful." (page 256, lines 15-20) What is wonderful? Why is it so important that the captain "understand"? What has the captain given to Leggatt besides the opportunity to escape from Archbold?

22. Why does the captain feel that it is a matter of conscience to shave the land so closely? (page 261, line 32)

23. Note the scene between the captain and the mate on page 263. How is this behavior on the captain's part uncharacteristic? What earlier scene in the story is it reminiscent of?

READING IN DEPTH

24. How is it ironic that the thing which finally saves the captain is his own white hat?

25. The plot of *The Secret Sharer* contains many ironical coincidences which combine to form a remarkably symmetrical pattern, like the two sides of an ink blot. What instances of this symmetry can you find? What incidents in the captain's life seem to parallel Leggatt's? In what way can the miracle of the white hat at the end of the story be said to mirror a similar miracle at the beginning?

VOCABULARY FOR ENRICHMENT

1. *graphic* (page 244, line 10)

   A. "After scoring over my calmness in this *graphic* way he nodded wisely."

B. Television coverage gives us a much more *graphic* picture of what war is like than what we used to get from the newspapers.

a. unusual   c. crude
b. mathematical   d. vivid

2. *tenacity* (page 244, line 33)

A. "His obscure *tenacity* on that point had in it something incomprehensible and a little awful. . . ."

B. Once he conceived of an idea, he hung on to it with the *tenacity* of a bulldog clinging to a burglar's ankle.

a. persistence   c. politeness
b. mysticism   d. wisdom

3. *countenancing* (page 244, line 36)

A. ". . . Something, as it were, mystical, quite apart from his anxiety that he should not be suspected of '*countenancing* any doings of that sort.'"

B. As long as I'm sheriff of this town, I am not *countenancing* illegal gambling and I'll do everything in my power to stop it.

a. needing   c. tolerating
b. challenging   d. stopping

4. *urbanely* (page 245, line 18)

A. "I smiled *urbanely*."

B. He behaved most *urbanely*, complimenting her dress and opening doors for her.

a. suavely   c. foolishly
b. wickedly   d. crazily

5. *punctilious* (page 246, line 5)

A. "From its novelty to him and from its nature, *punctilious* courtesy was the manner best calculated to restrain the man."

B. He didn't actually do a very good job but he was extremely *punctilious* about getting to work on time and wearing a clean shirt and tie.

a. sarcastic   c. proper
b. sad   d. simple

6. *arbitrarily* (page 253, line 5)

   A. "It was this maddening course of being . . . *arbitrarily* chased out of my cabin . . . that accounted for the growing wretchedness of his expression."

   B. Since everyone's entry was so good that it was impossible to declare one better than the rest, the judges were forced to award the prize *arbitrarily*.

a. angrily	*c.* bodily
b. not based on reason	*d.* suddenly

7. *maroon* (page 255, line 26)

   A. " 'You must *maroon* me as soon as ever you can get amongst these islands off the Cambodge shore,' he went on."

   B. Rather than take his life, the pirates voted to *maroon* the captain on a desert island where there was little chance of his ever escaping.

a. strand	*c.* help
b. purple	*d.* kill

8. *perplexity* (page 257, line 36)

   A. "All that afternoon he wore a dreamy, contemplative appearance which in him was a mark of *perplexity*."

   B. By that time I was in a state of complete *perplexity*, not knowing whether he wanted me to meet him at the station or whether he would come by cab.

a. intelligence	*c.* bewilderment
b. purposefulness	*d.* sincerity

9. *faltering* (page 259, line 32)

   A. " 'From first to last'—and for the first time there seemed to be a *faltering*, something strained in his whisper."

   B Confidently and without any *faltering* he recited the entire poem to the delight of all the adults in the room.

a. suspicion	*c.* hesitation
b. displeasure	*d.* contradiction

10. *desisted* (page 261, line 25)

A. "I wonder what he thought had come to me before he understood and suddenly *desisted*."

B. The film on the damages to health caused by cigarettes was so powerful that most former smokers who viewed it forever after *desisted*.

a. stopped   c. returned

b. thought   d. regretted